# THE
# RIVER
# SORROW

# CRAIG HOLDEN

# THE
# RIVER
# SORROW

Delacorte  Press

Published by

Delacorte Press

Bantam Doubleday Dell Publishing Group, Inc.

1540 Broadway

New York, New York 10036

Library of Congress Cataloging in Publication Data

Holden, Craig.

The river sorrow / by Craig Holden.

p.   cm.

ISBN 0-385-31207-5

1. Physicians—Michigan—Fiction. I. Title.

PS3558.347747R58   1994

813'.54—dc20

93-43571

CIP

Designed by Christine Swirnoff

Manufactured in the United States of America

Published simultaneously in Canada

October 1994

10   9   8   7   6   5   4   3   2   1

BVG

*FOR LISA, WHO ENDURED,*
*AND*
*FOR ALEX, WHO ARRIVED*

# THE
# RIVER
# SORROW

I see that man going back down with a heavy yet measured step towards the torment of which he will never know the end. That hour, like a breathing space which returns as surely as his suffering, that is the hour of consciousness. . . .

*ALBERT CAMUS*

What I got you gotta get it put it in you.

*RED HOT CHILI PEPPERS*

# THE
# FIRST
# WEEKEND

L ike some mythical dragon a helicopter screams down out of the night, its spotlights illuminating the white cross on the asphalt landing pad and blinding those on the ground. Dr. Adrian Lancaster and three of his team watch from just inside the end of the enclosed walkway leading out from the ER. The huge machine settles toward the earth, brilliant against the blackness of the night sky. Even in the tunnel the noise is deafening and the frigid wind whips their faces and stings their eyes.

The chopper, laced in red and blue running lights, stops cold two feet off the ground, then touches down. Heads bowed, the trauma team runs, pushing a stretcher before them.

"He's bottoming!" the flight doctor, Ann Palicki, shouts over the whacking of the blades. She has only one patient, a burn, on this flight, strapped into the lower berth. "Third degree on the face, chest, and full left arm. Respirations ten per minute and dropping."

Normally a case like this would go directly to one of the regional burn centers, in Toledo or Ann Arbor. But with respirations so shallow and slow, and no tracheal tube in place, this one wouldn't have made it.

When Lancaster steps up and inside he can see the damage. The left half of the face is destroyed, a mosaic of bloody exposed muscle, subdermal membrane, and strings of blackened hanging skin. The left eye is covered with a saline-soaked gauze pad. The left ear has burned partially away and the nose and lips are swollen and split from the flames.

An obstructed airway is the first enemy. Shock is second.

"I tried to intubate but the throat's swollen," Ann says. "He managed to keep breathing so I just kept it open as I could and used the ambu bag. I didn't want to risk cutting him in the air. Bumpy ride tonight."

"What happened?"

"His car hit a tree, but it didn't look too damaged. I don't know what caused the flames. They were limited to him for the most part. Also, there's a pretty bad contusion back on the head we'll have to watch."

Then Lancaster catches a whiff of something, gasoline maybe.

"There was no engine fire?" he says.

"No."

"Lower body?"

"Bloodstains around the left knee."

"No burns?"

"No."

"Weird," he says. He turns to a first-year trauma resident who's shifting nervously from foot to foot. "We're going to need a burn team in here. When we get inside, you get on the horn. I have to establish an airway before anything. This one's a fucking mess." To Ann he says, "How about an ID?"

"No."

"He's John Doe," Lancaster announces.

Ann and the pilot lift the wooden pallet and feed it down to the resident and the two trauma nurses. Then they hand down the two IV bags and the line in the man's arm. The team leaves, one pushing the stretcher, one working the ambu bag, one holding the bags up so the fluids will continue to feed into the patient's veins. Lancaster and Ann follow at a trot.

The official time of touchdown was 11:55 P.M., Saturday, January 12, 1991. By midnight only the pilot, an ex–Air Force lieutenant who once flew huge dual-propped Sikorski troop-movers over Vietnam, is left to clean out the bird.

Inside, under the halogen arc lamps of the trauma stall, it is all shouting out stats and orders for blood work and chemicals and equipment and X-rays, communication somehow happening in the cacophonous web of raised voices and mechanical noises. Dr. Lancaster swears and throws a hemostat at the tiled wall before he finishes the tracheostomy and gets a tube anchored so the ventilator can take over Doe's breathing.

"Next?" he says to the resident.

The resident stares back at him wide-eyed.

"It's a burn," Lancaster says.

"Fluids."

"Good boy. We've got a peripheral line in the right arm. Now we're going to start one subclavian, where we can really pump the juices."

While Lancaster worked on the tracheal tube, others were cutting away what was left of the patient's charred overcoat and flannel shirt. Except for the pad over his eye and a thin chain and medallion around his neck, he lies exposed from the waist up.

Lancaster is surprised to see that the unilateral burning of the face is continued on the body. The left arm and shoulder are damaged even worse than the face, with the tissue below the elbow scorched black. The left upper chest and left abdomen are burned badly too. But the surrounding tissues—the right chest and even the right side of the neck—show little burning at all.

"Look at that pattern," he says. "You've got a clear and distinct line." As he speaks, Lancaster snips the chain and tosses it on the pile of clothing. Then he drives a long latex-coated IV tip into the depression beneath the right clavicle. When he gets blood back, he removes the needle, leaving the latex tubing in place. Quickly, with help from the resident, he attaches the line and tapes it into place while one of the nurses opens the Y-valve connecting the line to bags of normal saline solution and plasma.

"Ever see anything like this?"

The resident looks up and shakes his head.

"Chemical burn," Lancaster says. "A spill. See it?"

The resident looks again. "I see it," he says. "But that's not what happened here. There were open flames. Look at the charring. Look at his clothes." The resident kicks at the pile of blackened cloth at his feet.

Lancaster nods in agreement, but something's not right.

With the establishment of the line Doe's blood pressure gradually stabilizes and starts to come up a little.

The first of the burn team is already arriving by chopper.

Ann is suturing the head wound.

The trauma nurses work with tweezers and sterile water to pick away the destroyed skin. With the fluid and blood-oxygen levels stabilized, the enemies now become infection and damaged tracheal and lung tissue. It will be a hard fight.

Since the staff is all busy, Lancaster hands his resident a pair of heavy bandage shears and nods at the legs. "Start with the belt, work down. Take everything off. Keep your eyes open, especially for that left leg."

The resident begins to cut.

★ ★ ★

The central glass-encased office of the Morgantown County General Hospital ER, the nerve center of the ward, was modeled after larger big-city trauma centers. Along one wall of the rectangular office, the wall just opposite the trauma room where John Doe is being debrided and detrousered, runs a white Formica work counter. A row of fluorescent lights illuminates its length. Stools sit waiting for staff who need to catch up on notes or chart work. Directly across from the counter two X-ray screens hang at eye level. Next to them a double automatic drip coffeemaker perpetually steams and sighs. One end of the room, nearest the doorways, is filled with the clerk's desk and phone bank and the shortwave radio connecting the ER to the rescue squads and the chopper. The other end holds a file cabinet and an old cracked vinyl couch with cigarette burns all along its arms and on which now sits a thin, long-legged sheriff's deputy, in from the cold of the night, both his hands wrapped around a cup of coffee as he breathes in its steam.

The office and the general layout were not like this when Lancaster, who's now thirty-four, came here to help bring this ER—an outpost of sorts for rural south-central Michigan—into the age of modern trauma medicine.

He sits on one of the stools and pulls off his mask and sterile bonnet. His dark straight hair is long and it falls over his shoulders. The hair is a vestige, a reminder of a rougher time and place. It used to bother some people around here, but no one except the kids he works with at the Free Clinic seems to pay much attention anymore.

Lancaster keeps himself lean and well toned. In his basement he has a set of weights he uses a couple times each week, and he runs when he can.

He pulls the hair back and rubber-bands it, his eyes on the deputy's.

"You called in the bird?"

"Yessir. I was the first one at the scene."

"What happened?"

The deputy pulls a pack of Kents from his shirt pocket and lights one. Lancaster lifts an ashtray from the counter and hands it over.

"Dispatcher called me."

"Who called it in in the first place?"

"Don't know. Some passerby. But I was right in the area. Went over and saw the flames. When I got closer I saw it was a man burning. Jesus Christ." Lancaster can see the tremble in the man's hands now, not from the cold but from the shock of seeing a human torch, something even cops don't see that often.

"No one else was there when you arrived?"

"No."

"How long from the call until you got there?"

"Three, four minutes."

"You put him out?"

"I carry a blanket in the trunk, you know. I filled it with snow and threw it over him, then radioed."

"It took some guts to lean in and smother those flames. You could've been burned yourself."

The deputy stares at his cigarette as he spins it between his fingers.

"So what's your theory? You were there first."

"About what happened?" The deputy takes a quick drag and exhales. "Not that uncommon. See it with truckers mostly. Guy pulls over, either dead tired or drunk or stoned. Lights a smoke, then dozes off. Cig falls into his clothing and smolders—no oxygen in there to really burn, see. Then later on, he wakes up. It's smoky. He cracks the window to get in a little fresh air."

"And poof."

"Combustion. Flames go right up in his face. I seen it happen once down on I-80. Truck stop down there. That guy was DOA. No face left at all."

"It's an idea," Lancaster says. He crosses the office and slaps one of Doe's cranial shots up on the X-ray screen. "So no one has investigated this, right?"

"You don't think that's what happened?"

Lancaster moves in close to the film and squints his eyes. "You want to look at the guy again?"

The cop shakes his head.

"Pattern's all wrong. Looks like a fluid accelerant. In the chopper I thought I smelled fuel."

"Maybe he'd spilled something there earlier. Gas or kerosene or something."

"Maybe. But figure it out. Someone saw him burning, then found a phone and called in, then dispatch got ahold of you, and then you took three or four minutes to get there. How long altogether, from first sighting until you put out the flames?"

He frowns. "Least ten, fifteen minutes. Maybe more."

"This guy would have been cinder if he'd been on fire for ten minutes."

"What're you saying?"

"He wasn't burning until after the call was placed and you were already on your way to the scene. I'd say not more than thirty seconds, a minute at the outside, before you got there. And that means he was torched by someone. Besides that, he was smacked on the *back* of his head." Lancaster snaps a finger on the backlighted X-ray film. "Explain that."

"I don't know."

"Who's on call for a homicide tonight?"

"Homicide? The guy ain't dead."

"Not yet."

The deputy smokes and sips at his coffee and thinks for a minute.

"I hate to call in a shield for a traffic accident in the middle of the night. If you're wrong I'll get chewed on hard."

"Or maybe we should call the arson squad." Lancaster laughs at his joke. The sheriff's department has one man trained in criminal investigation, and the city force only two full-time detectives, so whether it's homicide, arson, theft, or sex crimes, they're it. Third shifts, they alternate being on call. "I take full responsibility," he says. "Who's on?"

"City. Frank Brandon, I think."

"So it's not a lucky night." Calling Brandon out at 3:00 A.M. is on a par with poking sticks into a bear's hibernation den.

"Dr. Lancaster?" It's the resident. "I think you and the officer should see this."

The deputy follows Lancaster to the curtain draped across the front of the stall of the burned man. He does not look inside.

The resident has the jeans cut off but not the boots and socks. The left knee has been severely bruised and lacerated, but nothing below the waist is burned.

"I was cutting down alongside his fly, through the pocket. My scissors snagged up in something. Look." The resident hands Lancaster a packet of tan powder, lighter and finer than brown sugar but still grainy looking. Lancaster leans out around the curtain and hands it to the deputy, who fingers the packet and shakes his head. It is an image that will recur to Lancaster at odd moments for the rest of his life.

"Something else," the resident says. He's working on cutting through the heavy laces of the man's high-top work boots. Tucked into the top of the boot, inside the sock, is a thin leather wallet holding a couple of credit cards and a Michigan driver's license.

By now the deputy's curiosity has given him the strength to look around the curtain.

"Michael Straw," the resident says. "He's from Detroit."

"I better make my call," says the deputy.

Lancaster, too, had come back to Morgantown, the place of the latter half of his youth, from Detroit. When he came, he was running from some things, from the heart of the onetime greatest manufacturing city in the world, from a series of jobs in Detroit emergency rooms where fifteen minutes did not pass that didn't see some crisis and no shift passed without at least one trauma that would make a normal person's hair stand up just to hear it described. After a three-year trauma residency and a couple more years as a staff trauma doc, he was not normal. He had grief-proof latex skin and a heart of hospital stainless steel, and had become addicted to violence and despair. At home at night he thought of addicts and accident victims in the way other people think of their friends, as the comfortable old familiar.

During that time he had also ended up a patient himself, the graduate of a drug rehab clinic in Royal Oak, this after he was arrested for lifting hospital morphine. It was only through the efforts of a creative attorney and some doctors who, although they did not condone or even understand his addiction, believed in his abilities and his career, that he had been saved. Through legal and AMA probations, a closely supervised year of public service, and extensive outpatient therapy and peer evaluations, he had finally redeemed himself in the eyes of the state and avoided having his license revoked.

And in Detroit, finally but perhaps most importantly, he had seen the end of his relationship with a woman named Denise Richards. Sometimes he felt as if she had stolen his life away. At others, as if she had given it back to him. In weaker moments, although he always came back to knowing it was in his own self where the weakness had hidden, it was her he blamed for the drug problems, the breakdown. Most of the time, though, when he thought about her, he wished she were still here, where he could talk with her. But the drugs that had nearly ruined him had been worse for her, and had taken her away.

In any case, a time finally came three years ago when he knew he had to go somewhere and get human again. So he wandered west, following an instinct that pulled him toward the place that felt as much like home as anything he could identify, and ended up settling back in here, where the pace was a bit slower and the gruesome wasn't so frequent or so extreme, the place to which when he was seventeen he swore he'd never return.

In the cafeteria Lancaster orders a large coffee, and sits by the wide glass window on the central courtyard for a few minutes. The burn crew and surgeons are evaluating Straw and soon they'll be setting him up in the ICU. Lancaster sees the sheriff's deputy wander in and look around, not sure of what to do with himself, and waves him over.

"Fresh coffee at the counter," Lancaster says.

"Nah," says the deputy, slipping into a chair across the table. "I'll piss a damn river if I don't watch it. Weak kidneys."

"The old weak-kidney syndrome."

"Something," the deputy says. "Ought to have you check it out."

The funny thing about his addiction, arrest, and treatment, Lancaster has often thought, is that the people who know about it—and that includes all of the local law enforcement, grapevines being what they are—seem to admire him for having gone through it. He possesses a currency they appreciate.

One requirement of the settlement was that his file would accompany him wherever he went. But it wasn't something he particularly tried to hide anyway; rather, he utilized his image as an authority on the subject. After a year in Morgantown of watching indigents and drunks and the poor drag into the ER for treatment of their chronic problems, he'd helped a group of local doctors tap into state money to establish the Free Clinic on the north side of town not only to treat medical problems but to serve an addiction rehab function as well. Even now he volunteers there eight hours a week, still surprised after three years at the fact that, aside from scale, the underbelly here gives nothing away to the big city.

★   ★   ★

An hour later, just after 4:00 A.M., back in the ER's central office, Lancaster sits on a stool at the work counter; the deputy stands by the coffee machine; Morgantown police detective Lieutenant Frank Brandon, the department's chief investigator, rocks back in the clerk's chair. The clerk is on her break.

Lancaster stares out into the empty trauma stall where John Doe/ Michael Straw was treated. The room is hushed now, blood and other fluids spattered on the floor, syringes and tubes and bottles and bags lying around on counters and on the equipment trays. The halogen arc lamps still burn down on a now empty space. A sanitation worker is mopping while an aide restocks the pigeonholes of the supply rack along the back wall.

"So, you reading something that's got your imagination going?" Brandon says. "Good detective novel? Been watching movies?" Brandon, the unchallenged worst dresser on the force, has on a subdued outfit tonight—a brown polyester shirt, an orange Paisley tie, and a blue plaid sport coat.

"You really believe the guy dropped a cigarette on himself?"

"Me? Don't know. Maybe not. You seriously think that from a burned arm and a packet of drugs you can say he was set on fire? That someone tried to kill him? If that's the case, you're one hell of a detective, Doctor. My hat's off."

Brandon is fairly heavyset, not too tall, and his hairline has receded back to the top of his head. The hair around the sides is red and curly and he doesn't have it cut too often, so it bushes out. With his ruddy Irish face Lancaster thinks he looks faintly clownish, but he also believes Brandon exaggerates the look and the obnoxious clothing because it throws people off.

"You get an anonymous call—"

"Not anonymous," Brandon says. "Dispatch gave me the caller's name. They've got it on record. Alan something—" He flips back a page in his notebook and checks. "No, Arnie. Arnie Holt, the caller said. Kind of blows your theory, doesn't it?"

"What does that mean? You don't see anything suspicious about this?"

"Maybe. We can look into it. But we can look into it tomorrow morning."

"There it is," Lancaster says. "The real source of irritation. You got dragged out of bed."

"Knock it off."

"Listen, it's already tomorrow morning, Lieutenant. And I'm beat, too, and I've got a half day at the clinic starting at nine."

Brandon plays an air violin. "Who's fault is that?" he says. He was not a proponent of the idea of a publicly funded clinic. His argument was that it would not only encourage the lowlifes to stick around, but would attract more of the same.

"Anyway," says Lancaster, "I've heard most murders are solved within six hours of the crime."

Brandon snorts. "Sure," he says. "Murders. Accidental burnings by smacked-out hopheads who drive their cars off the road in the middle of the night are another story."

Ann Palicki has wandered into the room and is listening to the detective. She looks from him to Lancaster to the deputy and then back.

"What about the time-frame thing?" the deputy says.

"You're factoring in dozens of variables," says Brandon. "You're guessing on all the times, hypothesizing about how fast the flame burned, who first witnessed it. I mean the guy was very severely burned. He *was* on fire for a while."

"Not ten minutes," says Lancaster. "Nowhere near it."

"You don't know that it took ten minutes to get to him."

"Excuse me," says Ann. "Detective, you said something about him driving his car off the road."

"You were there, right? It was cracked up against a tree, I was told. It either slid off the road or he drove it there, right?"

"He was in the passenger seat."

14

There is a pause in the room, a moment of complete silence.

"What?" Brandon says.

"He was in the passenger seat."

"Well, he could have moved over there after he hit. He could have been—"

"He was seat-belted in. I know. I had to cut him out."

Brandon looks from Ann to the deputy.

"She's right," the deputy says. "It never even hit me in all the confusion. I was just thinking about the fire."

"Well, goddammit," Brandon says. He shakes his head and shakes a Camel from his pack. "So maybe we have a case of someone skipping the scene of an accident. That's still a long way from attempted murder."

"The clothes," Lancaster says. "Might be worth getting them tested for accelerants. Just to see."

Brandon looks at him hard for a couple seconds, then says, "Yeah. I'll get the lab going."

B y the time Brandon pulls into his driveway it's after six. He called Jimmy Mendez, Morgantown County's forensics scene man and crime lab guru, then drove the clothing to the justice building, which houses their small lab. Before ordering out the militia he wants corroboration of Lancaster's theory. He sent a couple uniforms out to tape off the scene and keep a watch until they heard from him. Besides, he's tired and it's not quite daylight yet. So he figures he'll go back to bed to wait. So what if he dozes off and gets a little sleep? It's the weekend. During the week he's up by six but weekends he figures he ought to get to sleep in a little before waking up his wife, Lorraine, and strapping her into her high-backed orthopedic wheeled chair, before slogging out through the slush at some scene or sitting in the smoky squad room listening to mindless bullshit.

But when he walks into his house the phone is ringing.

"Frank?" It's Jimmy Mendez. "I tested positive on the clothing."

"Already?"

"The spec threw bands all over the place. We are definitely dealing with a carbon-based fuel, probably gasoline, but it's not showing a homogeneous pattern. Some kind of exotic mix."

"I hate that word."

"The pattern was unusual. I'm sending the clothes by courier up to the state crime lab. They can do a specific qualitative. We should know by tomorrow."

Brandon loves to listen to Jimmy talk. His diction, even with a trace of his family's Hispanic accent, is the most careful and polished Brandon has ever heard.

"But you're sure there was something there."

"Positive."

"An accelerant."

"Whatever was there would have burned like all hell."

Brandon nods into the darkness of his kitchen. "Then let's get started. Make sure somebody up there also tests for fiber samples, blood, the complete workup."

"I already ran my own, and ordered more. The vehicle is still at the scene. We'll meet you out there. You sound rough."

"Goddamn cold." His head feels lousy with swollen sinuses and congestion. His throat burns. *Twenty degrees out and I'm working on four hours sleep,* he thinks. *Figure it out.*


As soon as he steps from the kitchen into the garage he coughs at the coldness of the air. Temperatures have dipped back down into the teens. It feels colder than in the middle of the night. The Buick starts all right, though. He stops for a coffee on his way into town and heads north on State Route 57, then west to a spot about fifteen miles out of the city, along the northern bank of the River Sorrow, which winds down out of the Irish Hills and eventually cuts through the southern section of Morgantown itself.

The two-lane dirt road is so badly pitted, he has to slow his car to nearly walking pace. He pulls into a gravel parking area, one end of which has been cordoned off with yellow crime-scene tape. A squad car, lights turning, an unmarked, and the blue scene van used by Jimmy Mendez are parked at the opposite end of the lot from the red two-door that is the object of their attention. Before approaching them Brandon crosses the parking area and walks the couple hundred feet down the sloping snow-covered park, following the tracks of someone who was here before him, to a green metal railing marking the edge of the cliff. To his left a heavy woods forms the western border of the park. This spot, which some call Suicide Park and others simply the Overlook, although it has no official name, is at the top of a high bluff above the river. He's heard it's the longest vertical drop in a four-county area.

The river, thickened by the cold, is a quarter its normal width, a rivulet hemmed between wide expanses of undercut ice extending out from either bank. Loose clots of ice float by in the black water. A filmy haze hangs in the air below the cliff, a blanket that distorts the view from above.

A light snow starts to fall, unusual in this kind of hard cold. Brandon is acutely aware at that instant of the sensation of the isolation of this place, of the cold and the colored flashing lights and the snow, and of feeling the same way he always has when an investigation begins. In nearly twenty-eight years as a cop he has never failed to feel, at this precursory moment, both unworthy and privileged.


The car, which bears Ohio plates, is butted up against a twisted old maple. The white vinyl of the passenger seat has melted where Michael Straw burned. Droplets of blood have dried on the seat and the door. Jimmy will make sure they match the victim. He has coated the wheel, dashboard, and gearshift with black ferrous oxide powder to lift any latent prints. He's vacuuming the carpet but stops to talk to Brandon.

"We lifted two sets of latents," Jimmy says. "They belong to the owner and Straw."

"Come again?"

"You haven't heard this already? A red 1988 Chevy Cabriolet was reported stolen from someone in Wauseon, Ohio, yesterday afternoon. This is it. The locals already faxed us the owner's prints."

"Story checks out?"

"From what we can tell. Anyway, the wheel and gear knob also have unridged markings—your perp wore latex gloves."

Not just gloves because it's cold out, but latex gloves, surgical gloves. A premeditated crime. A setup. The doc was right. Brandon grinds his teeth.

"Hey, boss!" someone shouts from the snow and weeds along the edge of the parking area. It's Morgantown's other detective, Sergeant Spinner Wharton, wearing his favorite winter field outfit of a badly oil-stained Carhartt work coat, jeans, boots, and a Tigers baseball hat. He tells people it blends him in, sort of an undercover thing, but Brandon wonders how in a place this small there could be anyone who doesn't know him already, especially since, at six two and only 170 pounds, he tends to stick in people's minds.

Spinner has made a find. Beyond a ridge of plowed snow, lodged between the twin trunks of a small pine, lies a tire iron, one end speckled with blackish droplets.

Brandon holds a clear plastic evidence sack open as Spinner picks up the iron with a cloth.

"Jimmy," Brandon yells back toward the car, "have someone get the trunk open. See if the tire iron is missing."

"I heard the guy got bashed," Spinner says.

"In the knee and the head."

"So we got a for-real attempted H."

"Maybe more than attempted, if you believe Lancaster. And listen, he seems to think the call had to come in before Straw was already on fire. We got the name of the caller, somebody Holtz or Holt, something. Find out and see what the story is."

"Sure. You get breakfast yet?"

Brandon looks at him. "You haven't eaten?"

"Yeah, but I thought you might wanna grab something."

No mystery the Morgantown force has ever faced compares with that of how Spinner Wharton stays so thin and yet eats so much. His metabolism, Brandon thinks, must be on a par with that of, say, a hummingbird. Resting heart rate of about 180 a minute. The benefit of this is that Spinner has more energy than a kid. He'll run legwork on a case for twenty hours straight if he's asked, and then want to do more. What he cannot do is sit and wait. Once, years before, Brandon made the mistake of bringing Spinner on a stakeout. It was the last time for that. Now, Brandon does surveillance alone.

A uniform waves from the rear of the red car.

"The iron's missing," Brandon says. "Exhibit A. And I grabbed a bite at the house, but thanks anyway."

Back at the car Brandon kneels next to Jimmy's feet, which protrude from beneath the jacked-up right front fender where he's searching for debris.

"All the snow is a pain in the ass," Jimmy says. "We'll scrape what we can, pull the grille and so forth, but I don't know."

Not a lot to go on, that's the message. "I'll have Spinner talk to the owner," Brandon says.

"You never know," comes back from beneath the car.


Michael Straw lies in a special isolation room of the intensive care unit at MCGH. As soon as he stabilizes, he'll be flown to the burn unit in Ann Arbor.

Brandon waits on a couch in the hallway, sipping what's left of a cold coffee, until a nurse hands him a gown and mask and leads him back.

Straw has another visitor already. His sister, Sarah Le Seure, sits in a hard plastic chair against the wall of the sterile cubicle. Brandon can only see her eyes between the mask and the surgical hair covering, but these eyes are striking, hazel and beautiful and wounded. She lives, she tells him, with her husband and daughter up in Emerald. Emerald is a nice little bedroom community outside the state's capital, Lansing, a couple of hours north.

She probably passed her brother's clothing on the drive down, Brandon thinks.

"Can't you even leave him in peace when he's dying?"

"Pardon?"

"You're a detective? Whatever you can get on him now can't matter much."

"He's been arrested before, then?"

She laughs a bitter laugh.

"I'm not here to investigate your brother's crimes, Mrs. Le Seure. How old is he?" Straw's face and head are bandaged totally. The tube from the ventilator snakes through the bandages and into his throat. His left arm, wrapped in thick layers of gauze, has been suspended from an overhead bar. The chest burns have thin gauze over them, but not enough to completely hide the raw pink flesh beneath. Brandon swallows hard and looks away.

"Twenty-nine. Pretty nauseating, isn't it?"

"He might be able to hear you."

She shrugs.

"You mind if I look?" Brandon indicates the sheet.

She shrugs again.

The left knee has swollen badly and turned green and a deep grayish-blue. It hasn't been wrapped. A sutured inch-long gash, surrounded by the darkest bruising, runs along the upper outside of the kneecap.

Brandon pulls the sheet back up and walks around to Straw's undamaged right side, thinking about the asymmetry of these injuries.

As he looks over the wounds he slips his hand into Straw's. It matters to him when a victim is still open to any sort of comforting. Then he notices the right arm. All along the inside, but especially concentrated in the crook of the elbow, are swollen crosshatchings of scar tissue punctuated here and there by the red spots of recent needle entry. The tracks are hard, pencillike, and run up and down the arm, as ruined as any he's ever seen. The whole area of the antecubital is a solid mass of needle-scar tissue. The forearm, inner wrist, and back of the hand, even the spaces between the knuckles, are scarred as well.

"Was your brother left handed?"

"No. Why?"

Brandon shakes his head. "He must have been a very heavy user if this is his backup arm."

"Only for about twelve years. If you're not after Mikey and didn't even know he's a junkie, why are you here?"

"One of the doctors who worked on him is a little excitable. He thinks there's some evidence the fire was set, that maybe Michael was the victim of a crime. I'm just following up."

Sarah stands.

"You don't believe it?"

"I'm investigating. I'm just looking at the evidence."

"And?"

"And there are a few anomalies I'd like to have explained. I don't want you getting excited. Anything definite turns up I'll let you know."

"If somebody did this to him—"

He's sure that when she first heard about her brother she was in shock, but now Brandon can see in her eyes that she has started on the roller coaster of emotions that follows a tragedy, anger and pain and disbelief and probably guilt. It's clear she hasn't slept much, and that she's spent some time crying too.

"Tell me something," he says. "Emerald is an expensive place to live. You're married. You got a good life."

"So how could I have a junkie for a brother?"

He watches the fury dance in her eyes.

"We didn't come from a place like Emerald. We grew up in West Detroit. Our dad left when Mike was little. I'm four years older than him." She shrugs. "I need to smoke. Do you mind?"

"You speak my language," he says. They leave the room and their gowns and masks behind and walk to a lounge on the far side of the floor. Sarah Le Seure has light brown hair that goes nicely with the eyes, Brandon thinks.

"I got lucky, to be blunt," she says. "I married a man who was destined to be successful."

Brandon offers her one of his Camels, then lights it and one for himself.

"Oddly enough, I never would have met him if it weren't for Michael and his problem. Jim was a DEA agent in Detroit. Eight or nine years ago Mike got caught dealing. It was Jim's case. He was very helpful to us. He got Mike into a treatment program and spent a lot of time talking with me."

"Your husband was a DEA agent and your brother was an addict." Every day something new.

"Jim understood Mike's habit. It didn't faze him."

She walks over to the wide glass windows overlooking the River Sorrow as it winds through south Morgantown.

"I'm surprised," Brandon says.

"I know it must sound strange. But I think Jim actually kept Mike out of a lot of trouble over the years. I mean, I think he intervened in certain situations. I stayed out of it."

"When did you last see him?"

"Only about ten days ago. And sometimes I'd go for months without hearing from him. Then he'd call just to talk or maybe to ask for money. I sent him money when he needed it."

"A lot of money?"

"Usually not."

"So what was ten days ago?"

She turns and faces him. "Out of nowhere he showed up at the house, agitated and looking for Jim. Jim was out of town.

"His hands were shaking. He said he was in on some new business. To be honest, I didn't really listen that carefully. I made lunch, we talked a little while, and he left."

"You say 'agitated.' "

"Maybe upset. Maybe excited. With him it was hard to tell. He could have just been coming down off something."

"Anything else about this business—where it was, who was running it, where he found out about it, anything like that?"

"No."

"Do you know any of his friends?"

"No, I'm afraid I don't."

"If your husband thinks of anything you'll ask him to call me?"

"I'll ask him."

"You need anything while you're here, please get in touch." He hands her his card.

She nods. "They're taking his fingers off today, you know."

"I didn't know."

"This afternoon. The doctors said they were already infected. They can't be saved."

For another moment he watches her smoke and stare out the window at the river. Then he turns to leave.

"Detective?"

"Yes?"

"Do you really think somebody did this to him?"

"No." Lies comfort.

"But you'll tell me if you change your mind."

"Of course."

★   ★   ★

He stops by home to check on Lorraine, then has to head into the office to start writing up this mess, but when he walks into the living room he finds his daughter Susan waiting. She watches him until he says something.

"No church today? It's pretty early."

"Rick left on a job."

"On a Sunday?"

"Why not? Roads are clear."

"So you here to be social or just to check up a little?"

"You left her alone in bed again, Dad. How many times do we have to go through this? She can't be left alone."

"She's fine, dear."

"She's *not* fine." Susan follows him into the kitchen, where he pours a glass of milk. "I talked with some people. There's a really good Catholic place right here in town."

"I'm not putting her in a goddamn nursing home."

"This isn't working."

"She has help."

"Eight hours, five days. That's not enough anymore."

The house, the one he and Lorraine moved into after they were married twenty-seven years ago, is on the northern edge of Morgantown, on the bank of Elmer Creek in what used to be an outlying neighborhood. Now it's all city around him, carryouts and prefab houses and gas stations and a three-plex theater, but he doesn't think much anymore about moving away. He paneled most of the house in knotty pine and they raised two daughters here.

Susan, the eldest, lives on some land east of town now, married to a long-haul trucker and making the best of that situation. The other, May, died two years ago in the same car accident that crippled Lorraine and took her mind, when some freak spaced out on Quaaludes and beer crossed the center line at seventy miles an hour.

Until a few months ago Lorraine was stable. She had a good day nurse and at night she slept. But she began to have problems with her breathing, waking Brandon up with horrible racking coughs. They had to run a humidifier constantly now and a respiratory therapist came in three times a week. Lorraine's behavior, what there was of it, changed too. She began to cry for hours at a time.

"I'm beat," he says. "And I have to go back out soon. Can you stay?"

She nods. "But we're not finished with this."

## THREE

M organtown is a small city of thirty thousand or so, one-half college town with old-money Victorian neighborhoods, one-half home to rusting has-been factories and underemployed blue-collar workers. It lies on the flat plains of southern Michigan, more than 90 miles west of the sprawl of Detroit.

Hard cold hit at the end of December and temperatures dropped steadily to a week-long trough in the early new year close to ten below. Then a warming trend up into the twenties brought with it the snows, heavy blankets that kept falling one on top of another. Now the major roads are lined by twelve-foot-high piles of frozen slush. People have gone into a kind of walking catatonia in which they do their jobs and get along, but are not happy about it.

Early Sunday morning Lancaster takes his own walking catatonia to the Free Clinic in the northeastern corner of Morgantown, a neighborhood of squat shingle-sided bungalows interrupted by the occasional rickety-looking duplex that had been solid blue-collar-prosperous a couple decades ago.

Lancaster's aunt Rose used to live here. When he was a little kid, before he lived here, too, he and his mother visited twice a year. This was a good place then, unlike his own neighborhood on Cleveland's east side where the families were rough and the games were rough and the streets were the only place to go. But now, this has gone rough too. The lawns and houses are deteriorating; along Rumford, a major cross street, a third of the houses are boarded up and most others have FOR SALE signs on the lawns, signs that have rusted and bent, they've been there so long.

The clinic itself is housed in a high-roofed four-bay garage that belongs to the city and was once used to maintain garbage trucks, but has been insulated and remodeled into a nice space. In addition to offices, four treatment bays, and a group conference room, it has its own small blood and urine lab and an X-ray machine circa 1963.

Lancaster parks his Bronco and looks around at the low gray sky and the tattered buildings covered with sooty layers of snow and the old beaten cars parked along the curbs.

When he was fourteen, after his father died and he and his mother moved here to live with Rose, he began to see how limiting life could be in a smallish tired city at the junction of a flat plain and a worn-down mountain range. And he began to want out again. The week after he graduated from high school he moved back to Cleveland, where he'd been accepted into the premed program at Case Western Reserve University.

A few years after that his mother and aunt moved to a condominium village in Santa Fe, New Mexico.

Once in a while when he comes to work at the clinic he fails to reflect a moment on the irony of his working here. But not too often. Most of the time it makes him smile.

★   ★   ★

Today he's just on to cover weekend walk-ins, a twice-monthly task. Most of his work here is with dependents, and occasionally he'll take appointments for one of the family practitioners who's sick or on vacation.

After treating a couple cases of strep and referring a homeless man with three frostbitten toes to the MCGH ER for probable admission, he finds no one else waiting. So Lancaster asks the desk nurse to keep an ear open and stretches out on an examination table in one of the treatment rooms.

He's nearly asleep, legs hanging off one end of the table, hair hanging over the other end, when he hears the outside door of the waiting room open and slam against the inside wall when it is caught by the wind. Another patient, but he is tired and it feels so good to lie with his eyes closed on this amazingly uncomfortable table. In his residency he learned how much difference ten or fifteen minutes could make. He decides he'll wait for the nurse to show the patient to another room and then come and get him. After a minute or two, though, when he's nearly dozed off again, he hears the nurse's voice rise, and then the patient's voice rise even higher, to nearly a screaming pitch. He hears the word *emergency* and then *Get him out here!* Then he hears another door slam open as feet pound the floor, and before he can swing his own feet to the floor and stand up, the door of the treatment room is flung open and a girl stumbles in.

At least Lancaster thinks so until he looks again and sees that he is wrong, that it is a woman, thin and young-looking, but a woman nevertheless. She wears a dark hooded shawl and beneath that a bright red nylon vest and a turtleneck sweater. Something about her seems remarkably familiar to him, as if he knew her once, as if he had known her very well. This familiarity is so powerful, it startles him. He sits up on the table and watches her as she throws back her hood.

She's only in her mid-twenties he guesses. He couldn't have known her after all, at least not in the long ago.

The nurse, who is holding with both hands on to the young

woman's shawl, says, "I'm sorry, Doctor. She has no appointment and I asked her to wait—"

"Dr. Lancaster, please," the woman says. "I need your help." Her face is slender and pretty, with dark hair that looks undisciplined despite the fact it's cut short, and dark eyes to match. Then she smiles and becomes all the more beautiful for the sadness that smile expresses. When it fades, though, her face changes, closes, and grows tense. She glances from him to the nurse who's waiting in the hallway, then tugs on the shawl and pulls it from the nurse's grip.

Lancaster remembers where he's seen her, why she looked familiar.

"Sit down," he says.

"I'd really rather not."

"I know you," he says then.

The woman nods. "I was here at the clinic last summer. I wasn't in your group—"

"No, I remember you," he says. He motions to the nurse that it's all right. She shakes her head in disgust and pulls the door closed, leaving Lancaster alone with this young woman.

"You sleep when you're on duty?" she says.

"I've been on duty for fourteen hours now, and you can see there aren't any patients here. Or weren't. All right?"

"I'm sorry," she says. "I'm upset. Anyway, thank you for seeing me."

"Could I have refused?"

He notices that the shawl, which looked elegant at first and would have once been expensive, is tattered, worn thin here and there, coming loose at one shoulder seam, its lining hanging below the bottom hem. A thrift-shop special, and too thin for this weather, which is why she's wearing the vest as well. She probably owns nothing warmer.

She decides to sit after all, and settles on the chair across from him, and as the shawl settles around her she suddenly looks elegant again, as if all she had to do was move to bring the illusion back to life. "It's about Kevin Babcock," she says, her voice low and tight. "Do you remember him? He's in trouble."

"Babcock," Lancaster says. "That's right. You two were buddies." He raises one leg and crosses it over the other and closes his eyes for a moment. The thought of Kevin Babcock makes him feel even more exhausted than he had. "What is it?" he says. "Phencyclidine again?"

Kevin Babcock had been an Angel Duster when Lancaster first met him. He'd been brought into the ER by a couple local cops who'd found him in a grocery-store parking lot smashing car windows with a crowbar. The kid sat motionless and silent on the stretcher, his eyeballs jerking around in their sockets. Lancaster ordered some blood work and an IV then went out to talk with the cops while a lab tech and a nurse went in. A moment later he heard a shout. Then the nurse flew out of the stall and into a wall.

When Lancaster ran in, the lab tech's tray, full of needles and syringes and test tubes, sailed past his head. With one hand Kevin was holding the tech, a middle-aged woman who must have weighed 150 pounds, up in the air by her collar.

Someone handed Lancaster a pair of leather restraints.

He was trying to decide how best to approach when the two cops moved past. One went for Kevin's feet while the other laid a nightstick across his head, opening a huge gash and stunning him long enough to get him down and secured to the metal rails of the stretcher. This would not have been Lancaster's first choice as to methodology, but cops are cops and ERs are ERs, and that is how it happened.

Kevin bucked so hard that the stretcher came up several inches off the floor. The laceration in his forehead was a blood faucet. He ended up breaking both wrists fighting the restraints. All Lancaster could do was administer diazepam and wait for the storm to pass.

"He hasn't done that in a long time," she says. "You really did help him a lot."

"Right," Lancaster says. "That's why he dropped out."

One of the things Lancaster liked best about the move from the big city to Morgantown was that, while MCGH had facilities for most cases that came in, it was still small enough that even an ER doc could get to know many of the people who came through and could follow up cases when he felt he could do some good.

The morning after the PCP episode, when Lancaster visited him on the ward, Kevin remembered nothing of the night before. But they'd talked for almost an hour that day, about the various drugs Kevin was into, how he wanted to quit, and then about his life in general. Lancaster remembered it well. At the end he mentioned the clinic and suggested Kevin drop by.

To his mild surprise, a week or so later, Kevin did. And by the end of the spring Kevin proclaimed to his group that he was chemical free, including alcohol and cigarettes. Lancaster promoted him to the position of group coleader, and through the summer Kevin spent three evenings a week at the clinic.

Then, in the early fall, he abruptly stopped coming. Lancaster had tried calling him a few times, but Kevin was distant and clearly did not want to talk.

"The door's always open," Lancaster remembered telling him, and left it at that. People move on. What could he do?

"He should have stayed," she says.

"I'm afraid I don't remember your name."

"Storm Summers."

"Right. Cocaine." It's a guess but he's nearly always right. He remembers she'd been in Dr. Delvecchio's group. Maybe Lancaster had said hello to her once or twice. She hung around after her meetings until Kevin was ready to go. They arrived and left together most of the time. Lancaster remembered because he'd referred to her once as Kevin's girlfriend but Kevin had corrected him, saying they were just friends.

"Yes," she says. "I had a little problem."

"You're still clean?"

She looks away and says, "Yes."

Although he doesn't believe her he says, "Good for you."

"Anyway, I'm hardly the issue. Kevin's not into PCP again but he is using other stuff."

"Such as?"

"I don't know. Different things, I think. He doesn't talk about it with me because I'm not using, but I can tell. He's just been distant, you know. And he's been having family problems. His mother's a born-again Jesus freak. Are you going to help me or not?"

"What problems?"

"The drugs. And sex. Kevin's been . . . experimenting."

"That's a problem?"

"Not to me."

"Look, if it's chemicals, he can always come back here. He knows that. Or maybe you, or rather Kevin and his family, should talk to someone else. A counselor. If he's having trouble at home, there are really good people who can help—"

"You don't understand." Her voice rises a notch in pitch and intensity. "I'm worried about him, not his family. And it's not the drugs, it's the people he's been hanging around with. There's something going on, something he's involved in."

"I don't see what I can do."

"He liked you. He listened to what you had to say. He talks about you sometimes, even now. But these people—"

"Who?"

"I don't really know them. I know they nearly killed a man last night."

"Last night—"

"They burned him, I guess. Badly."

"Christ," Lancaster says. He uncrosses his legs and plants his feet on the floor. "You have to call the police."

She looks pleased, he thinks, for the first time, now that she's got him to react. "I tried. They asked me what I wanted them to do, go and protect Kevin from his own friends?"

"No, listen. I'm talking about an investigation into this burning."

"I don't care about that!" She jumps to her feet. "I just don't want Kevin to end up the same way. That's why I'm asking you to talk to him. I'm begging you."

"Please don't beg. And sit down."

"You were the only one I could think of he'd listen to. He's leaving with these people this afternoon, he said. They're going on a trip or something. He won't tell me anything about it, and that's not like him. He tells me everything." She feels for the chair behind her and lowers herself into it. "Something's going to happen. Something horrible. I'm scared for him."

"Just hold on." Lancaster walks to the wall phone and asks the nurse to get him an outside line. He tries to reach Frank Brandon at the station. Not in, he's told, so he asks for the front desk and explains the situation. "Gotcha," the clerk says, around the food in his mouth. "We'll make a note of it."

"This is important," Lancaster says.

"Sure thing," says the clerk. "We'll look into it."

"You stupid ass," he says, and hangs up.

Next he calls information and gets Brandon's home number. A woman answers but says he's gone out and she doesn't know how to reach him.

When Lancaster hangs up he finds Storm watching him and smiling, but not so sadly this time. "What's funny?"

"Nothing," she says. "I'm just glad you're helping me."

"I thought it was Kevin you wanted me to help."

34

"Yes. Of course." Still she smiles. And he is glad of it. He has not seen a thing like her smile in some time.

"What's the Babcocks' number?"

"I've been calling every couple hours since late yesterday. At first I kept getting a busy signal, then later, nothing. He said his mother hadn't been paying the bill."

Lancaster remembers this happening last summer too. "I still don't know what you want me to do."

"Just talk to him."

"What's this really about, these friends of his? You don't know any of these people?"

"I haven't met them. I saw Kevin with some of them once, at a club we go to called Red's."

"Why'd you come in here now?"

"I'm afraid. Actually, I have met one of them, at least I've spoken with him. That is, maybe he's one of them, or maybe not."

"You lost me."

"A man called this morning. I'd spoken with him once before, two days ago. He called me at my apartment and just said he thought it'd be a good idea if I didn't see Kevin for a while. That's all he said, then hung up. This morning he was more talkative. He told me he'd seen me with Kevin at Red's and asked around about me. He told me again to stay away from Kevin. Only, this time it was less a suggestion and more an order. He said Kevin would tell him if I came around, and if he did, I might not like what would happen to me."

"He threatened you?"

"Yes, in a veiled sort of way."

"It doesn't sound too veiled to me."

"Actually, it doesn't to me either. That's partly why I'm here. I'm just so mad, I'm not sure what to do. I don't want to do anything rash."

"Heaven forbid."

Instead of glaring or rolling her eyes, which he expected, she startles him with another smile, then continues: "He said he was looking after Kevin now. He said Kevin was involved in some important business and I'd better keep my nose out of it."

"I ask again, what's this about?"

"I tell you again, I don't know, Doctor. Maybe he thinks Kevin would tell me things. Or maybe it's some kind of weird jealousy. But I've never had a physical relationship with Kevin."

"Who is this guy?"

"I never met him. He said his name was Mr. Holt."

"Holt?"

"Yes."

"Arnie Holt?"

"He didn't say his first name."

"Goddamn," Lancaster says. Holt was who Brandon said had called in the Straw burning. Lancaster sits back down on the table and checks his watch.

"I told you he was going on some trip this afternoon. I think he shouldn't go. But he won't listen to me."

Lancaster's head is full of it and he wants so badly to lie down that he feels dizzy. And the last thing he wants to do is get wrapped up in some excitable girl's paranoia. But images of Michael Straw's burned face pass through his mind. Kevin was a good kid. Among the dope-using population you don't find all that many.

"Look," he says. "I've got about an hour left before I can leave here. In the meantime I'm going to try again to reach the detective who's on the burn investigation. If I don't reach him, I'll talk to Kevin. I want him to come in and give a statement."

"Thank you."

"Don't thank me. I'm not doing it because I want to. But I was the one who got that burn last night."

"Bad?"

"Worse than that. You want to wait here and come with me?"

She smiles the sad smile again and shakes her head. "He'll be angry if he finds out I talked to you, that that's why you went out there. Don't tell him, okay? Just say you heard about it somewhere."

"Fine." He opens the examination-room door and follows her past the nurse's desk into the utilitarian waiting room with its green cinder-block walls and cheap linoleum floor.

"What would you have done if I'd refused?"

She turns to look at him. "Probably cried or fell down on the floor or something dramatic like that."

"So I figured."

"Here." She hands him a slip of paper with Kevin's address written on it. "You're doing us both, Kevin and me, a big favor. I don't know if I can return it, but thank you." Then, using both hands, she pulls the hood up over her head and steps back out into the cold.

Lancaster's Bronco hangs tight even on the snow-packed curves. He's well west of town, on a road named, aptly he thinks, Pitt. The first house in is old and leans to one side. It has no paint on it anywhere and the front yard is filled with rusted autos and farm equipment and other junk, all of it covered with snow and none of it any good. Next, a few hundred yards up, are three houses in a row, the last of which is the Babcock place. All three houses are sad looking, but the Babcocks' is the saddest. It's small and made of cinder blocks painted orange. Junk litters this yard, too, though not as much as at the first place up the road. A light fresh layer of snow has coated the driveway where a rusted green Dodge Duster, covered with deeper snow, sits with its front end up on blocks.

An old black dog comes around the house and growls at first, then sniffs hopefully. It shakes from cold and hangs close to Lancaster's legs as he walks.

A quick knock on the front door raises no response. The bell works but still no one answers. A pane in the window to the right of the door has been replaced by cardboard but the others are clear enough. Lancaster steps into a snowdrift and swears and looks through the greasy glass into the living room. The room has been destroyed. A couch lies upside down in the middle of the floor and next to it a smashed table lamp. Clothes are scattered about and the television is on. Bottles and glasses litter the floor and one wall has a jagged hole punched in it.

He knocks on the storm door again, then opens it and knocks on the wood one, which opens a little because it isn't latched. A weird tingle crawls up his spine and whispers in his ear that it's time to leave. But something is wrong here. He pushes the door open and steps inside.

The heat is off—he can see his breath. Some liquid that has been spilled on the rotten carpet has frozen solid. The smell of human waste floats on the air and makes him gag, but because it's so cold this odor is muted, thin and hard and contained.

The damage and disorder in the living room are even greater than he could see. He takes two steps farther inside and calls out: "Kevin?"

His voice disappears into the cold, fetid air.

He turns off the TV, then looks more carefully at the scattered garbage. Along with the overturned couch and clothing and lamp on the floor are some other things: a badly worn leather moccasin slipper, a handful of scattered coins, and what looks like a black jewelry box with its lid open. The box seems incongruous. Inside he finds a plastic Ziploc bag, and inside that is what he thought might be there: Kevin's stash—a couple buds of marijuana and a glass pipe, a vial of white powder that looks like cocaine, some white tablets, then a surprise. At the bottom he finds two glassine envelopes of the same grainy tan powder his resident pulled from Michael Straw's pocket. Kevin has graduated to smack.

He puts the drugs back as he found them, then notices the telephone lying with its receiver off the hook. After hanging it up, he lifts it to his ear. The dial tone is strong and clear, not disconnected after all. He stands.

The kitchen: nothing but more mess, dishes crusted and frozen in the sink, plates broken on the floor, the silver drawer pulled out and lying upside down on the table.

The house is small, only two bedrooms tacked on to a living room and kitchen. Three or four steps from the kitchen take him into the hallway. He finds one bedroom, the mother's, untouched by the mess of the rest of the house. The other has its door closed.

When he shoves it open he sees Kevin.

Lancaster hears a sound come out of his own mouth—a frightened cry, a defensive yell invented by some ape ancestor and fueled by a massive jolt of adrenaline. He hears this noise but has no sensation of having made it.

Kevin hangs by his neck from the closet door frame. From where Lancaster stands he can only see a part of the body, a blue leg and arm and half a blue face, but he knows who it is. He steps into the room. The blue tongue protrudes from the side of the mouth. The eyes are open and bulging. Kevin is naked. A small step stool lies overturned beside his legs, which are bent beneath him, his knees nearly touching the floor.

Some emotion takes control then, maybe an instinct to react that he has been trained to give in to, maybe sorrow or anger, maybe just the inability to leave a friend hanging so pathetic and exposed; probably all of these he feels at finding this boy dead. But knowing he should not touch the body, knowing Kevin is long dead, has been hanging for many hours, and that there is nothing here to save, knowing that he should back away, get to a phone, call the police, or just get out, he rushes forward and lifts the body with his left arm while loosening the noose with his right. Lancaster pulls the rough rope free and lowers Kevin to the floor.

As he looks at the deep indentation in the boy's throat, he finds himself sobbing without tears, his chest heaving, choking on air. He sees these bodies on his ER table, or in the chopper, but stumbling on one in a ransacked house is a new horror.

Still, the only reaction to death he knows is to act, so although the body is stiff, the skin temperature ice, the face and hands deeply cyanotic, the backs of the legs dark with purplish lividity, he does. The protocol of a trauma situation is like breathing to him. He feels the neck for a carotid pulse, tilts the head back and breathes into the mouth, and presses with piggybacked hands into the chest.

The chest rises and falls, rises and falls, then is still when he stops his breathing. He beats on it, then breathes again. Again it rises and falls. Again he clenches his fist and slams it down over the heart.

"Goddamn you," he says.

Not just anger at this waste of a life. Anger that he's been pulled in like this, anger that he's acted stupidly, rashly, emotionally.

"Goddamn both of us."

And then as suddenly as they came the insanity and panic leave. He feels dizzy and nauseous. He sits back on his heels, then pulls himself up to the unmade bed, closes his eyes, and waits to catch his breath.

His head clears.

With his rational mind he looks at the naked boy and sees what really happened. Straight suicides rarely do it with their clothes off. He's seen this before, or rather seen the cases when they came in. Autoerotic asphyxia, accidental strangulation during masturbation. Feels good to come when you're close to blacking out from lack of oxygen. His suspicions are corroborated by a quick examination. The penis is crusted with dried semen. Kevin's face is especially dusky and shows marked hemorrhages in the whites of his eyes and elsewhere, clear indication that he strangled.

From the phone in the living room Lancaster has an operator put him through to the police station in Morgantown. A lady with a nice voice answers.

"Get a squad car and an ambulance to fourteen twenty Pitt Road," he says. "A boy is dead."

"One moment, sir." He hears a click, then another, then she says, "Sir, Pitt Road is under the county sheriff's—"

But already sirens sound in the distance.

"What's happening?" he says.

"Sir?"

Lancaster sets the phone back into its cradle. A car has pulled along the berm in front of the house, a dark new Ford Taurus. The driver, who wears mirrored sunglasses, rolls down the window and studies the house and Lancaster's truck. He looks around, looks down at his lap as if he's writing something, then rolls the window up and drives off.

Then another car, this one old and beat up, pulls in behind the Bronco. A lady gets out. She carries a shopping bag and a small suitcase as she walks toward the house. The old black dog wags his tail as she comes up the walkway and in through the front door.

"Who're you?" she says. "What are you doing in my house?" Legitimate questions. She would not remember him. She's middle aged, but looks old. Her hair has gone to gray and her face is lined and tired. The depth and roughness of her voice say that she has smoked cigarettes for a long time. Lancaster knows who she is. He met her once when she came into the ER to find out about her son, Kevin Babcock.

"I'm Dr. Lancaster, from the hospital. I treated Kevin—"

She moves into the house, watching him, and sets her bags down. The old dog followed her in and has discovered Kevin's body. His barking, which is as hoarse as her voice, leads her into the bedroom. Lancaster wants to tell her before she sees, but he cannot speak, and then it's too late.

"Oh, God," she says. She drops down at Kevin's side. "Oh, *God!*" She looks at Lancaster.

From outside comes that lonely wail made by dying sirens. He goes back and looks out the front window. His tongue and the bottoms of his feet tingle. A sheriff's car pulls up and stops in the road. Two deputies run toward the house.

"Who *are* you!" Connie Babcock screams at him from the bedroom. "What'd you do to my boy?"

He moves away from the window and toward the bedroom. "I'm a doctor," he says. "I came here to help," but he does not think this makes any difference to her as she cries and chokes.

"He's dead."

And then, as he stands mutely listening to that mind-numbing final farewell, feeling helpless and sad and stupid, the two deputies come crashing through the front door, guns drawn and imaginations in high gear.

He leads them into the bedroom.

"He's dead!" Connie Babcock screams, and then she points at Lancaster. "He was in here and my Kevin's dead!"

They look at her and the blue boy she is holding to her chest, and then they look at Lancaster.

He holds his hands away from his sides, palms exposed, and says, "I'm a doctor. I came to help and found him dead. Someone asked me to come. He's been dead a long time. There's nothing you can do."

"Shut up," says one of the deputies, a short middle-aged guy with no neck.

"Who asked?" says the other, young, blond, with aviator-style glasses.

"A friend of his named Storm came in this morning and asked me to talk to Kevin. I treated him some time back, at Morgantown County General, and then at the Free Clinic. He knew me. She was worried about him. She was afraid he was in some sort of trouble."

"What kind of trouble?"

"I'm not sure, really."

"I never heard of no friend of his named Storm," Mrs. Babcock says.

"That her real name?" says the younger deputy.

"I suppose."

"Last name?"

"I don't remember."

"How can we reach her?"

"I—don't know. She was a patient once. There may be some records. She said she'd spoken with another friend of Kevin's, a man named Arnie Holt, and that she was afraid this Holt would—"

"Whoa," the younger deputy says. "You know this Holt?"

"No. As I said—"

The younger deputy leans over to the other and whispers something to him. Mrs. Babcock stands in the middle of the room now, hugging herself and looking at Lancaster with a scared and hateful expression.

"That right?" says the older deputy.

"Just came over about an hour ago."

"There's an all-points out on this Holt, you know that?"

"I'm not surprised," Lancaster says. "Last night—"

"You'd better come with us."

"I'm not going anywhere," Lancaster says. He starts toward the doorway of the bedroom, when the older deputy steps in his way and says, "Put 'em on top of your head, son."

Adrian Lancaster finds his breath hard to catch. He has never looked down a gun barrel before. He does what the man says.

"We're goin for a little ride."

"This is bullshit," he says.

And bullshit it may be, but the blond deputy cuffs him, takes him outside, and locks him in the back of a squad car before going back into the house.

★ ★ ★

A little later, after Lancaster's had a chance to get nice and frozen, after a few more officials have arrived, the neckless deputy comes out, starts the squad car, backs out of the driveway into the road, and guns it toward town and the sheriff's jail.

As they come to the end of Pitt Road, which with the snowbanks is barely wide enough for two vehicles, they encounter a car coming from the opposite direction, an old yellow Toyota. The deputy slows and pulls hard against one side to squeeze by. As they pass, Lancaster looks into the other car and sees Storm behind the wheel. Her eyes lock on his for a quick moment. She raises her hand to cover her mouth.

Lancaster twists in his seat and watches as she stops and gets out and stands by her open door. She watches him as the squad car pulls away. He watches her, too, until they turn and she's no longer in sight.

## FOUR

When Brandon gets back to the office after stepping out to buy his Sunday feast, fast food in a bag, he finds a visitor, a semireformed sex offender named Petie Boncaro. Petie is gaunt to the point he looks starved. He keeps his hair nearly shaved so that it's little more than a suggestion of darkness on his scalp, and always wears black: black jeans, black army boots, and a black coat. Petie's an on-again, off-again snitch and today he's on the broke side so he's looking for a buck. He leans across Brandon's desk and eyeballs the food so hard, Brandon loses his appetite and slides the half-eaten burger and fries over so Petie can inhale them.

Petie likes to come in and talk about sex. Morgantown has developed a surprisingly high closet-homosexual and swinger population, and was once even bashed in New York City's *Village Voice* when the local paper published the names of twelve people, including several successful business owners, two lawyers, and a doctor, arrested in the raid of a gay sex club. Occasional word drifts in of more unusual deviations—S & M groups, kiddie porn clubs, et cetera. All part of the general turning-to-shit of everything Brandon sees around him.

But Petie keeps Brandon tapped into the moanings and groanings of the underbelly and once in a while it turns out to be useful information. Today he babbles about some boy who he heard had died totally naked. Has Brandon heard about this?

Brandon laughs. "Here?" he says.

"Yeah, that's what I heard." Petie can't give any details, though. More importantly, he claims no knowledge of Michael Straw, which is all Brandon wants to hear about. Brandon gives him a five to keep him happy and boots him out.

Until the final labs come back on Straw's clothing and the car, the avenues are limited. There is no population around the Overlook to canvass for witnesses; the initial caller, Holt, hasn't been found. Brandon has a request in to Detroit Metro. He wants to talk with someone there who knew Straw, but figures he won't hear anything until Monday. Spinner is planning on driving down to Wauseon to interview the owner of the Cabriolet. That will lead just about nowhere.

He's about to call home to tell Susan he'll be there shortly when the phone rings and the county sheriff's department informs him they've just arrested Dr. Adrian Lancaster at the scene of the hanging of a twenty-three-year-old man named Kevin Babcock.

They wonder if he'd like to swing by, just to take a look-see. He calls upstairs for Jimmy, but Jimmy's assistant says he's already on his way.

Two sheriff's department cruisers, a white Bronco, an old Chevy, and a beat-up Duster on blocks, are parked in the Babcock driveway. A four-wheel Cherokee with sheriff's department markings and the crime-lab van are on the berm out front. Brandon hopes that someone has gone over the driveway and yard for any sort of evidence that might turn up, but he knows they haven't and it makes him angry to think about it. Yellow crime-scene tape hangs along the front of the house, a few feet out from the wall. The second such scene of the day. *Un-fucking-precedented* is all he can think.

Two sheriff's deputies stand outside the front door, both of them shifting from foot to foot and blowing into their gloved hands. Brandon shows his badge and one says, "Go right in, sir."

Brandon nods but doesn't go anywhere. He lights a cigarette, turns his back to the two deputies, and surveys the area.

"Who," he asks, "do you suppose, lives in a place like this?"

Neither deputy says anything.

"Hmm?"

"Sir?"

"Who? What kind of people. Half these houses aren't even painted. They're falling down. The yards are full of crap."

"Lot of them are just people who've always lived like this. They were born into it. I suppose they like it well enough."

"Do you?" Brandon says. "That's good to hear."

"Yes, sir. And some are city welfare people who moved out, you know."

"Easier to be poor out here than in the hard grind of the metropolis."

"Yes, sir."

"But how do you get a whole country block like this of run-down, crap-heap houses? You go over a few miles north or south and there are prosperous little farms, well kept. And here all the shit settled."

"The way it falls," the second deputy says.

Brandon looks at this one, a younger man than the first, and he can see a glint of something in the eye, some anger.

"Just natural," Brandon says.

"More or less," says the younger deputy.

"You get a lot of calls out here, to impoverished areas like this?"

"More than other places."

Brandon nods, crushes his cigarette on his sole, and drops it in his pocket. "No surprise there."

"No, sir," says the older deputy. Brandon remembers this one. He's never seen anybody with a shorter neck. The guy's head is bolted right to his shoulders.

"You boys go over this yard?"

"Sir?"

"Did anyone comb the yard for any evidence? You know what evidence is?"

"Yes, sir," says the older deputy. "No, I don't think anyone did."

"Thought not," Brandon says. "You think you're gonna have crowds of onlookers around here? You need to guard the front door? Or would you mind walking the yard for me?"

They look at each other, and the younger one nods.

"I'd appreciate it. Just start out there in the middle of the yard, and work your way out. Use a grid pattern, you know, like in the textbooks. See what you find."

"Sure," the younger says, as if he's glad to have a chance to do something.


Inside, an older woman—the mother, he figures—sits on a couch with a female deputy. This deputy points toward the hallway off the left side of the living room, and this leads him to the bedroom where Jimmy Mendez is snapping pics with a Pentax and flash unit.

"We runnin' a goddamn two-fer special today?" Brandon says, looking over the bedroom.

A white male, early twenties, lies on his back on the floor, arms frozen at his sides, mouth slightly open, dead gray eyes staring up at the dead gray ceiling. His face is turned a little to one side. He wears nothing except the brown paper bags Jimmy has tied over his hands and feet to preserve evidence. Two lines of dried blood run down from the nose.

Jimmy straddles the body, squats, and shoots the face from as close as he can get with his 50-mm lens, eight inches or so. Then he moves to one side to get a different angle, same distance.

The throat is exposed because of the position of the head and the damage is apparent—the larynx slightly flattened in on itself, the angling mark of the rope, marked purplish bruising.

The body stretches from near the bed into the closet.

"Where the fuck is everybody?"

"You just missed Harvey," says Jimmy, who talks as he shoots. Harvey Bennet is Morgantown County's medical examiner. "He looked around for a minute and said he wanted to do the rest in the shop."

"Why didn't he take the stiff?"

"I didn't have my shots and you had not seen it yet."

"I'm the man on this? This is a county job. I got the shit from last night, and that should have been county too."

"You can call Harvey. He was here for a minute, as I said, then called Sheriff Donner and Lou Adamski to clear it. They want you to take this from here, at least as far as the scene is concerned. The sheriff has Dr. Lancaster."

"Their people go over it at all?"

"Not really. They poked around."

"Just enough to fuck things up."

The county preferred to abdicate to experience in cases that looked like they might be messy. There was precedent for this. It happened a few times a year. And Brandon had more experience than all the other investigators in the county combined.

"So what's the story?"

"The body was lying like this when the first deputies arrived. Dr. Lancaster said it had been hanging but he took it down to try CPR.

He said he knew right when he started the victim had been deceased for some time. I got this from the deputies."

"What's it look like to you?"

"At first glance, autoasphyx." He points out the overturned stool, the noose.

"He ejaculated?"

"On the penis. Not on either hand."

"Pretty neat trick." So there it was, Brandon thinks. Anyone with half a brain—even a sheriff's deputy—knew this wasn't a clear-cut hang-'n'-bang. If the kid hadn't jacked himself off, smart money said he hadn't snuffed himself, either, or at least that he hadn't been alone when it happened.

Along with that, the Lancaster angle made everything weirder.

"Before you start," Jimmy says, "there's a box out in the living room. You might want to look."

"Just tell me."

"Drugs—coke, grass, some pills."

"So?"

"And two glassines identical to the one they pulled out of Straw's pocket."

Three strikes. No way the county was going to touch this.

Brandon says, "On top of everything else, now we've got some clever son of a bitch running in smack."

"Calm down."

"I'm gonna retire to Wyoming. This is shit."

"You don't know the extent."

"Two incidents in a day? I know the extent is more than I want it to be. What's your ETD?"

"He's been dead over sixteen hours. There was no heat in here so that may be a little off, but well before midnight anyway."

"So roughly the time Straw was getting barbecued, few hours earlier." Brandon kneels next to the body and looks it over first. Kevin Babcock was a skinny kid and his skin is white and papery. The muscles of his arms and his chest are so underdeveloped, he looks emaciated. Says druggie all over. On his face is a thin mustache that never quite came in right and a series of scratches on the right cheek. Brandon notices a broad fresh scrape on the left rib cage and another, narrower but more severe, on the point of the left hip.

"You get all this?" he asks, pointing.

"Yes."

He shines a penlight into one eye, then the other, while Jimmy takes pictures of each, then slips on gloves and examines the dried semen on the penis. He pushes the chin back in order to see the throat better. "Lot of damage," he says. Jimmy snaps off a few throat shots.

Next Brandon pulls down on Kevin's jaw and tries to open the mouth, but the muscles have set pretty hard.

"Let's turn him."

Brandon rolls the body toward Jimmy, who holds him while Brandon runs his hands along the backside and on the carpet beneath.

"No other apparent injuries than facial scratches, left-shoulder and hip abrasions, and profound damage to the throat."

Brandon balances the body on its side while Jimmy lays a nylon bag out on the floor, and then lowers it so it's lying facedown on the bag.

He scans the back now, pushes up the hair to see the neck, runs his hands down over the buttocks to the thighs. "There," he says. He pushes the cheeks apart and points at the dried blood at the back of the crotch and around the anus.

"Hold it." Jimmy's camera flashes four times.

"Keep an eye out for an instrument. Something or somebody was up there. We'll let Harvey go at it from here."

Brandon stands and flicks his rubber gloves into Jimmy's plastic debris bag. Jimmy has begun shooting other objects in the room, moving along each wall first, stopping every few feet to shoot again.

"Two in the same day, Jim. What a mind-fucker." He lights a cigarette and exhales hard through his nose to flush out the smell of death. "Did you send that drug sample up with the clothing to Lansing today?"

"Yeah. We also sent urines and bloods from Straw, per Harvey's request. He ran them here but didn't get anything."

"So why send them?"

"He asked."

Brandon picks at the white residue the gloves left on his hands. "Something feels wrong about this."

"Listen, Frank, I want to start dusting. Harvey's sending a crew out to haul the body in. Then I'm going to clear all the drain traps, sweep the rugs. I will be here all day. Prints could be anywhere in the house."

"I'll clear the place. Somebody ought to train these yokels out here how to investigate a scene, or at least preserve it. Christ knows how much good evidence has been ground into the snow and dirt." He pauses in the doorway. "How much they paying you these days?"

Jimmy Mendez, who grew up in the migrant workers' ghetto in East Morgantown, one of the few to claw his way up and out through college and graduate school, looks surprised at this question. He smiles.

"Over forty?"

Jimmy lets out a laugh.

"You're giving it away, man. You're way too good for us. You know that?"

Jimmy turns away and continues shooting.

Brandon tells everyone, the deputies and the mother, to get out and let Jimmy do his thing. The female deputy agrees to drive Mrs. Babcock down to her sister's house.

Outside, the no-neck deputy is back at his post at the door.

"Cold feet?" Brandon says.

"We did the yard. Nothing. How could you find anything in all the snow? Tom's on the driveway."

"Thanks for your help," Brandon says. "Hope you didn't strain yourself."

The blond deputy named Tom has found some things, though. He lays out his collection on the hood of Brandon's car: a wooden coat button, an eyelet that looks like it came from a work boot, a square of hard black plastic, a used condom, and a miniature blue flashlight—the type that turns on when the sides are squeezed.

"You think these mean anything?"

"I don't know if they have anything to do with the body, but they mean something to someone. Mind if I take them?"

Tom shrugs.

"How'd you find these in all the snow?" He holds out plastic evidence bags so the deputy can drop the items in.

"Didn't. They were mostly out along the road where it's been plowed. I decided to walk that 'cause I couldn't really see much in the snow. The flashlight and the rubber were in the driveway. The rubber was sticking out of a snow pile, like it got shoveled there. The flashlight was covered with snow. Here." The deputy walks Brandon back up toward the house and indicates with his boot the spot where he found it. Brandon kneels.

"I didn't even see it. I was kind of kicking along, seeing if anything came up."

Brandon feels the spot where it had been. "How much snow on top of it?"

"Just enough to cover it."

"So it hadn't been there too long," Brandon says.

The justice building houses the entire realm of law enforcement in Morgantown County: courtrooms, the city police force, the sheriff's department, the county jail, even Jimmy's forensics lab, which is on the sixth and top story, a half-floor that was once a storage attic. In the center is a black lab table and sink, and racks of tubes, chemicals, and other glass paraphernalia. On the south wall is a bank of machinery Jimmy has managed to pull together over the past few years: a gas chromatograph and a visible spectrophotometer, both picked up secondhand from larger labs around the state. Across the room is the library of identification texts, including county-wide print files, reference books and directories, and a couple of microscopes. Anything sophisticated goes to Lansing or Detroit, but Jimmy handles most of the requests that come up.

Brandon drops the plastic bags of debris on the central table with a note asking Jimmy to dust for latents, run them against the sweepings from the Straw scene, and run a type on the now thawing semen in the condom.

His cold and the cigarettes have combined to make his throat burn and his eyes continually water. He should be home in bed, he knows, but he still has Lancaster to interview, and before that some paperwork. Down three floors, in his own cramped office, he writes up a report on Kevin Babcock.

It is not until he has filed these notes and is in the elevator on the way up to Sheriff Donner's fifth-floor office that the recollection of his talk with Petie Boncaro strikes him and he realizes that when Petie said he'd heard of a boy who'd died naked, he must have been talking about Kevin Babcock. But word wasn't out about Kevin until Lancaster found the body, which would have been just about the time Petie was sitting in Brandon's office. So Petie had known about this death somehow before the body was discovered.

When the elevator opens Brandon rushes for the stairs and back down to his office, where he tries the half dozen phone numbers of places he knows where Petie hangs out, but none turn him up. Petie's a wanderer and a mooch. It could be days before he surfaces again.

## FIVE

**I**f they had just talked to him, tried to figure out the misunderstanding, he would have described every detail. Can they really believe he is involved in this death, that it could be anything other than his happening upon it through bad luck and bad judgment and maybe someone else's conniving? Maybe not. He's been locked in an empty interrogation room for three hours. Maybe they just like having him here where they can exercise their power, and they're playing it as long as they can.

When Lancaster took the job here, it happened that Michigan's governor Irving Jovanovich, the first independent in the state's history, had just initiated certain health-care funds for small and mid-sized cities, especially for drug treatment programs, which Jovanovich was big on. Within a year Lancaster had helped secure some of these funds as seed money for the clinic.

Sheriff Donner and Detective Brandon were both part of the counterforce that lobbied and circulated petitions to prevent its opening. It did open, though, and two years later is a model of its kind, much of its financing now coming from private sources.

Lancaster has been detained for questioning and left alone in this room "to think on things," a deputy said.

So he thinks about Storm and Arnie Holt and Kevin Babcock and his thoughts go wild at times. He thinks he may really kill someone. Then he comes back to sensibility and thinks he should cooperate fully. He thinks through everything that has happened and tries to find an explanation, a logical misunderstanding. But fear keeps coming back, the fear that there will be some horrible mistake and he will be convicted of murder and spend the rest of his life in a cell. The fear shoves itself down his throat until he cannot breathe, until he feels he must scream out.

But any of these thoughts are preferable to the physical memories that assault him from an earlier time when he spent two days in the Wayne County jail in Detroit. The jail wasn't far from the hospital where he was doing his residency, and where he was busted late one night on felony theft and narcotics charges. It wasn't that unusual for a doc to pop the occasional barbiturate or amphetamine, depending on the need of the moment. But Lancaster was caught with two full vials of pharmaceutical morphine in his lab-coat pocket, and he hadn't received those vials in the proper, documented way.

He remembers that cell with its cinder-block walls and exposed seatless toilet and wet concrete floor and cockroaches crawling and half-human creatures curled up in corners puking and bleeding and snoring and crying out. And the smell, how smell is the one aspect of the human condition that can make even a medical worker sick, and how the smell in the jail cell, more than any other thing about it, should not have to be experienced by any person, a smell which there is no describing except to say that there is no description for the combination of feces and vomit and alcohol breath and body odors and seeping sores that is produced there and soaks itself so deeply into the cement that it can never be cleansed, no describing it except to say that once smelled it never leaves a mind. It embeds itself there to come back later, in bad dreams and bad drunks, to haunt and warn.

Finally Lancaster cannot hold off these physical memories. They come on until he can smell the puke breath again and his own sweat, can hear the raspy whispers and grunts in his ear.

In the end he can only put his head into his arms and wait.

The only light in Sheriff Donner's office is from a swinging-arm lamp attached to the edge of a broad desk. Outside it grows dark. Lancaster sits in a hard chair across the desk from Donner. Brandon stands to the side of the desk by the window, wearing a hat that shadows his face but cannot hide the head of wild red hair. He smokes and he listens as the sheriff starts to ask questions.

"Wait a minute," Lancaster says. "First, let's talk about how I've been treated. You expect me to sit here and talk to you after what you've pulled?"

"Pulled?" Donner says. He's a stupid man, Lancaster has always thought, and he looks stupid with his broken-veined potato nose and droopy eyelids and his laconic drawl.

"False arrest," Lancaster says. "Battery, libel, prejudicial treatment." He has no idea what he's talking about now. His anger is driving his mouth. And before he has time to reconsider any of it Donner leaps across the desk, grabs Lancaster's shirtfront in his hands, and drags him to his feet.

"You threatening me, son?" Donner says. "In this office?"

"Do me a favor," Lancaster says. "Hit me a couple of times so it looks real good. Then I'll run some lawyers so far up your ass they'll be looking out your mouth."

"Put him down," Brandon growls. *"Now."*

Donner drops Lancaster back into his seat.

"We're not filing any charges against you at this time," Brandon says to Lancaster. "This is on tape, and you have my word. If you want to file charges against us, that's your business. But right now I've got a murder to solve, and time is not on my side. I, we, will appreciate your telling us everything you can about this situation so we can get on with the investigation."

Lancaster takes a breath and lets himself calm down. "When can I leave?"

"As soon as we're finished talking."

He looks from the sheriff, who's brooding in his anger, to Brandon, who tips his head toward the sheriff and rolls his eyes.

Lancaster smiles down into his lap. "All right," he says. "Let's just get it over with."

In an hour of talking Lancaster tells his story. But as he tells it again and again, as he watches the faces of Brandon and the sheriff and listens to himself, he imagines how crazy it must sound. A depressed girl with a strange name approaches him in the clinic and claims Kevin knew the people involved in last night's burning and that one of them was threatening her. Without question Lancaster takes the bait and after a few attempts to reach Brandon agrees to drive out on a Sunday afternoon to talk with this burned-out loser of a kid. How can he explain the bond he felt with this girl, the urge to intervene? And then he finds the same drug that was found on Straw. And then the body. Didn't he know not to touch it? Of course. How to describe the emotion of the moment, the feelings he had for Kevin, someone he had liked as well as treated?

Why didn't he call it in when he found Kevin? He did, sort of. He called and reported the body, but before giving his name he heard a car and hung up.

At least, they tell him, they do have a record of an anonymous call from Kevin's house at that time.

Brandon's face is set into a hard, impassive blank. "The thing you have going for you," he says, "is I don't know anyone who'd be nuts enough to make up a story like that."

They all fall silent for a moment when Donner's phone rings. He puts the call on hold, hands the phone to Brandon, and says, "Barnes."

Brandon curses under his breath but takes the call. Ken Barnes is the Morgantown County district attorney, and a friend of Lancaster's. He must have heard, Lancaster thinks.

Brandon grows more and more red faced as he listens. He says almost nothing. Lancaster can hear Barnes screaming at the other end of the line.

When Brandon hangs up he wipes his face with a handkerchief and says, "Just a few more questions, then you're free to go. You know a sleazeball named Petie Boncaro?"

"No."

"Sex deviant. Reformed except that sex crime is like alcohol— once you're addicted, you're always an addict. He still does some weirdness but to cover his ass he comes in and talks to me once every few weeks. He gets almost as much of a thrill talking about it as doing it."

"This concerns me?"

"Today around twelve-thirty, before I knew who Kevin Babcock was, Petie told me about a kid who maybe died with all his clothes off. Didn't make any sense to me at the time."

"I didn't leave the clinic until noon."

Brandon smokes and nods.

"Storm said Kevin was into some experimentation."

They are both quiet.

"These are the kinds of people who live here now, Doc. You see how it is?"

Lancaster ignores the remark. "So it's a sex crime."

"I don't know what it is. Sex. Hard drugs. You tell me." Brandon punches his cigarette into an ashtray. "Listen," he says. He exhales and inhales, then turns to face the window. "There might be more to this than you think. You know that Holt called in the Straw burning. Every call like that that comes in is recorded and held for twenty-four hours. The tapes are then rotated back through the next day and taped over. But a little while ago we pulled this tape."

"Only now—"

"Three minutes before your call from Kevin's house was received by the county dispatcher, another caller reported a disturbance at Kevin's address, saying there might be a murder taking place."

"I was still on the phone when I heard the sirens." The moment flashes back on Lancaster and he experiences again the sensation of surreality. He had forgotten already, or suppressed it. "I remember wondering how they could be so fast. It was impossible. I just—I didn't think about it after that. With the arrest—"

"I understand," Brandon says. "It's all very confusing."

"They knew he was dead. They waited until I was there, then they called. I was set up."

"The point is, although this time the caller didn't leave a name, it sounds like the same voice that reported Straw."

"Holt again."

"And someone, also a man, also anonymous, called Connie Babcock at her church retreat today around noon and told her to get home right away." He turns back from the window.

Lancaster's face is hot. His head pounds and his throat feels swollen and cracked. Swallowing is difficult. "Who is this guy?" he says. "Why would he do this?"

"Take it easy," Brandon says.

"And what about Storm? She sent me out there. She helped in the setup. I can dig out her medical records. We could—"

"We talked to her."

"You what?"

"That's why we held you, so we could talk to her first. She left here about an hour ago. She came in on her own, said she saw you getting hauled away from the Babcocks'. She was all broken up, sobbing and shit."

"What'd she say?"

"What she told you. This guy Holt called her, like you said. She felt threatened by him but she was more afraid for Kevin, who she'd been trying to reach for several days. Holt's call panicked her into talking to you. And there's a record of her calling us, like she said. We should have picked it up then."

"Why didn't she drive out there?"

"She says she did, yesterday. Kevin wasn't home. Then she gave us the name of another one of these friends of Kevin's she mentioned to you. The name was Petie Boncaro. I guess he and Kevin were real tight, and Kevin had been sort of excluding her."

Lancaster is silent.

"I don't think she knows much," Brandon says. "I think she was just what she says, Babcock's friend and someone who knew he'd fallen into a barrel of deep shit. She just waited too long to say something. What we have to do is find this guy Holt."

"I should go," says Lancaster. He gathers his coat and his belongings that the sheriff has handed back to him: keys, wallet, money. They feel strange, as if they're from some other country.

"You remember anything else?"

"The car I saw, it was just before Connie got there. Before the deputies."

"Yeah?"

"Black Ford, guy in a suit."

"Holt, maybe?"

"I wouldn't know."

"Anything else strange?"

"My life."

"Hey, we agree on something. Now get out of here. I'm sick of you today."


Lancaster had been working at MCGH for a little over a year when a county EMT squad brought in a double auto trauma one night—two women named Lorraine and May Brandon, mother and daughter. The girl, May, was hopeless. Her chest was flail and she had no pulse and no respirations when she presented. They got her intubated and a surgical resident was called down to open the chest right there in the ER. If Lancaster had had an extensive team around him he would have worked on her himself. But the mother was critical, too, and under the protocol of triage she was judged to have the only realistic chance of surviving. So Lancaster had turned his attention to her.

May was pronounced dead by the surgeon an hour later.

Lorraine was operated on by an on-call neurosurgeon flown in from Toledo. She was comatose for six weeks. When she came out, she had no language capability and very limited general cognitive functions.

On the night of the accident Lancaster had seen Frank Brandon as no man had seen him before or since. He wept and raged in the conference room where Lancaster gave him the news. He'd threatened death to the stoner scum who killed his daughter. He threatened Lancaster for coddling these people and encouraging them with his fucking clinic to stay around this city.

Brandon's chief, Lou Adamski, held him while a resident gave him a shot of Valium. Brandon wouldn't let Lancaster touch him.

The episode has never been mentioned by either of them. And in time Brandon came back to being who he was, and treated Lancaster like any other professional. But Lancaster knows there is a hole in his heart, a void he feels every time he looks at the man who told him his daughter was dead. And, Lancaster thinks, there's nothing difficult to understand about that.

The snow, which softened during the day, has frozen again, leaving a coating of ice on the world. More is falling, small hard pellets that sting when they hit. The cold air of the evening makes Lancaster's eyes water. He inhales deeply again and again. Daylight is just ending.

It's been twenty-six hours since he slept. He finds the Bronco in an adjacent city lot, jammed between two squad cars, and heads toward home. The hospital called to say they'd covered for him in the ER tonight.

In Detroit it had been Denise Richards who found the lawyer who eventually got Lancaster out and began the long process that would salvage his career. It started with his being driven directly from the jail to the detox program in Royal Oak.

He breathes in the cold air again and again and thinks of that moment, of leaving that horrid place, as he is leaving this one. Then, though, Denise disappeared from his life. By the time he got out of rehab, she had gone away for good.

# MONDAY

**E**arly Monday, Brandon awakens to find the house dark except for streetlight filtering in through the blinds. It's well before six. When he turns to fold back the blankets pushed up around Lorraine's chin he finds her damp with sweat, so he strips the top blankets off completely and loosens her gown. In the darkness with her eyes closed she looks like herself still, the pretty face he married. The vacancy only shows in her eyes, when she's awake.

She'd been so young, once. She'd wrap her body around his and whisper there was no getting away from her ever. He was young, too, and hard and handsome. He knew he was handsome. He could see it in the eyes of other women, even into his late forties. He couldn't remember exactly when that stopped, when he'd put on too much weight or lost too much hair to be handsome anymore. But Lorraine always told him he was. She said that now it was just a more mature sort of look. Established, she said.

A line of drool runs across her cheek. He wipes it away with the corner of a sheet and then dabs at her damp forehead. He fingers the crucifix that hangs around her neck, making sure it's not too tight.

He thinks often of the times in this house when two children made constant noise, busy with the importance of their projects and imaginations. It was a real family, his own family, the kind that used to be seen everywhere but isn't so much anymore. Susan has no children and Brandon realizes she probably won't. She's never spoken with him about it but he assumes it's a conscious decision.

What surprises him most is that he doesn't blame her. The world's shit, he told her once when she wasn't too old. She must have believed him.

It felt funny seeing Lancaster under lock yesterday, almost as if in his association with scum some of the trouble rubbed off and came back around to bite him. And this wasn't the first time for the doc. Brandon believed as much as anyone that if a man could pull himself back up after a fall he deserved a second shot. But isn't it strange that smack, which brought Lancaster down the first time, is tied to what put him down again yesterday?

Brandon's throat still burns, but the cold feels as if it's moving up farther into his head.

On the kitchen counter Susan has left a brochure from the Catholic nursing home. He tosses it in the trash on his way out.


The police lab is dark and quiet like the outside world, where the sun has yet to rise and the day shift, including Jimmy Mendez's assistant, won't be in for another couple hours. Brandon's eyes are puffy and his nose is a brick. Feeling weak from the bug and fatigue, he has parked himself at the black-tiled work counter in the center of the lab and lit a cigarette. For openers Jimmy turns on the faucet, plucks the smoke from Brandon's lips, and drops it in the sink where it dies with a hiss. Then he lays out his Babcock and Straw files.

"I wanted to see you before the meeting this morning. I hear shit's going to fly because of the Lancaster arrest."

"What of it?"

"I thought you might like to see what I have so far. And Harvey's going to have big news. I should get the autopsy notes by nine-thirty, so you'll have time to see them beforehand." Every Monday starts with a general meeting between the detectives and the Morgantown police chief, Lou Adamski. Today's will no doubt be a little more crowded, and a lot hotter, than usual.

"What news?"

"Kevin Babcock was no suicide."

"That's not news. That's corroboration. What showed?"

"The lividity patterns were all wrong, and under infrared a second ligature mark on his neck, probably from a belt, was visible. That's what killed him, not the rope. The body was hung later."

"How much later?"

"A couple of hours."

Brandon nods and sighs and says, "Okay. Let's go through what else you got."

"First we pulled some nice latents from the living room—the wooden couch arm, the television—and from some silverware in the kitchen and from the bathroom. These are from six different individuals, two being Kevin and his mother."

"I'm told there's a brother, Seth, who has a history."

"Yes, we'll have to get a set of his to cross."

"Run Petie Boncaro's too. I'm sure they're on file."

"Sure. Now the yard debris—the black plastic, the button, the boot eyelet—no prints and no ties to the Straw debris. Nothing significant. The condom was old but showed traces of feces on the exterior. I ran the semen over to Harvey. He got a match with Kevin's ABO blood type and some more specific factors. So Kevin had penetrated someone's anus. And there's no evidence that a foreign object was used on him. His own anus showed recent latex burns."

Brandon is silent.

"The flashlight from the driveway was the best. We lifted one nice partial latent, a central pocket loop with a good eight points, maybe a ninth. Certainly enough to make a positive ID. Whether or not it would stand up in court, I don't know. Size indicates it's a male."

"Match any of the six in the house?"

"No. This one is a stranger."

"Fantastic. The deputy who found it was wearing gloves. Start on the indexes, do eliminations on everyone who was there. We'll get a listing from the mother of anyone else who's visited recently and cross them too."

Jimmy grunts. "Now, bigger news. You know before I sent Straw's clothing up north I ran my own tests."

"For the fuel."

"That and I also jumped them through the usual hoops. I found a couple tiny fibers on the cuffs of his pants. He wore them long, so they dragged. He picked up something, a yellowish fiber, looks like nylon."

"So?"

"They're from the living-room carpet in Kevin Babcock's house. Straw had been there."

Brandon lets out a lungful of air, rubs his eyes, and says, "A package deal. This is good. I'd rather have one big shit pile than lots of little ones."

"I have not run Straw's prints yet—I'll get a set from Detroit. We did get something from the tires of the car he was burned in. Has Spinner talked with the owner yet?"

"Couldn't reach him all day yesterday."

"We scraped the treads and dried it out. Lots of little chunks of concrete, which could be helpful. Concrete's a composite and almost never made exactly the same way twice. You've got stone, sand, gravel, glass, whatever, mixed into a fairly unique cement matrix."

"So if we can find the place where this concrete came from, you can confirm that the car was there."

"Reasonably so. Keep in mind that there may not be a lot of snow down wherever this is, or the tires would not have picked up the debris. Maybe inside a warehouse, something like that."

"Okay."

"Finally, I got a call from a friend up at the state lab last night. He'll be faxing final results this morning. But he said it was looking a little unusual. I told you the residue in Straw's clothing—actually just around the burned-off left sleeve of the coat—didn't match any standard band pattern. They agree. They say it was a fast gasoline-based accelerant but it looked like it was hand synthesized. Custom made."

"What?"

"And the heroin, Frank. It's not heroin."

"Speed?"

"No, no. It's like heroin, but synthetic. Some sort of a fentanyl derivative. It also showed in Straw's urine."

"But Harvey ran that here and got nothing."

"He wouldn't have. Extremely low concentration because it's so potent and it breaks down fast. Takes very sophisticated testing to pick it up."

"All right. Let's see what comes in before the briefing."

Jimmy nods.


Half of the third floor of the justice building is used by the mayor's staff, the other half by the municipal police. Most of the cops' half is given over to a large central squad room and holding pen where the daily business takes place. Along the southern wall are smaller rooms —the chief's front corner office, an interrogation room, the oversized closet Brandon calls an office, and a long, narrow conference room used for everything from meetings to staff lunches.

In this conference room at 10:00 A.M. Brandon, Jimmy, and

Spinner, who's working on a huge buttered cinnamon roll, face their chief, Lou Adamski. Ken Barnes, the county DA, is sitting in as well. Two violent deaths on a Sunday aren't exactly Morgantown run-of-the-mill. Brandon, armed now with Harvey's reports and the results from the state lab, is ready to lay out a theory, but sees that this is going in a different direction.

Lou Adamski opens by saying, "The hell's goin' on here?" He is thick and square—square shoulders, square chest, square head, square hands—shaped like a stack of cinder blocks, someone once said. The image was accurate enough that people started calling him Cinder-ella until he got mad and put a stop to it. His dark, hairy eyebrows knit together into one strip when he's angry, as he is now, which Brandon thinks makes it look as if some long insect has crawled onto his face.

"It's all around the doctor," says Spinner.

"He a suspect?"

Spinner shrugs.

Lou says, "He treats a patient and sees the guy's been torched, then has to argue with us to be taken seriously. Later he checks on a former patient at the request of a friend who had called us, and after he, Lancaster, *again* tried to let us know. We talking major criminal activity here? Hello?"

Spinner shakes his head.

"No is right," says Lou. "If anyone fucked up, it's this department."

Silence.

"All right. So who has theories?"

Brandon chews a thumbnail and waits. One dead, one nearly, and some strange syntho-heroin flowing in, but the brass is pissed because a doctor got bounced around a little. Ken Barnes, a politician before anything, is tight with Lancaster and had a lot to do with getting his clinic funded. It was the next best thing to kissing babies, because the money was state and federal—free gifts and no tax increase. Vote for me.

Lou says, "Voice analysis confirmed that the caller of the burn and the first Babcock caller are a dead match."

"Arnie Holt," says Spinner.

"Apparently. Did you check out Lancaster's story?"

"Nurse said a woman fitting Storm Summers's description forced her way in to talk with him. Lancaster recognized her, and sent the nurse out. Later, he made some outside calls while the woman was still in the office with him."

"He's a victim here," Ken Barnes says, cutting in. "Nothing more."

Brandon grinds his teeth and watches the balding fortyish DA wave his slender fingers around. Barnes is the yang to Lou Adamski's yin; while Lou looks like the quintessential Teamster, with the smoked-out voice to match, Barnes is slender and groomed to the point Brandon thinks he looks effeminate, and he sounds more like a game-show host than a tough attorney.

But when it comes to attitude, they rival each other. Brandon is still burned about Barnes's call to Sheriff Donner's office during the Lancaster interrogation. Even over the phone Brandon could hear Barnes's blood vessels getting ready to burst, and his threats still ring in Brandon's ears.

But then things have never been good between them. They'd clashed when Barnes was elected DA six years ago, and clashed often since. The skirmishes went a long way toward explaining why Lou, ten years Brandon's junior and six years behind him in departmental seniority, had been named chief when the job opened a few years back. The excuse Brandon got at the time was that Lou had a master's degree in administration. *A degree,* Brandon thought, *he worked on while I was out busting ass.*

"But it don't make sense," Spinner says.

"Then get out there and make it make sense," says Lou. "You're in Wauseon this morning, talking to the car owner."

"Right."

"I want you to track down Kevin's brother too," Brandon says. "Seth Babcock. For one thing we have to do elim prints. But see what he knows about what Kevin was into. I pulled his sheet. Petty possessions going back, then a bust for moving quantities of hash and rock in '88. Smack a year later. Did six months." He looks at Adamski. "Can we get on with this now, or should we sit around and whine about the poor doctor some more?"

Lou sets his jaw and glances at Barnes.

Brandon opens his files and runs over the forensic findings he'd discussed with Jimmy earlier, highlighting the facts that Kevin was not a suicide and that Straw has been tied to the scene. "But we've got more now," he says.

In addition to the autopsy on Babcock, Harvey had gone to the ICU himself and examined Straw. The doctors up there, he said, were a little pissed at the medical examiner working over a live body. But given the magnitude of these two cases, he felt justified. And he was rewarded. Under a fingernail of Straw's right hand he found a fiber from the manila rope that hanged Kevin.

"Straw's now the leading suspect in Kevin's murder."

"That he was there and touched the rope doesn't show murder," Barnes says.

"His belt," says Jimmy Mendez. "The belt Straw wore when he presented in the ER matches in both width and texture the underlying ligature mark on Kevin Babcock's throat. Harvey will testify that Straw's belt, not the rope, actually did the killing. Also, blood samples from under Kevin's fingernails match Straw's type and Rh."

"Tied up with a bow," Brandon says. "But the forensics on Straw as victim aren't so clear."

"He was probably unconscious when he burned," says Jimmy. "It's his blood on the tire iron. He took a severe blow to the head. And we now have an ID on the accelerant. I detected petroleum, I told you, but wild band patterns. It turned out to be plain old gasoline. But there were also residues of complex fatty acids, aluminum, and plastics."

"Napalm," Brandon says.

"Essentially. Homemade napalm. Somebody made an aluminum soap and mixed it with gasoline. That's about all it takes. Just stir it for a few hours until it gels up."

"What the hell do you have going here?" Barnes says.

"I'll tell you," says Brandon. "Straw shows up at Kevin's pissed off over some bad dope deal and attacks him. Remember, Kevin had the house to himself because his mother was away at a retreat—she'd left about seven that evening, she said—and he'd had homosexual intercourse. Based on Kevin's injuries I think he was still naked during the struggle with Straw."

"Naked?"

"Abraded hip and chest. Rug burns. Couldn't have happened if he was dressed."

"Are you saying someone else was there? His lover?"

"Maybe. Or maybe the lover was gone. But Kevin was naked, and he'd had sex. Anyway, Straw strangles the kid, then panics and splits. A couple hours later he comes back to cover up by making it look like a suicide by hanging up the body."

"Maybe Straw raped him."

"Anyway, after Straw comes back someone either meets him there or intercepts him, someone on Kevin's side, maybe Kevin's lover, maybe someone else. I'm guessing Holt because that's who called. This person, Holt or whoever, convinces Straw to go for a drive, takes him out to the Overlook, and fries him."

"This is all guesswork," says Barnes.

Which goads Brandon on. "The thing that's curious is Straw's killer knew he was going to kill. He'd planned carefully. He wore latex gloves and had gone to the trouble of making a batch of napalm. Why napalm? Because it sticks. There's no way you can miss. A cigarette, a match, anything sets it off and then there's no escaping it.

But the killer didn't just set the fire. After he knocked out Straw and threw on the jelly, he called 911. Cellular phone, let's say. He waited until he heard the siren right up the road before setting the flame."

"Then where'd he go?"

"At the scene yesterday, before I looked at the car, I followed a set of footprints down across the park to the railing. There they cut left and went straight into the woods."

The others are silent, watching him.

"Why wait to light the fire? Uglier that way. It's a drug hit, done for show as much as anything. The guy lives, it's more horrible than if he's dead. People have to look at him then."

"You can't prove it," Barnes says.

"Give me a little time. And I'll tell you something else. One way or the other, whether he's a perp or a victim, we haven't heard the last from Dr. Lancaster."

"Leave him out of this!"

"You watch, Ken. This is big-city bullshit and he's got the right kind of past. This isn't some grand coincidence."

Barnes goes red. Choking noises rise from his throat.

Lou leans across into Brandon's face and says, "Hard evidence and nothing else, Lieutenant. Got it?"

Brandon lights a cigarette and says, "Jimmy, tell us about the drug so we can get the hell out of here."

"Three, four-methyl ethyl fentanyl. Actually, it's the acrylate salt of that drug—three, four-methyl ethyl fentanyl acrylate. An extremely potent synthetic heroin."

"Like other fentanyls?"

"Only more so, I guess. I'm still running it down, but it's real ass-kicking stuff from what I hear."

"There has to be word out about this," says Lou. "Start pulling in your people. We've got to cap this or major shit is going to hit a major fan."

Silence.

"So go."

Another call to the Detroit Metro Police headquarters and several transfers and connections lead Brandon to a personnel clerk who tells him that the request he placed the day before has been referred to a Detective Byers. Byers is temporarily working out of the River Rouge precinct station. A call to that station, another transfer, and a woman answers: "Narcotics."

"Detective Byers," Brandon says.

"Who's calling?"

"Detective Lieutenant Frank Brandon, Morgantown Municipal Police, Morgantown County."

"Morgantown?"

"We're about an hour and a half west of you. Can I have Byers?"

"Horse country, right? I've got a brother-in-law over there somewhere. Seems to me he raises horses."

"Horses do fine out here. I need to speak with the detective. Is he in?"

"He isn't. But I am."

"Who're you?"

"Detective Ellen Byers."

"Oh," Brandon says.

"What do you want?"

"You ever hear of Michael Straw?"

There's a pause. "Zipper they used to call him, because of a bad scar on his face. Yeah, I know him."

"The scar is gone, but I've got him here."

"In jail?"

"Not exactly. County hospital's putting him up for a few days. What's left of him, anyway. He got doused with jellied gasoline and torched Saturday night. He's not expected to survive. According to his sheet you arrested him once."

"He was a chronic loser. Busted for this and that. Needle freak. Couldn't get off it. Because of Le Seure—you know about Le Seure—"

"I talked to his wife."

"—well, we watched out for Michael. But, what the hell, a junkie's gonna take some raps no matter what. So what can I help you with, or you just calling to give me the good news?"

"Straw was found carrying what looked like everyday brown smack. Now I'm told it's a synthetic, some kind of fentanyl. I'm trying to put together his last days, and I thought—"

"What was it exactly?"

"I'll read it to you—three, four-methyl ethyl fentanyl acrylate."

"Do you know much about synthetics?"

"Not really."

"Me, either, and I'm a specialist. Fentanyls are heroin substitutes made in the lab. Powerful but usually short acting."

"Ten, twelve years ago, I remember, in California they started showing up."

"Only, then, other forms of it, variants of the basic fentanyl and hundreds of times more powerful, began appearing. Nearly eight years ago we began to see this stuff around here. And the lab told us it wasn't just any fent. This was some very concentrated and long-lasting chemical with a long and complicated name. And this particular variant did not appear anywhere else in the country. I mean it was a big thing. People were dying from ODs because if you don't cut the stuff way down it's lethal. Just the dust raised from testing some of these variants in their pure form can cause lethal overdoses.

"Anyway, the feds jumped in, managed to infiltrate, and made a sweep. They only used us for street-level busts, so I can't tell you all the details. Old Greek was at the head of it, though he never took the dive somehow."

"You remember his name?"

"Louie Papalanos. Fat Man they call him. Old Fat Louie."

"Greek mafia?"

"Not a mafia, really. A powerful family. Anyway, these Greeks, who hadn't been in the drug business up until then, managed to get a line on some synthetics."

"Fentanyls."

"Let me finish. I said they never nailed the big guys, but a lot of street-level busts were made and the manufacturing was shut down. The whole thing didn't last too long, a year and a half, until now."

"Now?"

"The chemical that was made then was three, four-methyl ethyl fentanyl acrylate. A one-of-a-kind drug, as I said. It only ever appeared in Detroit and only for that one year. It was a signature chemical. The same stuff you've got your hands on. And I, Detective, have a dime of it sitting on my desk right now, picked up in a buy-and-bust last week.

"Somebody's recently gone back into the trade."

"Papalanos?"

"No. His sons run the family now, but I have eyes in their pockets. They're not behind this. Fat Louie knew they had no business in narcotics. That was their one foray and he got them out quick. They were always big in real estate and construction. These days it's auto parts as well. No drugs."

"How much has been showing up?"

"Three months ago samples started to appear. That little bit has been growing. Maybe half a ki came in over the past couple weeks. Thing is, you test this stuff it's all cut—baby laxative, sugar, whatever. The amount of the actual chemical in a sample of street is almost immeasurably small."

"You said the feds were involved in that bust. Le Seure?"

"No. This was after he was out of the DEA, working for the chief. He had no involvement."

"Or Straw?"

"No. Not to my knowledge."

"And this variant has never appeared anywhere else?"

"Right. Just around here. Usually cut brown, which is the caramelized sugar. People started calling it Metal Fang, after the acronym MEFA. That got shortened to Fang."

"Can you fax me the list of people who were arrested before?"

"Sure. What I want to know now is how did Mikey end up getting burned out in horse-farm country? And what's it got to do with my drug?"

"You find an answer to that one, Detective, and I'll drive over there and buy you the biggest steak in Detroit."

"I'm vegetarian."

"Then I'll buy you a salad. Listen, what'd you mean when you said Le Seure was working for the chief?"

"I thought you talked to Sarah."

"She just said he'd been a DEA agent."

"He was more than an agent, Brandon. His last four years in he was head of the regional office. And he left that nice job for a good reason—to work for Irving Jovanovich."

"The governor?"

"Yessir."

Jovanovich, recently inaugurated into his second term as Michigan's first Independent head of state, was a runaway in the last election. At forty-five he had become the youngest governor in recent state history by accomplishing the unprecedented feat of developing strong support from both the liberal labor voters of Detroit and conservatives across the state.

"Le Seure's still with him?"

"He's chief of staff, so you'd best take care of young Michael."

# SEVEN

**O**n the leather couch in his den where he passed out the night before, Lancaster rises into a shallow sleep. And in this shallow sleep he dreams a memory.

Years before, in Ann Arbor and Detroit, a woman named Denise Richards was the center of his life. Mornings in bed she would whisper to him as he was just waking up. In his dream she is as real as life, kneeling naked next to him, her long sandy brown hair hanging in his face, tickling him until he opens his eyes and smiles up into her own smile, her pale breasts, blue veins visible on the sides, touching him too. She's older, already into her thirties. He can smell her breath, stale from the night but sweet anyway. Sometimes she would kiss him. In these early-morning first-of-the-day minutes there was no hunger, no longing, no chemical emptiness crying to be filled. He felt, and knew she felt, too, that this was the day they could stop, this was the day they could just keep on not needing it, could do without anything but what they woke up with—themselves. Some days, especially those rare days when neither of them had to work, or go to a class, or deal with the people who came to them for help—odd holidays, occasional Sundays—on these days they could make the illusion last sometimes until well past noon, taking in nothing stronger than coffee and cigarettes, sitting at opposite ends of her living-room couch, the *Detroit Free Press* spread out between them, Bugs yakking on the tube. Sometimes he'd think in the back of his mind that he wanted to freeze a moment like this and hold, just stay, the two of them in a posture that smacked so strongly of boring, mind-numbing suburban normalcy. Two people sitting around, waking up together, reading the paper.

But even on days like this the hunger came, more slowly, perhaps, but inexorably. He'd notice it first more in her than in himself, in the number of cigarettes she smoked. Early on, over the first steaming mug of coffee, she'd light a smoke, drag on it a couple times, then set it down. By noon she was chaining, sometimes to the point of lighting a fresh one off the dying butt she'd just taken out of her mouth. She smoked Kools because she liked the menthol anesthetic. He smoked, too, in those days, Marlboro Reds—he liked the thick, heavy smoke, the honest taste. The number of cigarettes escalated, ashtrays filled, the air grew dense with hanging smoke.

Eventually one or the other of them would go to the bathroom, stand on the toilet and get the kit from the top of the linen cabinet, bring it in, and set it on the newspaper on the couch between them. She usually did the honors, she the chemical wizard, the Candy Man to end all Candy Men, she whose brain could envision abstract theoretical designs and interminglings of the molecular structure of chemicals in the way a good cook could imagine the bit of individual flavor each ingredient would bring to a finished dish, the way a true conductor could hear distinctly each line of each instrument in a 120-piece orchestra. She, brilliant as she was, lit her Bic like any common street junkie under a silver spoon full of the magic dust, mixing a suspension in the normal saline solution he'd bring home from the hospital, cooking it for the tuberculin syringes they bought from John, his pharmacist friend, who pretended to believe Lancaster was a diabetic but who must have suspected the truth. No diabetic could ever have used that much insulin. Besides their own habit there were the others, customers he'd called them in Ann Arbor, friends-in-need in Detroit. They went through syringes by the gross. But he paid John a nice fee, cash only, of course, for keeping it quiet and John kept on believing what he wanted.

So she would hold the suspension up to the light, a band which had been growing around his chest now tightening so hard that he could barely breathe as he watched her, the humming in his head deafening him. His skin itched, it crawled, and how, Jesus, how could her hands stay so steady when he knew she needed it as badly as he?

But they did. They dipped the needle into the solution, sucked up a half cc into the tuberculin syringe, turned the set upward, snapped a fingernail against the side to bring the air bubbles up into the needle, and shot out a little spray. He always liked that precise moment, the moment she voided the syringe of air by sending a squirt up and out. He can see it in slow motion, the fluid arcing through the smoky late-morning air. That meant it was time. He tied on his own tourniquet, a rubber chest-drainage tube that pulled itself tight around his upper arm. He flexed, balled a hard fist, the veins popping up firm and clear, not so many tracks showing yet.

And then, after first applying the dark reddish Betadine antiseptic (their technique was always sterile), she would lay the needle against his flesh and slide it in and draw back on the plunger, pulling blood into the milky solution, pinkening it up, then pushing a little into the vein, then drawing back again. And on the second or third push he popped the rubber and the rush hit his brain and oh fucking christ. Sometimes it gave him an erection.

She would pull back and inject more, pull, inject, until the dose had been delivered. And now, hands steady as brick, head clear, no humming, no tightness in the chest, eyes open, he could take up the Bic lighter and the spoon and the powder and begin to cook hers.

Dr. Fix, they called him. They loved him.

And she loved him. She would love him for the rest of her life.

A dark-eyed girl stands over him.

"Denise," he says.

"Storm."

"What?" He's awake then, and badly startled. He jerks away from her, yanking up a couch cushion to use as a shield.

"What are you doing in here?"

"Your garage door was unlocked. I let myself in," she says.

"Are you crazy?"

"Maybe."

"I could have you arrested. I could shoot you." His heart pounds violently against his chest wall as he watches her, half expecting something horrible to happen, for her to pull a knife or for some friends of hers to burst through the door to rob him.

Instead, she sits down Indian style on the floor in front of him.

"How can you just walk into someone's house?"

"I told you, the garage door—"

"I mean how? How can you let yourself?"

Lancaster's heart settles in his chest as he watches her. She's wearing the same sweater and vest she had on yesterday, but without the shawl. In spite of himself he notices how good she makes the clothing look. But he wonders who this girl is. What kind of person just casually lets herself into a near stranger's house?

He has a sensation similar, he imagines, to what he would feel if he were alone with some semidomesticated animal, a wolf dog, say, that had only been partially trained, or a cat that had lived most of its life in the woods. He has no idea what to expect.

"It's not 'how' you should ask. It's 'why.' "

"I should ask why? I don't care why. Goddamn you." He rubs at his eyes, trying to clear his head and compose himself.

She shrugs. "Why, then?" she says. "I was hearing footsteps."

He turns his face away as if he does not want to listen to her.

"Someone's after me. I saw a car parked in front of my building."

"Go away," he says.

"You want to know what kind of car? I didn't notice. It was a dark color, and there was a man in it."

Lancaster pauses. "Was he wearing a suit?"

"Ah, you are interested. See?"

"I'm not interested. I think I'm going to call the police."

"I don't know what he was wearing. I didn't stay there and watch him. All I knew was it felt like he was there for me. Like he was waiting for me."

"I still don't know why you're here."

"I'm scared."

"So go to the cops. I can't make anything better for you."

The hurt look that flickers across her face makes him angry. And at what? At the fact that the needy come to him? At the fact that he's made them his mission? At the fact that even in his anger he can't help watching her face because he likes the way it looks?

He does not want to look at her. He wants as much distance between himself and anyone having anything to do with Kevin Babcock as he can get.

"I can't help you. I don't want to help you."

"What can I do?"

"I said go to the police if you're scared. Just like you did yesterday."

"Are you mad at me about that?"

"Mad? That I found a dead body and got arrested? That I was set up like some chump? Mad?"

"At me, I said. It wasn't my fault. I was set up, too, you know."

He doesn't look at her.

"It was all horrible," she says.

"That's a word for it."

"I was sincere; I hope you know that. If I had known—"

"All right. Just forget it. You gave the cops what you have. There's nothing more to do. Like I said, if you're scared, go back to them."

"I can't."

"Why not?"

"Because the police are in on this."

"What do you mean 'in on it'?"

"I don't know."

"You know more than you told me yesterday, though, don't you?"

"A little."

"Who told you the cops were in on it?"

"Kevin, a couple days ago."

"Local cops?"

"God, no. These incompetents?"

"Narcs?"

"Something like that."

"Narcs were onto Kevin?"

"Yes, I think so."

"Was Kevin dealing smack?"

"I don't know."

"He was, wasn't he? Jesus," Lancaster whispers. He sits up on the couch and leans forward with his head in his hands. "Why the hell didn't you tell me this before?"

She is silent.

"Who'd he deal with?"

"Different people, I think. He worked out of Red's, I told you. Do you know the place?"

"Sure." Red's, a bar and dance club isolated by design at the far eastern edge of the county, has a reputation for catering to clientele most people in the county would call strange. An alternative, it calls itself. He's heard people drive all the way from Ann Arbor and Toledo to go there, people who shave their heads and pierce their nostrils.

"The last time I saw him, at Red's last Friday night, he was with a friend of his named Petie Boncaro and a couple of guys from out of town."

"Brandon only said you told him about Boncaro."

"Yes."

"Why's that?"

"These other guys, I was told they were major dealers. Traffickers. Can I smoke?"

"Who were they?"

"I didn't hear their names. These are the kind of people who move strictly large weight. And that means they're killers. Real killers." She lights a cigarette and waves the match until it's cool, then sets it on her leg.

He watches her drag deeply and exhale, then flick ash onto her jeans and rub it in, and wonders again who she is, what sort of recklessness leads someone with her undeniable natural grace and self-possession to end up as the onetime confidante of a dead drug dealer, and in fear of killer traffickers. Perhaps, he reminds himself, the same sort that led a young medical resident into an addiction that almost ended his career before it began.

"You told me before you didn't know any of these people."

"I don't know them, not even their names. I know of them. And they're not the sort of people I want to be turning in. I didn't think it was necessary to explain all this to you. I just wanted you to help Kevin."

Brandon was right, he decides—she knows nothing. She's good for nothing but more grief and trouble.

"Well, I tried. Now do what I want."

"What's that?"

"Leave."

"Seriously?"

"Seriously. If you're scared, you should talk to the detective."

She shakes her head. "I don't trust anyone."

"Then why are you here?"

"You've got more to lose than anyone, so I know you're straight. With Kevin getting killed, I didn't know where—"

"Killed?"

"As in murdered."

"Kevin hanged himself. It's called autoerotic asphyxia."

"That's not true."

"No?"

"He wasn't stupid and he wasn't that deviant. I knew him. And I knew he was in way over his head. Somebody killed him."

"You're pretty smart, aren't you?"

"Maybe not. But I'm surprised you haven't heard this. Word's out on the street, Doctor. Kevin was eliminated, and Straw was, too, and they were connected. I heard they were doing some business that went bad. Word is, too, that you're mixed up in this. I don't believe it—"

Lancaster leans forward and gathers the front of her vest in his hands. He pulls her toward him until her pretty face is an inch from his own, until he can smell her sweet-stale breath and the remnants of her lilac perfume.

"What word?"

"A man gets burned. Then Kevin's found killed. You're arrested. People know you were a junkie once upon a time. The story is you were arrested for it then. Rumors spread."

*Set up*—the phrase he used when Brandon told him of the caller —comes back. He lets her vest go and she slumps toward the floor. "You'd better leave."

"I thought we could help each other. I thought since you were involved—"

"I'm not involved. I'm so far from being involved, it would stun you. I don't want to know you. I'm glad you got over your cocaine problem. I'm sorry for you if Kevin was your friend. Other than that, I can't help you."

Lancaster's mind spins with the ramifications—what a fragile thing a reputation is. How hard it was to reconstruct his career the last time, and how easy for some sick fuck to blow it away again. Ignoring Storm, he walks to the window and looks out at his snow-buried front yard and the walkway that needs shoveling so badly.

"I may not know these people, Dr. Lancaster," she says. "But I know this town and I know where they deal and I can get in there. I have friends. If you want to start looking, I'll help."

"Why?"

"Because I feel like I need some protection. I'm in it too. Like I said, someone was waiting for me. I knew Kevin well. Very well. Maybe he used my name when he shouldn't have. Maybe I was his excuse. Or maybe I really know things someone else wants to know. If Holt set you up, then he set me up too. All I'm sure of is I'm very scared. And I know that, whatever you want to be, you're not uninvolved. Not now."

"You really believe he was murdered?"

"I guarantee it."

"I appreciate your telling me," he says. "Everything." He walks to the front door and opens it. "But I have to think."

She zips up her down vest. "If I hear anything else, I'll call you." She hands him a slip of paper with her number written on it. "Let me know if you need to know anything. Believe me—I can find out." Then she is gone.

## EIGHT

S outh Morgantown, which is separated from the central city by the River Sorrow, has become a sprawl of prefabrication. Fast-food restaurants, gas stations, carryouts, cheap apartment buildings, and new roads spiral out from the nucleus that is Valleydale Mall at the intersection of Route 57 and the South Border Highway.

Brandon's headed toward a little pisshole bar called Spike's, which is next to an old trailer park behind the mall. All the nice old houses went, but the cheap-shit trailers and bars managed to survive the wave of development. At least they're consistent, Brandon thinks.

Spike's gravel parking area holds a couple pickups, a beat-up fifteen-year-old Pontiac Le Mans, three Harleys, and a lame-o Kawasaki 500. It's only lunchtime but Brandon knows the people he wants to see have probably been here all morning.

Inside it's dark. The smelly moist air—a mingling of sweat and beer with an undercurrent of vomit—gags him. The decor is early post-Neanderthal: bare concrete walls and pictures of centerfolds taped up in various strategic locations, and hanging over the bar an inflated life-sized anatomically accurate reproduction of a naked lady.

Brandon sits at the uninhabited end of the bar near the door, the wooden surface of which has been carved with intellectual drawings and sayings such as PUSSY HOUND 4 EVER and EAT ME. The place grew quiet when he walked in and it stays quiet as he orders a 7-Up. He feels lots of pig eyes on him, but the bartender serves him the soda, then stands with arms folded and watches him drink. From the corner of his eye Brandon sees someone wearing a green nylon jacket slip past the huge antiquated phone booth along the back wall and into the hallway leading to the men's room.

"Shirley," he says to the big man behind the bar, "I was driving by and had a sudden urge for something cold and wet."

"Stupid, Brandon." Shirley is maybe six five, maybe three hundred pounds. He has hair redder than Brandon's and eyebrows and beard to match. Shirley knows a few things about what goes on in Morgantown.

"Stupid?" Brandon says.

"You showing up here, man. Make this place look bad."

"Gosh. And you have such an image to uphold."

"Fuck you."

"Careful, boy," Brandon says. "Tell me about Kevin Babcock."

"Besides the fact he was a trashy little shit?"

"Maybe like what he was into, who was doing him?"

"Maybe like if I hear things I call you, remember?"

"You know him at all?"

"Know his brother real well."

"Seth?"

"Yeah."

"You see him, tell him I want to talk. I need to know if he knows anything about what Kevin was doing."

"All right. I don't know how much time they spent together. I only saw Kevin around now and then. He hung out with the freaks at

Red's. Tried coming in here a couple times before he figured out he was gonna get his ass kicked."

"Who'd he go around with?" Brandon takes out a tissue and wipes at his nose.

"Petie Boncaro, sometimes. Faggot trash like that."

"Tommy Winter?"

Shirley looks around. "Not that I know of."

"I thought you knew everything."

"Yeah, well keep it to yourself."

"You hear anything, you get on the horn, hear? Heat's up on this one."

"Yeah," he says. "Now get outta here."

"I'm gone," Brandon says, and he stands up. "Except I gotta take a leak. That 7–Up goes right through, you know?"

A doorway in the rear of Spike's leads to a narrow hallway, which in turn leads to the rest rooms. In the middle of this hallway, across from the doorway leading from the bar, is another door, an old wooden one leading outside to the back parking lot. The green-jacketed apparition Brandon saw either slipped out this doorway and escaped, or he's hiding.

The men's can is freezing and filthy, Magic Marker graffiti all over the concrete walls, dirt caked on the sink, half an inch of standing ice-edged water on the floor around the urinal and the single stall. Brandon tries the stall. It's locked, but when he bends and looks he sees no feet.

He turns on both faucets, then crouches next to the dividing wall.

"Tommy, you old son of a bitch, you haven't been around in a while."

No answer.

"You make me promises and then you don't keep your word."

No answer. Brandon lights a cigarette and blows the smoke under the wall of the stall.

"Kinda hacks me off."

More smoke into the stall. Now someone coughs behind the locked door. A voice says, "Damn, Brandon, you know I'm allergic."

"That's why you hang out in bars all day."

"What do you want?" The voice whines.

"I haven't seen you in two weeks, and all kinds of wacky fucking things've been happening. When I need you most, buddy, you disappear on me."

"I just been busy, that's all. Ain't had time to stop by. I ain't tryin' to avoid you or nothin'."

"Good, Tommy. I don't think I could sleep nights if I thought you were trying to avoid me. So talk. Mike Straw might be a place to start."

"Didn't know him."

"Who?"

"Straw."

"Who's Straw?"

"Stop it, Brandon. I didn't know no Mike Straw."

"You didn't hear about the guy got baked down at the Overlook?"

"Something about it. Junkie of some kind."

"That's all you heard."

"Yeah."

"Very disappointing, Thomas."

"Heard about the kid, though."

Brandon drops his cigarette. It hisses in the water on the floor.

"I know you think he was stroking off and hung himself. He wasn't, I heard. I heard maybe somebody hung him up."

"Where'd you hear it?"

"Don't know."

"Petie?"

"Ain't seen Petie in a while."

"Then where?"

"Around."

"You're slick as shit, Tommy." Brandon lights another cigarette, then rolls up a five-dollar bill and deposits it in the crack where the two walls of the stall form a corner. It rests there a second, then disappears. Now Tommy's feet come down, and Brandon can see his cowboy boots, so worn out, they've got silver duct tape wrapped around to hold them together.

"Your friend Petie Boncaro told me about that kid killing himself."

"He ain't no friend of mine."

"He told me before the body was discovered."

Silence. More smoke up into the stall. A cough.

"So?"

"So how'd he know that, Tom? How'd old Petie know that kid was dead out there in the country, and no one had even discovered the body? You think Petie had a hand in it?"

"He might of had something in it, but it probably wasn't his hand."

"Was Petie banging Kevin?"

"Brandon. You're so slow."

"That's why I need you, Thomas."

"Petie and Kevin were in love, man. Kevin's the first thing made Petie stop getting it wherever he could. They were tight." Tommy snickers at his joke.

"The night Kevin died, Petie and Kevin got it on, didn't they? They were together."

No answer.

"Petie was there when Kevin got killed, right? He saw who did it."

Again no answer.

"What about after Kevin got hung up?"

"Petie went back out there. . . ." Tommy's voice fades. He coughs.

"Did he see who met Straw?"

"I don't know."

"Who else is in this?"

"Couldn't say."

"You know anyone named Arnie Holt?"

"No." Silence. "Petie says you'll be hearing from him again real soon."

"That's good. I been looking for him. Must have dug himself a hole." Brandon rolls up another five and parks it in the slot.

"Guess so. No one called him that, Brandon."

"Who?"

"Mike Straw."

"You knew him?"

"No. All's I heard was he was maybe a runner, a bagman with some connection to Detroit."

"So what name did he go by?"

"Don't know. But it wasn't Straw."

"Zipper?"

"Yeah. Maybe that."

"So what's a big-city bagman doing coming over here?"

"Honest? I can't figure it out. You see much showing up on the streets? I don't."

"Who was he coming in here to?"

"Don't know. Got another five?"

"When we're finished. Kevin Babcock?"

"Warm."

"What's that mean? Kevin was part of the group?"

"Warmer."

"Petie was in it too."

"A balmy breeze is blowing."

Brandon stands up because his legs are starting to cramp. "Petie and Kevin were doing the dealing."

"Fucking sauna in here. Thing is, Petie's no dealer. Petie has a big mouth. He likes to brag on himself, how he's this up-and-coming businessman. He's gonna build him a nice little underground business and put away a lot of money. Him and Kevin and Seth didn't know what the fuck they were doing."

*Seth?*

Brandon holds his breath. "Seth Babcock was part of this?"

"Hot."

"He was involved directly in the trafficking?"

"Sweatin' my ass off, Brandon. I gotta get out of here. I don't know nothin' else."

"How about the doctor—Lancaster?"

"Heard what happened. I don't know what that's about. He was a junkster himself, busted in the Big for lifting morphine, that's the story. Once you're bit you're always bit, but why he'd fuck around with small-town white-trash dealers is beyond me."

"I need help on this, Thomas, so get out of there." He rolls up a ten and slips it into the stall. "You be in here tomorrow, same time. Unlock the back door and no one will know."

"I ain't sure about any of this."

"Then get sure."

"Give me time. Two days."

"I don't have time. You can have till tomorrow afternoon. Five o'clock, say."

No answer.

"I want to know about Kevin and Petie and Seth, who they were in with. None of this makes any sense."

Tommy doesn't answer.

On his way out Brandon slides a ten over the bar to Shirley. "House round on me," he says.

"Thanks," Shirley says. Then he slips the bill into his pocket and glances around to make sure no one else heard.

★   ★   ★

On the way back toward the downtown Brandon sees two men pushing a shopping cart along 57, past the piles of plowed snow and the old gingerbread Victorians. Traffic swings wide to avoid hitting them. He turns on the windshield flasher and pulls over.

"Ride?" he calls back.

The two stop when they get to his car. They're both fairly young, early forties, but they look old. Their beards are rough and matted, their clothes shiny with grease, and they stink. The closest he can come to naming the smell is rotting garbage, but that's not quite it. One has an open seeping sore on his cheek.

"What?"

"Where you headed?"

"North."

"You'll get hurt out here."

The two look at each other. No one says anything. And then Brandon doesn't care anymore. There's no way to fit the shopping cart and both men in his car anyway, and he knows they won't leave it behind. He tells them to be careful and drives away, watching them in his mirror until he turns out of sight.


On his desk is a pile of mail, a few phone messages, and a copy of Harvey's report on Kevin Babcock. Nothing from or about Petie Boncaro.

He calls Jimmy upstairs and learns he's matched three additional prints from the Babcock house to Petie, Lancaster, and Michael Straw. That leaves two unidentified latents including the one on the flashlight.

Before Brandon's phone makes it back to the cradle the interoffice buzzer goes off, rattling his teeth.

"I've got a visitor waiting to see me," Lou Adamski says. "You want to join us?"

"Who?"

"Guy named Kline. DEA."

Brandon feels a surge of quick anger rush through him. "I figured you'd be calling someone in."

"You got a problem with that?"

"No, sir," Brandon says. "Just not surprised, that's all." *Typical that anything beyond an ounce of weed you think we can't handle,* he wants to say.

"Anyway, smooth your fur. You don't get it. He wants to talk about the Straw thing for some reason."

"He called us?"

"That's it."

"Pretty damn quick," Brandon says. "Byers, the Detroit dick, must have called him. Maybe they know something we don't."

"Let's hope. Get in here."

The fed, Julian Kline, is young, thirty-fiveish, with curly blond hair and eyebrows and mustache, and neon-blue eyes behind red designer-framed glasses, the sort of pretty-boy face Brandon guesses has probably got him into trouble more than once or twice. His suit looks like it's designer as well—Brandon figures it probably cost more than his own entire wardrobe. Kline confirms that he's heard through the Detroit narcotics grapevine about the Straw killing. He's a special agent out of the Detroit bureau and has been working with the Motown police on the fent situation, as he calls it.

"So," Kline says, "Straw's down for the count. Homemade napalm. If that's not the most bizarre-o guano I've heard in a while. And Chief here tells me you've got a related killing?"

"Probably. Looks like Straw perped that one, then someone got him."

"Little turf war."

"Looks that way," Brandon says. "I didn't know there was any turf around here worth getting snuffed for."

"Like bad cancer, bud. It's spreading."

"Town's turning to shit."

"Yours and everyone else's. But in this case I'll admit it's a little strange. You're talking about Fang. Wickedly damaging Horsie. Dozen of ODs already directly attributed and more sure to come."

Lou says, "It's just a fentanyl. That's not so unusual."

"Sure. But what does that mean, 'just a fentanyl'? The variations are endless. Carfentanyl, sufentanyl, para-fluoro fentanyl, alpha-methyl fentanyl, benzyl fentanyl, on and on. You break off a side chain here, insert a carboxyl molecule there. All very effective synthetic opiates, all relatively easy to reproduce in a decent lab. Designer drugs. Endlessly variable. And endlessly various in their strength, with some testing at up to three thousand times the potency, gram for gram, as pure morphine.

"But this particular recipe, three, four-methyl ethyl fentanyl, has a mongo capability, maybe as high as six thousand times morphine. That's fifteen hundred times pure heroin. The quantity needed to cause an effect is unimaginably small, a microfraction of a percent of total volume. The street samples turning up, which actually contain the drug in the form of its water-soluble acrylate salt, are almost entirely caramelized sucrose. Ninety-nine point nine nine five percent."

Lou says, "Imagine how much final product you could produce at that ratio."

"Easy. One gram of pure Fang, at a ratio of fifteen hundred to one, conservative, cuts down to the equivalent of over three pounds, a kilo and a half, of good import-quality heroin. I mean major-weight quality, if you're buying kilos at a time—maybe ninety percent pure. At what, a hundred fifty large per key these days? So we're already talking two hundred twenty-five thousand dollars for one *gram* of this shit and that's only the first tier. Then it's going to be handled like any shipment of smack—let's say it gets stepped on one-to-one by the guy who buys the key, so now there's two at the equivalent potency of about forty-five percent heroin. His buyer will triple that to six keys at eleven or twelve percent purity. Those get spread around to distributors who'll each do another three-for-one split before they break it down into grams or balloons. That's eighteen keys on the street at a concentration equivalent to about four percent heroin, which is standard.

"But remember, it's not heroin. It's all from one gram of this super fent. The concentration is so low as to be almost immeasurable."

Brandon does some quick calculating of his own. At fifty bucks a gram, which is still really wholesale, that's nine hundred thousand dollars from one gram of pure Fang. On the street in dimes it's even higher. Numbers to die and die and die for.

"What we want to know is how this ties in," says Lou. "Was Straw trucking it over here, supplying?"

"Sounds like a theory to me," Kline says. He pushes the designer glasses up so they're on top of his curly blond head. "It's been showing on the streets again in Motown for months now."

Brandon and Lou look at each other for a second. How, Brandon wants to say, does a fed end up over here within twenty-four hours of the discovery of a body, within six hours of the indentification of a rogue synthetic heroin? Lou's look says that his guess is Brandon's guess. There's something big beneath this surface.

Then Lou gives the nod. "Tell him," he says.

"Get out your notebook," says Brandon. "Let's talk about Kevin Babcock and the doctor who found him."

**T**he general departments of radiology and pathology are kept in the basement under the main section of the hospital, out of sight of the average hospitalgoer. The medical examiner's office and labs are also underground, but even further separated in a far-flung wing of the basement shared with housekeeping and maintenance, and connected to the rest of the building by a narrow and poorly lit tunnel called the catacomb. Lancaster figured out the distances once and decided Harvey worked just about directly beneath the helipad outside the ER.

Harvey's sitting behind his desk, smoking the meerschaum-lined pipe he keeps in his mouth even when he autopsies.

"Adrian," he says, then settles back to puffing. He has a sharp nose and dark features—heavy black eyebrows and dark hair, which he combs straight back. He fixes his gaze about a foot over Lancaster's head and a little off to the right when he talks. Lancaster figures that people who work with the dead never really need to fine-tune their interpersonal skills as much as the rest of the world.

It's evening; Lancaster's in a little early for his 8:00 P.M. to 8:00 A.M. shift. Except for Harvey's voice all is silent. The autopsy rooms, which Lancaster can see through the open doorway, are dark. Somewhere in there Kevin Babcock lies in cold storage.

"I heard Babcock wasn't an autoasphyx. I heard he was maybe murdered."

From his top drawer Harvey removes a slender silver lighter, about the size and shape of a pencil, which puts out a special flame for pipe lighting.

"I can't talk about it."

"Is it true?"

"Goddammit. Professional privilege or not, if you so much as tell anyone you were down here, I get strung up."

Lancaster waits.

"Bad choice of words. Sorry." Harvey fires up, and a cloud of smoke rises around his head. "I'm declaring an inquest. And if Straw expires, on him too. I want a grand jury to start looking into this."

"So you can't tell me anything."

"Nope." For the first time he looks straight into Lancaster's eyes. "But I'm surprised at you. Think about what you saw. Babcock was suspended from a door frame by a manila rope clothesline. If you were going in for a little autoerotic fun, would you use something that rough to hang yourself?"

"No."

"You see a cloth or something else to lessen the abrasion?"

"No."

"All right. Now remember what else you saw, the body and how it was hanging."

Nearly the full weight was on the cord. The feet, actually just the toes, were resting on the floor. "I remember the legs being bent, the knees a few inches off the floor. The face and hands were deeply cyanotic. The chest and abdomen less so."

"Both hands?"

"I . . . don't know. I remember seeing the right one."

"How about the legs and feet?"

"I don't know."

"If the body had been hanging for some time, where would you expect to see lividity in the lower extremities? Think about the positioning, with the knees bent."

"The fronts of the lower legs should have been livid."

"That's right."

"But I don't remember seeing it. I looked when I lowered him. I don't . . ." Then he remembers: the lividity was along the *backs* of the legs. He looks up at Harvey.

The girl was right. Kevin hadn't hanged himself, because when he died he hadn't been hanging.

"Why wouldn't I have realized that?"

Harvey shrugs and lights his pipe again. "The lividity was all along the right side of the back, in the right hand, and along the backs of both legs. He was lying down after he died, with his right arm hanging lower than the body."

"Then why the cyanotic face?"

"Because he was asphyxiated. Listen. I meant it when I said I couldn't talk about this with you. But goddamn if I'm not out of tobacco. I have to run up to my car and get another can." And with that he stands and leaves.

Lancaster is in deep thought—it takes him a moment to notice the half-full can of Prince Albert sitting next to the Babcock file on Harvey's very organized desk.

He slips around behind the desk and opens the file. First are the scene photos of the body, including close-ups of the neck. The mark the rope left is clearly discernible, rising from lower left to upper right. But there is also an infrared photograph of Kevin's neck taken during autopsy in which a second eerily white ligature mark shows up as well, an inch wide and moving straight across the neck. No hanging mark this. Kevin was strangled by someone else, probably from behind.

He sits down in Harvey's chair, the effort of standing having become too much. The notes bear out what Harvey's just told him. Histological testing showed that the belt, not the rope, did the killing.

He starts to get up when a smaller piece of greenish paper—a carbon copy of a result sheet from the state crime lab—catches his eye. Across the top in red letters it says REQUEST FOR QUALITATIVE ANALYSIS. At the bottom, in a box marked RESULTS, someone has written, *3,4-methyl ethyl fentanyl acrylate.* Attached by staple to this sheet are two photos of packets of powder—the same grainy tan powder Straw was carrying and Kevin had in his living room.

Lancaster remembers this chemical, although he'd never tried it himself. In the Detroit days it hit the streets hard. ODs were coming in all over the city, and Lancaster was one who had to deal with them. The drug—Fang, they called it—just shut people down. Unless an OD victim made it in within a few minutes and was put on a respirator, there was little chance of survival. For over a year they had to deal with the shit, then it just disappeared.

Fang is back, he thinks, and flips through more of the papers in the file.

He's about through and hears Harvey coming down the hallway when he finds at the back of the file a few sheets on Michael Straw. He figures Harvey's keeping them in the Babcock file until Straw expires and gets a file of his own.

Lancaster scans the sheets quickly, trying to pick up what he can. Nothing jumps out and he stands up. And then his eye falls across a little notation at the bottom of one sheet—*AKA Zipper.*

Lancaster goes so dizzy, he falls back into the chair.

Behind this sheet is what looks like a driver's license photo of

Straw, showing clearly a long jagged scar running from his left eye down across his cheek.

When Harvey comes in, Lancaster looks up at him wide-eyed.

"The cliché," Harvey says, "has something to do with your having seen a ghost. Are you all right?"

Lancaster can feel the blood draining from his face. He's about to speak when a flat, neutral voice comes over the PA: "Dr. Lancaster to Emergency stat, Dr. Lancaster to the ER stat."

Harvey picks up the phone on his desk and dials an extension. Without a word he hands it over.

"This is Lancaster."

"I'm patching you through to unit thirty-five," says Eileen, the ER clerk. Then he hears, "Base, we have a male, approximately thirty years old, being pulled from the river at Juncket Street. Don't anticipate pulse or respirations."

"How long?" Lancaster says.

"Police reports started coming in twenty minutes ago that someone had fallen. Water temp here is thirty-seven degrees Fahrenheit."

"Get him in now," Lancaster says.

He gets on with one of the trauma nurses next and says, "Prep One. We've got a cold-water drowning, submerged approximately one half hour. Get lab and respiratory up stat. Track down Ann. Call ICU and let them know."

His life is about to change; he knows that now. But for this moment, all he can afford to think about is the job at hand.

As he runs from Harvey's office down the tunnel toward the elevators, the monotone voice comes back over the PA system—"Dr. Palicki to Emergency stat, Code Blue, ETA five minutes. Lab and respiratory to Emergency stat, Code Blue. . . ."


An EMT sits up on the dead man's belly, jamming her fists into the chest, compressing the heart, while her partner forces pure oxygen down the throat. They hit the wide glass pneumatic doors and burst into the lobby. Lancaster can see them from the trauma stall. The divers push the cart. Water runs off their black rubber skins onto the linoleum of the long hallway.

One of the fire crew jogs beside them in his yellow slicker. With them also are a couple cops and behind, outside, and not to be admitted, a news crew.

In the stall Ann removes the cervical collar and works with a respiratory tech to establish an airway. Lancaster drives a needle into the femoral artery and draws blood as he shouts at the lab tech, "Blood gas, lytes, CBC, and a type-only cross. I want one of packed red cells and one whole blood ready to go stat if there's a lot of hemolysis. Got it?"

The EMT is off the body now but still pumping on the chest.

"Stop," Ann says as she peers down the laryngoscope and tries to place the breathing tube.

The EMT steps back, shaking the fatigue from her arms.

"Let's establish two large-bore peripheral lines," Lancaster says. "We'll start with half a milligram of epi at one to ten thousand IV push, repeat at five minutes, and then atropine. Lidocaine and paddles should be standing by. We'll probably have to blast him sooner or later. We have an ID on this guy?"

"Pete something," one of the EMTs says. "Cop IDed him at the scene. Boncaro. Petie Boncaro, that's what he said."

Lancaster pulls away from the body and looks at the tech.

"What's wrong?" Ann Palicki says. "Adrian?"

Lancaster drifts backward until he runs into a shelf. The clamoring sounds of the ER fade. Everything goes silent. The absurdity overwhelms him for a moment. And the brilliance, if this is a setup. To plan it so that each time it's he who works on the body. Straw, then Kevin, now Boncaro. Is it possible?

And most horribly, Michael Straw was Zipper, Zipper from Ann Arbor, Zipper who—

"Lancaster!" Palicki shouts.

He snaps back, steps to the table again, and begins where he left off, trying to revive this drowned man. It is still his job.

The floor is slippery with river water until someone has the sense to lay down blankets for everyone to stand on.

**W**hen Brandon arrived at Juncket Street, a district of sprawling manufacturing plants and warehouses and an industrial park housing small businesses, the scene was only fifteen minutes old. The lights of the fire trucks and the squad cars and the rescue squad, blue and white and red lights flashing and popping, reflected from the snow and the asphalt and the black river.

Lou Adamski squatted at the crusty iced-over mud of the shoreline, looking out over the lip of ice at the middle of the River Sorrow where an aluminum skiff waited. A lone medic, bundled in a blaze-orange down parka with EMT written in huge black letters across its back, stared over the side into the dark waters. Brandon imagined he could just see the beams from the divers' sealed mercury lamps playing beneath the surface. The wind chill, he'd heard, was fifteen below.

"Those boys can't stay down long," he shouted over Lou's back.

"Five minutes a pop," Lou said. "But they've got on arctic suits.

They come up and get checked. If they're okay, they go down for five more."

"How do they know where to dive?"

Lou shifted his gaze from the river up to the bridge. "Go take a walk, Brandon. We've got it sealed off at both ends. Stay in the street, not on either sidewalk. You'll see."

So Brandon pulled his coat tighter, followed the edge of the river to the base of the bridge, ducked under the yellow tape, and walked up through the slush in the southbound lane. The streetlights threw off a grainy pinkish aura. Traffic had melted the snow here, but on the walkways on either side, next to the low concrete walls, he could see that the fresh snow, a couple inches of it, was intact. On the west side a single pair of feet had walked through that snow recently. He crossed over and looked at the other sidewalk—two pairs of prints, one heading in each direction, each made by the same set of studded boots. But the steps heading down were spaced much farther apart. Someone walked partway up this side and then ran back off.

The bridge had a slight arc to it. At its apex the single pair of prints was joined by a second pair coming from the other side. Where they met, the snow told a clear story. It had been scuffed away in a roughly circular area, outlines of an arm here, a head there, visible where the two bodies scuffled.

Brandon knelt. Spots of blood stood out in the cleared area and when he looked closely he saw that in the snow, too, blood droplets had fallen and left their trail.

He stepped carefully onto the sidewalk in the middle of the cleared area where the fight took place, and leaned out over the wall. He was directly over the skiff and beneath it, beneath the surface of the river, he could now see one of the divers' lights growing steadily brighter as it rushed toward the surface.

The diver broke through, one fist raised skyward. In his fist he held the end of a fluorescent yellow fly-fishing line. That meant the other end was tied to something. And that meant they had found the leaper.

But not a leaper, Brandon thought. They'd found the victim. The snow on top of the wall along the bridge was all scraped off right here where he stood, scraped off where a body had been pushed across it. And here, where the concrete wall was fitted with a steel expansion cuff, a small piece of black nylon cloth had snagged and lodged. A bit of clothing, a coat perhaps.

A second diver was surfacing now, his light not as bright as the first because he was not holding it above his head. Instead his hands were full of the body he was raising. The first diver sank back down to help lift the body the last few feet. Together they hoisted it up to the medic in the skiff. The three of them struggled with it until it rolled soaking over the side and onto its back. The dead man wore a black coat. His face was blue.

Brandon knew the coat. He knew the nearly shaved head. And even through the death mask he recognized the face of Petie Boncaro.

Then Lou started yelling from the shoreline. They had the hospital on the radio. Since the water was so cold, they had a chance at revival.

The two divers flopped in as the medic started the outboard and raced for shore.

Brandon stepped back off the sidewalk and ran from the bridge. Lou was waiting by the rescue squad.

"It's Boncaro," Brandon said, breathless.

Lou looked at him. "I got some things for you."

Brandon nodded.

"Let's talk, then. After, you go in and claim his clothing."


Brandon starts his engine to get the heaters going. Lou's in the passenger seat.

"So we got a tape of the caller."

"Same as the other two?" Brandon says.

"Yeah."

"Jesus Christ."

Lou rubs his thick hands under the car's heater. "Spinner came in to see me this afternoon. He tracked down the house where Seth Babcock lives with a woman named Carla Nye. You know those developments off Ridge North, by the country club? There's one called Cottonwood Hollow."

"Those aren't cheap homes."

"That's right. So we sent somebody over to the county clerk's to pull the deed. House is in Nye's name, but she turns out to be a former bank teller. And get this, she dropped a thirty-g down payment on the place two years ago when she bought it."

"Nice inheritance."

"Kline, through the magical power of the DEA, got copies of her recent tax returns. No inheritance. She lists all income from a business she owns called MTown, Inc."

"What sort of business?"

"Consulting. And who's listed as the president?"

"Seth Babcock," Brandon says.

"You got it."

"Seth boy must've graduated from small-time dime deals to weight."

"He's still nothing big time. How big could it be in Morgan-town?"

"That's what we're all wondering."

"No. We figure he's one of a handful of midlevel guys who buy and bring it into the county, that's all. Only, now he's dropped out of sight. Nye claims he took off when Kevin bought it and hasn't shown up since. She thinks he's holed up somewhere on a bender."

"So maybe there was a new business starting, Babcock and Babcock. And they were doing a little purchasing from Mr. Michael Straw."

"Might be like that," Lou says.

"You know what I wonder? How could a guy live in a house like that and let his mother and brother stay in a four-room shack?"

"Maybe his bringing Kevin into the business was his way of rectifying things. In any case, we have to find him now.

"As far as Arnie Holt's concerned we can't turn anything. No records, no social security number, nothing. Dick. Like the guy doesn't exist. But he's another son of a bitch we better get to."

Brandon says, "Byers in Detroit faxed me a list of names, everyone who was arrested in connection with Fang six years ago. Nothing yet. Straw's not on it. Not Holt, no locals."

"Okay," says Lou. "Now, here's your present." He hands Brandon a thin mottled-brown folder sealed with an orange label that has since been cut. "It's from Kline, DEA archives. It's about Lancaster, of all people."

"No shit."

"Read it. It's not that long."

Brandon skims through the first page, which is about Lancaster's habit and bust for lifting hospital morphine. But then it moves into more detailed history. Lancaster had been a heroin junkie for more than four years. He and his girlfriend, Denise Richards, had been connected to a dealer named Bobby Karnowski in Ann Arbor. There was some indication Lancaster and Richards had worked for him.

"He was trafficking, Lou."

"Maybe."

"And now he's a goddamn doctor in our hospital."

But the real shocker is the section of the report detailing Karnowski, which mentions a mule he used out of Detroit who went by the name Zipper because of a bad facial scar. Although Zipper was the only name he used then, his given name was known to be Michael Straw, the kid-glove-handled brother-in-law of District DEA Chief James Le Seure.

Brandon feels a rolling crest of anger rising up.

"Lancaster knew Straw in Ann Arbor."

"Under the alias," Lou says. "The report's clear on that point. Straw didn't use his real name. He was strict about that. And no way could Lancaster have recognized him when he came in. He may not have figured out who this guy is yet."

"Doesn't this all seem a little bizarre to you? Lancaster treating Straw and calling me in the middle of the night, then finding Babcock, and now having a known history with Straw?"

"Yes. Evidence of a current crime by Dr. Lancaster? No."

"What's that mean?"

"We let him lead us. If he's in this, we'll nail him. If someone's yanking his chain, then that's who we want."

"So who's watching him?"

"We'll talk about it in the morning. I want you to collect Boncaro's clothing now, but stay away from Lancaster. Then go home and get some rest. If Boncaro doesn't make it, we'll have autopsy results early."

"Jesus, Lou." Brandon chews his lower lip. "I want him brought in and questioned."

"You already did that."

"In light of this new information."

"It's not enough."

"Not enough . . . what the hell do you want? The son of a bitch is rotten."

"I don't want rotten, Brandon. I want guilty. I want a murderer and a trafficker. Rotten does me no good."

"He's guilty."

"How can you say that? You got nothing on him, no proof."

"The thought of him having these kinds of associations in his past and then coming over here to practice just grinds me."

"You really think he's killing people? You think he's dealing smack here?"

Brandon bites down hard on his lip and counts. Ten. Twenty.

No, he thinks. In his heart he doesn't believe it, he can't believe it. Despite the mammoth differences between them, the horrible associations Lancaster holds for him, despite the fact that Lancaster comes from a place and a life-style that turns his stomach, he admires this man. He knows what kind of a doctor he is, has seen him save life after life with his brains and his instinct and his balls. The gonzo doctor they call him, but Brandon has seen him pull back a few that everyone, the cops and the EMTs and the nurses, had written off.

"I don't know, Lou. It's all just crazy."

"Get the clothes, Frank." Lou opens the passenger door and the cold night swirls in. "We'll pick it up again tomorrow."

**T**hey shocked Boncaro six times in an hour and a half of trying. At seventeen minutes before ten Lancaster says, "That's it, people. I'm calling this one. Thank you."

Equipment is dropped, voices grow quiet, feet shuffle out as the curtain is thrown and a heavy sheet is pulled up over the face of the late Petie Boncaro.

The phone rings in the office and Eileen waves him in.

"It's for you. He's been calling every ten minutes for the past hour. Says it's important—"

Lancaster takes the phone. "Yeah," he says.

"Doctor," says a raspy, whispery, low-pitched voice.

"Who's this?"

"The name's not important. Mr. Boncaro's no longer with us, I take it."

"Who the hell is this?"

"My name's Holt, Dr. Lancaster."

Arnie Holt. Lancaster's breath catches in his throat.

"Doctor?"

"Did you kill Petie too?"

"Most certainly not. I didn't kill poor Kevin either."

"Who the fuck are you?" Outside the office, through the glass, Lancaster sees Frank Brandon carrying a plastic hospital Personal Belongings bag. Boncaro's clothing.

"Holt, I told you. An unimportant pawn. A trivial messenger with a crucial message."

"What was that all about with Kevin?"

"Mirrors, Doctor. Images. Reflections. Oneself." He hears a phlegmy laugh. "You with me, Doctor?"

"Yes."

"The selves of others."

"What—"

"Straw," Holt says. "Michael Straw, Dr. Lancaster. An image you should consider. He went by other names. Another name. A long time ago."

Brandon is moving toward the doors when his eyes meet Lancaster's.

*Signal,* Lancaster thinks. *Let him know.*

Brandon nods at him, touches the brim of his hat.

"In *your* long time ago. He had a bad facial scar. It was sutured poorly, so that little round scars were left on either side of the main scar, a regular pattern running down his face. So they called him Zipper. Do you remember?"

Brandon is gone now. Lancaster is silent but his hands have begun to shake. His face feels cold, yet damp with sweat.

"Doctor?" Holt says.

"Yes." Whispered.

"You knew him."

"What's this about?"

"Arnie Holt, Doctor. It is the perfect name, you'll discover.

Regal even, though you may not believe it. The name of a king, of a
beast."

"What have I done?"

"Don't be narcissistic. Listen: Kevin's out. Petie's out. But there
are still players. Seth Babcock, Kevin's brother, plays on."

"Who killed Kevin and Petie?"

"Ah, who indeed? There are other players too. Bad mystery men
have come out to play. Watch your back, Doctor."

"Who are you?"

"Next, part two, *The Petie Story.*"

The line goes dead. Holt is gone again.

Adrian Lancaster sits at the work counter.

"Doctor," Eileen says, "are you all right?"

He looks at her, at the crew in the stall with dead Petie, at the
emergency room.

"I'm going to need some time."

"Yessir. Are you all—"

"I mean several days, Eileen. There's been a death."

"Oh—" she says. "In your family, Doctor? Is that what he was
calling about? He should have said something to me. I'm so sorry."

"It's okay. I'll just need some time."

"How long?"

Lancaster says nothing.

"A week?" Eileen asks.

"Yes."

"I'll take care of it. I'll redraw the schedule for you to look at
before you go."

"Thanks," he says. He touches her shoulder, then heads toward
the staff lounge in the back. As he walks, he feels himself begin to
shake again. It starts in his hands, then moves up until his whole upper
body is trembling.

He should leave right now. He'll be no good here anymore.

He wanders from the ER into the main part of the hospital,

headed nowhere, and passes the in-house service window of the pharmacy.

He stops. A girl named Kelly is on tonight. He likes her.

"Kell," he says.

"What's up, Doc?" She laughs.

"Got a lady driving me nuts back there, a real wall bouncer. Think we can slide her some tranqs ASAP on my signature so I can get her out the door? Meprobamate, say. Time-released."

"Meprospan."

"Yeah. Four hundred milligrams, eight pops at Q twelve h. I'll write her a script for later."

"Give me a minute."

Meprobamate. The stray fact that something like 250 tons of the drug is manufactured and sold each year in the U.S. alone floats into Lancaster's head. Prescribed as a mild tranquilizer, in many ways it resembles a barbiturate in its actions. Lots of muscle relaxation and drowsiness if you take enough.

He moves on toward the cafeteria, where he buys a carton of milk to settle the burning in his stomach.

On his return Kelly hands him a small brown envelope containing the eight blue-and-white capsules. She slides a pad toward him, which he signs without reading. Next, he slips into the nearest men's room and makes sure he's alone, removes two of the pills, and slips the envelope with the remaining six into his lab-coat pocket.

He sits in a stall and holds the two pills in his palm. Eight hundred milligrams will counteract a lot of anxiety, he figures. Bad nerves will cause bad problems where he's going.

*Half an hour*, he thinks. *That's all it will take. Then I'll be okay again. Then I'll be on cruise.*

He has not taken any drug but aspirin or antibiotics in the six years since his rehabilitation. But life has taken on the texture of a dream, and in dreams there are no rules.

He holds the two pills between his fingers and looks at them. *It is always fear,* he understands. *Nothing more than that which drives us to do this, we addicts, present and reformed.*

But before the pills reach his lips his great anger surges and displaces the fear he feels. Anger is valuable. Anger protects and destroys. Anger is what will save him.

He stands and, before he can reconsider, empties his hand into the toilet, pulls the handle, and watches the two blue-and-white capsules swirl away.

# TUESDAY

**W**hen Brandon got home, Susan was waiting again. Crying. At nearly midnight.

"I can't deal with this," he yelled at her. "Spying on your own father. I got called out! I tucked her in! She's fine!"

"She's not fine," Susan said, breaking down into deep sobs.

"I'm going crazy, Sue. How long is he away this time?"

"Five days . . . what does that mean? You think I do this just because I'm *lonely*? Oh, Jesus, Daddy."

"I'm sorry."

"Jesus." She was on her knees in the middle of the living room floor, gagging from crying so hard.

"Susie, you're hysterical. We got to stop this."

"She needs help."

"You'll make yourself sick."

"I'm scared she'll die."

He got down on his knees on the floor with her and hugged her

123

to his chest. He heard her whispering and realized she was praying, something she'd taken to strongly since the accident.

When she was finished, and calmer, he helped her up to the couch and sat next to her. "Can you stay over?" he asked. "I got to go out again early."

"Why?"

"It's a mess, darling. A bad case. Just stay with me."

In the bedroom he found Lorraine crying and the pillow beneath her head soaked. He wanted to call Susan and tell her her mother reacted to their fighting, as if this proved something important, something that would convince Susan her mother belonged where she is.


He slept now and then, waking at five for good, no less angry than when he went to bed. Realizing there would be no more rest, although he was still exhausted and his virus felt like it had bloomed into a low-grade fever, he dressed and headed out into the cold again.

Now, at six-twenty, he's sitting in the Buick, engine running for warmth, sucking down a cupful of the thermos of coffee he brought, and watching the doors leading from the emergency room to the staff parking lot. He's parked out farther, in the guest lot, but his view is clear. It's crazy, he knows, but he wants to see the doctor, to watch what he does, to see if he drives like a guilty man. Lou said keep an eye on him.

The car's heater blasts away, and Brandon feels no chill anymore, even in his feet. His face is hot and damp. His eyes close and he nods, then snaps back and turns the radio on to some Ypsilanti jazz station. He hates jazz, but it's coming in clear and he needs the noise.

_Do something._ On the seat next to him he opens his briefcase and spreads out the information he's gathered: Byers's Fang list from the 1984 busts, the small leather portfolio containing all his notes from the past few days, the synopsized reports of Harvey and Jimmy, and Lancaster's DEA folder, which he's already been through a dozen times.

He's struck by the lack of detail it really contains, only a few double-spaced pages outlining Lancaster's life in Ann Arbor and Detroit.

As he begins to read it again, however, fatigue catches up. He sips cold coffee, turns off the engine, and rests his head back, closing his eyes. His chest burns right up into his throat and he can feel the fever building its head of steam inside him.

There are too many angles. *Napalm burns on Straw.*

He feels himself drifting off but does nothing to stop it.

*Napalm burns on Straw.* Jesus God. You want burns, he'd seen burns: Korea, 1952. There was a guy, a buddy, from . . . Wallace, Idaho. Brandon smiles. *How long ago has it been since you thought of him?* Theodore something. Brandon called him Ted once and had gotten snapped at, so Theodore it was. Pretentious son-of-a-bitch someone said, but Brandon understood the issue.

They'd been on patrol one afternoon, three of them in a Willys on a dirt road at the southern tip of a DMZ fifty miles north of Seoul. They'd passed a girl riding a bicycle, her long skirt floating out on the breeze as she rode. Theodore looked over at Brandon, shook his head, and pointed with forked fingers at his eyes. He wanted a look to see if she was carrying anything.

They waited for the girl to catch up and stopped her. With the end of his rifle Theodore lifted her skirt and saw it, a two-way radio strapped beneath the seat. She was Red; they knew immediately. Theodore grabbed her hair and dragged her screaming off into the bushes to do a strip search and then to shoot her in the head. They had standing orders.

Brandon and the driver kept an eye out to see if anyone had been following her.

When the blast came, it sounded more like a loud wheeze than a rifle report. Brandon wasn't sure what it was. Then he saw smoke.

He ran but it was too late. The girl was blown wide open, eviscerated by the bomb she'd worn strapped around her waist. Theodore was more or less whole, but the flash had destroyed his face and hands. He lay there screaming, burned black and smelling like scorched meat. He was dead within three days.

Theodore . . . *K,* something Polish. Brandon and . . . Kowalski. Mick & Stosh they were called. The Irishman and the Polack.

Brandon smiles and lifts the smoke to his lips.

Kowalski.

Kowalski. Jesus Christ.

He nearly drops the cigarette, manages to set it down in the ashtray, flip on the overhead light, and fumble through the papers on his lap for the alphabetized list of Fang arrests Byers sent. Here—he runs a finger down to the *K*'s, and sees it—*K* something Polish. Not Kowalski but Karnowski. Robert Karnowski.

He opens Lancaster's DEA file to be sure, and there on page two, in the same paragraph as Michael Straw, is the same name—Bobby Karnowski.

> Karnowski, an Ann Arbor dealer, and Richards were reported to be living in the same building as Lancaster, and Karnowski was apparently instrumental in Lancaster's becoming addicted. Lancaster, according to some reports, actually worked in some capacity for Karnowski in late 1981 and 1982. Karnowski and Richards had known each other since the late seventies and were thought at one time to have been sexually involved.

So Karnowski was Lancaster's Man for a year and a half. And Karnowski was arrested two years later, in 1984, in connection with the synthesis and distribution of the controlled substance 3,4-methyl ethyl fentanyl. Fang.

There were too many names on the Fang list; Brandon had missed the link the first time through.

But now pieces were connecting—Lancaster to Straw; Straw to Karnowski; Karnowski to Fang; Fang to Kevin and Straw and back to Lancaster.

*I got you,* is Brandon's first thought. *But what?* he thinks then. *It's the same question Lou asked. Do you really believe he's behind this?*

Brandon rubs his eyes. There are just too many connections, too much evidence pointing at the doctor. Maybe that's the point—it's too much.

But then these thoughts disappear. He tosses the coffee out the window and starts the engine. He's grown cold again and, besides, Lancaster is walking toward the parking lot.

It's 7:27. Dawn has begun.

Brandon watches him start his truck and pull out of the small front lot, then drops the Buick into gear and follows.

*Guilty or not, he's the one to follow,* he tells himself. *You can worry later about—*

Then something strange happens. A dark four-door pulls out from a side lot, cutting Brandon off. Two men in the front seat. Suits. They pull out after Lancaster's truck.

Brandon is so surprised, he doesn't react for a moment. He sits in the driveway of the hospital staring at the houses across the street until someone behind him, a night-shifter wanting to get the hell home, pounds the horn. Brandon guns it in the direction the car went.

He spots Lancaster's truck ahead, and behind it the dark car. The truck turns right onto Greenway, heading west toward the development where Lancaster lives. The car turns right too.

He maneuvers through the light early-morning traffic until he's close enough for a moment to see the license plate of the car. Then he drops back again and lifts his radio handset.

"Dispatch."

"This is four fifty-one," Brandon says. "Who's this? Bernie?"

"Yessir."

"I got a Michigan plate, looks like a Ford, license plate number AA-five—"

"Federal," Bernie says before Brandon gets the entire number out.

"You're sure?"

"There's only three prefixes they use in this state. That's one."

"Out."

*Kline.* Kline's got his boys on this. Sneaking around Brandon's town. Following his suspects.

Brandon pounds his fist on the steering wheel until he feels something give in his hand. But his rage passes and is replaced by a wrench in his gut as he thinks it through and realizes that Lou Adamski, and probably Ken Barnes, have been in on this since the beginning. Last night Lou said, "We have to watch him, Brandon. He'll lead us."

Who? Brandon had asked. Now he knows. Lou's been playing hanky-panky with the feds behind his back. That's why he kept Brandon from bringing Lancaster in. In the investigation Brandon was brought in to take over, he's being played for a patsy by his own brass.

He steps hard on the gas, wheels around a corner to the next street, and heads toward the justice building.


Lou's office door is open and Brandon can see Julian Kline in there, yakking it up. Brandon passes and enters his own office. It's not a minute before Lou and Kline are knocking on his door.

"Come." Brandon's ready to let loose, ready to jump down his chief's throat and kick around for a while, to ask why the hell Kline has his DEA boys following Lancaster when Brandon was told nothing about it.

But when Lou steps in he says, "We got Seth Babcock. We've been waiting for you."

Brandon shuts his mouth and follows.


Seth Babcock is beefier than his brother, going maybe two hundred pounds at five feet ten. His dark, oiled hair is just long enough that he can gather it into a small ponytail. He wears a knee-length black leather coat and a half-carat diamond in his ear. The small interrogation room smells like sweat and cologne.

The quick brief from Lou was that Babcock simply came home. He pulled into the driveway of his house, got out of the car, and stood there like he was waiting. The department had the house staked, of course. They jumped on him.

"He *was* waiting," Brandon said. "He wanted to come in. Whatever game he's playing has got way out of hand."

Lou Adamski and Julian Kline listen from Lou's office as Brandon's interrogation is piped in and taped.

"You on anything?" Brandon says.

"Darvon for my headache."

"That's it?"

A nod.

"You going to help us?"

"I get a lawyer?"

"This is voluntary."

"Then I want to leave."

Brandon, still standing, rests one foot on the seat of a wooden chair then leans on his knee. He closes his eyes and rolls his head around to relieve the kinks he already feels forming in his neck. "I was there last night when they pulled Boncaro out of the river. I saw the burn, too, Straw. Torched. I was in his room. He's a goddamn mess. I was there with Kevin too—"

"Shut up."

"You're scared you'll be next."

"I want to leave."

"Petie was scared. He had this chance and passed it up. Who's Straw connected to?"

No answer.

"Your own brother, for Christ's sake. I'd think you'd like to get the bastards who did that."

No answer.

"We've been told there's a setup to distribute manufactured heroin in Morgantown and you're involved. I want to know who's bringing it in and why people are dying. Is this a territorial war? Someone cut in on your action? Vice versa?"

"I don't know nothing about it. I don't have no idea why they were killed. I don't want no action."

"Where's the shit coming from?"

"I ain't bringing no dope into this dive town."

"Who, then? And why isn't there more? I don't see any big money flying around and frankly very little product. Maybe you're just the fall guy for some scam. Who's behind you?"

Seth says nothing.

"You really think I'm going to just let you walk?"

"You said you ain't got nothin' on me."

"I said it's voluntary, Babcock, and you're the volunteer. Don't play hard-to-get now that you're here. I don't have the patience for it."

He says nothing again. This is the game. He wants to see Brandon's hand, what the stakes are going to be.

"Okay," Brandon says. "You don't want to talk, I have alternatives. One, we cook up some bullshit story to hold you long enough to find real dirt. That won't be hard. DEA's in here. They can start tearing apart the records of MTown, Inc. You know what they can do if they find a hint that any drug money was laundered there. They'll take it all, Seth. Or two, we cut you loose right now and make it nice and visible. We put out word that you spilled, that you gave the goods big time. And I'm inclined toward the second choice because that way I get something out of it. News like that'll flush someone. Somebody panics, runs in, and starts chattering. Never fails."

"You don't know dick."

"We're not after you anyway." Brandon walks over to the gated window and looks down onto a back-alley drive. He sucks air in

between his two front teeth, making it whistle. His sinuses ache.
"Won't do us any good to hold you except the satisfaction of it."

Brandon nods as if he's considering the options.

"You're so fucking dumb," Seth says.

"Then educate me."

"There ain't no shit being brought *into* Morgantown. You
thought about it for half a second you'd figure it out."

Brandon looks out the window. And then he laughs, because he
gets it. A beat passes before he says, "It's being manufactured here.
You're shipping it out."

"Kevin was the only one who knew the chemist. He'd pass it to
me with a ratio of how to cut it down. This shit stretches. I could sit
on it hard."

And whoever buys cuts the stuff again and again. Brandon holds
his forehead and sits down with the shock of the insight. "And then it
goes into Detroit."

"Eventually. Greatest junk market in the world. Understand, I'm
not on the street, nowhere near it. I got to deal with the top of the
food chain, man. I dump the whole weight at once."

So the Fang Byers and Kline have been seeing on their streets
isn't Detroit dope; it's all imported from Morgantown.

"How's it work now with Kevin out?"

"Uh-uh," Seth says. "You want in, we cut a deal first. Things are
set to go big time." He fingers the diamond stud in his ear.

"What d'you want?"

"First, I talk, I walk, and you don't say nothin' to no one.
*Nothin'*. I'll feed back to you. Any busts go down, I get hauled like
everyone else, then I get protection. Second, you and the DEA stay
off the business. Anything I made up to this point is free and clear.
You catch me again in the future, then you can run it up my ass."

"How big is big?"

"Key of concentrate to start."

"What's concentrate?"

"Equivalent of pure smack, which I pick up for a C. Bargain basement."

"A hundred thousand? You got that kind of cash?"

"Look, I'm just the middle here. They know I'm good for it."

"You'll sell it first, then pay for it."

He nods. "But I'll turn it over once, which makes two keys I pass at eighty per. That's sixty long left for me. Lot of jack, but I'll trade that for my ass any day."

So the deal is made: Seth will be secreted back home. He'll play it like nothing happened.

"Where's it coming from?"

"I really don't know. It was all backwards. My kid brother, who couldn't sell his ass to make a nickel, comes to me three, four months ago with a bag of this shit. I let a few people check it out. Next thing, they're asking for more, and we're trucking the stuff out of here, not much, maybe a couple bags a month. I ask him who's making it, but he says if anyone finds out it'll all go away. Who'm I to fuck with that?"

"Who's buying?"

"It was going through hands up in Jackson, then over. Now I got new buyers coming out direct from the city, volume buyers."

"That's who Straw represented."

"Yeah."

"Now what, with Kevin out?"

"I won't know nothin' till the last second."

"They'll call you?"

He shrugs. "After Kevin died, I got a call that a new batch was ready."

"From the chemist."

"Whoever. Petie was supposed to make the pickup. That was the drop that got him killed."

"Kevin ever mention a guy named Arnie Holt?"

Seth throws Brandon a quick glance, then looks down at the tabletop.

"He the chemist?"

"I told you I don't know. I only saw the guy once."

"You saw him?"

"Once. He showed up in Red's. I just caught a quick look."

"What'd he look like?"

"Little guy. Skinny, weasely looking, black goatee, round glasses. Wore one of those orange hunting hats, gloves with no fingers. Weird."

"You talk to him?"

"No."

"Anyone else see him?"

Seth shrugs. "He was there at the bar. People seen him."

"Anyway," Brandon says, "we assume whoever contacted you before, from either side, will do it again. We'll wire you."

"I'm not wearing any fucking wire."

"Calm down."

"Fuck calm! These are killers. You don't have no idea. I oughta have my own fucking head examined."

"Then why don't you just run?"

"They want me in, man. Can't run when they want you in."

*Arrogant greaseball,* Brandon thinks. "You need us to be there when it goes down," he says. "Don't ever forget that. Now or later, they'll do you like they did Petie."

"I'll get word to you. I'll figure something out."

Brandon looks out the window at the alley again. It's a thin shot, but it's the best they have right now.

"I ask you something? Why'd you never buy your mother a decent house?"

"I tried, man. She won't have nothing to do with it. She thinks my money's dirty."

"Silly her," Brandon says.

★  ★  ★

Jimmy rings down just before lunch to make sure Brandon saw his note ID'ing all six latents from inside the Babcock house. The last one belonged to Seth.

"Nothing on the flashlight yet?" Brandon says.

"Nope. I ran eliminations against anyone who was at the scene. We've been keeping up with any names you guys bring in, anyone connected. We ran the lists of Kevin's friends. *Nada.*"

"Can you get me a good hard-copy enlargement? Faxable?"

"It'll be on your desk after lunch."


Spinner hunches over a deep bowl of linguine marinara in Elio's Italian on Singer Street, on the edge of the campus of Waite College. Brandon, ignoring the veal in front of him, is smoking and working on a whiskey and soda.

"I love this shit," Spinner says. His wife has him on a budget so she packs him cold-cut sandwiches and chips to bring to work for lunch. Brandon wants his mind on the case at hand, not on his stomach, so this is his treat today. He figures Spinner can use the sandwich for an afternoon snack, anyway.

"The guy's nervous, you said," Brandon says. Late Monday Spinner finally reached the owner of the stolen red Cabriolet in which Straw was burned.

"He was up to something," says Spinner. "Ditching me for two days. All I wanted to do was verify where the car was when it was lifted, that kind of shit. People, if they just wouldn't be so fucking dumb, you know. Guy sends up a red flag that something's goofy by avoiding me, bullshitting me over the phone, 'Now's not a good time, officer.' Moron. I finally surprise him last night, he's in his driveway working on another car. He about wets his pants when I walk up."

"What d'you think? Should we pull him?"

"Naw, fuck no. But he proceeds to tell me how the car was right there in his driveway when it was stolen. 'Where were you?' I ask. 'Inside,' he says. I get his wife out there. She was in Toledo at the time, didn't see nothing, but now with her there the guy's really turning red, sweat's running off. How'd they come to steal a car right out of his driveway? I wonder. Does that make any sense? Someone wants a car to perp a knock-off, they're gonna pick this bright red jobbie and right in some guy's driveway in Wauseon, Ohio? So I excuse the wife, the guy and I go for a little walk in his backyard. I tell him now there's a murder involved, his car was used. He don't want to be wrapped up in that shit, right? But if he's yanking my putz, he's gonna find himself in a real nightmare mess."

Spinner stops and shovels another forkful of the pasta into his skinny face.

"And?" Brandon says.

"The damn guy starts to bawl on me, then comes out with it."

Brandon knows what it is now. He smiles.

"Got some chickee up here he's been balling off and on for a year," Spinner says, grinning and nodding, his mouth full of noodles and bread.

"The car was stolen here, wasn't it?"

Spinner nods again.

"You know where?"

"They'd taken a room for the afternoon at the Ramada, right in beautiful downtown Morgantown, two blocks from the damn justice building. Car got lifted from the parking lot. The guy was so excited to get naked he left his keys in the ignition."

*It's never complicated,* Brandon thinks. "So it may have been someone staying there."

"There or maybe at the Washington." The Washington Hotel, on Washington Street at the northern edge of the true downtown, was once an elegant institution. But when developers put up the Ramada directly across the street, and cut rates and offered amenities such as a weight room and swimming pool, the Washington began a slide. Now, it's basically become a welfare flophouse.

"You've got a toehold," Brandon says. "Check it out."

Spinner nods and chews.

"We should also interview friends of Kevin Babcock," says Brandon. "And someone should hit Red's, see if someone who works there remembers seeing Holt. Maybe we can get a description."

"I'll take care of all that. How about you? You look like shit."

"People to see," Brandon says. "And that's how I feel." The fever seems to have abated, but his eyes and head and throat are as bad as ever. Even the whiskey is having no effect.

"Hey," says Spinner, "you gonna eat that veal?"


FAX

Date:   January 16, 1991

To:     Detective Ellen Byers
        River Rouge Precinct

From:   Detective Frank Brandon
        Morgantown Municipal Police Department

I'm faxing herewith a print found on a compact flashlight at the scene of a murder tied to Michael Straw. Cross-reference with all available prints in connection with either case has led nowhere.

Could you have this checked against any known associates of Straw, or anyone connected with Fang six years ago who might be a factor in this? This may be a flyer, but I want to cover all the angles and will appreciate any light you can shed.

Thanks in advance for your help, and we'll talk soon.

F or the third time today Lancaster calls the office of his good friend DA Ken Barnes.

"Mr. Barnes is still in a meeting," the secretary says. "Can he call you back?"

"This is important."

"I'm sorry, Doctor—"

He hangs up. It's a brush-off and he knows it. Barnes has stopped taking his calls. Something's changed that's turned Ken cold. No doubt he knows about the Straw connection. And now the idea of Lancaster's being involved in this mess isn't so absurd after all.

So cut the lines; jettison the bad association.

"Fuck yourself, Ken," Adrian Lancaster says into the air.

On the way home he stopped and bought some things he hadn't been sure yet he was going to use. Now he knows he has no choice.

★ ★ ★

He is exhausted from the night's work. He lies down on the leather couch in his den to rest a minute, but the next thing he's aware of is the doorbell ringing. He sits up. His head feels thick.

The doorbell again. He looks at his watch: 3:42. Five hours he slept. He jumps up from the couch, then has to steady himself on the mantel. There's so much left to do.

The doorbell.

It's a messenger, from the only courier service in town.

"Package."

"What is it?"

"Dunno."

"Who from?"

"Days Inn Motel. A Mr. Regal Crusader." The kid gives him a funny look and shakes his head. Lancaster's ears start to ring. He signs the book, gives the kid a buck, and closes the door.

It's a plain brown envelope, no markings other than the word *Doctor* and his address printed on the front.

He opens it and removes the single sheet of paper:

Doctor L,

I was shadowing Petie Boncaro up the bridge when I saw, or sensed rather, someone approaching from the other side. But no one else was supposed to be there, just Petie and the package he was to retrieve. Seth Babcock was to meet Petie later, but he would come from the north, the city side, same as me. I stopped, crept forward, until I was just high enough to see the crest where Boncaro waited. Caution pays big dividends. When this new approacher turned out not to be Seth, I smiled at the setup. Petie had been tailed.

These are wicked people. Remember that, Doctor.

The assailant—I could make out no facial features, could see no hair, since the man was wearing a black mask on his face—tucked the bag of precious powder, the bag Petie was to deliver to Seth, into his coat, then proceeded to pummel Petie Boncaro. Petie did not fight back. He only tried to cover his face. Finally, the man pulled Petie to his feet and hefted him up and over the railing. Petie screamed until the waters closed over his head and shut off the sound for good.

Facing the light at the top of the bridge, I walked backward until I was out of sight of Petie's murderer. Then I turned and ran and at the first pay phone, good citizen that I am, called the police.

At that moment I saw someone else slithering toward the bridge—Seth Babcock. He is an animal; he smelled danger before he got close, slunk along the shoreline looking up. He must have seen the masked man, because suddenly he ran.

I hung up and wandered away from the lighted bridge into the dark streets of Morgantown, into a part of the city made up of warehouses and rough industrial plants—stamping factories and metal shops and steel reclamation centers. It all had a particular odor to it, the slightly acrid, metallic smell of oil and grease and tar.

Away, back toward the bridge, sirens converged. Petie was dead. Kevin was dead. My friends. Someone was killing them. Someone had come out to play.

I smiled again. My heart was breaking, and I was happy.

Back in my little room, Doctor, I opened the windows and let in the cold air. I have a picture of you taped on the wall. In it you are walking from the front door of the hospital. The grass is green; think how long ago that must have been.

Whisper: (I'm your biggest fan!)

Always,
Arnie Holt

Upstairs, time is short. This madman Holt is dogging him for what? Lancaster pulls clothing from his closet and shoves it into a shoulder bag. There's much to do. Then he pulls a slip of paper from his wallet and dials the number on it. No answer.

*Calm,* he thinks. *The only way you'll get out is to be like ice. Think. Step one, gathering. Step two—*

He hears a noise downstairs.

139

Someone is in the house. From his medical bag in the bedroom he removes a scalpel and slips the plastic sheath from the blade. He slides along the hallway wall to the stairs.

The staircase creaks.

"Dr. Lancaster?" a small voice says. "Doctor?" A girl's voice.

He exhales and takes deep breaths, blood rushing back into his head as the adrenaline rush abates. "Up here." He drops the blade into his shirt pocket.

Storm walks up the stairs, watching his face. She's wearing Levi's and a black T-shirt. Her red down vest hangs on the banister post below. Her hair has been moussed and combed straight back from her face, the first time he's seen her like this. She looks older, he decides.

When she reaches him, he draws up before her. She's taller than he realized, nearly his height, and her eyes lock on his.

"You shouldn't have come here. I just tried calling to say we could meet."

She wears the same tense look he saw at the clinic, and carries herself with the same grace, but now there's something else, a frailty, a vulnerability, he hadn't noticed before. Her slenderness adds to the effect, as do her eyes, which are so dark he cannot distinguish pupil from iris.

She puts her arms around his neck and hugs him. He holds his hands free for a moment, then places them on the small of her back. He imagines his hands could encircle her waist entirely. He smells her hair. He breathes it in.

"I'm scared," she says into his shoulder.

A vacuum opens in his belly, a hollowness he has felt before but which surprises him now, here, with this girl.

She says, "A car's been following me. People came to my apartment. I snuck out the back."

"We're leaving," he says. "We have to get ready. You have to help."

"I can help you." She pulls away from him. "You were glad to see me." She states this as a fact.

"What?"

"You were smiling the whole time I was walking up the stair-case."

"I was?" He feels foolish when he realizes it's true. And doubly foolish because he hadn't realized it until she said so.

But he wants her now, this girl about whom he knows nothing, whom he finds it impossible to predict, who even frightens him somehow. She knows how to find the people he wants to get to, the network of scum he wants to trace. Despite her frailty she has strength about her, and an abandon he needs. There is nothing to be lost. So what if he doesn't know her? No one he knows now can help him. The people he knew who could help him left his life long ago. He is alone. And when one is alone, the company of an attractive stranger can be a welcome thing.

In the bathroom she begins to chop with scissors at his foot-long hair. Following his instructions, she lays each lock of hair on a paper towel spread out on the toilet seat.

"What's this about, really?" she says.

"Really, I don't know. I know it involves an old boring story, but I can't see any answer in it."

"So tell me the old story anyway. Unless you can't talk about it."

"I can talk about it. It was a long time ago."

"Tell."

"Where to start? I grew up in Cleveland and later, in high school, moved to Michigan. Here, in fact. To Morgantown."

"You did? You lived here then?"

"Yes. Then I got myself a scholarship degree from Case Western, and then an admission to one of the best medical schools in the country—the University of Michigan at Ann Arbor. I had no money, of course, and my mother, who had since moved on to Santa Fe, had even less, so I borrowed heavily."

As he settles into his story, he finds it easier than he would have thought to tell. He's ready. It's that simple.

Since he was going to be a doctor, banks were perfectly willing to loan him enough for his tuition and books and fees and even a little extra to pay rent. Still, he had to live, so he was forced to pull from his savings and to do odd jobs, waiting tables, working as an orderly, things like that, to get by. And for the first couple years in med school this was how it was.

He had been living in a grad dorm, but in the summer between his second and third years he decided it was time to get a life, as it were, so he found a roommate, another medical student, and moved into an apartment on the northern outskirts of the city, near the VA where he was doing some rotations. The apartment building was in bad repair, with paint peeling and the lights burning out and the stairwells being dark and smelly, but the price was right, it had two bedrooms and was close enough to campus and the hospital.

Now, in this same apartment building, in fact on the same floor as the medical students, lived another couple, a man and a woman. The students didn't know much about them except that they didn't seem to have regular jobs and that the woman was very beautiful.

His hair is down to a couple of uneven inches. Storm gathers the cut hair, careful to leave no evidence, and rubber-bands it together at one end forming a long strand, a disembodied ponytail, which she lays carefully on the back of the sink. Lancaster nods his approval.

Next she opens the bag he brought from the pharmacy, removing the contents, including a pair of plastic gloves, which she slips on. She opens a squirt bottle, and then two larger plastic bottles labeled DEVELOPER and CREAM BLEACH. He watches as she pours equal portions into the squirt bottle and shakes it. The strong ammonia odor burns his nose and makes his eyes water.

He sits on the toilet, towels draped over his shoulders, as she begins to lay the solution on his hair and knead it in.

"Afterward, I'll give you a more even cut."

"Just hurry."

"We have to wait for now. Your hair's dark. This will take a little time. Go on with the story."

One night this beautiful woman knocked on their door. She was bleeding from the nose and lip, and one of her eyes was swollen shut. She was crying.

They looked at her injuries, which weren't anything that wouldn't heal on their own. They gave her ice wrapped in a washcloth and let her stay the night. She wouldn't say what had happened, only that it didn't matter and not to worry about it.

Storm finishes working the dye into his hair and covers it with a plastic shower cap he bought. She follows him into his bedroom, where he continues to pack his small bag.

Soon after that, the story continues, the woman, Denise, invited the two medical students over for dinner. After dinner her partner, his name was Bobby, brought out a couple bottles of wine, some marijuana, and some cocaine. The four of them sat around and drank and got stoned, and then started snorting coke. Adrian Lancaster the med student had never tried cocaine, but his roommate had, and so he thought he'd try it just to see. It was pretty good. He liked the elation that came with the drug, and he even liked the physical sensations, the numb teeth, the medicine taste running down the throat. They had fun that evening, and would repeat it a number of times in the coming months, he and his roommate and the man and woman sitting around sipping wine, cutting up lines of coke on a mirror and sucking them up. Adrian discovered a kind of release in these chemicals he had never imagined. He was a very tightly wrapped guy, you might say, anal, but under the influence he felt his intensely rational and control-hungry mind relax and open up.

What was especially remarkable to him was his first exposure to mind-expanding drugs, psychedelics. Bobby gave him a tab of acid one night and his life was never the same. He began to experiment, in a controlled sort of way, with nonpharmaceutical organics, peyote and psilocybin, primarily. It was amazing. For the first time he realized that there was an entire valid way of looking at the world that was completely outside the intensely rational, linear approach he had always taken. And he saw that this was valuable. To put it to a test he once took some psilocybin mushrooms before going back to work on a very intricate biochemical problem a professor had proposed to him and that had been giving him fits because he couldn't come up with a solution. It was a minute thing, something about the way certain protein molecules bonded in the presence of certain enzymes in the liver. The exact mechanism of this specific reaction was apparently not really understood by anyone. Under the influence of the drug he came up with a theory, a hypothesis, that was brilliantly weird, and very impressive. It was, as his professor said, "Out of left field, but fascinating." The professor mentioned it in a longer article he was writing, and gave Lancaster his first publication credential. He was dumbfounded. Here he had been given insight to the most concrete, scientific sort of problem through what amounted to an essentially psychotic hallucination. He began to experiment more, and even considered a career in research.

But these psychedelics weren't a problem. He used them as tools. He saw himself as a modern-day Aldous Huxley. Gradually, however, Lancaster, enchanted by now with the miracles of modern pharmacology, began to use other drugs to help him through the grind of school. It was terrific. Unlike your basic heads, he knew exactly what he was taking, what it would do, and how to counteract it. He used Dexedrine to study and Seconal to sleep at night. And nothing particularly bad came of any of this. Months passed. He had things under control.

He looks into a mirror. "It's working," he says.

"Leave it on a while longer. Let it work."

He sits on the edge of the bed. "They were following you, you said. Did you come in through the garage again?"

"Yeah, don't worry. I parked on the next block over and cut through the yard behind yours. No one saw me."

"What makes you so smart about all this?"

"Paranoia," she says. "That's not the end of the story."

"No. Of course not."

"Please go on with it."

The following summer, between his third and fourth years, brought some changes. His roommate graduated and left to start his residency out of state, leaving Adrian in a bit of a pinch. His financial situation hadn't improved any. In fact, it had gone downhill. He had little savings—for one thing, the drugs cost a lot of money—and there was no way he could carry the rent on the two-bedroom apartment himself. Of course he could have found another roommate, or moved, but he didn't have the energy to think about these things, and before long another solution presented itself.

He spent more time now with the couple across the hall, the three of them drinking bottles of wine and doing grams of coke and discussing anything that was on their minds. Adrian liked these two, looked up to them, especially the woman. She was very bright. One night he was talking about his situation when the man, Bobby, made a suggestion, a way to make the extra money our student needed, and to put the vacant second bedroom to good use as well. And not just a little extra to cover the rent. "Real money," he said.

Bobby of course made his living dealing. He had recently come into a line on some of the heroin coming into Ann Arbor, and had thought of a way to make it as profitable as possible. His idea was this: Adrian was to get himself a good supply of clean needles and syringes, a supply he could keep stocked. And since he was adept with a needle, and knew a thing or two about dosages, he would use the second bedroom as an unusual shooting gallery. A place for respectable junkies—students, professionals who needed someplace. No lowlifes. No violence. Bobby could truthfully tell his clientele that they would be getting the safest smack in town, injected by an almost doctor. Sort of a clinic. And for his trouble our student would make enough extra cash to pay the rent and put some in his pocket. It would be very discreet. Bobby would take care of handling the stuff and getting the clients.

And what was best of all, perhaps, from a medical standpoint, was that he would be guaranteeing these junkies clean drugs and clean needles. They were going to use no matter what. This was just a way of ensuring their safety.

Adrian refused outright. The idea was abhorrent. It would be an incredible risk. His entire career could be ruined if he were discovered. He'd been living for three years on almost no money. One more and he'd be in a residency program that would at least pay him a semiliving wage. He could find a cheaper place to live, or another roommate.

Then one night in September he heard shouts from the apartment across the hall, and soon a pounding on his door. It was Denise, whose face had been bloodied again. He dressed the abrasions as best he could, applied ice to take down the swelling, and put her to bed on the couch. Later that night a noise awakened him. The door to his bedroom opened, and Denise came in. She sat down on the edge of the bed and started to talk to him about how attracted to him she'd been ever since they met. He wanted to say something, but she put a hand over his mouth and she got into bed with him. He figured she was wired on something or other. Whatever it was, he knew he should stop her but of course he didn't. He'd been in love with her for a long time. And she went wild. They made love off and on until sunrise.

That night did something to him. He was hooked on her like he'd never been hooked on anything before.

Over the next few days she and a friend of hers, a junkie named Sandra who was also one of Bobby's main runners, took him around to some of the places where junkies gathered to get high, where they shared needles and syringes and tourniquets. These were the most horrible places he had ever seen—dingy stinking rooms in basements and empty houses, broken-out windows and garbage on the floors.

It wasn't long before she'd talked him into taking Bobby up on his offer. She started spending more time in his apartment, sleeping with him two or three nights a week, sometimes spending the weekend, and Bobby didn't seem to mind particularly, especially in light of the arrangement they'd worked out.

It started out slowly, a couple of customers a week, but business picked up. He became the heroin doctor to the junkies of Ann Arbor. Dr. Fix, they called him. Incredible as it seems, he saw himself as a kind of capitalist Albert Schweitzer of the counterculture. He put a lot of money away and he never got caught. Then, a couple months before he was to graduate in May, Bobby and Denise had the fight of fights. Adrian thought he was going to have to take Denise to the emergency room this time. Her nose and mouth were bleeding and she was cut badly. But she asked him not to. "You fix me," she had said.

So he did what he could.

Bobby moved out soon after that, and with him went the connection, so the shooting-gallery business closed for good. It was time. Our student was not one to push his luck. Besides, he got something from it. He and Denise decided it made no sense for them both to have apartments on the same floor. They were sleeping together anyway, so she moved in with him, and when our student started his residency at Henry Ford Hospital in Detroit the next fall, Denise moved with him, commuting back to Ann Arbor during the week to continue her studies. She was doing graduate work in chemistry.

The only bad thing in all of it was that Adrian had gotten nipped by the drug that fed him. He'd become something of a heroin user himself. At first it had been an experiment, like the psychedelics. Then it became an easy way to come down at night, to sleep. Denise had been an addict for over two years, it turned out. Soon they were shooting up and drifting off together. Finally, it simply became their life.

Time passed.

He sustained his addiction, and she hers, well into his residency, until at the end of his second year, almost four years after he'd met Denise, more than two years after he started using, he was arrested as he left Henry Ford Hospital. The security guards and the Detroit police were waiting for him when he came out the front door one fall night. They found two 50-cc vials of pharmaceutical morphine in his lab-coat pockets.

His life collapsed around him. He spent two nights in jail and tried contacting an attorney on his own. But before he reached anyone a Detroit criminal lawyer worked a deal with the hospital and the authorities. Denise had hired him—Adrian wasn't sure if she had been busted too. But he did not see her for a while after his arrest, only the lawyer she had hired.

As part of the deal he was put immediately into a two-month residential detox program at Beaumont Hospital up in Royal Oak, and the daze of withdrawal has blanketed most of his memories of that time. The deal the lawyer made stipulated that if Lancaster could stay clean and do public service, his license would be salvaged. Henry Ford would not allow him to continue his residency but wouldn't stand in the way of his finishing at another Detroit hospital, so he worked for the Michigan Clinic for a year, then finished up at the Detroit Medical Center, in the heart of the city.

He only saw Denise twice after his arrest, when she visited him at Beaumont, and even these visits had to be negotiated by the lawyer and were chaperoned. By the time he got out she'd moved away from the area. She was gone. He heard from someone that she had moved somewhere out west, to the coast. The two months in detox seemed like years to him, and in his heart he knew the best thing he could do was to not follow her, to forget her and let her forget him. Later, he heard she'd died from liver failure as a result of hepatitis.


Storm wipes tears away from her face.

"What most people don't understand," he says, "is that junkies can lead very normal clean lives. If they watch their dosages and use clean equipment, they can work and have families and no one ever has to know. I once met a seventy-six-year-old man who'd been addicted for forty-two years. True story. What's wrong with you?"

"It's just sad," she says.

"Yeah. But it's old history."

"Then what does it all have to do with Kevin Babcock?"

"I don't know," he says. "But it's connected. There was another murder attempt here on the same night Kevin died, a hard-core named Michael Straw. He was the bad burn patient you heard about, and as you know I treated him when he came in. He had a packet of brown powder in his pocket, the same drug I saw at Kevin's.

"I didn't know Straw's name, and I didn't recognize him because of the burns. I'd only ever known him as Zipper. He was one of Bobby Karnowski's supply lines. Bobby Karnowski was the dealer who lived across the hall, Denise's boyfriend."

"Then who's Holt?"

"No idea. But now he's contacting me. He called me last night in the ER. Today I got this letter." He slides the envelope across the bed at her.

"Listen," she says after she's read it. "I told you Kevin used Red's. I used to go there with him. He'd disappear for hours making the rounds. Whatever he was running was out of there. I never met Holt in person, but I've got a lot of contacts in this town and I know Red's. I'll take you. Tonight."

"For what?"

"People hear things, but you have to be aggressive. If you want answers, you'll have to go after them. They're not going to knock on your door."

"All right. But first we have to disappear."

In the bathroom he fills the sink with water, plunges his head in, and rinses. He uses the blow dryer and, when he's done, studies himself in the mirror. What was long and dark is now short and white-blond. In addition, he hasn't shaved in a day and a half. The growth is starting to look heavy, which helps alter his face a little.

"Can I trim your hair now? It looks pretty bad."

He looks in the mirror again, turns his head from one side to the other. "Be quick," he says.

As she begins to cut, he says, "Are you ready for this?"

"I'm ready," she says. "I'm glad you're with me."

When she's finished, he begins closing up the house, unplugging appliances, locking all windows and doors, turning off the water pipes. He does one sink-load of dishes, which takes care of about half those that are dirty. The rest he throws into a garbage bag and hauls out to the curb. He is careful to wear a hat.

Down the street a few houses sits a black Taurus, the same car Lancaster saw outside Kevin's house just before the deputies arrived. Lancaster is not surprised. He has been waiting. As he watches, the car U-turns away from the curb and drives off.

**B**randon, you're busting my balls for nothin', man. This town has gone cold. I got dick for you." Little Tommy Winter is on his perch again, feet up on the toilet seat, stall locked against the world. Brandon crouches on the frozen shit-water floor, talking and listening under the divider.

Outside dusk will fall soon. Brandon's cold is at full throttle in his throat and head and feels as if it's moving into his chest. He managed to steal a nap this afternoon, though, after lunch with Spinner. Considering the cold and the fact he only had three hours sleep last night, he feels fairly functional.

"Just tell me where to look, Tom. We've got two dead and another critical within two days."

"No 'critical,' " Tommy says. "Word's out on the torch."

"Straw?"

"Snuffo. Flameout. You're out of touch, Brandon."

"When?"

"This afternoon, couple hours ago."

Sarah Le Seure—he needs to talk to her again and she may still be here. He'll hit the hospital next. He says, "The city has every spare man working on this. We're running ongoing canvasses around the Babcocks' and in the vicinity of Juncket Street."

"So?"

"So nothing's turning up."

"Brandon—"

"And your buddy Pete; how does that make you feel?"

"Terrible, Brandon. Petie was a fucking saint and we all knew it."

"Tell me what you know, Tom. I don't have time for this."

"We were wrong. Ain't shit coming into town."

"I already know that."

"Who'd told you?"

"It's being synthesized here. Kevin was getting it to his brother. His brother was getting it out to distributors."

Silence from the stall.

"Hot? Are you sweating?"

"Yeah, that's right. See, there wasn't no scag on the street. Didn't make no sense. So I nosed around. It's all going out, man. Pure stuff, I hear."

"Fang."

"Fang, Fang, what a bang. Make Petie drown and Kevin hang."

"Talk to me some more about Seth Babcock."

Silence again.

"That name scare you? When you mentioned him yesterday you didn't tell me he was such an active member of our little community."

"Whatever this is, Brandon, it ain't nickel-and-dime shit and it ain't all incompetents. You don't just go read about it in the paper. Kevin was some kind of contact for Seth. Kevin was who Seth was coming *to*. Kevin was the *man* this time, Brandon. Honest to shit, I don't know what the game was. But whatever it was, Kevin was at the center. There was some guy, nobody knows who. Kevin was seen with him. He always wore this orange hat."

"Holt."

"Yeah, I guess so. I never knew his name. No one did."

"Tell me about him."

"Not much to tell."

"You saw him?"

"Here and there. Ugly fucker with these brown rotten teeth."

"Beard?"

"Yeah, nappy little thing."

"Who is he?"

"Nobody knows him. Nobody but Kevin ever saw the guy before this. Brandon, I heard this ain't nothing to fuck around with. I heard—"

"Where did you hear it, Tom? Who tells you these things?"

"Man, I'm shaking. Jesus Christ."

"You saw Petie before he died, didn't you?" Brandon slips a pint of brandy from his jacket and hands it up under the divider.

"Yeah. After you and I talked yesterday I managed to get in touch with him. He was scared. He told me this was way big, Brandon, he wanted out. He only ever wanted to turn a few bucks selling a little and now the world was falling down. But, Brandon, Petie was more than you think."

"He and Kevin . . ."

"Yeah, yeah. He was Kevin's bagman and Kevin's fag man. But he was a snitch, too, B. That's what you don't understand."

"He worked for me. He talked to me Monday morning."

"Not you. He yanked your dick. He was getting substantial *dinero,* big-league payola."

"From?"

"I can't, Brandon."

"Listen to me, Thomas—who the fuck is in my town?" Brandon feels angry, suddenly, indignant even, and it surprises him. But what's happening here is way beyond some local boys running a little lab.

"I don't know who."

"Who was Petie talking to?"

"I don't know. He wouldn't tell me. But they were working on the people Seth was dealing with, the big people, the money. They didn't care about Petie's small-time bullshit, or Kevin's, or even Seth's, really."

"They wanted cut in?"

"No, man! Brandon. Oh." Tommy's voice breaks. "He was working for the fucking government, Brandon."

Brandon takes a beat to collect himself. "The government's a big organization." Very soft, almost a whisper.

"Some deep investigation they were working him on. They didn't want Seth or Kevin or any of those guys. They wanted to know who they were tapped into."

They followed Straw in, no doubt, Brandon thinks. Straw led them to the Babcocks. Kevin Babcock was the conduit to the unknown Holt and whatever big league he belongs to. Think about how fast Julian Kline and the other DEA shadows showed up. They've probably had watchers here for weeks.

"At first Petie bragged how Kevin was the main jake, how he was running this, how Kevin was gonna deal some volume, use Seth to move the shit. But then Petie got real nervous because of Kevin and he changed his tune. The last time I saw Petie he was babbling about Kevin and how the Man was gonna find out about him and the Man was big and angry. He said the Man knew about me, Brandon. Then today I got a call."

"What call?"

"I don't know. I think they know me—"

The lights go out.

It's very dark in the can with Tommy, black velvet because there are no windows. Brandon couldn't see his own hand but for the light of the cigarette he holds.

With fear in his voice Tommy says, "Hey."

"Don't move."

"Brandon."

Brandon feels his way into the hallway and along the wall to the doorway into the barroom. The last of the day's fading sunlight leaks in through the gaps around the outside door.

He opens the inside door and steps around the old phone booth next to the doorway and into the barroom, which is dark, too, because the windows have been painted. People are yelling and laughing and Shirley's voice rises above them all: "It ain't funny! Now turn on the lights." A glass breaks somewhere, followed by more drunken laughs.

And then behind him, from down the hallway toward the men's room, Brandon hears a strange and powerful whisper—*pffft*. It's a sound he's heard before. Again, *pffft,* then again.

Three times the sound of a silenced handgun.

Every nerve and muscle in his body knows what's happening. He kicks open the hallway door and flips his cigarette into the empty black space, then drops to the side and pulls his pistol from the holster beneath his arm. In the same instant several things happen: as Brandon moves he stumbles over a chair and falls against the phone booth; a brilliant flame flashes from the hallway and the silenced handgun spits again, louder now that it's directed at him. Small gauge, he can tell. Twenty-two probably. The handgun of choice for close-range hits. The glass in the phone booth above him explodes and shards rain down over his head. He feels a cut open up on his ear. Someone in the barroom screams.

The outside doorway opens, letting in light, then closes.

Brandon's landed awkwardly on his side, pinning his gun hand against the wall, but manages to shift, aim at the outside door, and fire. His .38 roars, splintering the wood and deafening him.

When the echoes have cleared, he realizes how very quiet it has grown in the bar. He waits, not breathing. A second, two, not moving for fear there may be someone waiting to get a bearing. But in his gut he knows it's already finished.

Voices now, footsteps run back from the bar and a flashlight shines in his eyes.

"Shit, it's Brandon. He's gone nuts."

Big Red Shirley, the bartender.

"Get some lights back on, fast."

"The hell's going on?"

"Stay back," he says. He takes the flashlight from Shirley and aims it at the hole he blew in the outside door. Nothing apparently on the other side, and then he hears a car screaming away. By the time he opens the door and runs out into the lot, the sound is off in the distance and there's nothing to see.

Back in the cold can again he says, "Tommy?"

No answer. He sees bullet holes in the thin wall of the stall, kicks the door, breaking the latch, and points the light.

Tommy's still crouched up on the toilet seat, but he's leaning funny off to one side. Blood runs from behind his left ear where a bullet or fragment has penetrated the skull. His breathing is rapid and shallow. Brandon lifts the eyelids and sees that the two pupils are not in agreement, one widely dilated, the other a pinprick.

The top half of the brandy bottle is still clutched in his hand. The bottom has been shot away.

"Goddammit. Shirley, call an ambulance. And get some squads down here. Hurry up. Just take it easy, Tom." Brandon picks him up from the toilet and carries him out into the hallway, where he holds his head until EMTs arrive.

★   ★   ★

Five squads, three sheriff's and two city, respond. Spinner Wharton and Lou Adamski are there within minutes. Shirley found that the lock on the fuse box in the back hallway had been snipped and the master circuit control thrown, cutting off all juice to the building.

Brandon sits in the backseat of an unmarked, smoking and trembling. Spinner and Lou are up front. A flasher on the dashboard turns, washing them in waves of red light. It's dark outside now.

"It's been a while," he says. "Last time was '74, and that guy was so drunk, he about couldn't hit the ground from falling." Brandon drags on the cigarette and blows smoke against the glass. "He shot a hole in the clouds, and I blew his kneecap off."

Spinner, in the driver's seat, watches Brandon in the rearview mirror. "You all right?"

"Just a little jumpy."

"Comes on after it's over, don't it. Funny thing, nerves. I bet that in there you were as fast as you needed to be."

"Tommy got hit. I think that was the idea all along."

"You go look at where that last bullet went, and figure where it would of hit you if you were standing upright."

"Yeah?"

"Right where it counts, buddy. Right in the old gearbox."

"I was just lucky. And if I hadn't gone out of the can to see what was going on—" He rolls down the window, flips out the butt, and lights another one. "Anyone else get hurt?"

"Couple people got glass cuts, nothing serious. You want somebody to call your daughter or something?"

"No."

Brandon watches Jimmy Mendez and a ballistics man from the highway patrol walk around in the circle of light thrown by the pink security lamp on the back of the building.

"It was like he was wired and somebody heard him. Somebody knew I was here. Anybody question for witnesses?" Brandon asks.

"You're it," Spinner says. "No one else saw nothing."

"Tommy?"

"He's alive. That's all. You hear Straw expired about three hours ago?"

"Word filtered down. Anything on Lancaster? We got someone watching him yet, Lou?" He reaches forward and pokes Lou's arm.

Lou is quiet for a moment, then says, "There's a search warrant coming down tonight. We've got men on his house. We'll go in in the morning. Interested?"

"Wouldn't miss it," Brandon says. "Always glad to be involved."

He drives back into the city by himself and on over to MCGH to check on Tommy. He rides up to the ICU, figuring they'll know what's going on.

"He'll be out of surgery soon," a resident tells him. "Within the hour. The penetration wasn't too deep, but with head injuries all you can do is wait."

There's no reason to hang around, really, but Brandon sits in the hallway, thinking. He has work to do—so much work, he can't see straight—and yet the next step is not clear to him.

"Excuse me," Brandon says to a nurse. "There was a patient up here, a burn. Michael Straw. I know he died today. I'm a friend of the family and wondered if they'd left yet."

"The sister was up here until about an hour ago, when her husband came in. They had some arrangements to make."

"Where would they go to make those arrangements."

"Social services usually—"

"Where is that?"

"Fifth floor," she says. "B wing."

★   ★   ★

*Exhausted,* he thinks. *She looks as bad as I feel.*

Sarah Le Seure waits in a chair in an outer office. Her hair's pinned up and she's not wearing any makeup. He can see her through a glass pane next to the door. He knocks on the glass. She looks at him, her face blank for a moment, then she gets up and opens the door.

"Detective."

"I won't bother you," he says. "I heard. I'm very sorry."

"It's better," she says. "Are you still pretending this was an accident? Don't answer. I've done a little checking."

He nods.

"You lied to me."

"You didn't tell me your husband was the governor's right-hand. You don't think that's relevant?"

"Why would it be?" a deep voice says. A lean, silver-haired man approaches from a hallway leading back farther into the office.

"This is Detective Brandon," Sarah says. "He spoke with me on Monday. I told you."

"Yaaas," Le Seure says. "Who didn't think anyone had deliberately done this to Michael. You've revised your assessment of the situation?"

"We're looking into it."

"My God, man, the boy was immolated by some maniac. I hope you're doing more than looking into it."

"We are. Of course we are."

"Good," he says. "I want to see this animal caught. Now, about my position. We're as discreet about that as we can be. With Michael in the family . . . you understand."

*Governor's Chief of Staff has Junkie for Brother-in-Law.*

"I can imagine."

"We've gone so far as to hire a public relations firm to keep any mention of Michael *out* of the press. I trust you'll bear this in mind."

"We were officially ashamed of him," Sarah says. "When he was useful, we used him. But otherwise we had to look the other way." There's more than a little bitterness in her voice.

"Sarah," Le Seure says.

"You didn't have to sit there and look at him," she says. "You didn't have to watch him die."

Brandon clears his throat. "We wouldn't release any personal information without clearing it with you first. I wanted to express my condolences. I'm sure you have other matters to attend."

Sarah Le Seure offers her hand. Her husband, though, turns away. Brandon nods again and backs through the door.


He leaves through the ER and pokes his head into the office. The swing-shift clerk is sipping a Coke and reading.

"Dr. Lancaster," Brandon says to her. "He gets in around seven-thirty, right?"

She nods.

"He here yet?" He wants a word. No busts. No pressure. Just to come straight out and ask for what he wants—help.

"He's not on tonight."

"Oh."

"He took a personal leave, a whole week off, sudden like. Death in the family or something."

Brandon's running before she's finished the sentence. Out through the snow and into the parking lot, fumbling with the keys to the Buick, turning over the old engine. *Come on, Baby.* The 350 whines and catches. He pulls it into gear and takes off, bouncing so hard coming out of the driveway that the muffler scrapes the road.

As he runs a stoplight, he pounds his fist into his forehead, self-chastisement for not playing his gut, for letting Lou talk him out of it. Fed tail or no, he knows what's happening. The doctor's going to fly. These things always come down to hunch, instinct. You either call it right or you don't. And all the goddamn police tricks and tests and techniques, and all the fed tails in the world, can't help you when you're wrong.

His only hope is that Lancaster hasn't gone yet. He drives like a madman toward Sunnyvale Street in west Morgantown.

# FIFTEEN

**I**n his basement, in an abandoned sump pit covered by rotting boards, Lancaster keeps a stainless steel Smith & Wesson .357 Magnum revolver wrapped in an oiled cloth and then sealed in an airtight plastic bag. He unwraps it and holds it to the thin streetlight coming in through the ground-level half window. No rust; no pitting. It's as perfect as it was the day his father bought it for him.

Lancaster was thirteen. They lived in north Cleveland near the Lake Erie shoreline, where his father worked on the docks when he was working. It was an on-again, off-again situation, between the layoffs and the whims of his father. But on this day his father had gotten the first real paycheck in a while, and a fat check at that. He said he saw the gun in a pawnshop window and knew it was a deal. It'd belonged to some lady, the broker told him, who wanted to protect herself. She'd died in her sleep and this was part of the estate. The broker was asking a hundred dollars. Lancaster's father got it for seventy-five. He laid it on the kitchen table and told Adrian there were two things to remember about it. One was that it was something that would be good forever if he took care of it. Few things you could buy were like that. Second was that it was the closest thing to pure power an average guy could get his hands on. The power of chemistry contained in the gunpowder, and the power of death when released.

"Like having a handful of sun," he'd said. "It can burn you badly. Or it can burn some other poor son of a bitch."

His mother hadn't said anything. She just stood in the kitchen doorway looking on and rubbing her arms.

Lancaster never fired it. They'd talked of going out into the country to a shooting range somewhere and taking aim on targets, or of just finding some empty woods and blasting away at stumps and cans and shadows. But before they ever had the chance his father was killed in an accident at the docks that was never explained very well. All they knew was that there wasn't much of a body left to bury. Just a sealed coffin with a picture on top. It was only a month later that they moved to Morgantown to live with Adrian's aunt Rose.

"They're out there waiting," he says. "Can you get out clean?"

"I told you how I came in." Storm is holding the gun up to the light and examining it.

"Wait for me to get in my truck and drive off. They'll follow me. Then you go."

"Dr. Lancaster. Let's just do it."

He packs the gun in his overnight bag and looks at her. She holds her face high, almost proudly, some of the anxiety of earlier having disappeared. He doesn't understand yet what this girl has to be so proud of, but he likes the look.

"Valleydale Mall," he says.

The black Taurus is not in sight on Sunnyvale, but there's no doubt in Lancaster's mind it's around.

Lancaster parked the Bronco beneath a streetlight so he would be clearly visible although it's been dark outside for a couple hours.

His breath crystallizes on the white scarf hiding the lower half of his face. He pauses to make sure they get a good view, looks up at the sky, and tugs his hat lower over his ears. He wears a bright yellow stocking cap. To the back of the inside of this hat he has sewn the long black ponytail that used to be attached to his scalp. It hangs, as usual, down the middle of his back.

He zips up his neon-orange parka, throws his bag in the truck, and gets in.

There, three cars back—as he makes a wide turn he catches a glimpse in the side mirror of a dull black paint job. He heads toward the center of town, then south on Center Street, which turns into 57, which leads over the River Sorrow and on to the mall where it intersects the South Border Highway.

Out at the fringe of the mall parking lot he pulls into a Sunoco station and tells the mechanic the truck's been running a little rough. Could they give it a going-over, tune it up, whatever it needs? The mechanic's eyes light up.

"Take your time," Lancaster says.

He grabs the shoulder bag and hikes across the wide parking lot to the main entrance of the mall. Just inside the glass double-doors he stops and watches the Taurus slide up outside. A suit gets out of the passenger side and heads in after him. Lancaster walks slowly into the mall.

In the hunting department of Sears he buys a box of shells. The suit pauses across the aisle to look at a boot display.

Back in the central courtyard, with its vaulted glass dome and dancing water fountain, Lancaster notices a flash of red hair and a bright-green-and-yellow plaid sport jacket. Brandon? He turns to look, but sees nothing.

Enough, he thinks. He heads into the L-shaped utility hallway, which leads from the back of the central courtyard to the rest rooms. Around the corner he crouches and listens for footsteps.

When they arrive, Lancaster drives upward, catching the man in the hip with his shoulder and driving him into the wall. Unbalanced as much from surprise as anything, the suit loses his footing and falls.

Lancaster bolts back toward the crowds, dodges through the shoppers around the fountain, and dashes into a clothing store where a rock station pounds from ceiling speakers.

From behind a display of Hawaiian print shirts he watches the suit run past, yelling into a hand-held radio.

"May I help you?" a girl says. Lancaster waves her off and duckwalks between the racks of clothing and the teenagers toward the back of the store.

"Sir," she says, more loudly.

He spins and grabs her collar, dragging her down behind a rack of clothing. "Shut the fuck up," he hisses.

"Hey!" the thick-necked manager yells.

"Show me the rear entrance."

"What kind of an asshole are you?"

The salesgirl has regained her feet, and she backpedals and stumbles into a display.

"You want trouble?" Lancaster says. He pulls the butt of the unloaded .357 from his bag so the manager can see it. "Make some more noise. Create a little ruckus. Or show me the goddamn back door."

The manager points.

"Lead. Both of you."

He follows them behind the checkout counter and into the storeroom, twists through stacks of boxes and empty racks to the door, and hits the bar marked EMERGENCY EXIT ONLY. This sets off an obnoxious siren, which causes the girl to start screaming. But he finds himself out in the night, on the loading docks, beside a six-foot-high pile of plowed snow.

As he jogs along beside the loading bays he strips off the yellow ski cap with the ponytail sewn to it, the orange jacket, and the white scarf and tosses them all into a Dumpster. Underneath he wears a heavy gray wool sweater and a dark scarf, which he wraps around his neck and lower face. He puts on a pair of clear glass horn-rims, transfers everything else from the shoulder bag into a small nylon backpack, tosses the bag into the Dumpster, and runs toward the closest group of cars.

After he's covered fifty yards or so, he looks back through the windows of a parked car. The suit is standing under a security light outside the clothing store, radio in one hand, a gun in the other.

Keeping low, Lancaster runs again until he reaches the outer edge of the lot.

The Taurus has arrived at the loading docks. He watches the suit get in. Before the door is even closed the car begins to creep along the back of the mall.

When it's out of sight, he forces himself to walk as casually as he can manage toward the highway. His ears are humming.

At the corner, a crew-cut blondie waiting for the light to change, he sees the headlights of the Taurus coming up the road.

*Ice,* he tells himself.

The car slows as the man in the passenger seat looks him over and says something to the driver. Then a station wagon pulls out from the mall driveway into traffic, cutting off the Ford and forcing the driver to hit his brakes hard to avoid a collision. His tires screech. In that confused moment Lancaster crosses the street.

He dodges into a carryout, cuts through and out the back door, and walks around toward the Taco Bell sign.

Beneath the sign sits a faded yellow Toyota Celica.

"Very nice," says Storm when he gets in.

"Ride," he says to her.

Outside the Best Western Motel in Tecumseh, Michigan, thirty or so miles from Morgantown, Brandon rubs his hands beneath the stream of hot air pouring from beneath the Buick's dashboard. He is chilled, although the car's been running for hours. He's watching room number 134, rented to Lancaster and the girl named Storm. Attractive. Friend of Kevin Babcock's, now traveling with Dr. Adrian Lancaster.

Brandon smiles in self-satisfaction. No one knows where he is. No one knows where Lancaster is. They are alone together.

He watched it all unfold.

He made it to Lancaster's house in time, and cruised until he found where the fed boys were hiding on a side street. Two men. Engine idling. This time they had no idea he was there.

On the next side street he cut over, doubled back a couple

blocks, and parked between the feds and Lancaster's house. He could see Lancaster's truck parked beneath a streetlight.

When one of the feds followed Lancaster into the mall, Brandon went in, too, and watched Lancaster make a nonsense run, watched him lose the tail and duck into a store, and knew he wasn't coming out again.

In the adjacent record store he flashed his badge, and was about to hit the back door when the alarm went off. He opened the door a crack and peeked in time to see the hat and hair come off together to reveal Lancaster's blond crew cut, and to watch the colorful jacket and scarf and bag all disappear. *They don't make stupid doctors,* he thought. Again he actually felt something approaching admiration for this man.

But what did all this mean? Was Lancaster really scamming all of them? He'd obviously put some planning into this.

Lancaster ran for the cars. Brandon, hidden from view by a high pile of snow, slipped through the door and headed toward the parked cars too. He made it seconds before the idiot goon fed appeared out back.

Lancaster crossed the South Border Highway; the black government car circled and came right past him, never getting it at all. Brandon laughed again.

But when the doctor crossed the street and got into a waiting yellow car, Brandon realized he'd screwed himself. His car was out in front of the mall. The yellow car, which Brandon saw was missing a taillight, headed west on the South Border Highway toward 57, then turned north, into town.

He sprinted back to the mall, back through the door to the record store, which to his great good fortune had not closed and locked as it should have, and out toward the central fountain. A woman shrieked at this heavy official-looking man moving very hard and very fast.

His car was idling in the fire lane out front. From there it was a mad haul to the far north end, past the Sears Auto Center, left toward the stoplight leading on to 57, dashboard flasher helping to clear the way. Maybe two minutes had passed.

His chest burned and wheezed. His head was pounding so hard, he saw colors.

He gunned the big old engine and blasted around as much other traffic as he could until 57 narrowed to two lanes after the bridge over the Sorrow and became Center Street, then switched off the flasher and hoped the yellow car was going straight through town.

Finally, in the downtown where traffic looped around the Mc-Kinley Street detour to miss the heart of the business district, in a line of cars backed up behind a semi, he spotted a car with a missing rear light. As he got closer, he saw it was the yellow car.

It continued north past the city limits, past the new multiplex cinema and the TFG farm supply store, back into the darkness of the frozen farmland. Five miles north of town the car turned east on State Route 15.

Then it was only a matter of hanging back and watching the single taillight.

And watching brought him to Tecumseh, to the Best Western. After Lancaster and Storm had taken the room, they went back out and rented a midsized Chrysler. Then they bought some food and went back to the room.

Brandon found a pay phone, called his daughter, and told her he was going to be out again tonight, maybe all night. But the trucker wasn't back yet so she didn't mind staying over, and he thought she sounded relieved that this time he had called her instead of leaving her to discover on her own that he was gone.

He grabbed a couple burgers and coffees and settled in for what he expected would be a long cold asshole of a night spent shivering in his front seat.

★   ★   ★

He awakens from a doze to see that the door to room 134 is open. Storm waves back into the room, gets into her yellow car, and leaves. Brandon's heart rate rises and falls. Then it's back to dozing until, an hour and a half or so later, Lancaster himself comes out and gets in the rental Chrysler and pulls away.

*Good,* Brandon thinks. More than anything he hates sitting.

## SEVENTEEN

For one thing, it is misnamed—Red's is yellow. The bare light bulbs are yellow, the floor is yellow, and the walls are maybe white but the lights make them yellow. The decor looks as if some crew of renovators started in with sledgehammers pounding holes here and there, knocking off loose plaster, exposing the underlying studs and wire mesh, and then suddenly stopped and left things in that half-destroyed state. The ceiling is exposed pipes, flaking plaster, and raw beams. Music videos play on the television screens mounted in every corner. The accompanying music is run through a powerful system and beats out into the rooms, enveloping Lancaster when he steps inside.

Red's is built down into the ground, the ceiling low in the front chamber and opening back and down into the sunken main room, which has a height, or depth, of fifteen or twenty feet. This room is dark, the yellow bulbs spread far apart, creating large pockets of shadow. Garden-style wrought-iron tables and chairs are scattered around a dance area in the middle of the floor. There are two bars, one near the entrance in the front chamber and one at the back of the larger room with the dance floor. Lancaster, who is still wearing the horn-rimmed glasses, finds a table against a wall of the large room in an inset corner. He wants something solid behind his back.

The place whirs and pulses and shakes. Three women dressed entirely in black leather take the table next to his. One, whose red hair is streaked with blue, sneers and looks as if she's ready to pound anyone who looks at her in the wrong way. Another one, slim with spiked white-blond hair and blue eyes, slips off her black leather jacket, revealing nothing underneath but a loose-fitting vest, and then stares straight at him. He looks away, then back. She is still looking. She wears heavy black eyeliner and black lipstick. She looks familiar.

A moment later Lancaster's busy staring into his drink when he senses someone else standing over him.

"Hey, blondie." It's the slender black-lipped girl with the vest. "Do you know who's sitting at the bar?" He looks up at her, then realizes with a small shock it's Storm.

"Sit down," he says, kicking out the chair across the table. "I really didn't recognize you."

"Good." She points and says, "See the guy in the long leather coat, down to his knees? He has black hair."

It's difficult to see this far in the weird lighting, but Lancaster can make out the man at the bar. "Yeah."

"Seth Babcock." Kevin's brother, who Holt said was supposed to meet Petie after the pickup on the bridge.

"Really?"

"Really."

He looks over at the next table again, at her friends.

"What would you think if you didn't know me, just saw me hanging out with people who looked like that?"

He shrugs.

She laughs. "You'd probably think I'm a dyke or something."

"Maybe."

"Listen, I could turn you on and off like a light switch all night long. I'm willing to bet you've never known a woman like me."

True enough, he thinks. Even with the black lipstick, blue contact lenses, orange eye shadow, and heavy-as-paint rouge she's got a beautiful face. But she's so changed from two hours ago, he feels dizzy from disorientation. He cannot reconcile the looks, let alone the personalities, as one person. Any trace of the girl from earlier is sublimated, no tense look around the eyes, no sadness or hesitancy, no vulnerability.

She's wired on something, he thinks. He was right in the clinic when he figured she was lying about being clean.

Storm lights a cigarette. "When Seth's around, it means something. He doesn't usually come out where he can be seen. He's kind of a shadow, if you know what I mean. Most people could walk by him on the street—or even see him in a bar like this—and they'd have no idea."

"Kevin's brother is a dealer?"

"And he was working with Kevin."

"You know him."

"I know people who know him. They talk to me. That's my talent—people talk to me. Witness yourself."

"Yeah, but—"

She holds up her hand. "Present tense. Seth's supposed to have a finger in the traffic in this county, but very low profile. He just floats around behind the scenes but knows everything."

"And he's here tonight."

Storm looks into his eyes and says, "See how important you are?"

"I didn't even know I was coming here until a couple hours ago."

"An eternity."

"There's no way anyone else knew I was coming here."

"You're right."

"You told."

"I set things up."

"Your friends."

"They know people. They help me out." She glances back at her table.

"So you told everyone I was going to be here. Why did I bother going through this whole charade with the hair?"

"You lost your tail. It worked. Seth has never seen you in his life, hair or no hair. What does he care? You either want to figure some things out or not. No pussyfooting now, Mr. Junkie Doctor. Not at this point."

"You tell all your friends my little story too?"

"Thanks for the good faith. I wouldn't betray you like that."

Lancaster feels as if he's on the face of a smooth cliff. He's lost his grip and has begun to slide. As he slides he picks up speed; faster and faster he goes with no way to stop it now.

"You should have done what I did if it was such an issue." She tugs at her platinum spikes. "Wig, in case you couldn't guess. I have quite a few."

"You look different."

"Better?"

"Different."

"Exciting?"

"Yeah."

"I change myself often. I like to change."

Lancaster looks back into his drink.

"What do you see in there?"

"The future. You want to hear about it?"

"Why are you still wearing the glasses?"

"Camouflage. You never really told me what you do. School?"

"No."

"You work."

"I don't want to talk about it. So what's my future?"

Lancaster looks back down into the Scotch, swirls it around in the glass. "It's still a little murky," he says. "But I see a big change coming."

"Really?" This interests her. She leans forward, her bare arms on the table. "What kind of change?"

"Murky," he says. "But it will come soon."

"I could use a change in my life."

"What's wrong with your life?"

"It's boring." She hits off the cigarette and spits the smoke out Bette Davis style, without inhaling. "That's what I like about you. You're not boring."

"I thought you were scared."

"Boredom can be scary."

"Well, I can tell you it won't be boring much longer. I can tell you that much."

"You're right. Want to make a buy?"

He shakes his head. "Why would I?"

"What're we doing here? You said you wanted to come. I arranged it so Seth Babcock, who does not make many public appearances, is here for you to meet. Now do something with it."

"I wanted to find Holt."

"He's not here. Seth is. And he knows, believe me. You want to make a buy?"

"For what?"

"Make a buy."

"I don't want to make a buy. I don't buy anymore."

"If you want to learn something, Adrian, you have to get back down in the muck. You have to lower yourself again." It's the first time she's called him by his first name.

He hears truth in what she says, and it scares him. He lifts his empty glass toward the waitress.

"When you asked me to help, I took it seriously. I've set things up for you. But the people who are in this aren't going to walk over and sit on your lap. Listen to me—you should make a buy. And a good buy, no nickel-and-dime business. Pay some money."

"What's available?"

"Smack. Coke. Pills, up and down. Psycho. Experimental. Pharm speed. Street speed. Grass. Gas. Crystal. You name it, I can have it in front of you inside a half an hour."

"I see danger," he says, into the empty glass. "This change that will come."

She looks at him a moment and says, "You're very strange."

"*I'm* strange." He laughs.

"Talk, talk. We need a break. Let's dance." She puts on an obviously often-practiced expression of boredom, but he can see her heart beating in the V of the vest.

The waitress sets a new glass in front of him. He slides her a five and waves her off. "Fresh medium. Things are clearer."

"You can see the future now?"

He sucks it all down in one long pull, then says, "Yeah. It tells me we're going to dance."

It is a golden seventies oldie, a Johnny Rotten jam, the Sex Pistols, fast and nasty early punk, a twisted and sarcastic version of "Rock Around the Clock." Six, three, seven, nine, two o'clock rock. Storm is wild. She gets down low and comes up fast and inside. She holds the front of his shirt when she moves, and he holds the chains on her black leather vest. They move hard together, slamming their bodies into those around them, and they hold on harder, as if there is nothing else for them. She tears his shirt. Under her chains he can feel breast, nipples firm and turned on. He pulls her close to him.

She throws her arms around his neck, presses her lips to his ear, and says, "I can make it better. You want?"

He shakes his head. "I can't."

"Come on." She pulls him by the hand toward the back of the bar. He tries to resist, but has no will. They cut off down the dim hallway that leads to the rest rooms, stopping in front of an unmarked door. She looks around and pulls him in. It is just a small storeroom, empty gray plastic garbage cans stacked in one corner, mops and buckets in another. Storm locks the door, then she takes a knife from somewhere in her pockets, flicks the blade open, and holds the flat cold side of it against his face. He closes his eyes.

"Kneel," she says.

He drops.

"Do you like it that I set you up to make a buy? You can see the trash that lives around here in their element, the people Kevin hung out with."

Lancaster is eye-level with her black leather crotch. A black-capped brown glass vial appears in her hand. "I can get you your own if you want, eighty-five a gram. That's a bargain." She taps some onto the tip of the blade and holds it out for him. Cocaine.

He looks into her fake blue eyes and whispers, "I really can't."

"Come on, Doc. Coke wasn't your bête noire. It's like the Scotch—it doesn't mean anything. Do one for me. Then we'll rock and roll." She kneels now, too, and leans in so he's breathing her breath. She closes her eyes. "Join me where I am," she says. "Come on down."

What she says is true; cocaine was never a drug he'd been hung up on. He used it when he wanted, then walked away. Even so, it's something he knows he has no business with now. But her kneeling there, breath hot on his face, a thin line of perspiration dotting her upper lip, the Scotch spinning his own brain, makes the temptation strong, not so much because he wants the drug but because he wants to share it with her, to be with her in this way, to lower himself, as she says. This is a passage rite of sorts, his commitment to following her back, his demonstration to her that he will go where she will take him.

He plugs one nostril and begins to suck in with the other but at the last moment changes his mind and pulls his head back before he takes the hit. He shakes his head.

So she lowers her face to the powder and inhales it herself. As he watches, he imagines the whang of the drug into his brain, imagines closing his eyes as she is doing, tilting his face up and rocking back on his heels, his face going numb.

He imagines that it is strong coke, clean and pure, maybe the cleanest he's ever done.

"Clean?" he says to her.

"Clean and good," she answers.

"Like you," he says.

"Ralph, Adrian," Storm says by way of introductions. Ralph is skinny to the point he looks sick. His skull face cracks a quick half-smile, then goes back to sucking on a beer bottle. He sits with his cowboy-booted feet up on the table, his chin pressed down toward his chest. Lancaster can see scalp through his hair.

He slaps the beer down and says, "What?"

"Fang," she says.

"Uh-uh. Nobody's movin' that shit around here. China, I got. That's it."

China white. Used to be, in the days when Lancaster started, China was the finest street heroin you could buy. But it eventually became just another generic name for any dogshit smack somebody wanted to tie up in a plastic bag.

Lancaster nods.

"Dime?"

"Gram," he says.

Ralph purses his lips and nods. *Nice score,* his eyes say to Storm. *I owe you, baby.*

"Sixty-five."

"Fifty," Lancaster says. Play the game; the game means showing that you know.

"Sixty. You don't like it, try someplace else."

"Fifty. And if it's good, I want an ounce as soon as you can get it. Tomorrow, say."

This is enough to bring Ralph's feet from the table down to the floor.

"That'll run you a grand."

Lancaster nods.

Ralph says, "I gotta take a walk outside. You wait a minute and meet me out there, but don't look like you're following me."


Away from the building the parking lot is dark. Storm leans on the fender of a parked pickup truck, puffing nervously on a cigarette. Lancaster paces to keep warm. The temp is in the teens again, and a stiff breeze blowing in from the west has the chill factor down in the arctic range.

"Hey, hey," Ralph says as he comes to them out of the darkness. He tosses Lancaster an acorn-sized plastic-wrapped packet of white powder. "It's the real thing," he says. "You'll see. You'll want your ounce, man. Be here tomorrow night, same time, same station. A cool G and you're in."

"Let me check this out." He passes a fifty to Ralph.

"All right, man," Ralph says, holding out his hand. Then his look changes as he watches something over Lancaster's shoulder. "Gotta go," he says, pulling back the hand.

"Wait up, Ralphie," a smooth new voice says. Seth Babcock moves out from the dark beyond the cars into the circle of dim light that reaches from the building. "Stick around, buddy." Seth holds what looks like a .45 auto in his left hand.

"Sure," Ralph says. Ralph is clearly not comfortable being a party to this meeting.

"Kevin's doctor makes a score," Seth says. "Ralph says you're in for more. Buying weight these days. Times have changed."

"Doctor?" Ralph says.

Seth Babcock is striking in his plainness, Lancaster thinks. His features seem to shift; he has a face you couldn't remember for trying. And with his long black coat and dark greased-back hair he blends into the night. That's his skill. The only noticeable element is the large diamond in his left ear that catches and refracts light when he turns his head.

Lancaster holds his hands away from his sides.

"What's it all about, Doc? Don't make sense, you being out here. You want to clue me in?"

"I'm here because I don't know either. I wanted to find Holt."

Seth nods. "Holt's a comedian."

"You know him, then."

"Of him. That is, we ain't actually met face-to-face. But we know each other. Let's go someplace warm. I got a place I can use not too far from here, nice quiet country house. We could have a drink, catch up on things."

"Did you know Straw?"

"Dr. Lancaster, let's—"

"Tell me."

"I knew him. That's all. He represented some people I needed to deal with. I don't know who did him. I wish I did know. I wish I knew who did my brother." *Pity that person,* Lancaster thinks. He can hear the death wish in Seth's voice, has no doubt at all that he could easily, would easily, kill whomever he had to to stop the craziness, to get revenge for his botched business affairs and for Kevin.

"You ever meet his people?"

"If I'd met them, there would of been no need for Straw, would there? Now"—he waves the end of the gun—"let's go. I'm getting cold."

Storm walks a few steps away and turns to light a cigarette, shielding the flame from the wind. Then Lancaster sees the cigarette fly from her hands. It hits the ground and a shower of embers flashes up and disappears. She turns back toward the group holding a gun of her own, a small silver automatic. But Seth doesn't see it right away, not until she has it pointed at his head.

"Storm," says Lancaster, "we're just having a talk. We all want the same thing here."

"Think about it, Adrian. We don't want the same thing at all. Seth just wants things to go away, including us. We want daylight. Daylight would melt him. Drop the gun, Seth. And take your other hand out of your pocket."

"Storm," Seth says, "if you walk right now, I'll let you."

"Do it."

"Storm." Seth is smiling.

She swings the gun toward the truck behind them and fires through the cab window, leaving a nickel-sized hole and a spiderweb of shattered safety glass.

"Shit!" Ralph yells, and hits the ground.

Seth Babcock watches her, making his decision. Then he shakes his head. The .45 falls to the gravel. He holds his hands out from his sides, just like Lancaster.

"Take off your coat and lay it down too. Then back off."

"You little psycho cunt," he says. But he drops the coat and backpedals, dragging Ralph with him.

"Pick it up, Adrian."

He stares at her as she waves her gun at him, giving him directions. She looks as comfortable with the gun, he thinks, as she does with a cigarette.

"Storm."

"Pick it up! In the inside pocket is an address book. Take it out."

"You're dead," Seth says. "You just killed yourself."

Lancaster finds a black Filofax.

"Now pick up the gun. Seth, you lay down next to Ralphie there, hands behind your head."

He watches her, waiting for an opening.

"Seth, I swear to God."

He kneels, then lies face forward on the asphalt and clasps his fingers behind his head.

Lancaster holds Seth's heavy .45 in one hand and the address book in the other.

"Now let's go."

"You're dead!" Seth screams at them as they walk away. "You're both fucking dead and buried!"

Storm walks with her back pressed to Lancaster's so she can watch Seth and Ralph.

"Don't move," she says.

Then as if on cue she and Lancaster run.

As Lancaster fumbles to unlock the rental, a cherry-red Chevy four-wheeler, jacked up high and sitting on oversized mud-crushers, bleats and tears into the parking lot.

"Hurry up," says Storm.

Seth is charging toward them. He flags down the cherry-red truck and points at Lancaster.

"Hurry up, Adrian."

The rental car starts fine and Lancaster guns it, sizzles back on the icy asphalt, locks up the brakes, and spins the front end around in a neat 180.

"Ride, cowboy," says Storm. Lancaster lays it down, out of the parking lot and on the road back toward Morgantown.

"Casual." Storm wipes at her face, smearing the makeup worse than it already is.

"You want to tell me what that was all about?"

"Nothing," she says. "It was about nothing. Seth wanted you to go for a ride you'd have never come back from."

"I mean the whole stupid thing."

"Just rattling their cages, Doctor. That's the game."

"You knew him after all."

She doesn't answer.

"I don't even think Seth or his people are the ones doing the killing."

"Everybody's doing the killing, Adrian. Find one, you find them all. Like snakes. You just have to keep flipping rocks."

"Is that why you wanted the book?"

"This?" She rolls down the window and tosses Seth's Filofax out into the night. "You think he'd really write down any important numbers?"

"Why'd you take it?"

"Just to piss him off. He's scum and he deserves it. I blame him for getting Kevin involved in his shitty business."

In the rearview Lancaster sees a big angry pair of truck headlights coming up the road after him.

"Any quick game plan? They're right on our ass."

"Drive fast."

"Genius," he says. The road is two lanes bordered tightly by banks of plowed snow, a continuous white blur whipping by in the outside headlight beam. It's well traveled, though, so the surface is scraped and dry, and Lancaster pushes the car for all it will give. He hits seventy-five and the truck's still riding right behind. Eighty he opens a little space. Eighty-five and he can almost breathe.

Then something startlingly loud cracks into the back end.

"They're shooting," Storm says. "I guess this is what you call hardball."

"Je-sus."

"You're coming up to a gas station at the next intersection. Act like you're going through the light as long as possible, then make the cut into the station, but keep it so your side of the car is still facing the road. You can do it. They'll never make the turn in the truck."

"Then what?"

"That'll bring them right up past us and they'll be surprised. And I'll have an angle."

She takes both guns, climbs over into the backseat, and rolls down the rear driver-side window. The wind is deafening.

Around a tight curve at fifty-five and there, a hundred yards up, is an intersection, light green, and on the right a Shell station. He presses it hard right up to the light. Then at the last possible moment, maybe thirty yards from the gas station driveway, he hits the brakes as hard as he can without locking up, cuts the wheel, and squeals into the station, then swings left to stay parallel with the road, barely missing the first set of pumps. Behind him comes a tearing screech of burning Goodyear as the truck ties up into a skid. It slides by sideways, its front end pointing at the station and at Storm.

She fires three shots with the little .25 and two booms with Seth's .45.

"Go!" she screams. Lancaster jumps back on the gas, through the station, past the open-jawed stares of the local shit-shooters inside, out onto the less well-traveled crossroad, and north into the night.

There's nothing behind them.

"From one moving vehicle to another, and I shot out their tire," she says. "Am I hot?"

"You're crazy."

"You got what you wanted."

"I did? All I got was a gram of cut-down everyday street smack, a dealer who's ready to put a bullet in my head, and still no Arnie Holt."

"Yeah," she says, crawling back up front. "But they know who we are now. And they respect us."

"You really hit one of their tires?"

"Would you like to go back and look?"

"That's an impossible shot."

"My father," she says. "He had me target-shooting from the time I was six. One of the many benefits of not having a brother."

They crest the top of a long downgrade coated in hard pack and glare ice. Lancaster touches the brakes and nearly sends them into a spin, but he pulls it out and sits back for a long coast.

He's about to ask her what's really going on, what's with this craziness she set up at Red's, the fact that she obviously knows more about Kevin's connections than she's led him to believe, the lie about not doing drugs anymore. Is she really directly involved in this after all? Was she dealing along with Kevin? What does she want, and why has she brought him along with her? These thoughts fill his mind, and he's looking for a way to sort them out when he checks the rearview mirror.

He opens his mouth but it's already too late. The truck has come up over the grade so fast, its tires nearly leave the ground. Lancaster has time to grab the collar of Storm's leather jacket and pull her head down toward the seat. He tenses and on instinct yanks the wheel toward the snowbanked berm so they don't take the impact straight on. At this speed the truck would kill them.

And then all he knows is it's snowing again. Snow is everywhere and they're spinning and sliding and slamming into earth and ice and rock. A hole appears in the floor of the car beneath his feet. Storm screams. He catches a glimpse of sky. Something smashes into the windshield, buckling it. Snow shoots up through the floor hole into his lap.

Then it stops.

They've come to rest against a fence post fifteen yards off the road. Lancaster's dizzy. He feels sticky blood on his face, running down from his scalp somewhere. He doesn't remember the impact of hitting. The car is buried in snow and utter darkness. The wind, he hears that. Something's ticking. The engine. Otherwise, the world is silent.

# WEDNESDAY

## EIGHTEEN

B y Wednesday, early afternoon, the sickness has settled in Brandon's lungs, turning his cough into a resonant bark. Pneumonia, he figures. Double pneumonia. Maybe lung cancer. He lights a cigarette and after a few drags the coughing subsides.

The conference room has been commandeered by this case. Detailed county and city maps hang on one wall, dotted with colored pins. A cork board holds autopsy photos of Kevin's ligature-marked throat and Straw's burned face.

The boys are having a working lunch, sandwiches brought in from the diner across the street. Julian Kline, in his red designer glasses and another new-looking wool suit, sits at one end of the conference table, Ken Barnes and Lou Adamski at the other. Spinner is at the counter, unwrapping a sandwich. Brandon leans against the windowsill, holding the bridge of his nose and willing an end to the pounding in his sinuses.

"Where were you, Brandon?" Lou says.

"Following out a lead." They executed the warrant to search Lancaster's house this morning, and Brandon wasn't there. Lou was, in his own words, a little disappointed. "I had to go with it, Lou. No choice." Brandon's voice is hollow and hoarse.

"You gonna be all right? You should see a doctor."

"Should take a couple'a weeks in Florida too. What'd you find?"

Lou sets a medium-sized Pyrex flask, narrow in the throat, wide at the bottom, on the table. "From Lancaster's basement. Two more like this one. DEA flew them to Detroit. All three tested out: one had residue of three, four-methyl ethyl fentanyl acrylate. The other two had residues of two of the chemicals needed to make it. Lancaster's in it."

"Prints?"

"Latex gloves again."

"It looks like he's gone too," Kline says. "We can't find him anywhere. In an upstairs wastebasket we found a freshly used hair-dyeing kit."

Brandon looks from Kline to Lou and shakes his head. He can see the redness creeping up from Lou's neck.

"But get this." Spinner holds a roast beef and mayo in one hand, a coffee in the other. "Car-truck wreck last night out on Flanders leaves the driver of the truck dead. But no one from the car's around when crews arrive. All they find is a .45 in the backseat and a little Spears .25 semiauto under the passenger seat. Prints all over them. It was an Avis car—rented by Dr. Adrian Lancaster."

Ken Barnes clears his throat and says, "You were right, Brandon. I owe you an apology. We should have pulled him in."

In his mind Brandon starts to laugh like a madman at Barnes's joke. He wants to tell the punch line—*You're wrong. Lancaster's not it at all. Not guilty! Three handy stray jars with drug residues, no prints, no drug, no apparatus? His getting caught with Kevin Babcock's frozen body? The presentation of Michael Straw in the ER with his face conveniently burned off?*

In his mind Brandon's falling to the floor from laughing. He's going to die. At the window in the conference room, though, he does not even smile. He only nods a solemn nod.

He got to the wreck seconds after it happened. The truck lay on its side, one headlight still on and shining back up the road. The head of the driver was crushed against the wheel, his face a mass of pulp. Brandon knelt and felt for a carotid pulse that wasn't there.

Seth Babcock walked around from behind the truck. When he saw Brandon, he held out his hands, then turned and walked away, up the middle of the road.

Back behind him fifty yards or so Lancaster had made his way through the snow to the asphalt. His face was bloody.

Brandon backed his car up and opened the passenger door.

"Get in."

"Storm," Lancaster said.

"You've got to get out of here right now."

"Help me get her."

Brandon and Lancaster waded back through the snow to the car. Brandon couldn't believe how destroyed it was, that either of them could have survived.

"Storm?"

They couldn't see the girl in the darkness.

They couldn't hear her.

"Storm?"

"I guess I didn't hit their tire," she said then.

Brandon found her hair lying on the seat, then moved his hand down to her sticky face.

Lancaster found his medical bag in the car. On the drive back to Tecumseh they bought extra tape and gauze and some food and bottled water.

In the motel room Lancaster and Brandon worked on her. After the cleaning it was a matter of seven stitches just beneath the hairline. Lancaster had no anesthetic so Storm had to grit her teeth.

"You'll have a scar," he told her. "I'm only putting enough in to hold it together."

"Souvenir," she said, her voice weak.

Afterward Brandon himself looked over Lancaster. There were cuts; there would be some nice bruises, but nothing bad, nothing that couldn't be taped back together well enough.

"You're lucky," Brandon said.

"Is that what you call it?"

They spent the night together in the motel room, Lancaster and Storm on one bed, Brandon on the other—he knew if he left them now they'd be gone when he got back. And they were all so exhausted, they slept right through. Brandon had meant to get up at eight for the search of Lancaster's house. When he finally awoke, though, it was after eleven.

At one o'clock he had to be in for the meeting. He made sure they each ate a little breakfast and had some water. They could both barely wake up enough to eat, which was good, he thought. Then he handcuffed them together on the bed, and handcuffed the handcuffs to the headboard.

"I'm sorry," he said.

Lancaster shook his head and lay back on the pillow. Already his eyes were closing again.


The rest of the meeting whirls by. Spinner has a handful of concrete chunks that match the debris from the Cabriolet. He tells the story of how, outside a heavy-equipment storage yard behind the Washington Hotel, under a free-standing roof, he started crunching the stuff under his boots. How the stored equipment belonged to a company called Abood Contractors based up north of town. How he drove up there and started asking around, how finally one guy remembered seeing the red Cabriolet there behind the hotel Saturday afternoon. He remembered because he'd just bought his daughter the same model, only in blue.

"We'll start canvassing this afternoon," Spinner says.

Kline's bringing in a DEA artist today to put together a sketch of Arnie Holt based on the recollections of a couple of barmaids at Red's.

Lou says the number Straw called from Kevin's house on Saturday night has been traced out. It went to a small motel, to a cash-paying guest registered as John Smith. Dead end.

It's as if there's a thick pane of glass separating Brandon from some key. And all his scratching doesn't mar the surface.

In the middle of a statement by Lou Adamski, Brandon stands up in his daze and wanders out of the room and into his own office.

"Frank," Lou shouts after him. "What the hell?"


It's an overcast day, the wan early-afternoon sun too weak to do much good, but Brandon prefers the semidarkness to artificial light. He lights a cigarette, which this time sets off a coughing fit.

Then a knock comes on the door. Kline.

"Can we talk?"

"You talk." Brandon coughs hard into a handkerchief and then sniffs. His eyes are watering.

"You really ought to take care of yourself."

"Who's running this show?"

"Who? You are—"

"I know you've had a tail on Lancaster. I wasn't informed. Lou know?"

Kline nods.

"Barnes?"

Yes.

"Why they keeping me out?"

"You should ask them."

"I'm asking you. I don't want to ask them."

"I don't know," says Kline. He wipes his hand across his face. "I think they just wanted an outside source, someone independent. Someone separate."

"Lancaster saw your goons' car out front of the Babcocks', before the deputies got there. Black Ford, man in a suit driving. You didn't show up here till the next day."

Kline crosses his legs, then uncrosses them again. "All right. We've been following this drug for two months. We've been in Morgantown for a couple weeks."

"Straw."

"That's who led us here, yeah. But listen: I can't crack this, Brandon. Honestly, I can't figure the source. I'm baffled. I suggested Lou and Ken keep our presence here as quiet as possible so as not to stir anything up. Things surface better that way. You know that."

"It's my investigation."

Kline shrugs. "Federal presence makes people do things differently. I didn't want you or the manufacturers changing your procedures."

Brandon nods.

"We really did lose Lancaster last night."

Brandon looks away, out the window at the rooftops of the stores across the street, and squints his eyes.

"If he comes back in, Brandon, he'll come to you."

Brandon grinds out the Camel and watches this too-cool DEA man through the smoke. "Might," he says.

"We need him."

"Too bad we're not working together on this, then, isn't it?"

"Frank."

*Let him in,* a part of him says. *Give him the details he doesn't already have. Work together, tell him about Lancaster—*

But no. Brandon realizes this is a different sort of game than he's used to playing, the moving-shell scam, an under-the-table and be-hind-the-back charade of information. This isn't about drugs. It isn't about murder. It's about knowledge. And rule number one is protect what you've got.

He's got to get back to Tecumseh, to the motel, but before he can get out a call comes in. Ellen Byers, the board says, so he takes it.

"Don't you return messages?"

"I've been out. I'm sorry."

"Well, I have something you'd better hear. The latent on the flashlight. I wasn't sure we were going to get anywhere with it. Now I'm afraid we might get too far."

"You got a match?"

"My lab started with Straw's file and ran any names that came up, per your suggestion. Then they broadened out to the entire list of Fang arrests. Still nothing. So I started fishing. You know about MALPAS, of course."

The Michigan Automated Latent Print Analysis System is a de-veloping computer data base that will eventually hold the entire set of the Department of Justice's five million–plus existing fingerprint cards, and any new ones that come in. This means that anyone finger-printed in the state in the past twenty years, or in the future, will be able to be matched within hours by computer to a single unidentified latent. An incredible technology, Brandon thinks, when it's ready. The last he heard, it wouldn't be fully operational for another two years.

"I didn't know they were using it."

"They've got about a quarter of the JD latents fed in now," she says. "And the bugs aren't out of the program. But I figured small odds are better than none. Right?"

"Sure."

"But here's the thing. They're also using it to organize noncriminal print files—state employees, law enforcement personnel, that sort of thing."

"These are all referenced in a general criminal search?"

"It's a separate data base, but I guess everything in the system is referenced in any search. So get this—the print on the flashlight found a match."

"To a government employee?"

"Yes."

"DEA?"

"It holds state personnel files, Brandon. Not federal."

"I don't see—"

"To someone listed as an employee of the governor's office."

The hair on the back of Brandon's neck stands up. "Who?"

"Try the governor's chief of staff."

"Le Seure," says Brandon. "I can see if he had someone else on his brother-in-law. But to go himself . . ."

"I'm working on it," she says with no prompting. "You've definitely got some interesting problems out there."


On the drive back toward Tecumseh Brandon feels paranoia creeping up. He watches the rearview, makes several unnecessary turns, and stops to see who's there, but he's alone.

It's after four by the time he gets there. He buys some plastic-wrapped chicken salad sandwiches and more water before going to the motel.

In the room Lancaster is awake and staring at the ceiling.

Storm, minus the blond wig and wearing only a leather vest and panties, sleeps next to him. The jacket she wore is bunched around the cuffs. Brandon's struck by how fragile she looks, her slender arms and calves and thighs and abdomen.

"All right," he says, unlocking them. Lancaster sits up and rubs his wrists.

"What a shitty thing to do," he says.

"So call a cop." Brandon lights up and spins the desk chair around to the foot of the bed. "Talk to me."

"Go to hell," says Lancaster.

Storm opens her eyes and turns toward him. "Tell him, Adrian. Tell him what you told me. And I'd like a cigarette, if you don't mind."

"Two choices," Brandon says. He tosses Storm a Camel and his lighter. "I take you in, or I let you go. When you're done talking, I'll decide. I'm the court, so make it good."

Brandon sets the sandwiches and water on the bed and waits.

"Why'd you bail us out last night, then?"

"So you could come clean with me," Brandon says. "If you're legit, I need your help. World of trouble's coming down and I'll take any angle I can find. You know what Fang is?"

Lancaster nods.

"You should know my people went into your house this morning. In the basement they found three pieces of glassware containing residues of the drug. Even your buddy Ken Barnes is after your ass now. He's got egg on his face, and he figures you put it there. He doesn't know if you're pushing or buying or what, but he's pissed and he's gonna get you."

"Then why don't you just arrest me?"

"I think Ken Barnes is an asshole. Besides, whatever I think about you, one thing I know you're not is stupid. The crap with Holt and Kevin, now you split but conveniently leave three dope-encrusted bottles in your house? No way."

"You believe me."

"At least that you're being set up now. Maybe in the past you committed indiscretions. That's none of my business.

"So let's talk," Brandon says. "Let's start at the beginning."

A part of him still almost hopes this junkie doctor will refuse, or make it clear that he's guilty of some present-day crime, to justify

Brandon's cuffing him again. But mostly he's curious to hear where the heart of all these troubles lies, and he knows he is closer than he has been since they began.

Lancaster unwraps a sandwich and begins to eat. He chews slowly and deliberately, saying nothing, staring at the cheap carpeting. When the sandwich is gone he looks up at Brandon and nods and begins.

He talks for a long time.

**L**ancaster tells the same story he told Storm. It's a good, true story and he can see it makes an impression. Brandon sits silent for a minute when Lancaster finishes.

Finally he nods. "That's a start," he says. "Now let's deal with the present."

"I want her to rest," Lancaster says. "She was in shock. She has some recuperating to do."

He looks hard into Brandon's watery blue eyes, and can see that the detective understands what Lancaster wants him to understand— there are things to be discussed in private, away from Storm.

"Sure," Brandon says.

"Stay," says Storm. "I want to hear too."

From his medical bag Lancaster takes the envelope of the six remaining Meprospan tablets he got from the pharmacy after Holt called him, removes one, and hands it to Storm. She swallows it with some of the bottled water. Then he locks himself in the bathroom, where he looks at himself in the mirror. His hair shocks him at first. He'd forgotten about it. He looks one way, then the other, realizing he looks different but not really because of the hair. There's something else, something in the eyes and in the mouth, a desperation that hasn't been there for a long time. The desperation of a man who needs something and isn't sure he's going to be able to get it.

He does not know what to do. He has escaped only to find himself shackled with a strange and dangerous girl and a cop who seems to be making up his own rules as he goes along. He needs to free himself of these people. He was mistaken, he realizes, to think he could follow the maze back from Morgantown, to figure it out here. It has nothing to do with this place. It's himself he has to find, and no one here can help him anymore.

His hands have begun to shake again. The panic he felt at Kevin's house, then after Holt's call, then after receiving the letter, and again when Seth approached them outside Red's has gripped him once more. The violence of the accident last night comes back, images of what the victims of car wrecks look like, how incredibly lucky he and Storm were to walk away, how when it happens again, whether it's a car or a gun or a fall out a window, he probably won't be so lucky. And there's little doubt that something else will happen. Violence lives where he is going, with the people he must try to find. Violence is the only language they all share.

He must be as calm as he can be. He must not panic again. He cannot tremble. He has to be able to find what he needs to find, and regard it, horrible as it may be.

Once again he removes two of the capsules and looks at them lying in his hand. Six years it has been since he last narcotized himself, six years since he has used. But he cannot face it alone anymore.

*Afterward, I can stop again,* he tells himself. *It's only pills, to get through one day.*

And then the pills are in his mouth, dry and sticky, and he cups some water from the faucet and lifts it to his mouth and swallows.

*It's so easy,* he thinks. Like that, his resolve and his abstinence and his promise to himself are washed away.

"I need to," he whispers to the haggard face looking back from the mirror. "Only for right now. Then no more."

When he opens the door, Brandon's waiting with his coat on. Storm has fallen asleep again.

Brandon lets Lancaster drive. Dusk is falling.

"The present," Brandon says.

"The night Petie died, right after I'd pronounced him, Arnie Holt called me in the ER."

Brandon doesn't speak.

"I later wrote down as much of the conversation as I could remember." He hands Brandon an envelope.

"Then, when I got home in the morning, a courier arrived. He gave me this typed letter. You can check with the service, but I'm sure it's a dead end."

"No doubt." Brandon reads as they drive.

"Unit four fifty-one, confidential," says a voice from the radio.

"I have a call," Brandon says. "There's a gas station up ahead. They'll have a phone."

Lancaster pulls in and watches Brandon run over to the phone, dial once, listen, then dial again.

When he gets back in the car he says, "How about a drink?"

"Sure."

"Head back toward town, the South Border Highway. We're going to a place called Spike's. Got to see a man named Shirley."

Using a flashlight, Brandon goes back to the reading again. He reads each of the two documents three times. Finally he says, "You must have some idea."

"I really don't."

"A plan?"

"Go back."

"What was that about with Seth last night?"

"Like everyone else, he thinks I know something."

"Why'd you go there?"

"I was looking for Holt. I found Seth instead. Or he found me. I'm still not sure how it worked."

The noise of the drinkers at Spike's makes it difficult for Lancaster to listen in on Brandon's conversation with the huge bartender named Shirley. He strains to hear.

They're seated together at the bar. Brandon leans forward so he and Shirley are nose to nose. Brandon's got a smoke hanging from his lips and Shirley has a Tiparillo burning in the ashtray. Lancaster can't get over the number of cigarettes Brandon puts away. He must top two packs a day.

Shirley sucks on the Tiparillo and says, "So listen. Petie was the runner. You know they were shipping out."

Brandon nods.

"Petie was making pickups on the bridge where he got popped. After Kevin got it, Petie was gonna make one last run, then get out of town. He should of gone when he had the urge. Anyway, it was Seth who was meeting him after the pickup and I know he didn't pop Petie. Even if Petie was stiffing him, he'd of just kicked his ass.

"Now I hear that Petie and Kevin's deaths have slowed the flow, and they were on the verge of going into large weight. My hunch says there'll be at least one more meeting if the people still want to buy. I bet they do."

"On the bridge?"

"Would you use that spot again?"

Brandon shakes his head.

"So they're no stupider than you. There'll be another drop point. You just gotta figure out where."

"And you have an educated guess."

"Might."

"Shirl."

"Kinda preoccupied. Got my eye on this '59 Hog a friend of mine's sellin' down in Montpelier. His old lady's knocked, see, and she told him he's gotta dump it, a daddy can't own no bike. 'Bout broke his heart, poor son of a bitch, but I told him I'd take it off—"

"Fifty help you out?"

"Wouldn't hurt, bud. But I gotta pay for this information myself. I'm the middleman here."

"C note?"

Shirley nods.

"Damn. This better be top drawer or you'll be sliding me freebies for a long time." Brandon lays five twenties on the bar and waits for Shirley to fold them up real tight and stuff them down into his Levi's.

Then Shirley says, "Now we wait. I'll top you off."

"Wait for what?"

"Call," he says, pouring bourbon into Brandon's glass and Scotch into Lancaster's. "I'll be gettin' a call."


Lancaster sips at the Scotch and ice and watches Brandon. "How's your wife?" he says, finally.

Brandon looks at him. "What do you think?"

Lancaster nods.

"Can I ask you something?" says Brandon.

"Sure."

"Someone like that, in her condition, you think she'd be better off in a home?"

"I don't know her condition."

"She's having breathing problems, lots of congestion. We have a therapist in three days."

"Does that work?"

"More or less."

"You're alone with her?"

"Usually. Sometimes she's just alone."

"Like now?"

"I got a daughter keeps an eye on her."

Lancaster sips Scotch and stares straight ahead.

"You can't answer, can you?" says Brandon.

"It's one of those calls only you can make. If you want me to take a look at her—"

"Nah. I wasn't asking that."

"Okay."

"I'll figure something out."


Half an hour they wait before the phone rings. Shirley listens, hangs up, then leans over the bar toward Brandon again.

"You ever drive around back of the airfield, on that service road there?"

"Sure." It's a longstanding make-out spot for local high-school students. When Brandon was a uniform, long long ago, his beat for a while included rousting these kids on Friday nights. He used to get teased that he was the most effective birth control device in the whole county.

"Might want to hang there tonight after sundown."

It's already going on six. "Sundown just happened."

"How'd you think it would work? They set it up and knock it down as fast as possible. Amazing thing is I still got a lead on it. You best appreciate me."

"Shirley, goddammit, is this reliable? The drop is happening right now?"

Shirley winks and picks up the cigar. "Seth Babcock says to say hey."

So he came through after all.

"Something else, Brandon. I know you been thinking about how anyone could of known you and Tommy were holed up in convo in the head, how anybody knew to take a shot like that. But people knew. Tommy was no secret. Even the bigs knew about him, man."

"Feds?"

"Uh-huh."

"Who?"

"Tommy wouldn't say. I don't think he knew who. He just knew they were watching him."

Brandon glances at Lancaster. "You want to go? It's up to you."

"I'll go," Lancaster says.

## TWENTY

**T**hey drive. The sunset, which painted the sky orange and pink, has all but faded. The roads are dark with the wetness of ice, which has melted under sunlight but soon will be freezing again. Brandon gets on the radio and has the dispatcher patch him through to an outside line so he can raise Lou and Kline. But when the motel rings Kline's room, no one answers, and Lou's fifteen-year-old daughter says her parents are out to dinner but she doesn't know where. Finally Brandon reaches Spinner's wife, who says he went to the store. He'll be back in twenty minutes. Brandon tells her to write down what he says, then outlines the situation. He says Spinner should set up at the west end of the access road so Brandon can take the east. Spinner should get some backup help moving as soon as possible.

They stop a few hundred yards from the east entrance to the service road, on a rural stretch of Blair Highway where the houses are spaced well apart from each other. In the trunk Brandon keeps a couple Kevlar bulletproof vests. He hands one to Lancaster and slips the other on under his overcoat. He checks the standard issue .38

Special under his arm. Then from an old green military ammo box he removes his backup gun, a modified late-1950s .44 Magnum revolver, a speed-loader, and a dozen rounds of ammo each loaded with a 225-grain half-jacketed mercury-core bullet and 22 grains of Hercules 2400 powder. He fits six of the rounds into the speed-loader and slips it into his coat pocket. The remaining six he loads.

A gunsmith friend of his named Erv Orrison had done the modifications, throating the gun to take the speed-loader and adding a new set of rubber grips, and designed the load to fit Brandon's requirement—a one-shot drop, no question.

Orrison took him out to a woods and fired an over-the-counter .38 round into a stump. It made a hole going in all right. Nothing coming out.

Then he fired one of the .44's. The muzzle blast made Brandon jump; it sounded like lightning had struck next to him. The recoil kicked Orrison's arms over his head and moved him backward a step. Again the stump showed a nice little hole going in. This time the bullet came out, but Brandon couldn't really call it an exit hole because a good portion of the back half of the stump was simply gone. He walked beyond it, looking at the dust, which stretched for thirty yards or so.

"Hit a man in his shoulder, it'll take his arm off," Orrison said. "Hit him in the knee, no leg. Hit him anywhere in the abdomen or chest . . ."

Brandon turns his collar up and sets out toward what he hopes will be a rendezvous with Seth Babcock and whoever else has taken over for Petie Boncaro and Kevin Babcock. Lancaster follows.

The service road runs in a broad ninety-degree curve, heading due east from Blair and ending due north at Sampson Highway. Its length is well over a mile, far too much ground for two men to cover. Brandon, swearing to himself at the fact he's here in street shoes, a suit, and overcoat instead of good outdoor gear, trudges along the snow-packed gravel road until he figures they're about halfway in. To their left is a high wire fence and then the airfield, dark now except for the deep blue lights outlining the north-south runway. To the right is a wide and wild swatch of heavy brush that stretches for at least a hundred yards before it opens into snow-blanketed fields. Brandon finds a vantage off the road on an elevated knoll from which they can see the surrounding area. As if it matters, Brandon thinks. It's dark now, he's underarmed and essentially alone. Lancaster, he realizes, is more a liability than any help.

Lancaster stomps his feet and blows into his hands.

"Why don't you send up a flare?" Brandon asks.

"Do you know what you're doing? Do you have any idea?" the doc snaps back.

It's a good question. Brandon imagines how this could have been done if he'd gotten the information sooner—hunting clothes, insulated boots, a mug of coffee, five or six good men posted at intervals. He kneels at Lancaster's feet, getting nice and lost in this fantasy, his toes completely numb already, and his mind ready to say screw it and go home.

Then Lancaster touches his shoulder and says, "There."

A light. It's happening.

He's confused at first. He expected it would come from one end of the service road or the other. But this light, a single headlamp, bounces across the open empty field to the south. Now they hear the high whine of the engine.

"Snowmobile," Lancaster says.

*Spinner, where are you?*

The snowmobile slows when it gets to the beginning of the brush, and picks its way in along a trail the driver's apparently familiar with. For a moment Brandon is afraid it will come so close that they'll be discovered. But the light veers away and joins the road about fifty yards down from their knoll.

The machine pulls up alongside the fence and stops, headlight facing them, engine still running. Someone gets off and comes around in front of the light.

"Let's move closer," Brandon whispers. The snow's eight inches deep and hasn't crusted over too badly, so their movements are muffled. He leads Lancaster through the small trees and bushes along the road. At times he loses sight of the light, and once has to get on his hands and knees to move under a limb, but now the cold, the tears in his suit, and the numb fingers and toes don't exist.

They come into an opening, a wide flattened circle that seems to be a bedding area for deer, only a dozen yards or so from the snowmobile, a few yards in from the edge of the road. Brandon crawls up to the edge of the road and pushes his way between some brush and a wide tree trunk. Lancaster creeps up next to him.

"Tell me if you know them," Brandon whispers.

There are two men, one squatting, the other standing, both in front of the snowmobile, clearly illuminated by the light. The squatter, facing the light so his back is to Brandon, smokes a cigarette. Brandon smells the smoke wafting toward him. But the one standing turns. He wears an orange hunting hat and a black beard, army fatigues and round glasses.

"Holt," Brandon says.

Lancaster lets out a strangled growl and starts to get up, to run toward the orange hat. Brandon grabs him around the neck and drives his face into the snow.

The squatting man stops talking and looks in their direction. He listens for a moment, then flicks his cigarette away and turns back to the conversation.

Brandon presses his lips to Lancaster's ear. "One sound and we're fucked. Keep—your—cool. All right?" He can smell the chemicals Lancaster used to dye his hair. Finally, after a long, tense moment of stasis, Lancaster sags against him and Brandon loosens his grip.

Now the squatter is talking loudly, angrily. Brandon can make out a few words—"Son of a bitch . . . forget it. . . ." And then he hears a clear sentence: "My brother was killed by these fuckers. Remember?"

"Babcock," Brandon says. "Holt and Seth Babcock."

*Where are Kline's men?* Brandon wonders. At the end of their talk this morning Kline told him he was going to put a tail on Babcock, so whatever happened, they'd be there to witness it. But these incompetents must have lost him in the same way they lost Lancaster.

Holt is speaking now, but too softly for them to hear.

From their left comes the sudden noise of a larger engine. Brandon grabs Lancaster again and ducks back into the weeds only seconds before headlights wash over the spot from which they had been watching. Brandon's heart races; his mind grows light with the rush of adrenaline.

*Where in the hell is Spinner?*

A truck, a big boxy pickup on wide tires, stops directly in front of Brandon and Lancaster, its brights meeting the small single head-lamp of the snowmobile. A man gets out of the cab. Brandon crawls forward again to watch. He finds the truck blocking much of his view, however, so, motioning for Lancaster to stay back, he creeps out from the bushes, up over the edge of the road, and alongside the truck's right front tire.

This new man is dressed in hunting camo and when he turns for a moment Brandon sees that he wears a black winter face mask.

*I could make out no facial features,* Holt had written of Petie's murderer, *since the man was wearing a black mask on his face.*

This man has his back to Brandon. Seth stands and faces him as Holt gets back on the snowmobile.

So the transaction begins.

Brandon cannot make out everything that's said. Seth and the man do most of the talking. After a minute Holt stands, lifts the seat of the snowmobile, and removes a package he tosses to Seth, who in turn hands it to the man.

It's a large package, heavy, wrapped in plastic and silver duct tape. At least a full kilo brick.

The man in the face mask holds up his hand, then motions back toward the truck and starts to walk away with the brick.

"Leave it where we can see it," Seth says, so the man drops the brick in the snow before continuing toward the truck.

Brandon rolls to his side, toward the brush again, and falls off the lip of the edge of the road into the snow and out of sight. He listens to the man move around to the back of the truck, hears the rear door open, then close. Then the man in the mask walks back around into the light.

When he's past, Brandon gets up on his knees. Lancaster's next to him now.

"What are they doing?"

"Shhh."

"I've got something for you," the man yells toward Seth and Holt. He's carrying a briefcase. And strapped across his back, which only Brandon and Lancaster can see, is a pistol-gripped, sawed-off 12-gauge that wasn't there before. Next to him, in the beam of the truck's lights, lies the kilo brick.

The man tosses the briefcase to Seth, who tugs off a glove so he can open it.

Brandon, who's alongside the truck again, pulls the .38 from his shoulder holster and hands it back to Lancaster.

"Stay out of sight," he says. "Defend yourself only. If something happens, get out of here." Then he takes the .44 from his coat pocket and cocks the hammer back.

Holt starts the snowmobile.

Seth holds up the empty open briefcase. "What the fuck's going on?" he hollers. Brandon hears fear in his voice. *Yes, boy,* he thinks. *Now's the time.* Seth drops the briefcase and fumbles for something in his jacket, when he sees the 12-gauge the man in the mask is now pointing at him.

"No!" Babcock yells. When he raises his arms in self-defense, the man fires, hitting Seth in midbody, ripping through his coat and blowing him wide open. Down feathers and a mist of blood float in the lighted air between the snowmobile and the truck.

Brandon fires the .44 into the air, a deafening cannon blast that freezes everyone for an instant.

Then Holt revs the engine of the snowmobile and kicks it into gear.

The man looks at Holt, then turns toward Brandon.

The snowmobile careens off into the brush and cuts a crazy arc out across the field. Arnie Holt makes his escape.

Brandon is leaning across the hood of the truck, the .44 out in front of him in a two-fisted grip. "Police!" he yells.

But the man in the mask does not even hesitate to think. He fires. The blast kicks snow from in front of the truck back up into Brandon's face. Brandon fires, too, the gun booming again and kicking back hard in his hands. But the snow distracted him. He felt himself pull the shot wide.

And then he tastes a bitter taste and feels an awesome heat coursing through him. His head goes light. His mind spins and slows. He sees flashing red and blue lights tearing toward them from the northern end of the service road. Two sets of lights. Spinner and Lou. And then he notices that the shotgun blast has torn open the kilo package. That, along with snow, powdered Fang was blown into the air and back into his face.

The drug, Fang, in him.

Consciousness warps.

The man with the shotgun watches. In a dream Brandon steps away from the truck. The .44 falls with a thunk onto the hood and slides off into the snow.

And then the man in the mask fires again.

# THURSDAY

# TWENTY-ONE

Ann Arbor, the archetypal midwestern college town, blooms even in the coldest grip of winter—the ancient houses and wide lawns along Washetenaw Avenue on the way in from the expressway are always pretty, even if most of them are now frat houses or offices, and in the downtown students perpetually schlepping to class clog the sidewalks and squares. The storefronts display clothing or records or travel posters or jewelry, and in spite of the cold, street musicians play.

It has been twelve hours since Lancaster made his second run, but despite the Meprospans—he took two more when he checked into this room—he has been a wreck since it happened.

As he lay in the snow and brush at the edge of the service road listening to the gun blasts and the shouting, the hard shaking began—his legs, his arms and body, his face. Everything moved. He pushed his face into the snow and screamed. There was another gun blast. When he looked up, Brandon was lying near him in the weeds.

He shut up. He was sure the man with the mask and the shotgun was going to come over and kill him too. But the man got in his truck and drove away.

Even with the flak vest Brandon could be dead, Lancaster knew. In spite of the trembling and the panic he pulled himself to his knees and tore open Brandon's coat. There, embedded in the vest, was a flattened slug, a single mass of lead instead of dozens of shot. The foot-pounds of energy at that short distance would have been enormous, maybe enough to stop a heart even through the vest.

But Brandon tried to say something. *Go,* it sounded like.

Lancaster hesitated as sirens wailed up the service road. His shaking grew worse, his whole body racked by uncontrollable spasms. He could barely control his hands.

*Go.*

He rifled Brandon's coat pockets until he found the keys, then ran, crashing blindly through the thickets and snowbanks out into the crusted field. He stumbled on frozen covered furrows plowed the previous fall, tripped when his foot broke through a skin of ice, landed face-first, cutting himself, struggled up and ran again.

Halfway across the field, caught midway between the brush line he had left and a distant stand of woods, he saw a spotlight washing over the snow toward him. He dove into a furrow, frantically shoveled snow over his dark trousers, then covered his head with his arms and prayed he'd blend in. When the lights passed he ran again.

At the woods he cut west, back toward Blair Highway. The car sat undisturbed where they had left it. Lancaster ran up along the berm of the road, unlocked the passenger door, and got in. He slid over into the driver's seat. Then, in the rearview, he saw flashers, a squad car speeding up the road toward him. He lay down on the seat and waited.

He listened to the squad car as it approached, slowed, stopped.

Another spotlight beam cut through the windows of the car into the darkness. He held his breath and looked up at the hot white light a few inches above his nose. He could hear the crackle of the radio, the voices of the two cops inside.

Then the light went out. The squad car hurried on. He sat up and watched it turn into the entrance of the service road.

He started Brandon's car, pulled a U, and drove.

He's in an Ann Arbor motel not far from the Wolverine football stadium south of the town center. In the mirror he looks at his face: his forehead is bruised; an inch-long gash runs across the bridge of his nose; his left cheek jumps with a rhythmic nervous tic; his nostrils flare with each breath, as if he has a fever.

He imagines himself at work, bent over some broken body, his hands steady, his thinking fast and clear. Then he laughs at his image now, at what a weak wreck he's turned into in just a few days. But there's no point in comparing. Work is other people's lives, other people's disasters. This is his own, and that makes all the difference.

He found a pack of Storm's Marlboro Lights, the only evidence of her, in his coat pocket. He lights one, sets it in an ashtray, and watches the smoke curl upward.

On the cheap vinyl-veneered table before him rests Brandon's .38 Special, his father's .357, and the gram of street heroin from Red's. The Meprospans aren't helping. He needs something else. The nerves will kill him, he thinks, if he doesn't get them under control. He can't stand the trembling anymore, the fear that possesses him, that has driven him into this room and will not let him out. Too much depends on his staying rational, on his being able to function.

He knows what this means. And the only solution here and now is this gram of street scag.

He was prepared for this to be a difficult decision. He was prepared to have to struggle against himself, to feel some sense of defeat.

217

But there is no struggle. He has already given in; he gave in when he took the first pills. It is merely a fact he has already accepted. He feels no remorse, no fear, no misgiving, only longing.

He sold himself to the Drug a long time ago, and once sold he was owned forever. They taught him that in Royal Oak—all he could do was be vigilant day by day. Avoid it at all cost. Get help if you feel the need. Always remember that it owns you.

But now a time has come when he has to go back to the Drug, to confess his weakness and his need. The Drug promises strength and clear thought. The Drug promises to save him. He will have to pay again for this, and the price will be dearer now than it ever was before. In fact, he knows, he may never come back. But there is no choice. It is either this or die quaking in some ignominious room.

He sets the black plastic tray from under the ice bucket on the table. Using a scalpel he slices open the gram bag.

The powder flows out onto the tray. He pushes it around with the blade, looking at it, listening to it talk to him, although he cannot hear it very well yet.

He must begin slowly, inefficiently, because he has no tolerance. Using the tip of the blade he lifts a sampling of the powder to his nose and inhales it. For all Ralph the Pusher's claims of greatness for this sample, Lancaster can tell it's cut way down. But the Drug is there. He feels the fire coursing through from his face to his fingers and his feet. His lungs open and his headache disappears and his eyelids grow heavy. Like an old lover, he thinks. It fits so well.

He lifts the blade to his other nostril and sucks again.

Then he lies back on the bed to wait and see. The Drug can be fierce; he must not overdo it now. But he feels it working.

After a few minutes he holds his palm above his belly. It is rock steady.

★   ★   ★

The terrain in a certain west Ann Arbor neighborhood turns hilly, and some of the houses built up these inclines, with high porches supported by long stiltlike legs, look almost exotic. On one block, sandwiched between two of these houses, he finds a worn-out duplex with a rickety gray staircase nailed to one side. Lancaster parks his newly rented LTD and double-checks the address, although he recognizes the house.

The woman who opens the door at the top of the staircase looks like she could be fifty, but she is only thirty-four, Lancaster's age. Her smile forms lines around her eyes. Then the smile passes from her face as the shock of seeing him hits her. Her mouth twists and tightens and her eyes turn cold.

"You," she says. Her name is Sandra Lear, Bobby's old runner, Denise's friend. A loose strand of her dirty gray-streaked hair hangs down in her face. Her mouth is thin and hard, her eyes black. Animal eyes, he used to call them to Denise. Denise laughed, because it was true. Sandra had the eyes of a badger or a ferret. Something that lived in the ground.

Lancaster says, "I need to talk with you. I'm sorry."

She looks around, down the street and up, as if she wants to call out to someone for help, as if she wants to escape. Then she spins and disappears back inside. He follows her into the same mess she lived in the last time he was here, in 1983. Dirty plates and glasses clutter the end tables. An ironing board hangs out from one wall. The couch is covered with clothing she is perpetually in the process of folding, and an empty laundry basket lies overturned on the floor. A cigarette burns in an already stuffed ashtray.

"Kid'll be home soon."

"I won't be long," he says.

"Drink?"

"No. I just want to find out some things I should have known."

She laughs at this. "You had me worried. I thought it was something serious."

"It is something serious." He gives her an abridged rundown of the situation, and ends by saying, "I couldn't let myself believe it had anything to do with"—he raises his hands, palms up, in front of him —"this. With us. But it's all started again. I'm completely set up. I may be looking at murder charges."

She jumps to her feet and leaves, as if she can't stand the sight of him. He follows her down a narrow carpeted hallway to the kitchen at the rear of the house.

He remembers this room. Denise came here a lot. They were unlikely friends, Sandra, a high-school dropout and double divorcée by the age of twenty-three, and Denise with her degrees and her poise. But Denise needed her. Lancaster had always thought Sandra reminded Denise of people she knew in Kentucky, where she was from. He also believed it was Sandra, not Bobby, who'd gotten Denise started using heroin.

Sandra looks hard into his eyes and says, "What the hell are you doin' in my house? I don't want you here."

"What happened after I was arrested?"

"You saw her."

"In detox. But when I was released I went home and her things were gone. And she was gone. *You* were gone. I couldn't find anybody."

"You didn't seem to try very hard."

He walks to the kitchen sink and looks out the window at the backyard and the backs of the houses on the next block over.

"Was I supposed to? I assumed you all wanted it this way, that she didn't want to see me again. Otherwise she'd have left word at least. And then I thought maybe it was for the best. The lawyer said she was in Seattle."

"She paid him to say a lot of things."

"What does that mean?"

"Adrian." When he looks at her, her eyes have filled with tears. She sits down and picks up a napkin from the table and presses it to her face. "She left me, too, you know, but she never went out west. She never went anywhere. She died here, Adrian. She was dead before you even got out, maybe a week after the last time she visited you."

Lancaster leans over the kitchen sink and gags. His stomach heaves but he's had nothing to eat in nearly twenty-four hours, so nothing comes up. It's the reflex of shock, nothing more.

"I just ran," Sandra says. "I couldn't face no one here. I ended up driving down for the funeral. She's next to her folks. There's a little churchyard. I met her sister there."

He leans on the sink and tries to catch his breath. "She never talked about her family. As if they didn't exist."

"There were lots of things you never knew about her, things she didn't want you to know. Even that she died."

"Why?"

"I don't know. She used to say it was enough to her that you loved her. She admired you. She told me once your medicine was a noble sacrifice. That's what she called it."

"Sacrifice."

"That you spent your life and your education helping people one at a time. See, Adrian, she wasn't like no one I ever met. Denise had a mind that was so . . . I don't know the word."

*Conceptual,* he thinks.

"Not brilliant," Sandra says. "On this campus here you can find lots of brilliant people. Hundreds, I bet. Denise wasn't like them. She was a real–life genius. I don't think you knew that. I think that's what got her in so much trouble."

"What's all this about trouble and dying? What the hell was going on?"

"I don't know, exactly. I don't think anyone knew. But it had to do with her work here."

"On campus?" When they lived in Detroit, while he was doing his residency, she commuted back to Ann Arbor to work on her

Ph.D. She already had a doctorate in pharmacy, a Pharm.D., from Ohio State. Here she was finishing the research for some sort of an interdepartmental degree in pharmacy and organic chemistry in a field known as medicinal chemistry, which had to do with designing new medicines by altering existing molecules or inventing new ones. She was good, too, he knew, although she didn't often talk about her work. She was very good. She'd begun to publish regularly, and showed him some of the pieces she'd collaborated on. "No. I would have known."

"Not on campus. There were other things she worked hard to keep you from knowing. She said you were the one doing the real work, and it wouldn't be fair to burden you."

"It doesn't make sense."

"Does it make sense that you got involved with her at all? That you did what you did with her here? You were as bad as anyone. A doctor and a pharmacist injecting street drugs into people's arms. It's not very hard for someone to believe they're completely safe in those hands, that it must not just be okay. It must be a good thing."

"We never encouraged anyone. We just helped people who needed it."

"Look, *I* was there, remember. I used. I know what it felt like. It felt good. It felt right, Adrian, to have a doctor shooting you up. It felt . . . legal."

"I wasn't a doctor yet. And they, you, would have done it anyway. Besides, Sandra, you helped convince me, remember? I wasn't going to do it until you and she took me on the grand tour of every shithole shooting gallery in this city. Our way was just safer. No one would die from ODs or dirty needles." He stops, embarrassed to hear the rhetoric he hasn't believed in so long. "I don't understand it anymore. But at the time we saw good in it."

"I admit I did wrong. I was pretty messed up back then. But you two should have known better. You kept people going who might have quit. You were two self-righteous criminals."

"Well, we stopped. That was years before I got arrested. Before she died. In Detroit that was all over. We only gave to each other, and a few friends who needed help."

"She never stopped, Adrian. That's what I'm trying to tell you. She just cut you out of it. I suppose that's what you really came here to hear, isn't it?"

"What?"

"That she kept right on working with Bobby. They moved a lot of volume in and out of here when you lived in Detroit. She was in right up until the end. She wasn't just coming over here to work on a Ph.D."

Lancaster cannot believe this. It's impossible that she kept dealing without his knowing. He shuts his eyes and concentrates on holding his composure.

"You were both in way over your heads."

And yet, he realizes that it would not only have been possible for her to continue surreptitiously dealing for Bobby, given that it all took place in Ann Arbor, far away from him, but he realizes she would have been able to do it and never tell him. She had that power, the ability to hold many things inside herself, to lock them away and live day-to-day as if they didn't exist. She supplied the heroin they used in Detroit. She only ever told him she bought it from someone safe. If he questioned that, he never brought it up to her. He didn't like her having contact with a dealer still, but knew they needed a supply. That the dealer was Bobby Karnowski does not shock him. That she was still working for him does. What he wonders is why she would have done it? She hated Bobby and what he did. Why go back to work for him? Why take that sort of chance when she was so close to finishing her degree anyway?

Icarus and Daedalus. The last time he saw Denise, on her second visit to the hospital in Royal Oak, that's who she'd said they were like. They'd flown too close to the sun, and now one of them had fallen into the waters of sorrow. She was referring to him, but she'd had it backward. She was Icarus. She was the one who melted and died. He was the one left to suffer.

"Then I have to see Bobby," he says.

"He don't want to see you."

"I want to see him. And I don't want him hearing I'm around and deciding it's a good time to take off for a few weeks."

She picks up her phone, dials, and listens. "Not home."

"I'll be around. I want to see him. You don't need to tell him that. Right?"

"Yeah."

"Just get in touch. Find out his schedule."

"What're you gonna do to him?"

"Just talk, Sandra. Like you and me. Do you ever hear about Harpo Epstein?" Epstein was the attorney Denise hired to save them.

"Guess he still practices in Detroit. I hear his name every so often. He gets a lot of press for his pro bono work."

"Yeah."

"Jesus Lord, Adrian. I thought you made it."

"I did," he says. "Now I'm back."


That evening, in a strip-mall near U.S. 23 on the eastern fringes of Ann Arbor, in the back room of Piscadero's Lounge, Lancaster sits alone at a corner table and nurses a Scotch. The people he once knew here are long gone, but the place is the same and the business is the same. He sits for no longer than twenty minutes before he can tell who he needs to talk to.

The man looks young, early twenties probably. He is thin and muscular and savvy-looking in spite of his unsuccessful attempt at a beard. Lancaster motions that he wants to have a conversation. The man slides over and sits down.

With no prompting Lancaster lays his hospital ID badge and

driver's license on the table. Cops can't falsely ID themselves. "Boy," he says. "Dollar's worth. Two g's."

The man gets up and walks out of the bar.

A few minutes later a different man, stockier, with swollen slits for eyes, comes in, looks at Lancaster, and goes in the john. When he comes back out, he sits across from Lancaster and says, "Hey there, partner."

Lancaster slides a hundred-dollar bill under a napkin. The guy balls up the napkin and stuffs it in his pocket. He says, "Second stall," gets up, and leaves.

In the second stall, stuffed behind the toilet works, is a brown paper bag. In the bag are two mini-Ziplocs of white heroin, supposedly a gram each, probably a little light.

When Lancaster leaves, neither man is in the bar. He knows they're watching from somewhere. When they see him leave, they'll be back. He's a stranger in town now and they have to take their precautions.

## TWENTY-TWO

**W**hen the pain returns, it starts in his feet. His door is ajar and he can see a clock in the lighted antiseptic hallway; it's after one A.M., but his feet still burn like they're frozen. He remembers the snow, and ruining a good suit. He remembers firing the gun. But he cannot remember what happened.

His room is dark except for the green light from a monitor hanging over the bed. He can't see it, can only hear the rhythmic beeping, and finally understands it is his own heart being measured. His left hand is immobilized. He raises his right to feel the pads and wires glued to his chest. He feels a bandage there, too, and pain when he presses on it. He wonders if he's been shot. Yet there are no tubes, no breathing machines. He takes an experimental deep breath, coughs, and then the pain really hits, searing jolts that shoot into his belly, across his chest, and down both arms. He groans.

A nurse comes in.

"Detective?"

He can see her face in the green light.

"What happened to me?" His voice is barely a whisper.

"The vest saved you but you've got three broken ribs and a bruised lung. On top of that you took a pretty heavy dose of narcotic. Apparently you inhaled some when a bag ruptured."

Fang.

"Are you in pain?"

He nods.

"I'll see what we can do," she says. "The doctors want to make sure your blood levels are down before giving you any painkiller. The lab took samples a half hour ago. We should know soon. Rest for now."

He doesn't really understand much of what she says. She adjusts something on the monitor over his head and leaves, her padded shoes making tiny sucking noises on the floor.


Later, he remembers Lancaster and the motel in Tecumseh. He remembers that he kept that to himself, didn't even tell Spinner. He remembers Shirley, a conversation at Spike's, and after that he leaps and remembers the final moments.

He lay in the snow, in the weeds, looking up through the branches of a tree at the black star-spotted sky. Years seemed to roll by. He didn't know where he was. He was cold and he couldn't breathe.

When the lights from the snowmobile and the truck left, it had grown dark and quiet. But now suddenly it was light again. Voices shouted. Radios crackled. Colored lights spun. It was beautiful.

But this time the dizziness was too strong. His tongue went numb. His breath was gone; he was drowning in the world of air and snow and light.

He remembers looking up at the clear night sky, the stars bright at first. But as he watched they began to fade to distant dim points of light. And then they faded to nothing as darkness returned and the cold snow where he lay grew warmer around his head.

He tries to follow the thoughts backward, to reconstruct exactly what had happened, but his chest hurts so badly now that he finds it harder and harder to breathe.

When they come in finally an hour later he's bathed in sweat and moaning with every breath.

"Ten milligrams," someone says. A nurse drives the needle into his thigh. From the time she presses the plunger he watches the clock in the hallway. He doesn't make it ten minutes before he's asleep again.

While it's still dark, he awakens again. The hospital is quiet. On the wall across from him he notices a crucifix he hadn't seen before, a courtesy the hospital sees is added to the rooms of its Catholic patients. Jesus' eyes, in his agony, are rolled up toward heaven. *I'm a Catholic,* Brandon thinks. *Susan must have told them.* It seems strange. It's been so many years since he's been to a Mass. He and Lorraine took the girls every week when they were little, but around their teenage years they lost interest and Brandon didn't seem to have the time or the inclination to pursue it. He hasn't prayed in a decade.

But now he folds his hands across his burning chest and closes his eyes.

"*Keep my family,*" he whispers. "*Don't worry about me, but thank you for the break this time. I know I came close.*"

In the morning he wakes to find his daughter sitting next to him.

"You didn't say anything to your mother?" He still asks these questions although he doesn't believe Lorraine could understand anyway.

Susan cries when she sees him awake and talking.

"No, Daddy. She knows something's wrong because I called a nurse in. And you're not there. But she's okay."

He lies back on the pillow and closes his eyes. His breathing sounds rough; the chest cold has not gone away just because of a bullet.

"You were lucky, Daddy."

He remembers saying the same stupid thing to Lancaster a day or so ago. "Keep reminding me," he says.

"I lied," she says. "I didn't call a nurse in."

"Where is she?"

Susan sits with her hand pressed over her mouth.

"What'd you do with her?"

"I told you a spot opened up."

"You put her in the home? Don't I have to approve this?"

"The spot was going to be filled. You were in the hospital. They told me I could take it now. When you're released, if you want her out, you can take her out. But someone had to take care of her now."

"I've only been in here twelve hours."

"She went in this morning. Rick's back. I can't stay over anymore."

Strangely, his rage doesn't rise to meet this. "Listen, little girl," he says. "I've got a lot of work to do. So when I get out of here I still may not take her out right away. But when it's over, she comes back home where she belongs."

"That's up to you, Daddy."

"Don't forget it, Sue."


After lunch Lou, Kline, and Spinner show up. Brandon plays dumb, although by now he remembers much of what happened, at least up through Seth getting shot and falling in the truck's headlights. He still doesn't remember actually taking a hit himself.

"Who died?" he says.

"Babcock," says Lou. "Took a load of number-one buckshot just below the rib cage. His mother'll bury both her sons in the same fucking week."

"How'd buckshot break three of my ribs?"

"You took a slug," Spinner says.

"Guy wasn't taking any chances," says Lou. "Figured he'd spray the first couple, then aim. I know hunters who load like that. How the hell'd you end up out there, Brandon?"

"I don't remember. I got a tip somewhere. Phone maybe."

"Why go alone?"

"It was happening then, at that moment. I called you and Kline, then Spinner. It just happened too fast." He looks at Kline. "Who was following Babcock?"

"I had two men on him."

"The same morons who lost Lancaster?"

"They were set up. They got cut off cold by a second car. Babcock was bullshitting you all the way. He'd made arrangements. He had help in losing the tail."

"Too bad for him." But Brandon knows the truth. It wasn't "us" he didn't want. It was the feds. He wanted Brandon alone. That's who he got word to.

"And I got called back to Detroit for a briefing. I'm sorry."

"Don't know what we'd do around here without your expertise."

"Look, Brandon, I know you're injured. I'm not one to trash a guy when he's laying in the hospital but I'm a little sick of your attitude."

"I'm a little sick of your fuck-ups. I'm a little sick of catching slugs with my Kevlar."

"You shouldn't have gone in."

230

"No? I should sit around with my thumb up my ass like you?"

"You fuck—"

"Knock it off," says Lou through his teeth.

But Brandon falls back onto the bed, his chest heaving and burning. Then some monitor on him goes off, a shrill screeching that brings nurses running and ends the briefing.

When he calms down a little, one of the nurses brings a syringe and swabs his thigh again. He watches as she jabs the needle in and injects a clear liquid. He lies back and closes his eyes. He relaxes. His breathing evens out. The pain fades.

Before he sleeps Brandon experiments with the feeling the narcotic brings on. This is what it felt like, he thinks, the cocoon that Lancaster needed so badly. If he lets go a little he can almost understand the rationale. Better than alcohol; alcohol is hard and jarring. But this is pure seduction. This is a mistress.

Then he sleeps again.

In the evening he comes out of a light doze to find a woman he does not know standing at the side of his bed, watching him over the tops of her glasses.

"I heard on the radio that you were shot. You know you made news across the state?" Her voice, quiet and deep and strong, is familiar to him. "This case is famous, and you're getting famous with it."

Maybe she's a reporter. He hasn't thought much about the PR aspects of things, understanding only that Lou is getting a lot of heat from the DA and the mayor to wrap things up.

"And the first reports were pretty damned vague, Frank. They didn't know if you were dead or not—"

"You're Ellen Byers," he says.

She smiles a half-smile and he likes her already. He's surprised, though. He imagined her tough looking, maybe a little on the heavy side judging from her voice, the sort of matronly powerful type. But

Ellen Byers, who's in her early to mid-forties, is anything but matronly or overpowering. She looks soft, in fact, gentle even. Her face is attractive and surprisingly expressive. Emotions seem to pass over it, especially through her eyes, and announce themselves as they go. She wears her hair, a sort of streaked brown, cut straight and neat along the line of her jaw. She looks more like Brandon's idea of a grade-school teacher, especially with the way she peers over her glasses, than a Motown narco dick.

"You're the first woman shield I ever met."

"Too bad, isn't it? But the world's changing fast. Soon we'll be everywhere."

He laughs a little, then grimaces. "You didn't have to come all the way out here to pay your respects."

"I wanted to meet you. Besides, we have work to do."

"One condition," he says. "You and me, whatever gets said is between us. Period. Your superiors are out for now. Mine are too. No DEA, no one. Otherwise you can turn around and drive home right now."

"What's bothering you?"

"Lots of things. If we have a deal, sit down."


He tells her everything he knows. Maybe it's weakness from the injuries or the drugs. Maybe it's just loneliness from having no one to share with, from trusting not even his fellow cops. But once he starts talking he can't hold anything back.

He finishes by saying, "Le Seure must have come over here to get his fuck-up brother-in-law out of another mess. He just ended up being too late."

She says, "Maybe. Probably. But I've been doing a little poking around myself since that print came in. I've got something I think you'll be very interested in seeing. But you need some background first.

"Le Seure worked for the DEA from '66 till '84, when Jovanovich got elected. He'd been working as one of Jovanovich's campaign advisors for about eighteen months before the election."

"What qualifications—" Brandon begins, but she holds up a hand to stop him and again lowers her face and looks at him over the glasses.

"Hear me first. Jovanovich knew one of the planks in his platform would be a strong antidrug stance. Presumably Le Seure was chosen to organize this. And in fact his first position after the 1984 election was as head of the special drug task-force the governor created."

"How'd he jump from that to chief of staff?"

"I don't know. Will you just listen? Jovanovich had to overcome the huge hurdle of being an independent. He needed to draw strongly from both the conservative and liberal sides of the fence. Follow?"

Brandon nods. He'd been feeling better but something must have worn off because his chest has begun to burn again; each breath makes it worse.

"His strength was outside the Detroit area," Ellen says. "Among the conservatives. For one thing the Republican candidate in that election was weak. The Democrat, Lieutenant Governor Charles Johnson, was stronger, but his power base was broad, spread out, as opposed to being very concentrated in the Detroit political machine. Jovanovich saw his opening and went hard for the city. He recruited strong, high-profile Detroit Democrats, one of whom was Le Seure. The others were all big labor-movement people, pols, union leaders, that type."

"They took a big chance backing an independent."

"And they won big. Are you okay?"

He nods and says, "Hand me that cloth."

She picks it up and folds it and wipes his forehead, which has broken out in sweat.

"Maybe I should call someone."

"Tell me the rest," he says.

"There was a political reporter at the *Free Press* I knew who'd done a lot of work on that campaign. I tracked him down and told him I was interested in James Le Seure. He'd said he never published anything but he'd done some stories, which were canned by his editors. He faxed them."

She hands Brandon the typescript of an unpublished article dated June 1983. He reads the beginning, which describes Le Seure's history in drug enforcement and his recruitment by Jovanovich for his gubernatorial campaign. But Brandon can't focus. He lays the page on the bed and says, "Just tell me."

"Le Seure's father and uncle were real estate developers with connections. Government grants, reduced taxes, all that stuff. They made a fortune in tract housing after the late-sixties exodus out to the suburbs. Then, in '75, they were indicted for building-code violations, income-tax evasion, racketeering."

"Racketeering?"

"They'd been working with another developer who also supplied them with materials. Cheap, poorly made materials they paid a lot of money for. Government money. See?"

"Yeah. So? They were playing the kickback game."

"Uh-huh, and this supplier also provided most of their labor, without fair bidding and all that. Know who that supplier was?"

"Come on." Brandon shuts his eyes against the pain in his chest. He needs a shot and begins pressing the nurses' call button.

"Louie Papalanos."

He opens his eyes and looks at her. "Le Seure knew Papalanos?"

"He must have if his father was one of Fat Louie's business partners."

"Jesus Christ. Can you get me a nurse?" Brandon presses the button again and again until a night nurse sticks her head in and says, "Problem? You got a spasm in your finger?"

"He's in a lot of pain," Ellen says.

"Tell him he only needs to press the button once, honey. We'll come."

"Fine, honey," Ellen says. "Can you do something?"

The nurse checks her watch and says, "Yeah. He's right on schedule." She's back a minute later with the injection, and soon after that Brandon watches Ellen's face as he fades into sleep.

She's still there when he awakens. It's dark outside now. His chest feels better but his head is fuzzy. "You should go home," he says.

"I will. I want to finish this. Can you talk now?"

"Yeah. Where were we?"

"We think Le Seure knew Papalanos. We also know Papalanos was distributing Fang, although it was never proved."

"How do you know?"

"Informant. In late '84, when the DEA really started to hammer on this drug, one guy, a district-level boss, finally talked. He'd gone on a buy with his supplier, who was drunk at the time. The supplier started to blab, told him Fang was coming through Fat Louie Papalanos and his sons. They weren't even cutting it, just jumping the price and passing it on, so the supplier had to step on it extra hard. At the buy this guy, the informant, even got to talk to the bagman, who was a Greek. He said he'd never talked to a Greek before. You following?"

"I'm all right. Just go on."

"See, it makes sense because Papalanos had gotten into big money trouble. He was close to bankruptcy. Fang first hit the streets in April of '83. I remember because it was the month of that big Easter tornado. My mom's house got wiped out. I was running around alternately trying to get insurance estimates and tracking down samples of this new shit we were just hearing about. I'd only been in narco about six months. Anyway, by late summer, four months or so later, Papalanos was out of trouble again. Major construction loans were paid, new developments begun; he even replaced most of his fleet of trucks."

"Okay," says Brandon. "Let's say you're right, that Papalanos wholesaled the drug out. And let's say you're right again, that Le Seure had met him through his father. So what?"

"Now Le Seure's brother-in-law is killed here, years later, with the same stuff on him. A drug that has never reappeared anywhere, *ever,* Brandon. And it turns out Papalanos was an old Le Seure family crony? Coincidence?"

"Are you accusing Le Seure of dealing too? A DEA chief?"

She shrugs. "No. I'm just saying it's a lot of coincidence to swallow. Le Seure and Papalanos had old ties. Now Le Seure's brother-in-law turns up with this drug that Papalanos had an exclusive line on. And Le Seure himself leaves a print at the scene of a murder perped by this brother-in-law the same night. I'm saying there're a lot of connections here that bother me. And it's worth doing some more digging. When will you be back up?"

"Tomorrow. I'm checking myself out of here."

"With the pain you're in? Brandon."

"Screw it. They can give me some pills. I'm not laying around another day. Maybe I'll be gimpy but I'll be out there."

"I was going to suggest you come over for a day or two."

"Maybe. This is just between us, right? Like we said?"

"Trust someone." She gives his hand a squeeze. "And rest."

"Listen, can you slip me a pack of Camels before you go?"

She laughs and pats him on the top of his bald head. "You're a bad boy," she says. "But you're kind of cute. I'll call you tomorrow."

# FRIDAY

# TWENTY-THREE

Lancaster finds the number of the law firm, Greene, Epstein, Sawyer and Simpkins, easily enough but when he calls he's told Harpo Epstein is in court all day and won't be back in the office.

So he dials information. Working from a list he made of the wealthier suburbs—Grosse Ile, St. Clair Shores, Rochester Hills, Troy, Birmingham, Farmington Hills—he finds numbers for four H. Epsteins. On the third try, to a number in Bloomfield Village, a very wealthy little town just west of Birmingham, well north and west of the city, he hits.

"Harpo's at the office," the woman says. "What're you, a salesman?"

The building he lived in when he met Denise and Bobby still stands on Nixon Road, north of the VA Med Center in the northeastern quadrant of town, the portion separated by the Huron River. It still looks like a run-down rat-trap tenement for students, which is what it is, but better than the days when he lived here. It's been aluminum-sided, for one thing; no more of the perpetually peeling paint with weathered wood showing through. Black shutters have been hung outside the windows. But the snow on the walk is still left unshoveled and junk-heap cars fill the lot. The front storm door hangs at the same broken angle it did when he left eight and half years ago. Uncanny.

Lancaster parks on the berm across the street and watches as a carload of students pulls in and files into the building.

When Denise came across the hall that last time, she had more than just a bloody nose and some cuts. Bobby had broken her nose and her right clavicle. Her chin was so badly lacerated, Lancaster could see bone when he cleaned it. The first thing she said to him was that she would never set foot in Bobby's apartment again. The second was that she wasn't going to any emergency room either.

He stitched the chin first. For the nose he used a suspension of liquid cocaine as a local anesthetic and set the break himself, right there on his living-room couch. He remembers vividly her lack of reaction when he snapped her nasal bone and cartilage back into place. Her eyes were dead. He'd never seen anyone not react to the procedure, and even though he was still a student he hung out in the ER whenever he could so he'd seen more than a few. Later he thought that maybe he could have done it with no anesthetic at all, that she was numb to everything because she was narced out already. Then he wondered if it was just sheer will on her part not to feel the pain.

The collarbone took a figure-eight Ace bandage for support while it healed. He would arrange for a clandestine X-ray the next day to make sure it didn't need setting. He packed ice on her face, laid her down on the couch, and told her to sleep. Then he shut the lights off and went to bed, not really believing her vow, not believing that she'd even be there when he woke up.

But when he came out of the bedroom in the morning she was

sitting at his kitchen table, black eyes, swollen face, and all, writing in a notebook. A pot of fresh coffee sat on the stove, and a cigarette burned in her ashtray.

"How are you?"

"Fine," she said. "You're out of business as of today. We're moving out of here."

"Yeah?"

"You're done with school in a month. Bobby's moving out this week. I'll find us a place in the city, then I'll commute back."

"Us. You and Bobby?"

"Us you and me, and I don't ever want to hear his name again."

"Okay. Is this going to be a sort of platonic thing or are we living together as in Living Together?"

"Do you have to ask?"

"I know how I feel. The question is whether you're in any way in love with me."

"Do you want me to be?"

"It'd be nice if we're going to try this. I don't want to end up in a few months with us dating other people and acting like goddamn brother and sister. I don't need that. I don't want you to do to me what you did to Bobby."

"You don't know what our relationship was. You don't have a clue, so don't pretend you do."

"You were lovers."

"What difference does that make?"

"Maybe none. Is that what you're saying? He had something you needed, and you gave him something back. Is that it?"

"That's cruel."

"I just don't want to be the next one, Denise."

She smoked and thought for a few moments, then said, "Adrian, do you believe that there are only a few people in life you can fall in love with?"

He didn't know.

"I think love is something you grow, like a plant," she said. "It can begin anywhere, but then it has to be cultivated, no matter who it is. You know what makes people stay in love, what makes people fall more in love?"

"Tell me."

"The desire to be in love. If you want to be in love, then you'll be in love. If you want to stay in love, then you'll stay."

"You're saying you can force yourself."

"Just the opposite. I love you or I wouldn't be sleeping with you. I wouldn't be here now. I wouldn't have got beat up last night."

"He hit you because of me?"

"Just forget it," she says.

"No. I want to know. He hit you because you've started seeing me?"

"It's not that simple. He hit me for a lot of reasons, some of which have to do with you. It's not common jealousy. He's not the type. And it doesn't matter anymore. I love you now. I love you in a way I've never loved anyone, least of all Bobby. I never wanted to love him; I always wished we'd never met. But I risked a lot for this, for you. And all I'm saying is that as time goes on I'll fall more in love with you because I *want* to be in love with you, I want to stay in love with you. And you'll fall more in love with me. If we're careful and if that's what we want."

He wasn't sure if it was the most callous or the most sincere thing he'd ever heard anyone say, but he believed it.

And it turned out to be true.

In the early afternoon he gets Sandra on the phone.

"I don't know," she says. "I been callin' since you left yesterday. No answer. But Bobby never goes that far, and he never stays away overnight. He's too paranoid something will happen. I don't know what's going on."

"I'm coming over. You'll take me to his place."

"I just said he's not there."

"You said he's not answering. I'll be there in fifteen."


She drives him to a new apartment village he's never seen before, a whole community of identical two-story beige buildings of motel-style apartments, which open directly to the outside rather than into a central hallway. All the doors are red.

They park in the back and walk through an unsecured black metal gate into a courtyard, which is empty except for a swimming pool covered for winter with a blue plastic tarp.

He follows her up a set of stairs and halfway down the second-story balcony before she stops in front of apartment 242.

She knocks but gets no answer.

"Where is he?" Lancaster says.

"Anywhere. I don't know. Hey, look at that. In all this cold." The window to the right of the door is wide open. Lancaster tries to look in. A closed blind blocks his view, but a strange odor gives him a funny feeling.

"Try the door," he says.

"Why?"

"Just try it."

"Why?"

"We'll wait for him."

"Oh, God. You're crazy."

He pushes her aside and tries the handle himself. The door opens. And Adrian Lancaster knows what he's going to find.

"Wait out here," he says.

Sandra backs toward the metal railing. He pushes the door open, steps in, steps back out, and closes the door.

"Let's go."

"What's in there?"

"Come on." He pulls her by her arm toward the stairs.

"What?" she says, twisting free and running back into the apartment. Her scream travels nicely through the frigid January air, up and down the long balcony so all the people can hear. When she begins a second scream, this one louder than the first, Lancaster goes in after her and pushes the door closed behind him, to contain the sound.

Then it's just the three of them: Lancaster, Sandra, and the rotting, swollen corpse of Bobby Karnowski. Bobby's slashed throat smiles up at them, exposing white tracheal cartilages. Cakes of blackened blood cover his shirt and the floor around his head. One leg is twisted sideways at the knee.

Despite the sickening smell, Lancaster crouches next to the body and the large sticky-looking bloodstain beneath it. The hands and fingers show deep gashes, a clear sign of self-defense against a knife attack. Now he notices other wounds: a puncture of the left cheek so profound that molars show through, deep penetration wounds to the abdomen and chest, and slice marks across the throat above and below the major cut.

Smeared blood has dried on the walls and furniture.

"This was a real battle," he says, and then notices something else. On Bobby's exposed belly rests a glassine envelope of light-brown powder.

Sandra's curled into a fetal position in the corner by the door, whimpering. He drags her to her feet. "Quietly," he says, pressing his fingers over her lips. "We just walk away."

"What about Bobby?"

"Bobby isn't going to give a shit. Now come on." Outside, the balcony is still deserted. He wipes the doorknob, then moves her down the stairs, through the gate, and back to the car. She sobs silently. Lancaster finds her keys and drives them away.

After a little while she says, "You gonna report this?"

"Nope."

"Why not?"

"You want your name tied up in this shit, you call."

"No," she says.

"Somebody'll find him. You just pretend like this never happened. And if anybody does talk to you, don't say a word about me. For both our sakes."

When they're nearly back to her house she says, "I was you right now, I'd run, Adrian. I'd run as fast and as far as I could. It's a big country."

"I can't do that. I have a life."

"That's my point."

"Thanks for your help. I'm sorry to drag you in."

"Do me a favor. From now on, don't come around no more. Let's just let our fond memories be enough."

At 5:00 P.M. he tries the attorney's number again. A young girl answers this time and tells him to hold on a minute.

He listens to the noise in the background, the faint voice calling, "Dad! Phone!" And then an old familiar voice that once meant nothing less than salvation, the voice that said, "Everything has been taken care of. You still have a career in front of you, and you'll be free of all this in a matter of months," now says simply, "Yes?"

Lancaster finds his own voice. "Harpo, this is Adrian Lancaster."

A pause at the other end, a throat clearing, and then, "I've been waiting."

"You know what's been happening?"

"No."

It rushes out. Straw's murder, the Babcock setup, the glassines of fentanyl, tails and gun battles and now Bobby Karnowski's dead—

"Adrian, calm down."

"You don't know about any of this?"

"No."

"You said you've been waiting."

245

"For years. She said you'd come back someday, either needing help or just wanting to know what happened. She said to help you when that time came."

Lancaster sprinkles heroin on the tabletop, then scrapes it back and forth with a credit card, forming it into a neat line.

"How could she know?"

"She paid me a retainer then, ten thousand dollars, to do whatever you needed. We've got a lot to talk about. Are you safe?"

"I'm underground, Harpo. I'm in a hotel in Ann Arbor under an alias. I know there's an APB. I shook a tail two days ago."

"Be at my office tomorrow morning. It'll be quiet on the weekend. I have something for you."

"From her?"

"Something she left you."

"Why didn't you give it to me then?"

"It was part of the deal, Adrian. Her instructions were to tell you nothing until a year had passed. Then when, if, you ever came back, to give this to you."

"You could have called me."

"I couldn't."

"Harpo, I thought she moved out west and died later from hepatitis. But an old friend of hers just told me she was dead before I even got out of rehab."

"The deal, Adrian. All part of the deal she structured. I'll explain what I can."

"She died right away?"

A pause. Then, "We'll go over all of it tomorrow. Just stay under until we can talk. Don't see anyone."

Lancaster leans forward and uses a section of a McDonald's straw to suck up the powder.

"Adrian?"

"Yeah. All right."

"Tomorrow morning? Nine, say."

"Okay."

"I'll see you then. Stay cool."

Lancaster lies back on the unmade bed and weeps for the first time since the nightmare began almost a week ago.

Later that night he's lying on the motel bed in the dark. He remembers a night in Detroit in that first fall after they moved. Their apartment had no shower, only an old-fashioned tub that sat up on four clawed feet. He'd always hated baths, so he rushed through them as quickly as he could. But on this evening Denise filled the tub with warm water and suds and made him get in with her. It was different like this, the two of them barely fitting. She lay between his legs, with her back to his front, and they stayed for a long time. He wanted to make love to her there, in the warm and soapy water, but she wouldn't let him. Finally she told him to run, without rinsing or drying, to the bed and get in.

"Go!" she said.

So he ran. The air that night was chilly and he was soaking and cold as he threw himself between the sheets and then turned toward the doorway. She followed, dripping, her body shiny with soap, her breasts full, the patch of hair matted and wet.

He sees her in midstride like this, laughing, her body forever shining as it shone that night. In the real moment she continued toward him, climbing wet into the bed and wrapping her body around his, warming them both. But now, in his mind, in his half-dream of remembrance, she remains frozen, suspended on her way to their bed, giving the illusion of movement but never arriving.

# TWENTY-FOUR

**T**he press has moved into Morgantown, not only from Toledo and Detroit, but from the AP, the UPI, and from one of the Chicago papers. The case, first reported as a possible serial situation, is now rumored to be a drug war, and has begun to generate national attention. No one involved is pleased by this.

In Morgantown the Thursday-evening headline covered the entire top half of the front page: 27-YEAR COP VET GUNNED DOWN IN DRUG BATTLE, *Survives Bullet and Accidental Overdose.*

Ken Barnes is in Lou Adamski's office, yelling, undoubtedly because he got yelled at earlier by some politician. The discussion centers on turning the entire case and all authority over to the DEA. Barnes wants this. But the final decision has been left to the chief.

Then the door opens and Brandon shuffles in, taking his breath and his steps in careful measure. As if to demonstrate that his edge is still sharp he's dressed in one of his wildest numbers, a black silk tie with a dancing girl painted on it, a black-and-white check jacket, red flannel shirt, and tan trousers.

"Who started this son of a bitch without me?" he says. He eyeballs Lou, then Barnes.

"What the hell," Lou says.

"Don't start," says Brandon. "I'll be goddamned if I'm going to lay in bed for the next week." Then he takes a shuddering breath and sags forward. Barnes jumps up and helps him into a chair.

After Brandon is seated, Lou looks at Barnes and nods.


"I'm out," Brandon says.

He and Spinner are in a back booth at the Shu Fong Yu on South Main. Spinner's eating a huge lunch of orange beef and scallion pancakes, but Brandon can only handle soup today. His stomach hasn't been able to take much solid food since the shooting. His chest aches continually, and the pain has spread all the way down his back.

"Not that I can't use the rest."

"Ah, you still got the angles," Spinner says. "Let 'em run around."

"They finding anything?"

"Sure. They tracked out the snowmobile from where you got shot. Someone had loaded it on a truck about a mile away. They even determined it was a Yamaha 300 Enticer made between the years 1982 and 1986. I don't know what we'd do without them."

Brandon laughs. "How about you?"

"Those apartments again, the Washington Hotel. We conducted interviews and record searches. Of the thirty-two rooms in that building, twenty-four are rented. We got the list of tenants and started asking questions, narrowing it down. To start, two are women, both older, one forty-five, one fifty-two. That leaves twenty-two names. Now, none of this is scientific, okay, but this is what I did. I found out who on the list is a new tenant, figuring if somebody's using that place as a base for these recent crimes, they haven't lived there very long."

"Okay."

"Seven guys been there less than two months. We found all of them. None fits Holt's description. None recognized the sketch. By the way, this came in from the feds yesterday." He pulls a color copy from his jacket, and a face looks up from the table—orange hat, black beard, narrow eyes behind round glasses, high cheekbones, slightly protruding front teeth. Arnie Holt.

"Three people at Red's remembered seeing him, not that you'd forget something that looked like this."

"He looks like a rat," Brandon says.

"Yeah. Anyway, so maybe the hotel's a dead end. I wanted to take the sketch around to every resident and also show it to all the desk personnel, the staff, anyone, but Lou said it might spook Holt if word got out his face was going around."

"Lou was right. But now we have no choice. So do it. Just don't tell him." Brandon sets down his spoon, leans back in the booth, and rubs the burning, aching spot over his right lung.

Spinner says, "The prints on the .25 cal from that wrecked rental car aren't Lancaster's. Jimmy thinks they belong to a woman."

Brandon lights a cigarette, which he puffs without inhaling. "I've got something for you," he says. "You know I was all out to get Lancaster. But the more I see, the more I think he's being fucked with."

"Even with the glassware we found? The car wreck?"

"Don't ask. Just trust me. I know what happened that night."

"Damn, Brandon. You're over the edge on this, aren't you?"

"It's gotten a little personal. Anyway, I had some time to think in the hospital and I got to postulating. Whoever's doing this knows things about Lancaster, where he works, where he'll be at certain times. Someone has an inside line."

"At the hospital?"

"Either there or at the Free Clinic, I figure. Remember, Lancaster and the girl, Storm, knew each other from the clinic, and that's where Kevin was a patient. He made friends there. So I made some calls this morning, pulled some favors. I talked to some people in the ER, and then got hold of a nurse I know at the clinic. They're not supposed to release information on their patients, but I lied and told her I had a subpoena coming in anyway. Get this: In the past year Petie Boncaro had been in treatment there. And so had Tommy Winter."

"Hello."

"Now, this is an area we've investigated very lightly up to now and I'm kicking myself in the ass, right? It starts with Lancaster and Kevin Babcock and Storm, and they're all involved with the Free Clinic. But we haven't touched it."

"You want me on it?"

"Hell, yes. Punch the buttons. Go talk to people. Get subpoenas if you have to. But be discreet."

"Sure."

"You want some help for the hotel, I'll swing it. I know guys that'll help you work it on the QT and keep their mouths shut around the station."

"Sure. That's all legwork there."

"It's done. Just keep it quiet. I'll be away this afternoon, maybe out of town for the weekend. You need anything, I'll give you a name. But no one, *no* one, but you gets this. All right? Anyone asks, you know nothing. Then you call me."

"No problem."

Brandon scrawls Ellen Byers's name and number on a napkin and slides it across the table.

"Some shit, this whole thing, ain't it?" Spinner belches and slips the napkin into his pocket.

★ ★ ★

Emerald, Michigan, is a quiet village of impressive houses ranging from starters—three-bedroom red brick colonials—to minimansions varying in style from huge columned classical Georgians to multi-winged contemporaries. Even the starters, Brandon figures, would require twice his salary to carry. Le Seure's home is the epitome of tastefulness, a three-story white green-shuttered clapboard that probably goes four bedrooms, Brandon figures, and a cool quarter of a million anyway. The long driveway leads on to a separate three-bay garage and a new Peugot parked in the driveway.

Sarah answers the door. She's surprised to see him here, of course, but she's gracious as he would expect the matron of such a house to be. The edge he saw in the hospital is hidden.

"Didn't I read something about your getting shot?" she says.

"News sure travels."

"And yet here you are, good as new. You're something of an amazement, Detective. My husband even talks about you."

"Nice things, I hope."

"No. Alternately what an incompetent you are and what a hick. But he only ever talks about people who impress him. So you should take heart from that."

"I'll put it right in my notes. How does he even know what I'm doing?"

She looks at him and smiles, the first one he's ever seen on her. The eyes are still green and ferocious, but with the smile beneath they're much more beautiful than before.

A daughter whom she introduces as Rachel, a dark and quiet girl of ten or so, says hello and then disappears. She shows him to the den in the back of the house, a wood-paneled room that overlooks an in-ground pool.

"I'm trying to tie up loose ends," he says. "Michael, as you may know, is being credited with killing Kevin Babcock."

"What about all the others? The papers make it sound like a bloodbath down there."

"I think it's all evening out. The doers are getting done, if you know what I mean. Anyway, I brought you this." He removes a plastic evidence bag from his coat pocket and lays it on the end table between them. Inside are her brother's gold St. Christopher medallion and chain.

"We had to send the clothing out, so this got separated. The ER sent it over to me this morning. They should have done it sooner, but sometimes it's a little crazy down there."

She picks up the chain and lets it slide through her fingers. It's obvious that she hasn't slept much.

"Thank you."

"What's your husband doing in all this, Sarah?"

She looks up at him, startled for a moment before the composure settles again.

Brandon says, "I know he was in Morgantown. I know he was at Kevin Babcock's house around the time Babcock was killed. I know the DEA is in there, and I can't believe he doesn't still have a finger in that pie. All I want to know is what it's about."

"It was only about Michael," she says, staring off at nothing through the wide glass sliding doors. "We wanted him back. When we heard he was down there, involved in something, Jim did what he could. He called his friends. He went himself. They were just too late."

"It's more than that."

"Not to my knowledge. Detective, I want to give you something in return for this. Can you wait a minute?"

"Sure."

When she leaves he holds his bandaged ribs and looks out the back door for a moment. Then he walks to the far wall, which is covered by framed photographs of all sizes. Photos of Michael Straw and Sarah as teenagers. Photos of James and Sarah and Rachel Le Seure as a growing family. Photos of the house and the pets. Photos of

Le Seure in his office, with the governor, with senators, even one with President Reagan.

And then, off to one side, he notices a framed *Detroit Free Press* photo and caption. It's old and yellowed. In it a less-silver-haired James Le Seure stands next to then-Senator Irving Jovanovich. Le Seure is smiling broadly, the look of a man who suspects that he may have managed to find the next rung up the ladder. The caption says: "Independent Gubernatorial Candidate Jovanovich and his newest advisor, Regional DEA Chief James Le Seure." The date at the top is April 5, 1983, a full year and half before the election.

April 1983 . . . Brandon squeezes the bridge of his nose and shuts his eyes. April of '83 was the month of the famous easter tornado, the same month, Ellen said, that Fang first hit the streets in Detroit. The article tying Le Seure to Papalanos was dated a few months later. By late that summer Papalanos was out of financial trouble. Quite a busy spring for Louie Papalanos, who began marketing Fang and paid off his mountain of debt, and for James Le Seure, who began his political career. And it all began the same month.

Byers is right, he thinks. It's too much to swallow.

"You found my gallery," Sarah says. "I take pictures of everything. That's what I wanted to give you." She hands him a small photo of a boy who looks like he's fourteen or fifteen. His curly hair hangs down over his ears and collar. He's sitting on a couch, smirking at the camera.

"Mikey his sophomore year. See what a normal kid he was?"

Brandon nods.

"That's all. He was just normal. I don't know where it went."

"It went where all heroin junkies go. Where all the scum who put that shit on the streets send those junkies. Ever think about that?"

"What do you mean?"

He shrugs. "Ever hear the name Louie Papalanos?"

"No," she says, too quickly.

"Funny, your father-in-law did business with him. Got into all kinds of trouble. A regular federal case."

"Why would I know about that?"

"Just seems like the name would have come up. Your husband must know him."

"He might. I don't see what—"

"Just that Papalanos is one of those scum I was referring to, one of the people who put junk out on the street so people can die from it. Only, Papalanos put out a special kind of junk, a synthetic heroin called Fang. Ever hear of it?"

"Detective, why are you asking me this?"

"A glassine full of it came into the ER in Morgantown in your brother's pocket. Strange thing is, no one's heard of the stuff for over six years. Last time it was seen was in Detroit in late 1984. Just about the time your husband's new boss was getting elected governor."

"Are you trying to imply something?"

"No. Not at all. It doesn't make a damn bit of sense, does it?" He laughs. "Pardon my rudeness. I'm just blocked here. There's some connection in all of this and I'm damned if I can find it. I didn't really believe it until just now, when I saw a picture over there on your wall. And suddenly, it was too much, all the connections. Everything fits just a little too tightly."

"What are you talking about?"

"I don't know. I mean, really, why would your husband be involved? He's the great crusader against drugs, right? He saves lives; he doesn't take them. He tried to save your brother's life, right?"

She knows something, he can tell. Maybe only a little, but something.

"Or is that wrong? I mean, when I saw you and your husband in the hospital, arranging to have the body sent back here, you were mad at him. I thought it was just because of the public-relations thing, the handlers and all that. But now I'm not so sure."

Sarah Le Seure's face has changed. Some of the anger Brandon saw at the hospital has crept back, but she's gone paler as well, as if something has suddenly frightened her. She sits down on one of the couches and folds her hands in her lap.

"Did your brother die because of this mess your husband pulled him into?" Brandon has no idea what to expect from her. Whether she'll scream and send him away, or threaten him, he does not know.

"Tell me what you're thinking," she says, coldly.

"I really don't know." He sits down across from her. "I know Papalanos moved Fang into Detroit starting in April of '83. How he got the drug, how he knew where to sell it, how he made those kinds of connections, I don't know. But I also know your husband first got selected by the governor-to-be in the same month, April of '83." Brandon stands and takes the newspaper photo down from the wall and hands it to her. "I know the drug disappeared just before the election the following year. I know that your husband knew Papalanos, that the families had done a lot of business together. I know that last week your brother carried one of the first new samples of that drug seen in six years into the Morgantown County Hospital ER. I know your husband was at the scene of Kevin Babcock's murder. Do you see all these correlations? They're amazing. But I can't explain them."

"They don't prove anything."

"You're right. They prove absolutely nothing. But I'm an old cop, Sarah. I've been doing this a long time. And I know how rare a true coincidence is. You know how rare? Never. I've never in my life seen a bona fide coincidence when it came to a murder case. People love to throw that word around. 'Circumstantial evidence,' they'll say. 'I just happened to be there.' But it's never true. When the same names or dates or locations start turning up over and over again, you can bet your life itself they're connected in some meaningful way that has to do with the case at hand. You just have to find the proof.

"The question here is how many more people have to get killed before I can prove something? We have five dead and another barely hanging on. How many—"

"Louie Papalanos was at our house," she says. Brandon shuts up and watches her. "We lived in Allen Park then. He came by a few times, once for dinner. They called him Fat Louie, although by then he was losing weight."

"When was this?"

"Then, in early '83, a couple months before Jim was selected by Jovanovich."

"You'd never seen Papalanos before that?"

"Nor since."

"But you didn't hear anything of what they said."

"No, of course not." Then she drops the next bomb: "Michael was there then too."

"He met with the two of them?"

"Yes." She seems so distant now, he's not sure she's even aware of him. Her voice has grown thin and quiet. Her stare is fixed on the photographs across the room but he knows she is not seeing anything but the past.

"Michael Straw, James Le Seure, and Louie Papalanos all met together at your house in early 1983?"

"Yes. One time they were all there together. Jim had an office in the basement. They were down there for over an hour. I know it was that year because Jim was in discussions with Jovanovich at the same time.

"I don't know anything else, except this: You might think about going back and reading the newspapers from then. There was a huge heroin bust in Detroit by the DEA, something they'd been working on for a long time. It was one of Jim's coups. The supply of heroin on the streets of the city dropped by maybe fifteen or twenty percent. Understand?"

"It created a vacuum," Brandon says. So if someone knew about it ahead of time, had that kind of inside information, and was waiting to step into it with a new supply of, say, a hot synthetic heroin, this someone would stand to make a fast fortune.

"Listen, Sarah—why are you telling me this?"

"Telling you what, Detective? And don't ask me to repeat anything, or testify, or even acknowledge this conversation."

Why do people decide finally to talk? It's an old mystery. Brandon figures the answer is something as simple as the fact that they just get tired of carrying it around, like any other burden. And in the end the "why" of it doesn't really matter.

When he stands to leave he holds the picture of her brother out to her.

"Keep it, if you don't mind," she says. "I'd like you to have that as your last image of him. And if anybody ever asks you where junkies start out, you can show them. Say they start out just like the rest of us, hopeful and confused."


As Brandon's backing out of the driveway, a BMW turns in hard. He hits his brakes and just avoids a collision.

The Beamer backs into the street again and Brandon pulls out after it. Through his rear window he can see the shining hair, the lean face, of the driver, James Le Seure.

They regard each other. Brandon nods. Le Seure holds his gaze for a moment, then, with an expression of great disinterest, looks away.

# THE
# SECOND
# SATURDAY

## TWENTY - FIVE

**H**arpo Epstein's hair has changed since Lancaster last saw him, gone on toward white on the sides and down into the otherwise dark closely cropped beard he wore then and still wears. He's past forty-five now, Lancaster figures, knocking on the door of middle age. But other than the white and a few more lines, he looks good— skin tanned and healthy, ice-blue eyes still intense as ever, chalk-striped navy wool suit undoubtedly hand tailored.

Harpo sits in a red leather chair behind his desk, his back to the wide plate-glass wall overlooking the central downtown, and beyond that the Renaissance Center on the banks of the Detroit River, and beyond that the low tree line of Windsor, Ontario.

"Nice view," says Lancaster, who's sitting directly across the desk. "Better than your last place."

"For being in a city that's falling apart, we've been doing well," Harpo says. "But then half our business these days comes from other parts of the country."

"You still doing mostly litigation?"

"Entirely. I've got a staff of three other full-time litigators under me. It's all we can do to keep up with business. But most of it these days is on the corporate side of things, spin-offs from the other partners' work. I still like to tie into a good criminal case now and then, but I don't do it as often as I used to. How about you?"

Lancaster smiles. "Great until recently. Still a trauma doc. I'm one of the heads of the ER at Morgantown County General. The work keeps me busy, but it's not the warfare I had to deal with here. I got my fill of that insanity."

"I hear you."

They regard each other for a moment and then Lancaster says, "You did a lot more than just keep me out of jail, didn't you?"

Harpo nods. "Your little problem wasn't much more than a sidebar, really, to what was going on with her."

"Well, there's the question."

"I only know so much. She kept me in the dark about certain things too. I know there were, still are, royalties generated from a couple drug patents she held jointly."

"From her drug designs?"

"Yes."

"I knew she was working on some things, in collaboration with some others. She said they had patents pending, but I didn't know anything had actually gone far enough to begin paying royalties."

"Medicinal chemistry, drug synthesis, is, I'm told, a hot field. Pharmaceutical molecular design is big business. There's a virtually endless demand for new product. And she and her group were on the cutting edge, from what I know. In a very specialized field she was something of a star. And she lived under a lot of pressure."

"I knew about that. I mean, maybe not that she was a star. She would have never said that. But I read the pieces she published. I read the reactions. I knew how good she was. Her collaborators were not other students, you know. They were full professors living off her insight. My fear was always that she was the one who didn't know how good she was, that she was being taken advantage of."

"She knew, trust me. She covered all her bases very carefully. No one was putting anything over on her."

"Were you her attorney for the patents?"

"No. That was another firm entirely. They protected her nicely, I believe. They handle all the royalties that come in now. She was very judicious, Adrian, in who she gave information to, and explicit in her instructions as to how she wanted that information handled. She was much more manipulative than I think you ever knew."

"How much are these royalties?"

"Understand that what she patented wasn't mainstream commercial fare. These were specific chemicals with limited application. And she had to split everything with the university. Even so, I'd guess about fifty thousand a year. But I also don't think that's the big money. Her royalties are legitimate legal income. Denise was involved in other business as well, as you seem to be learning. Highly profitable illegal business."

"She was still dealing. For Bobby Karnowski, I heard."

"Not exactly dealing. She was a designer. She invented new chemicals, and new variants of old chemicals. Think about it. You have all the pieces. Come on."

"My God. Three, four-methyl ethyl fentanyl."

"That was one of her drugs, yes. Extraordinary potency, and much longer acting than most."

Lancaster stands up because he cannot sit still any longer. "She was making that shit and selling it, Harpo?" He walks in a daze to the wide window and stands at the edge of the twentieth floor, looking nearly straight down. "She manufactured fentanyls on the side for Bobby Karnowski to sell? It's incredible." And it makes such perfect sense, he has to believe it. He laughs. "Jesus, how can a person be so blind?"

"Of course, she didn't fill even me in on all the details. Some of it I had to know."

"Why?"

"Did she have to come to me? To save herself, Adrian. And more importantly to save you."

"From the people she was selling it to?"

"Not really, although in the end they were her worst enemies. But the drug was so strong, so incredibly concentrated, that it was only a matter of time before badly cut batches hit the street. When that happened, people died. Nearly thirty in one month. All from ODs."

Lancaster turns from the window and faces Harpo again. "I got some of those cases in at Henry Ford. I remember them. One kid was seventeen. It just shut him down." He has a foul metallic taste in his mouth.

"Finally she broke. She couldn't let more people die. This is when she came to me. She realized what a horrible mistake had been made, not just in these deaths but in her whole involvement with the people she was working for. And in your exposure, Adrian. She told me about the business you ran several years earlier in Ann Arbor, and about your addiction, and hers.

"She wanted out as cleanly as possible, and she wanted you out. She was really more worried about your safety and career than her own. She would have thrown herself away to save you. In fact, that may be what happened.

"Anyway, we started to work out a plan. We'd go to the authorities, tell them everything. But, as you may remember, you two were having trouble supporting your habit at that time because she'd stopped manufacturing anything. In the last year you were together you almost never used natural heroin, you know."

"Fang?"

"No, I don't think she used that herself, or let you use it. It wasn't her only fentanyl variant; she had a whole group. Fang was valuable commercially because such a small quantity produced so much in the end. But she knew it was dangerous. You used other, less potent, of her synthetics. It was more controlled that way, she said, the effects were better, cleaner, higher, than the crude natural stuff. She didn't trust what you could buy on the street. She was paranoid. . . ."

"The morphine," Lancaster says. He was stealing morphine because her supply had dried up.

"You remember this?"

"Of course," he says. "I didn't really connect it to anything. I mean I didn't think about her supply. I never knew she'd been manufacturing it. I thought she just had a dealer who'd gotten busted. That's what she told me."

"She had just stopped manufacturing altogether."

"So I started lifting vials from the hospital to tide us over."

"And you got caught. Her worst nightmare. But it forced us into moving very quickly. In addition to saving other lives she had to save you. I called the federal authorities and your superiors and the state medical bureaucrats, and we had a meeting. She told them everything. Everything, Adrian. And we made the deal—the Henry Ford administrators and the state people agreed that if you went through rehab and did some public service, and agreed not to try to suppress the record, they wouldn't press charges. Denise would disappear. In return she'd give the DEA every name and every connection she had, and even some she didn't have. The buyers and distributors, the whole network including the people at the top of it all. That's who the feds wanted. They weren't interested in the middlemen. They wanted the money people behind the whole operation. It was a big deal. The DEA estimated that the chemicals Denise's group supplied had generated, at street level, somewhere between thirty and fifty million dollars in the previous fifteen months. And it was growing. There was evidence the Hamtramck buyers were planning on supplying people in Cleveland, Chicago, Columbus. They may have been making inroads to East Coast cities."

Lancaster takes a deep, head-clearing breath, turns back to the window, and looks out toward the river. "So what happened to her?"

"That's where it gets messy. She gave them everything she had—notes, records, photographs, account books. But they wanted more. She didn't have it. So she agreed to go in with a wire. The arrangement was that she would set up meetings with the people at the top, the ones the DEA wanted. And then immediately after these meetings, whatever she got, usable or not, she'd be disappeared, relocated with a new ID. Several meetings took place. She turned up a lot of very valuable evidence. Just before that final meeting with the biggest fish of all was the last time I saw her. I never learned exactly what happened. Certain government officials told me afterward that everything played out and she immediately left this area."

"For Seattle."

"Somewhere out there. But I never heard from her again. Nothing, not a call or a note. I always thought she'd touch back one last time. And then word filtered in she was dead. I called the federal people back. They said it was a ruse, to cover tracks. That she was safe somewhere." Harpo levels his gaze at Lancaster and purses his mouth. "She may never have made it out of the meeting, Adrian. For all we know, she may have been discovered and killed right then. It didn't matter."

"Didn't matter?"

"To the terms of the deal and of her instructions to me. It was finished legally. My hands were tied. We have no way of ever knowing how it really played out. I do know that she wasn't buried in her grave."

"*What?*" Lancaster comes back to his chair and sits down.

"I was there when they sealed the empty coffin. The funeral was a setup, as was the whole story of the hepatitis. She worked it out in advance, to cover her tracks just in case."

"She's alive," he says. "She's doing this. No one else could manage it. The same chemical she made before, no one else would know how. She's alive, Harpo."

"I don't know. But if she is, can you explain why she'd do this, why she'd drag you in like this, commit murders?"

"I can't explain it. But she can. And someone else may be murdering these people."

Harpo gets up from the desk and walks across the wide office to a recessed file cabinet hidden behind a sliding mahogany door. He unlocks the bottom drawer and removes a manila folder.

"This is yours," he says. "I told you yesterday why I couldn't call you. She was explicit in her instructions that I hold this until one year had passed, and then until you came to me and asked about her. To be honest, I thought you would have contacted me long before this."

"I just moved on. She obviously wanted me to, and looking back seemed pretty pointless. If I had known she'd left something—"

"Yes. Anyway, I think it's mostly personal stuff, although I haven't read it." He hands over the folder. "Maybe your solution is in here."

Lancaster stands on trembling legs. "Harpo, do you know who was behind it?"

"Not really. That was between her and the authorities. Once we'd reached an agreement protecting her and you, they insisted that when she briefed them I not be there. I understood that. Nothing she said could have hurt her legally at that point. But I do know the drug came in to a group based in Greektown." Harpo presses his fingers together in front of his chin.

"Whoever was distributing was based there. People have told me the organization went out of the drug business when all of this happened. They made their money, got out clean, and haven't gone back since."

"Thank you," Adrian says, taking his hand.

"If you do get somewhere on this, it will in all likelihood be messy. You understand that."

"Yes."

"I'm paid for. When it's over, don't talk to anyone before you call me. I'll be there."


Greektown, Detroit: a fifteen-minute walk from Harpo's office building. Wanting nothing but to read, and feeling drawn by circumstance to this place, Lancaster finds an empty corner booth in a quiet family restaurant on Kovach Street called The Athenian, and orders a Greek salad, souvlaki, and a bottle of retsina. A part of him feels a little silly about this but, notwithstanding the fact of some Greek drug lord in his past, he likes this place, enjoys the food and the ambience of an old-world bazaar, and can't think of a better way to kill the afternoon while he reads a bit of the history of himself and his lover, Denise Richards, which up until now has been kept from him.

But before reading, he drinks. The strong sweet wine goes down well. After a few glasses the meal comes and he eats. When he is through, he finally begins. He picks up the yellowed slip of paper on top, and reads:

October 8, 1984

Dear Adrian:

Long after it is finished, you will perhaps one day read this. I hope so, and I hope that long ago you will have forgiven me for whatever pain you felt. If it is half the pain I feel on leaving you, then I can never apologize enough, and won't try. I only hope that you know, or have learned, that what I did I did out of love and necessity. There are many things you don't know about me, things you are better off not knowing, and you can blame me for not sharing all of my life with you but again it was because I wished to shield, not to withhold. Perhaps I was wrong. I have been wrong in many things.

Lancaster stops, takes a breath, pours another glass of wine. It is unmistakably her voice, and it pierces him, making her seem that much closer. His belief that she is still living grows stronger.

There are some things I want you to have, mostly things about me, about us. First, copies of some letters you wrote me. They are beautiful letters and although you may have forgotten them, I haven't. When you are not around I take them out and read them. I have done this often, as you will tell from their condition.

There is a picture of me with my family, a long time ago, when we were all still alive. This is my life outside you, before you, before Ann Arbor.

In the picture she is a much younger woman than he had known, college age, standing with her arms around her mother and father, a younger sister wedged in between them. She never once mentioned these people. He had never met any of them, knew nothing about them. He wonders now why, if they mattered enough to her that she would leave him this picture, she could not speak of them.

Also, there is a picture, taken by some med student friend of yours that time I brought you the apple pie from Mrs. Tong's bakery on State Street, the ten-dollar kind you always loved but never felt you could afford. You'd been cramming for three days and looked half sick from starvation and exhaustion.

This is a shot of him holed up in the library, his stockinged feet up on a desk, a thick text open in his lap. She sneaked in with the pie and a thermos of coffee but forgot utensils, so they locked themselves in an empty carrel and tore the pie apart with their fingers. They finished it all. He still remembers the sensation of his jaws aching from

269

salivating so hard, and how he felt both sick and rejuvenated afterward from the massive sugar load.

> I know you remember all this, but I like seeing it written on the page. It helps me to remember it better.
>
> Finally, there is a key to a safe deposit box in the Michigan United Trust, West Woodward branch. The box is registered in both our names, either/or. It's been paid for for ten years from today. If a decade has not passed, you will find in the box some answers.
>
> Love,
>
> Denise

Woodward's not too far, he thinks, until he realizes it's Saturday. He finds a pay phone in the back of the restaurant and calls the bank. They're open until one, but it's already a few minutes after noon. So he throws a twenty on the table and sprints toward the garage where his car is parked.

## TWENTY SIX

On Saturday morning Brandon drives to Detroit to meet with Ellen. His first stop, however, is the basement of the main branch of the Wayne County Library in downtown Detroit, where he finds the articles Sarah mentioned about the heroin bust in early 1983. It took place in the last week of March.

Then he finds the photograph dated April 5 he saw on Sarah's wall. He pages forward through the municipal sections. In the April 12 edition he sees the first mention of the drug. "Samples of a new and highly potent fentanyl, a form of heroin, have been appearing for the past several weeks, especially in Hamtramck. Local hospitals have already reported three overdoses due to the drug, which authorities warn can be far more concentrated than what street buyers are used to. Authorities are presently testing the drug to determine its precise makeup."

And then, a few weeks later, when Fang had been identified as 3,4-methyl ethyl fentanyl acrylate, a city editorialist, commenting on the futility of the drug war, wrote: "Just when one inroad is blocked, another seems to open. The void created by the earlier arrests, it seems, is already being filled by this new and far more dangerous substitute."

Brandon pumps quarters into the machine to makes copies of all these articles. Then he runs. He's meeting Ellen for lunch.

When he arrives, she stands up on her toes, presses her cheek against his, and says, "I'm glad you're here." They stand like this for a moment, and his chest aches because of how hard his heart is beating.

"I'm glad I could get out of bed to make it," he says as they sit.

"You're really feeling okay?"

"I wouldn't say that. I can walk and breathe. What else is there?"

Her eye catches his for a moment and again he's aware of his heart in his bruised chest. "Anyway," she says, "you look good. Really."

After he's briefed her on his new information, she forks a tomato slice from her salad and waves it between them. "All speculation, but damned seductive, isn't it?" In her habitual manner she's looking at him over the tops of her glasses.

"Le Seure can offer Papalanos an opportunity to make back all his money in a shot," Brandon says. "He knows there's going to be an undersupplied market for heroin. The family can bring it in, wholesale it out real fast, without even getting involved in cutting or packaging or parceling out. They only have to find the new source.

"The source they find is high-grade synthetics. Safe, fast, low-volume. And who better to make the actual deliveries than Michael Straw, old drug horse and a member of the family to boot, so he's as safe and secure as he can be. And remember, he had worked with Bobby Karnowski, and Bobby was arrested in the '84 Fang sweep."

Ellen says, "Le Seure could have served up to Papalanos a no-lose situation: information that the heroin supply to the city would be cut off, protection, and a way of creating a new supply from thin air.

"Still," she continues, "the ultimate question is why. Le Seure's planning a career in politics. Why would he risk it to help his dad's old real estate partner sell dope? We have no evidence against him, but if we could answer that question, we'd have a much stronger argument."

"There's a reason," Brandon says. She smiles at him and nods.

In the afternoon he finds himself in another basement, this time in a police archive. Ellen has cleared him. On the isolated corner desk he's using are a phone and stacks of files from the 1983–1984 investigation into Fang—clippings and photos, detectives' reports, warrants, evidence notes, trial transcripts, and even a report from an independent chemist who was brought in as a consultant.

Almost everything has to do with the series of arrests and prosecutions of lower-level people, which do him no good. But he finds one photo that is unlabeled, a fairly distant shot through a partially opened window into a hotel room. It looks like it was taken from the window of another building across an alley or courtyard.

Six people can be seen in the room. The center is a woman sitting at a round conference table. Her face is striking but from this distance her eyes look like the eyes of a corpse. A man sits on a couch across the room, facing the window. Another man stands at the doorway, smoking. Two other men and a woman sit across the table from her. They all seem to be listening intently to what she says.

Brandon rings Ellen's office and describes the photo to her.

"I remember," she says. "There was a high-level informant, the one who broke the whole thing. She was only ever identified to a very few people, all federal. But somehow one of our surveillance teams ended up where they weren't supposed to be and got the shot. If the DEA had known, they'd have demanded the negative and all copies. So we never told them."

## TWENTY-SEVEN

L ancaster makes the bank with ten minutes to spare. He convinces the manager to let him see the box, that he'll only be a few seconds, just long enough to collect what's there. To gain access he has to show ID, which makes him a little jumpy, but there is no way around it.

He finds a cassette tape and small sealed envelope addressed to him, in her handwriting, and a rubber-banded stack of papers.

Time for a new motel room, and the most convenient is the Howard Johnson's at the intersection of Route 696 and Woodward Avenue, also known as State Route 1, the major northwest-to-southeast thoroughfare connecting Pontiac with Detroit. Lancaster pays cash for the room for two nights and registers under a false name, as he has been doing.

Before beginning he makes a quick shopping trip to pick up a cassette recorder.

Then he settles in. He tapes the photos from Denise to the wall over the small desk in his room, then lays out the folder and envelope and tape player. It is two-thirty in the afternoon.

The papers turn out to be dozens of personal letters, mostly from her family, a few from him, receipts and clippings she just threw together and kept in the box. As he looks through everything, though, he finds himself growing more and more incredulous at what he didn't know about her.

A few items stand out as somehow outlining the parameters of her life. He arranges them on the bed so he can see them all at once, starting with a yellowed newspaper article:

---

LEXINGTON GAZETTE
*November 30, 1977*

Martha Gelles Richards, 48, was killed yesterday when her car was struck broadside by a tractor-trailer rig at the intersection of Glann Road and Redding Avenue. This intersection has been the subject of debate by city planners because of its history of accident-related fatalities (see story on page three).

Mrs. Richards, an administrative assistant at Lexington Memorial Hospital, was on her way home from work when the accident occurred. She is survived by her husband, Jeremy Richards, 51, a partner in a plumbing firm, daughter Denise, 25, a student at the Ohio State University, and daughter Elizabeth, 14, a freshman at Glen Ridge High School.

The family requests that any donations be made to the Lexington Memorial Hospital Children's Fund. Private services will be held at the Ottumwa Ridge Cemetery tomorrow.

---

He had known her mother was dead because of something Sandra said once, but had no idea she'd died so violently or so recently, only four years before he and Denise met. His amazement is at the fact that she never needed to mention it to him, never needed to talk about it.

Next comes a series of letters:

*Postmarked Lexington, Ky., March 15, 1981*

Dear Denise,

Just like you said, I got the part! Kattrin in *Mother Courage*! I can't believe it! They said it's the first time a high-school student has gotten a role in a major U of K production. Now I'm scared.

I really wish you could make it. Please try!

Love,
Liz

Lexington, Ky.

July 1981

Dear Denise,

You have a lot to be proud of in your sister. We have just been told that Ohio State will give her a full ride scholarship to study theater arts. She is beside herself with joy.

Since your mother passed and you have been away so long, I have been worried about her, not knowing exactly what a young woman needs in the way of encouragement and advice. I know you have written her lots, and I want you to know I appreciate it. It has made the difference.

With love,
Dad

He carries the letters to the window and stares out at the motel parking lot and another Michigan sky, unbroken backlighted grayness, no sun showing through.

He had of course asked about her family early in the relationship. She always brushed the questions away, responding by not responding, so that he eventually came to believe she was estranged from them in some way she could not discuss. But this was not so, he sees now. They wrote; she must have seen them from time to time. How could she have not told him? He laughs. What had he meant to her?

*Postmarked Lexington, Ky., October 1982*

Dear D:

I know I should just keep going, but with Daddy so sick now and with the prognosis so bad, I have to be here. I'll go back to school when it's over.

Besides, acting doesn't seem as important as it did once. Maybe I'll go into the sciences now, nursing or pharmacy or med tech. Like you. Or maybe I'll just get a job somewhere. Taking care of him like this has changed the way I feel.

I wanted to talk with you about this but found it easier to write.

Love,
L

*Postmarked Lexington, Ky., December 1982*

Dear D:

You know how much it meant to him that you were here. He went in peace, and now joins Mother. I liked our talk, and appreciate that you think I have such talent, but you're wrong. I don't have the kind of talent it really takes. Besides, school is one thing I cannot think about right now. I don't know what I'm going to do.

Love,

L

More incredible than the facts of what he didn't know is the fact that all this had happened when he was with her, as they were falling in love. Her father had died the autumn Lancaster began his residency at Henry Ford; he'd been dying throughout the summer of their move, the beginning of their living together. And she said nothing. Not even an unexplained depression. She'd gone away at times that year, but said it was for academic reasons, conferences or symposiums. She'd been going home to see her father.

Lancaster's immediate reaction is not to believe it. She made it up for some reason to confuse him, to alienate him as she was leaving him. The letters are forged.

Or, if they're real, then maybe she hated him. Or worse, felt indifference. Maybe he'd simply been a convenience for her, someone with whom she had no desire to share her real life.

But he does not believe this. Then he is angry; he wants her there so he can yell, so he can ask her why she couldn't talk to him.

Then he wonders if it was his fault, if he were so self-involved that she could not find a way to bring him into the rest of her life. This possibility frightens him the most.

*Undated, handwritten*

Dear Neese:

Out for a long session with the books, so won't be back until late. Don't wait up. I'll have trouble studying because of thinking about you. These boards past me, I'll be off, and you too. On to Detroit. On to a new life.

On to us.

I can't say how much I love you.

Always,

A.L.

Finally there is a series of receipts, starting in March 1983, and dated every couple of months up until September 1984:

THE MCGIVVONS INSTITUTE

17 W. Reynolds Hwy.

Lexington, Ky. 43875

INVOICE

Date: March 22, 1983

To: Denise Richards

Re: E. Richards, treatments performed and ongoing

| | Due | $1,290.00 |
|---|---|---|
| | Rec'd | $2,500.00 |

Bal.    [$1,210.00]

Lancaster opens the sealed envelope next, and reads:

10/1/84

Adrian:

This tape contains a full list of the names and information I gave the DEA. This is the only copy besides the one they have. You may need it someday.

Denise

279

He has not heard her voice since that last time in his hospital room in 1984. He plays the tape:

> "There is no explaining I can do, Adrian, no justifying that would mean anything to you, so I won't try. Listen: I did things that you might someday need to know, but which I do not want you to know until I am long ago gone. I am neither proud nor ashamed right now. I am numb. But I am not so numb that I cannot see what needs to happen.
>
> "I have killed people; I am responsible for deaths. There is a drug, with which you may be familiar from your ER, called Fang. . . ."

It is her voice that breaks him. He cries as he listens, not hard, only a few tears, and he's not sure whether they're from anger or sadness or something else. It's not as if he still feels the emptiness of their separation.

Then he remembers that he has never cried for her before, and he understands that this is his payment for these artifacts she has left him. These are the tears he has owed her, as she has owed him this explanation.


By seven he is hungry and runs across Woodward to a Kentucky Fried for greasy chicken and biscuits. It is filling and fast, the only considerations.

When he gets back he scrapes out a couple of lines of heroin and does one, then lies back and rests for twenty minutes or so, until the sedative effect has passed. He's finding, though, that it does not calm him as it had. His hands have taken on a tremble again. He'll have to do more later, but now he has to finish this.

At ten, his head crammed with thoughts and questions, he lies down on the bed and tries to sleep, but the hum of his brain keeps him near the surface. He dozes for a little while.

Even shallow sleep is good. Sleep consolidates. Sleep connects.

When he awakens, he realizes it is time to go home. It is time to make the leap.

He listens to the tape one last time, does another line to make sure he's solid, then picks up the phone.

The Morgantown dispatcher tells him Detective Brandon is not available until Lancaster convinces him it's an emergency having to do with the case Brandon's working on. He is put on hold for a long time, several minutes, before a man comes on and identifies himself as Detective Wharton.

"I need to talk to Brandon, right away."

"Who is this?"

"Just get him."

"He's out of town."

"Tell him the Tecumseh connection wants to talk."

There's a pause. "Give me your number."

"Uh-uh. I'll call you back in fifteen."

"Call the dispatcher again. Tell him to put you through to Wharton."

Fifteen minutes later Wharton gives him a Detroit number.

Lancaster dials. A woman answers.

"Brandon," he says.

She does not ask any questions. Then Brandon's on the line.

"Sorry to bother you. I didn't know if you were okay."

"I'm fine."

"I have a file. Denise Richards was a top-drawer drug designer. I knew that was her field but I swear I never put it together. She was the one manufacturing Fang in '83 and '84, Brandon. She invented it."

Lancaster listens as Brandon moves the phone away from his mouth and speaks to someone else: "He found the link. Richards was the chemist."

281

A woman's voice in the background says, "She'd worked for Karnowski; Straw knew her. It's perfect. And she must have been the DEA informant!"

"She was," says Lancaster.

"He says that's right," Brandon says to the woman, then to Lancaster, "This helps, Adrian."

"People were dying. She turned herself in. I didn't know any of this until today."

"How could you not have known?"

"I don't know, Brandon. Really. I was buried in hospital work. She drove back to Ann Arbor most days to work on her thesis and that's where it all happened, but I wonder if maybe I just didn't want to know."

"Yeah."

"She left me a tape explaining everything, all the details. Bobby Karnowski and Michael Straw were her main contacts—Bobby set up the deals and Straw was some kind of connection to Detroit."

"Listen, there's something I haven't told you," Brandon says. "The drug is being manufactured in Morgantown this time. Kevin was the point man. It was coming from the chemist through him and Petie to Seth, then out. That's what we didn't understand."

"In some way she's here, Brandon."

"You think she's alive?"

"Her casket was empty—"

"Is she doing this?"

"I don't know. They used me to get to her. They knew about the operation we ran out of my apartment." Lancaster is lying flat on the bed, staring at the cracks and stains in the cheap tile ceiling. "They knew what she could do, that she was a designer. I guess she had patented some important new molecules. She had also made some synthetic narcotics, experimenting around. She'd given some to Bobby, who tried them on people. After that, when I was ready to graduate and was getting ready to move to Detroit, he beat her up pretty badly one night. I fixed her. She said she wanted to move with me, so we made plans. But that fight, that was when he first came to her with a new offer—he wanted her to keep manufacturing for him. She would get a percentage of profits. Or else he was turning us both in. It would have cost us our careers. So she went along.

"Then, later that year, just after we'd moved, he brought her a huge offer. She was to find the best synthetic heroin she could, and make it in volume. Big volume. That's when she started making Fang."

It occurs to him that again this was the same fall, of 1982, her father died. She must have been just shattered. Lancaster rolls on to one side and closes his eyes to try to stop the sickness that he feels.

"By early 1983 they had stockpiles of the shit. She said there was power involved. You can extrapolate out from the quantities of pure drug she made. The street value when it was all cut down was a hell of a lot of money. Tens of millions."

"Did she know who?"

"No. She was close. She cut a deal with the feds and told them what she knew. They wanted more. The last stage was that she'd try to get to whoever was running it. She went back to Karnowski and Straw and played like she wanted more money. She wanted to see the main people. They set up a meeting."

"And they knew."

"I think so. Either they killed her or she read it and escaped somehow and had to disappear to save her life." He's in the fetal position now, head tucked down toward his knees, eyes shut, phone pressed to his ear.

"Adrian, think about this. How would they know Denise had gone in? How would these people know about that? There's one explanation—the people she was talking to, the authorities, whoever they were."

"It was inside," Lancaster says.

"Do you see what you're up against?"

"And you."

"And me. But I'm close to the bastard behind it."

"Who?"

"Not on the phone."

"Who's Holt?"

"No idea."

"Listen to me. I'll turn over this material but only to you."

"Where are you?"

"I'm in Detroit too."

"You want to meet?"

"Can't."

"Then leave it somewhere safe. Call this number tomorrow and tell me where. If the woman answers, tell her."

"All right."

"One more thing—I had a call from another detective tonight. I had him on the Free Clinic. Kevin, Winter, Boncaro, Storm, and you all had ties there. We knew everything was running through Kevin. It turns out he was using the clinic. Late last year, when the drug first reappeared, there was a series of calls from the clinic to Straw's number in Detroit. We should have picked it up sooner."

He uncurls now, sits up on the bed, and puts his feet on the floor. "Exactly when were the calls?"

"From October twenty-third through November fifteenth. Tuesday and Thursday evenings."

"Thanks."

"Watch your back. Deal only with me. I mean it. One more thing—we got word today from Ann Arbor. Bobby Karnowski was found slashed up in his apartment. Dead for probably a week."

"Poor Bobby," Lancaster says.

He hangs up and dials a Morgantown number. He expects to get an answering machine, but after three rings a woman answers.

"It's me."

"Adrian?"

"Yes."

"God! Where are you? I've wanted you to call so badly. Did you find anything?"

"Listen to me. Listen carefully. I'm sorry for skipping out. I had to do this alone. Are you okay with me?"

"I understand. I stayed that night in the motel, then I just came back here. I didn't know where else to go."

"I want you to get out of there tonight. Pack a small bag and disappear. Don't get in your car. Don't turn any lights on. Is there a back way you can leave?"

"There's a basement. I can go out through there."

"Is there anyplace close that would be open? A bar?"

"Pretty close."

"Go there. Call a cab. You have some money?"

"Yes."

"Just make sure you're not followed. You know Bunnies' Restaurant on the South Border Highway?"

"Grease pit."

"It's open all night. Take a cab there. Sit alone, in a back booth. Get a paper to read. Order something. And wait."

"Adrian, what's happening?"

"Just go."


What is most amazing is the degree to which he remained ignorant of her life and her past. Was this all by design on her part? No. It was his fault too. Maybe mostly his fault. Junkies, he supposes, are at root and by necessity inherently selfish. For the two of them the immediacy of the moment of each other and the continual carnal satisfaction of the drug smothered the normal urges to truly know each other. But even this is a sad excuse for his not noticing the trauma she had suffered, was still suffering. In the end, he thinks, whatever happened, she was probably right to leave.

# SUNDAY

## TWENTY-EIGHT

Late Saturday night, after Brandon's calls from Spinner and Lancaster, Ellen got a call of her own. She wouldn't tell him about it. She only said, "Something may be developing."

Brandon sat on the living-room floor of her suburban town-house, rolling his head around on his shoulders, trying to relieve some of the tension he felt. Besides that, his chest hurt from its bruising and his cold had become an ongoing irritation of lung and sinus congestion.

She handed him a hot whiskey with sugar stirred into it. Then he felt her hands on his shoulders, rubbing and kneading in the way Lorraine had once done.

"Take your shirt off," Ellen said. He did, exposing his barrel torso with its spectacular bruise, and she continued to massage him until he felt the muscles let go and his head grow heavy with fatigue.

"You're a woman of true talent," he said.

"And you're a man who's going to collapse if you don't get some sleep. You should still be in the hospital."

They unfolded the sofa within the couch and she laid out blankets and sheets for him. As she turned to head upstairs to her own bed, he grabbed her wrist and held her for a moment.

She looked at him, and smiled. Then he let her go.


Sunday morning, over bagels and coffee at a local deli, he says, "How did it happen? Once the DEA had their informant in '84, how did it work?"

"Well," says Ellen, "we, Detroit PD Narco, had been involved with the DEA for over a year in trying to nail down the source of the drug. But once they got this informant, who we now know was Denise Richards, they shut us out. Word was they were afraid of a leak."

"Someone inside."

"Right. I heard that even within the agency only certain people were given access to this new informant, only people at the highest levels. The street-level DEA agents were shut out too. What happened was Le Seure decided to bring in special agents from other jurisdictions."

"DEA agents?"

"Yes, but from other parts of the country. People he knew would be totally clean. And they came incognito. The DEA guys I knew didn't even know who these people were. Deep-cover sort of shit."

"And that's who took in Denise," says Brandon.

"To my knowledge."

"Which would have been perfect except under one condition. If Le Seure himself was the leak."

"You got it," she says. "Then it would have been nothing but an elaborate smoke screen he set up to hide himself."

"What we still don't know is why he'd do it. For what possible gain? I still just can't make sense of that."

"I told you last night I was working on something."

"Trust me?" It's still before noon. Ellen's lying on her living-room sofa, feet up on the arm, sipping from a bottle of orange seltzer. She looks at her watch.

Brandon doesn't answer.

"You don't trust anyone, do you?"

"Not completely. Not now."

"Ha. You don't trust me. Think I could be the leak? I could have known. I was there for the whole thing."

"Could be. I'm fucked if you are. You've got me where you want me."

"Well, think hard about it, Frank, and make up your mind. If you're with me still, go outside and turn left. Walk until you're out of the complex and in the front parking lot. Stand on the curb and look lonely."

"You serious?"

"Yessir. But only if you trust me."

She looks nice lying on the couch like that, in a long sweater and a flowery skirt that's been hiked up over her knees. She's maybe fifteen years younger than him. "You got nice legs," he says.

"Thanks."

"That doesn't mean I trust you. But I'm a sucker for a good-looking gam."

" 'Gam,' " she says, and laughs. "That dates you, old-timer."

He puts on his coat and heads out to the appointed spot. It had been drizzling earlier. Now the drizzle has intensified into full-blown rain and it's cold, just barely above freezing. His cold is just breaking; this will probably set it off again. His chest hurts, both inside and out. He slides a hand into his coat and rubs the bruise where the bullet hit.

★  ★  ★

Five minutes later a new El Dorado spins up and stops dead in front of him. The front passenger door opens and a huge thick-necked monster steps out and without giving him a glance just opens the back door.

"Get in," the monster says.

"Who for?"

"We gonna play games or you gonna get the fuck in? You got about three seconds."

Brandon gets in. He's alone in back. The car takes off fast and heads back into the city, to the downtown. When they get off the expressway twenty minutes later, he knows where he is. He was here once years ago with Lorraine: Greektown.

They drive through most of it to a wide dead-end street lined with ornate but tired-looking five- and six-story pre–Depression era buildings. Most have high steel-caged windows, which have been painted over black. They stop in front of one such red brick building, which could be a warehouse or a tenement. The driver jumps out. The monster in the passenger seat looks around at Brandon and says, "Let's go." Brandon follows them through a rusted and badly dented steel security door, into a beat-up lobby and onto an antique elevator complete with manual gate and sliding brass lift lever.

As they're rising, an electronic wand appears in the driver's hand. He waves it all over Brandon's body, down the back and front, between the legs.

Brandon offers the man his gun.

The man shakes his head. "Wires," he says.

The pebbled glass in the fifth-floor office door says JACOB JOSEPH GAMBOLOS, PC, ATTORNEY-AT-LAW. The office isn't much—a small reception room, where a thick-legged and thin-mustachioed secretary stops her typing to announce them, and a dingy back room where the lawyer waits behind his desk.

Brandon is surprised. He expected a big man, a Greek with thick arms and neck and slick hair and a thousand-dollar suit. But Gambolos is tiny, half the size of the secretary in the outer office, and very very old. His face is a maze of folds and creases, so many that it's impossible to tell what he once looked like. And his hands are tiny, with long delicate fingers, barely larger around than pencils, capped with pink nails. He unfolds these slender fingers and motions at Brandon to come in, to sit, to be comfortable.

One of the pencil fingers presses a button on the desk, and the secretary appears with two cups of coffee and a creamer. Gambolos speaks to her with a movement of his head. She leaves.

"You know who I am?"

"No," Brandon says.

"I'm an attorney. I have one client, the Papalanos Construction Company." The voice is as folded and worn as the face, the croak of a frog from far across a pond. "I can't tell you anything, Detective. You realize that, I'm sure. I can't admit anything on behalf of my client. I can't tell you the answers to the mysteries you're trying to solve because I don't know the answers. Still, your friends here in my city brought you to my attention. They made it clear to me they could exert a lot of pressure if they needed to."

"Ellen Byers?"

"She's more than you think. She's probably one of the three or four best-connected narcs in Detroit. My point is, I told her no pressure was necessary. I'd be glad to talk to you. I want you to understand that what's happening has my client very upset. Very upset. His name has been dragged into this, it hurts him, hurts his reputation, hurts his business. He'll do anything to put an end to it."

"If you can't tell me anything, then what am I doing here?"

"Why don't you tell me what you know, what you believe? Maybe I can guide you."

Brandon goes right to the heart of it—he lays out his theory of the collusion between James Le Seure and Louie Papalanos in 1983 and '84. That for some reason Le Seure let Papalanos know that there would be a reduction in the supply of heroin to the city, and that Papalanos could profit from that by supplying synthetics. That Le Seure's brother-in-law helped in this by actually getting the synthetic heroin to Papalanos. That Le Seure protected them the entire time.

Brandon knows that this is speculation, that he is guessing at the mechanics of how it worked and at Le Seure's collusion with Papalanos, but when he sees the lawyer's hands go flat on the desk, sees him rise in his chair and push himself up so he's looking down at Brandon, sees the red anger creep into his face, Brandon knows he has struck a nerve. For an instant Brandon can see the younger man, can sense what he must have looked like forty years ago.

He waits, and Gambolos settles back down, folds his hands, and gets old again.

"This is as much so you can see what I know as it is to help me out, isn't it?" Brandon says.

"The world's a marketplace."

"Am I right?"

The old man shrugs and turns slightly to look out the window at the drizzle.

"Are your clients involved in this present situation? Are they behind the manufacture of Fang?"

"No."

"Are they in any way connected with the murders that have surrounded this drug? Michael Straw? The Babcock brothers? Petie Boncaro? The shooting of Tommy Winter?"

"No."

"Would they have any reason to feel threatened by the fact that this specific chemical has reappeared?"

No answer.

"Would James Le Seure?"

"I can't answer that. I wouldn't know."

"Do your clients have an ongoing relationship with Le Seure?"

"That's none of your business."

"It's very much my business. If they do, then they're suspects. And if they're suspects I can have arrest warrants issued by my colleagues here in the Detroit PD or by the DEA, which is participating in this investigation."

Gambolos shakes his head and drums his tiny fingers on the desk. "Don't you threaten me. I did not bring you here so I could hear threats."

"Why did you bring me here?"

"You're a bull, Detective. Has anyone ever told you that?"

"No, that's one thing I haven't been called."

"This problem is intricate, delicate. You don't untie a complex knot by yanking on the ends. You tease it. You finesse it out. Follow?"

"The question is what can you tell me?"

"Ask me a question I can answer."

"All right. In my theory of the Le Seure/Papalanos conspiracy, there's a hole I can't fill. Why would Le Seure do it? Why would he risk everything just on the verge of his political success? Money? Doesn't seem to fit."

"On the *verge* of political success. There's your answer. James Le Seure was one of the people Jovanovich was considering here. He'd already chosen three others. You know who they were?"

"Yes."

"Have you thought about the reasons he named them?"

"They could help him."

"Of course they could help him. It's how they could help him that's the issue. What's this city really about? What's its power?"

"Manufacturing."

"And what makes manufacturing run?"

Brandon shrugs.

"Imagine you're a politician. Looking for lots of votes. Think about it. Where's the power?"

"Unions," Brandon says.

Gambolos throws himself back in his chair and rubs his whiskers. Then he opens the top desk drawer and removes a pack of Kents and an ashtray. "I'm supposed to have quit. But I allow myself one or two a day." He offers the pack to Brandon, who happily accepts a smoke for himself.

"Unions," the lawyer says. "That's what Jovanovich had to have as an independent. And you know that unions are hardly democratically run. They're controlled by a small handful of powerful people. Sometimes one person. Each union is different. With some it's the traditional mafia. Some it's a handful of labor leaders who've pulled themselves up. Some it's other families. . . ." He shrugs.

"So these advisors were people who controlled unions."

"Or at least had influence. Jovanovich needed large blocks of organized voters. That's what he felt these so-called advisors of his could help deliver. But like anything, one needs momentum. Now, what do you suppose was the first union to endorse the candidate?"

Brandon shrugs. "AFL?"

"Wrong. You should have done a little more homework—this is all a matter of the public record. Give up? The first union to officially endorse Mr. Jovanovich was the Ironworkers' Union. And after them came the Pipefitters and the Electricians."

"All building trades."

"Right. So who had that connection? Of the real power brokers in Detroit, who were biggest in real estate? Who were the most powerful in development?"

He nods, coaxing Brandon toward an answer. When it doesn't come, he answers himself. "There were three men," he says. "But the biggest, and the one who controlled most of those unions . . . was Louie Papalanos."

"There it is," says Brandon. "Jesus Christ."

"Later, other unions came as well, the garment and auto workers were next. But the Papalanos influence began the trend."

"The man who could deliver Papalanos, then, would hold a lot of power with Jovanovich."

"And a lot of power in general if Jovanovich got elected, which the unions would certainly help to do."

So that's what Le Seure had to have. He went to Papalanos and asked for the construction unions. If he got them, he'd be in for sure. Jovanovich would not only get a campaign advisor with an image as a crusader against drugs, training as a lawyer, and expertise in law enforcement, but the crucial backing he needed to begin to lock up the Detroit vote. But old family ties weren't enough for that kind of favor. Le Seure had to offer something big in return. And what did he have to offer? Information. Information that could fill the Papalanos family coffers again, and in a very short time.

"Why are you telling me this?"

"I'm not telling you anything. I just gave you a little lesson in local political history. There's nothing surprising or illegal in any of that. Finesse, remember."

"You're angry at Le Seure, aren't you?"

Gambolos sits stonily, his lips drawn together into a pout. "Personally? No. I'm angry that this isn't being handled better, that it's got all out of control. Everyone's being hurt. I want it finished. I don't care how."

Brandon smokes and Gambolos smokes. After a moment Gambolos says, "The people you're after all have many secrets to hide. All of them. You understand that any information you find will be only for your own digestion. You won't be able to introduce it as evidence. You won't be able to say where you got it. It won't be the kind of information you can use in a court of law."

"I understand."

"Do you understand that none of this will ever come to a court, that if justice is done it will happen spontaneously?"

"I'm not sure I follow."

"These aren't normal people you're dealing with. They can't be

297

got at in the normal ways. You don't arrest and try them." Gambolos leans far forward across the desk. Brandon can smell his dusty, smoky breath. "You learn what is and what is not. You learn what's true. And you act accordingly. And you act swiftly. And you act definitively. Understand?"

Brandon stares into the black eyes of this ancient man and realizes that he does understand exactly what he's being told. He understands more than that too. This isn't just an admonition; it's an offer. Help is available. Many things can be accomplished. Many things.

Then Gambolos falls back and becomes the lawyer again.

"That's all, Detective. Follow the yellow brick road. And good day."

Not until he's in the El Dorado and on the expressway back out to Ellen's suburb does he get the joke. The yellow brick road leads to only one place—the Emerald City.


Lancaster called Ellen and left directions to his motel so Brandon could pick up Denise's notes and tape; he'd left them in a desk drawer, and taped the door so it couldn't lock. Spinner had also called with something urgent.

But before anything Brandon sits down next to Ellen and fills her in. "They want you to take Le Seure down for them," she says. "I'll be damned."

"Listen," Brandon says. "I want prints of the photo of Denise Richards—first a clear enlargement of her face, then enlargements of each section so we can see the faces of everyone around her."

"Sure."

He picks up the phone to call back Spinner, but before he can dial she has her hand on his arm. "Frank, pay attention to me. After you find out what you have to find out, but before you move on anyone, call me. I'll be there. This is all poison now. Touch it and you die. Keep that thought in your mind."

"You think I'm not gonna talk to you again?"

"No. I think you're compulsive and you have a temper. Those are your worst enemies right now."

He reaches Spinner at home.

"Oh Brandon," says Spinner. "It's about time."

"What is it?"

"Something broke at the Washington Hotel. We had it covered. Nobody going in or out looked like this Arnie Holt. And I thought we'd questioned everyone. But we were giving it one more go, we're up on the sixth floor. Only, this time I noticed an old woman we hadn't talked to watching us through a crack in her door. I called out. She shut the door, but I knocked and she opened it again. I showed her the sketch of Holt. And she just pointed."

"Where?"

"She came out into the hallway and pointed at room six thirty-eight."

"And?"

"That was twenty minutes ago."

"You haven't gone in?"

"No."

"Don't. And don't call it in. Wait for me. Secure the floor. Put a man undercover in the lobby. If there's an empty room on that floor, get set up in it. Anybody goes near that room, grab 'em. I've got a quick stop to make, then I'm on my way. I want first crack before we turn this over."

"Don't we need a warrant?"

"I got one glued to the bottom of my shoe."

## TWENTY-NINE

**S**he lies in the bed, covers pulled up so far that only her eyes and her dark hair show. He imagines that she has a smile on her face, a faint enigmatic smile the result of some dream satisfaction. He waits for her to awaken. He sits in a comfortable overstuffed easy chair he's pulled across the room to within a few feet of the bed. In front of this chair, separating him from her, he has set up a small folding table that holds the .357 Magnum his father bought him, a pack of cigarettes and ashtray for her, a bottle of Johnnie Walker Black and two glasses, and his heroin stash.

She'll be hungry when she wakes up, but now is not a time for nourishment. Alcohol and cigarettes are what he'll feed her. They will stay in this room all day. They will drink and they will talk. There is no world, no life. There are no responsibilities. There is only history.

★   ★   ★

She was waiting as he had instructed her, peering over the top of a *USA Today,* sipping coffee, looking nervous and tired. She must have been there for two hours, waiting. He'd meant to come sooner but he wanted a copy of Denise's tape, and drove around for over an hour until he found an all-night drugstore where he could buy a second cassette deck and a blank tape.

He stepped into Bunnies' and asked the girl at the register for change so he could make a call. Storm watched him. He caught her eye for one quick moment, then looked away.

He waited in the rental car until she came out a minute later. Then he drove around back of the building and waited again until she caught up with him. She was wearing the black shawl he'd last seen on her at the clinic.

She seemed glad to see him, threw her arms around his neck and hugged him. "I was afraid for you," she said.

"I for you," he answered. "Where can we go?"

"I know a place. A friend's out of town. I have a key."

It was their only conversation. She asked no questions on the drive to the apartment, none as they climbed the flight of stairs and dumped their bags in the living room. Lancaster took a shower. When he came out Storm was already asleep on the bed.

The apartment turned out to be the perfect place, in an anonymous complex in the western suburbs, not too far from his own house. Too perfect, really. He was not surprised.


She smiles when she awakens, and sits up a little.

"Hi," he whispers.

"What're you doing?"

"I like how you look."

"I bet I look awful. I should get cleaned up." She pushes her fingers through her hair.

"No. Don't get up."

"Adrian." She sits up a little more and sees the gun. "What's that for?"

"Protection."

"It makes me nervous."

He nods and inhales a line of the heroin.

"Is something wrong?"

He nods again.

"You're scaring me."

"I just want to talk, Storm. Here." He pours a little Scotch into a glass and offers it to her.

"Are you kidding?

He drinks it himself and pours more. "You should start," he tells her. "You'll want to keep up."

She sits up fully now, legs crossed under the covers, arms crossed over her chest.

"You think you know something?"

He nods again. "Should I start at the end or at the beginning?"

"Stop it, Adrian." She throws the covers back and starts to get up.

"Get back in the goddamn bed." He picks up the gun and stands over her until she folds her legs under the covers again. "This won't be easy. And I just want to get over it. Then we can go on to whatever we're going on to. But right now we're going to do this, and nothing else. If it takes all day, we're going to sit here."

"Don't you screw this up," she says. "Not now." Her eyes are different. He can see something he has not seen in her before, an anger, a potential he couldn't have guessed at. And her voice is changed too—subtly, nothing he can even name, maybe an accent underlying these few words that has not been there before.

"Last night, before I met you, I spoke with Brandon. He told me Kevin was selling Fang that was being made right here in Morgantown. He also said that a series of calls was made, starting in October, from the clinic to Straw's apartment in Detroit. He assumed Kevin had made these calls, but you and I both know that even though Kevin was registered for therapy there, he hadn't been coming for some time. The calls were all made Tuesday or Thursday evenings. So this morning, early, I called one of the administrators over there."

"And she told you I helped out then with a new group those nights. So what?"

"You were Kevin's friend. You were close enough that you knew about the people he was dealing with. At the very least you should know who made those calls if it wasn't you." Lancaster pours another taste of the Johnnie.

"You don't know anything."

"Are you going to make me drink alone?"

This time she takes the glass he offers.

"So," he continues, "the question now is what's the game? Where was Kevin getting the drugs? And were you in on it?"

"I was just helping him."

"But that makes no sense. How could he get ahold of a rogue fentanyl variant that disappeared years ago? How could that exact molecule, which I just learned was designed by Denise Richards, suddenly turn up in Kevin Babcock's hands?"

She pours him another drink, several fingers this time, and another for herself as well. They regard each other, then kill the glasses. The Scotch, this early and on empty stomachs, is making itself felt quickly and hard. Good, he thinks. He pours for them both again, and lights her a cigarette.

"What's logic tell you about that?" she asks.

"Logic, I don't know. Intuition? That you're the supplier. Are you drunk yet?"

She nods.

"So'm I. The reason you came to me was no accident, and it wasn't just because I was someone who'd treated Kevin. You knew exactly who I was, and that's why you came to my house later. Not because you were afraid. You knew who I was long before you approached me."

She watches, weaving slightly.

"So. Now to logic. How could you be supplying a drug that was invented by and died with Denise?"

She slumps back against the headboard, waiting for him to answer his own question. He answers it with another question.

"Why here in this little place? You could have done it anywhere. It would have been safer in the city, more anonymous. Here, everything's so exposed."

"Why do you think?"

"Me."

She smiles sweetly. "I wanted you to see it. I wanted you to know what happened, because I don't think you ever knew. I think you thought she went on and lived somewhere."

"Did she?"

"No. They killed her, Adrian."

His stomach drops; this is the truth and he knows it. He's surprised at his reaction, at this new sense of loss, at the hope he allowed himself to coddle again.

"Did you see the body?"

"What difference does that make? She told me everything, she sent me every scrap about her life, about you and how much she loved you, about the bastards she was working for, about the setup she made, how she was going to finger the scum who organized it and cut him down. But she knew she might never come out, Adrian. The one thing she promised—as soon as she got out she'd come home. Without you I was all she had. She never even called. I knew it then, that they killed her. What I could never understand was if she was working with drug enforcement people, why didn't they do anything? How could they let her go in and never come out and just not do a thing?"

It's not only the accent, a Kentucky twang, but her diction too. Polished, as before, but different.

"You're an actress."

"Yes, I'm an actress. She thought I was good, so I went back after she died and finished my degree at the University of Cincinnati."

"For her?"

"For me. And for her revenge. It's a skill that comes in handy. What else did I have to do?"

"How much money did she leave? Royalties?"

Storm snakes a cigarette from the table between them and lights it. "Varies. This year won't be so much, forty-five, fifty. Last year was almost seventy-five thousand."

"And."

"There's an account. Swiss, in a bank in the Bahamas. She left me just under eight hundred thousand dollars."

"God." He shoves his chair back from the table and stands up.

"Angry?"

"No. I don't know." Just stunned again at the magnitude of what he didn't know.

He says, "So you've dedicated yourself to this. Why'd you wait so long?"

"It had to be that exact chemical. That was the one way the whole thing would run itself. She sent me all her notes just after you got arrested, when she knew it was over. She sent me everything for storage—textbooks, diagrams, tapes of lectures. Of course, I didn't know what it meant. I paid a Ph.D. candidate I knew a lot of money to resynthesize that drug and to keep quiet about it. He had a wife and kid to support. You wouldn't believe the work that went into it."

"I'd believe anything, Storm. Or Liz?" He walks around to the foot of the bed and looks down at her.

"Storm has a ring, doesn't it?"

"I like it best. Who've you killed so far?"

"I haven't killed anyone. Are you taping this? You have your police buddies waiting outside with their cages?"

"No one's here."

"Sit down, will you? You make me nervous like that." When he's back in the chair she says, "I didn't have to kill anyone. That was the beauty of it all along. All I had to do was get that poison back out on the streets and get out of the way. I knew the bastards would all kill each other after that."

"Who?"

"Michael Straw and Bobby Karnowski first. Beyond that I don't know. You're going to help me find out."

He laughs.

"It was Michael and Bobby who took her in, you know. She called me on the way to Bobby's house. I remember the day. It was beautiful, autumn. The leaves were all just turned, and the air had that edge to it. She said up here the last leaves were coming down. She was crying, Adrian."

Storm sits up in the bed, animated suddenly with the memory of a day that must have been so agonizing, Lancaster cannot imagine it. Her face has changed again; her eyes are open, staring, her cheeks flushed.

"She was afraid. I waited all that day, hours and hours, for her to call again. She never did. You know how you hope and hope, but gradually hope slips away. Still you don't want to admit to yourself it's over. But by night I knew she was dead, and I knew they'd done it to her, they were at least in on it."

She looks at him now, her mouth twisted with emotion. She closes her eyes. "I swore those two would pay. Now Straw has."

"So has Karnowski. He's been dead a week. Slashed."

"Then I'm happy." She shakes her head then takes another drink and regains her control.

"What about Kevin?" he says.

"A horrible mistake. He helped me the most. Once I'd managed to re-create the drug it was just a matter of leaking it. I figured this was as good a spot as any, and you were here so you'd eventually figure it out. I moved here, set up a life, pretended I was a coke addict, and enrolled at the clinic for treatment and group therapy.

"Which is where you met Kevin."

"Can you think of a better way into the drug subculture of any town?"

"How'd you know about his brother?"

"I just paid attention, knowing I'd find someone. I was there almost a year before I made my move. I'd made a few buys from Seth through Kevin just to see if he really could deliver."

"So you found out how to get the drug out."

"Yes. I convinced Kevin to give a little smack, so he thought, to people he knew, which of course included Seth and his friends. They were small-time traffickers. I told him to tell them there was more where that came from. I told him to tell them we wanted to go big time, everybody could get rich if they could tap the Detroit market. If there's one thing you can always rely on it's people's greed. Seth's partners in Jackson knew people in Detroit. Before I knew it the drug was on the street there. Then it was only a matter of time before the right people ran across it, figured out what it was, and came looking to find out what was going on. The thing I can't believe is how fast they knew. I leaked the first samples at the end of October. Not even three months."

"Kevin knew who you really were?"

"No. He's the only one who knew I was the chemist, though. He knew he had to keep quiet about his true source. So he was my front. But he was a friend, truly a friend. I liked him. I felt sick that they got to him."

"He also started using again. You know at one time he'd gotten himself off everything."

"That was Petie's influence, not mine. I was just doing business."

"Business. You had to know a lot of innocent people would be dragged down by this. I mean, I'll give you credit—it's a brilliant plan in one way but terribly messy in another."

"There was no other way."

"Seth is dead now. The detective and I stumbled onto a drop; Seth and Holt delivering to someone who ended up taking a shotgun to Seth. Brandon got it, too, but survived."

"I read about it."

"Nice, huh? But Holt got away. Who is he? You hire him?"

"No. Kevin did."

"You said he called you about Kevin. Did he set that up? Or did you know Kevin was dead already, was that just you having fun with me?"

"I didn't know it, Adrian. That happened like I told you. Holt called me. It's true I wanted to involve you, but not like that. Not to find Kevin dead."

"Holt was there the night Petie got killed, watching the pickup. Holt was with Seth when he got shot. You have to know who he is. You were making this stuff. Holt's obviously on your side, Storm."

"I told Kevin to get rid of him!" she says. "But he saw him as his protection. At first I thought he was someone Kevin had known. Later I realized that Holt and Kevin had only met recently, through Petie. Holt just got to him, convinced him he needed his own muscle. Kevin liked that, the idea of having a sort of bodyguard/companion. Kevin knew no one could ever find out about my deception, but this made him nervous. He felt like he was the only one who was exposed. Holt gave him a buffer. Holt, who always carries a gun, made him feel good and safe and powerful. Holt went everywhere with him."

"He wasn't enough protection to save him. Did Holt know about you?"

"No. Kevin swore he never told. He knew I'd leave. But Holt saw Kevin and me together a lot. He knew something, but he doesn't know I'm the chemist. All the drug he's handled since Kevin died, the drop you saw at the airport, had been made already and was just in storage. I haven't passed anything in weeks. He just switched over to working directly with Petie and Seth."

"But listen—just after I'd found Kevin, Holt called the police. He reported a murder at that address. Why would he call at that moment? How did he know I was there?"

"People knew you had helped Kevin before. Maybe he followed you—"

"Bullshit!" Lancaster slams his open palm down on the table, knocking the ashtray and bottle to the floor. "I was involved six years ago. Now you just happen to convince me to find a dead kid, and Holt just happens to be watching me? Stop it."

She shrugs. "Maybe I told him I was going to talk to you."

"Maybe you'd told him about me before you ever came in that morning. Maybe because you wanted to protect your position. Maybe you wanted Holt to think you were just some bimbo contact—that's obviously what Seth thought. So you dropped my name at some point in such a way that they would think I might be the chemist. There's no more logical choice than me. I lived with her for over two years. I dealt for her. I was Kevin's doctor."

She watches him in his anger.

He continues: "Holt did call you that morning, to set it up so you'd come into the clinic and convince me to drive out to Kevin's house—maybe you didn't know Kevin was dead, and maybe you did. Holt got you to flush me out because he wanted to see if I knew anything about what was going on. He knew about Kevin whether or not you did. He called the cops so I'd get caught there with the body. But that was perfect for you; it played right into your hands, because *you* gave him my name in the first place so you could drag me in. You knew I'd eventually put the pieces together with Straw and Karnowski involved."

"I did it for you."

"And the rumors about me? You started them. And the glassware in my basement? You were the only one there. I left the house that night to start the chase to lose the cops. You were going to stay for a few minutes, then cut out the back and meet me later. Which you did, except before you left you slipped downstairs and planted enough evidence to convict me of manufacturing synthetic heroin.''

Her chin rests on her chest, her mouth pulled down into a tight line.

''Was that for me too?'' he says. ''Thanks for the fucking favor.''

''You were part of them!'' she screams at him. ''You were one of the ones she was with! You were a dealer, too, goddammit. You killed her!''

''I never knew about this drug, Storm. I never knew what she did. When we left Ann Arbor that was all over. All I did was shoot up with her; for two years all I knew was that we were junkies. I had no idea she was still dealing. I had no idea she manufactured. I only found out three days ago, when I went back to Ann Arbor and talked to a friend of hers.''

''I don't believe you.''

He sets the cassette player on the small table and puts in the copy he made of the tape Denise left him. Her voice fills the room as she tells him all the things he did not know, making it clear he was never involved in any of the Fang business, that he could not have known anything about it.

At the end Storm is sobbing.

Lancaster reaches into the breast pocket of his shirt and removes a snapshot, one of the two left for him in Denise's folder, the one of her family. Storm, known then as Elizabeth Richards, is a young girl, longhaired, skinny. She is maybe twelve, with braces on her teeth. She stands between Denise and her mother and father, the four of them smiling at the camera one summer's day in Kentucky. Lancaster tosses it on the bed.

''I looked at that last night when I got it and didn't even know it was you. It was only when Brandon told me about the phone calls that I put it together. Funny how one little detail crystallizes everything. The letters you wrote. How much you knew. Your being in my house that morning. The beakers in the basement. Even the pointless craziness with Seth at Red's. Everything suddenly fit.

"I thought I was pretty good, figuring this out. I thought you'd be shocked when I told you. But I'm nothing; even this conversation, my realizing all of it, is just part of the plan."

"More or less. Someone had to show you the truth."

"She never talked about you. I didn't know she had a sister at all."

"She sent me everything about you. I had a crush!" Storm laughs a little and wipes her eyes with the sheet. "Even when she first met you, long before you two got together, she'd talk about you in her letters. She loved you before you knew she did. I think she fell in love with you the moment you met. I was sixteen the first time I heard your name.

"I remember, we were sitting upstairs in my bedroom. I didn't understand because she was living with Bobby. My father knew about that and wasn't happy. But here she was telling me about this other guy, a future doctor with the strange name of Adrian, she'd just met!

"I only started hating you after she died. I wanted to hate every-one then."

"Why wouldn't she have told me anything about you?" says Lancaster. "All of you. Do you know the first fall we lived together was when your father died? She never mentioned it. And this was just after she started making Fang. Jesus Christ." He puts his hands to his forehead. "It's my fault. It has to be. I shut her off somehow—"

"Don't," Storm says. "She was always like that. Everything was compartments with her. She had trouble synthesizing. I think she needed to do that to keep from exploding. She felt everything too intensely. She'd hold things, big things, inside for months."

"No. It could have been different if I'd really been there, watched how she was feeling, paid attention. I could have worked things out of her. I made it possible for her to be like that."

"She was so strong, Adrian. I don't think you understand yet how strong. She was my parent, you know."

"What?"

"Not literally, of course. But emotionally I think of her as the one who raised me—not raised—the one who formed me. She was the strong one, the one who taught me. Our mother and father weren't like that, and they both worked my whole childhood so they were gone anyway. But she was there.

"When I was in the third grade it was a very hard time because she'd gone away for her first year of college. I was really alone. I was having trouble with a boy in school. On the way home every day he'd corner and harass me until I got mad. Then he'd hit me. It happened a lot. My parents called the school and had meetings with his parents. Once he even got suspended. It'd stop for a while, but always started up again.

"Things got to where I was having regular nightmares.

"So one day I came home scraped up because he'd tripped me. Denise had just come in for the weekend. She took one look and dragged me by the arm over to that boy's house. His name was Rodney. He was playing out in his yard.

" 'Now you go over there and make it right,' she said.

"I refused. I started to cry. She said, 'I'm not leaving here until you do it.' I cried so hard I was gagging. Rodney came over to see what was going on. He stood there grinning.

"I got so mad and humiliated I couldn't stand it, but she wouldn't let me go, and he just stood there enjoying it.

" 'Sissy,' he said to me. And it was as if something burst. With no thought I just raised up and brought my fist down square on his nose. I'd never seen blood like that in all my life. I thought for sure I'd killed him.

"Later, Denise held me and apologized over and over, but she said it was the only way to put an end to it.

"And that was the end, you know. That boy never raised a fist or his voice against me again. And so the dreams stopped."

Lancaster feels hollow, as if he has cast off a part of himself he will not pick up again. But this hollowness is not altogether bad; it brings with it lightness, too, roominess. His lungs feel freer. His breath comes more easily.

He stands up and moves the gun from the table to the floor. Then he carries the table away from the bed, and pulls the chair back to its original spot.

"That's it," he says. "I'll make some food if you want."

"Come," she says. He sits on the edge of the bed. She hugs him to her, puts her arms around him, and rests her face at the base of his neck.

"I've known you for so many years," she whispers.

"What are we going to do?"

She pulls away and looks at his hair, his eyes and nose. Then she leans forward into him, into his face, until her lips find his. Her kisses are like those of a child, he thinks, small and hesitant but curious. After a moment he begins to return them. Their kisses grow more earnest, neither hesitating in what neither wants to stop.

He peels off her T-shirt. They fall together sideways until they're lying on the bed, his cheek pressed to her naked belly. She kisses his head. Her skin is so hot that for a moment he is frightened, thinking she's sick. Then he becomes aware of the glow around his own face, of the sweat running down. She pulls away again so that she can finish undressing him, she who is already naked before him.

"Look at you," he says as he runs his hands over her small breasts, down her sides, and around her hips.

He pulls her down so she is lying beneath him, his hand supporting her head, her dark eyes as round and open as any eyes can be, and he enters her that way. She wraps her legs up around his waist. She is wet, there is wetness between them, on their bellies and on their legs, and when they kiss again her hands tear at his hair and at his neck.

313

The warrant on the bottom of Brandon's shoe doesn't have to be called into play. Twenty dollars and a smile works for the wrinkled desk clerk.

Room 638 is registered to one Zeke Bade. The clerk knows him.

"Old Sterno Head. Been around here for a year or so. Ain't here right now. Ain't seen him in a month, in fact. He hits the road sometimes."

"Mind if we take a look?" Brandon slides the double saw over the desk. The clerk slides a pass key back.

The Washington was once upon a time a top-rate boardinghouse and hotel, but now the lobby smells musty and the lights are mostly burned out and the carpeting has worn through. Inside the stairwells —which they're forced to use because the elevators are out—pools of mystery fluids have collected, the lighting is even worse than in the lobby, and the stench makes them gag.

Brandon's lungs feel raw and he has to stop several times on the way up. He's dizzy by the time they get to the top. His chest throbs where the ribs cracked, and burns from exertion.

There's no answer at 638 when they knock. The floor is dead still, so Brandon passes them in.

Spinner goes first and Brandon hears him say, "Holy shit."

The bare mattress shoved up against the far wall is covered with artillery—a .40 caliber Glock 23 autopistol with an extended twenty-five-round magazine and two hundred and fifty boxed rounds; a Remington Model 740 semiautomatic 30.06 hunting rifle with a Nikon 5X scope, fifty full-jacketed rounds and fifty hollow points; a tear gas gun and canisters; and a 150,000-volt stun gun.

Blankets are folded and stacked in a corner.

Across the room, on the wall over a small desk, eight-by-ten medium-range shots of both Bobby Karnowski and Mike Straw have been taped. Lower, just above the desk, is a picture of Adrian Lancaster.

Clothing is scattered about the room: military fatigues, a snowmobile suit.

Spinner points. On the windowsill rests the ubiquitous orange ear-flapped hunting hat.

Brandon's first comment is "Don't touch a goddamn thing. Get Jimmy up here now, on the hush-hush. We're gonna turn this place over fast, then wipe it clean. After that you can call it in to Lou."

He walks gingerly backward from the room, pulling Spinner with him.


Jimmy Mendez distributes surgical gloves before they go back in. First, he photographs the whole room as it lies. Then they start looking.

More books are discovered in the closet, ballistics guides, marine training manuals, a well-thumbed copy of Machiavelli's *The Prince*.

And along with more ammunition there's a box of splinter grenades. Behind the box of grenades is another box, this one containing stolen pairs of license plates from six different states, a Canon 35-mm camera with a long-range 120-mm lens, a Panasonic mobile phone and charger, and a glass jar of a clear jelly-like substance.

"This fucker was planning a war," Spinner says.

"Hair," Jimmy says, holding up a pair of tweezers. He's been going over the hunting hat. "Fairly short, fine, dark."

Jimmy uses a specialized white powder on the gun metal, but prints are hard to come by until the clip of the 30.06 yields a beauty. He lifts it off on tape, seals it in an envelope, then wipes the whole gun down with alcohol to remove any evidence of the powder or the starch from his gloves.

"Get out," Brandon says. "Leave the jelly jar for the feds. It's probably the napalm. I'll pay that desk man downstairs to get sick enough he has to go home. Spinner, find that old lady again and tell her not to open her door for anyone the rest of the day. Then give me a half hour to get back to the station and settle in before you call Lou. Tell him just what you told me when I was in Detroit. They'll have to execute a warrant and then they'll be all over this.

"Let's go."

When Brandon walks into the justice building he knows that something has changed. He's only in the front lobby, the desk sergeant peering at him through the opening in the smoked glass partition, but in this look Brandon reads a warning. The few people in the lobby, a couple of uniforms and a clerk, act cagey as well.

Upstairs on three, it is all bustle and haste, this at a time when the floor should be getting quiet for the night shift. People are running here and there; maintenance men carry a desk past him as he tries to get off the elevator. He sees a uniform he knows well and raises his eyebrows to say, *What gives?*

The cop mouths back three words. Brandon doesn't get it at first, so the cop says it again.

DEA. The feds are here in force. Kline's people are moving in. Brandon does not feel angry or defeated. What he feels is something he didn't expect. He doesn't care. He feels lighter, of all things.

Brandon can see strange men and women in suits, maybe half a dozen of them, taking over a set of desks near the windows.

"Lou couldn't help it," the cop says. "I heard he got splattered today. Besides Ken Barnes, Mayor Davies himself was up here too. And two councilmen. And someone from the county. Dump-truck loads of steaming bullshit."

Brandon walks into Lou Adamski's office. Adamski the brick pile sits behind his desk, and Julian Kline in yet another fine suit is sitting on the couch.

"I'm back," Brandon says.

"Brandon," Lou says. "There's been a change—"

"That's fine, Lou," Brandon says. Lou's block of a face has a strange, almost apologetic look, something Brandon has not seen before. It makes him want to laugh. "It's the right thing. Let me give you what I got today. Then, I'm going to go home and sleep. My chest hurts like hell and I'm exhausted."

"A trauma like yours takes a long time to get over," says Kline.

Brandon nods and tosses him a file and cassette tape. "That came to us from Adrian Lancaster. I didn't see him, just picked it up. That's how he wanted it. It's got documents Denise Richards left him six years ago. Letters, lists of information, and a tape detailing everything she told the feds, and everything she never told him. Maybe it'll help. For one thing you'll get a clearer picture of how the group was structured. Beyond that I couldn't see anything too useful."

Brandon thought hard about whether to turn over this information or not. He finally decided to, not because of the hard information, most of which was already in the DEA files, but because it's clear proof that Lancaster had no knowledge of the original plot to manufacture Fang. Maybe it will begin to lay the groundwork that will exonerate him when this is over.

Brandon looks at Kline. "You got a minute?"

The two of them walk across the hall to Brandon's office and close the door.

"I thought you might like to work out of here."

"I was going to use the conference room."

"That's for the group. Use my office. I won't need it."

"You're not going to walk away on us."

"I'm going to rest. I'll be as close as the phone. Listen, there's something else."

Kline sits down behind the desk in Brandon's chair.

"I'm playing this one pretty close," Brandon says.

"As it should be played. You've understood this more than anyone, Brandon. From the beginning. I knew that. Maybe you thought I was dicking with you. Maybe you thought I was cutting in on your turf. But I knew that you knew how to play it—alone and with your mouth shut. I had to help create the right environment for that. We were right, you and I. Case in point: Lancaster got in touch with you after he ditched, just like I said he would.

"If you weren't so closemouthed, if he'd had any hint you would come to us with that information, or that you were sucking up to the feds like the rest of the bozos around here, he never would have cut loose with the file and tape. Right?"

"Yeah."

"So you were dead on. You just have to know when to give up what you've got."

"Now it's time," Brandon says. He rubs his eyes and thinks hard. The magnitude of the thing is too much now. He needs help. He needs some power behind him. It's time to let the big boys play the big boys' game.

But what to keep and what to give? Keep Ellen back for now.

She knows everything he knows. He may need her. And access to Lancaster, of course. He's the hole card.

"All right." Kline leans forward, waiting.

"It's James Le Seure. He ran everything, Julian. He was the brains behind it all. And because he was the head of the DEA, he controlled all aspects. There never could have been a complete solution to the case, because he was the one who would have had to solve it."

"How do you know this?"

Brandon lays out his theory, running through the research and his meetings in Detroit.

Kline says, "We've been working the Papalanos angle, but from what you say he's completely out. But Le Seure . . ."

Brandon nods.

"Does anyone else know what you know about him?"

"I don't think so. You guys really had no idea? Even with Straw's turning up like that?"

Kline nods. "The official line is that we think he's being set up for something."

"Is this straight? You think that's a possibility?"

Kline shrugs. "Yes. And no. You don't just accuse your former boss of these kinds of crimes. We watch and we wait and we gather evidence. And we see where that takes us. Who can tell?"

Brandon nods again and puts an unlit Camel in his mouth.

"This is goddamn nice work, Frank."

Across the hall he hears Lou's phone rings. A moment later his own intercom buzzes. Kline picks it up. Brandon can tell by the reaction it's Spinner calling in his discovery at the Washington Hotel. Brandon smiles as Lou and Kline run like crazy people for the elevator. Then he puts his feet up on the desk and lights the smoke.

## THIRTY-ONE

Lancaster feels for the first time this season that a snowfall would be nice. Even in November when the earliest flurries created a general mood of anticipation, as season changes do, he wished for warmth, for sun. Now, sitting in front of the fireplace in the dusk-darkened living room of this apartment, Storm snug between his legs, a blanket wrapped around his shoulders, a good fire burning, he wishes for a deep, thick snow to fall over the world, to hush and insulate. But outside it rains instead, a hard, cold rain that will turn the already fallen snow to icy February mush. It is the same every year.

The Scotch is pretty much killed. It's growing dark.

"The key was Straw," Storm says. "Denise wrote that it was only when Straw started coming around more often that Bobby talked about manufacturing in any kind of volume, and that he wanted something new and really good. He said he'd tapped into an incredible market. Still she didn't piece it together right away. She made a little extra and Bobby started pressing her for more. She refused. Then

Straw came to her and told her either she played or they turned you over. He had all the dirt on you, even things Bobby could never have known. So she went along."

"She told you all of this?"

"At the end, and in so many words. So I looked for Straw but couldn't find him. Unlisted number, no job. Karnowski was easy enough, but I didn't approach him. I just watched, and waited."

She smokes cigarette after cigarette, finishing one halfway, then grinding it out and lighting another. This is all nerves, he can tell. He can feel her tension just from being in contact with her skin. It is as if her skin can barely contain the energy she holds within.

"In December people from Detroit came to Seth acting like they wanted to cut in. They told him they could send him big time, cut out the middlemen, they could distribute as much as he could supply. I told Kevin to tell Seth to tell them we could talk. But I would make the contact."

"Seth never knowing your identity."

"Mm. So they gave him a number, which he passed along to Kevin. I didn't know where I'd be calling, only that it was in Detroit. But I paid someone to trace it back and learned that it was the apartment of Michael Straw. I knew then my plan had worked. They had realized what this drug was and had come looking. So I began to play it out. Call, wait a couple days, string them along. Some of these were the calls from the clinic."

"Wouldn't it have been easier to use a pay phone?"

"I did sometimes. But you were at the clinic. It was another way to draw you in. Bread crumbs in the woods.

"The first few times I led Straw to believe I wanted to make the deal. Then I started playing with him. I mentioned Denise's name. Finally, I told him that I'd been talking to Bobby Karnowski, that he'd told me what had happened, what they'd done. They would have killed him right away, but I'd been calling him, too, warming him up. I got to know Bobby Karnowski pretty well."

"What'd you tell him?"

"Lies. I was a friend of Denise's. She'd talked about him. But then I asked him if he knew there was Fang floating around the streets and Straw and his people believed it was Karnowski who was making it. Then I told him I was a narc. He started to cry. I told him we could work with him, he played, we'd play. I wanted names. See, once I told Straw about Karnowski, time grew very short. That was less then a month ago."

"Why'd you tell?"

"Karnowski didn't know any names. He only ever knew Straw. They kept him in the dark. But it still scared Michael. That was the point. It heated things up. He and his people knew they had to put an end to this. So they came here.

"There was a meeting set up. I knew it would be a bloodbath. I was going to pull Kevin at the last minute, just let whoever showed up go at each other. But then Straw came in early, found Kevin, and found the drug there. I guess he went crazy.

"They, whoever 'they' are, were watching everyone by then. They knew where Kevin lived."

"But who killed Straw?"

"I don't know. Holt maybe, but I don't know why."

"And magically within range of my hospital. He came in to me, you know."

"Gorgeous luck. I could never have planned that. It just worked out. Not only did he die, but you got to see him."

The light from the fire plays around her head, giving her an aura as if she is some kind of angel. An angel of revenge. He rubs her shoulders and feels an exotic warmth coursing through him, from his hands to his shoulders to his body.


He has about a quarter of the heroin left and he does a line every so often to keep up the effect.

"You're compulsive, you know," she says.

"You opened the door again. More revenge?"

"I suppose. But do you understand that all of this, all your suffering, has been as much for the sake of knowledge as for revenge?"

"Knowledge."

"Framing you was the way to pull you in, with no chance of your not coming along. You'd have no choice but to go back, to learn what really happened. That was the most important thing. You had to see."

"But you hated me too."

"Yes. Wrongly, I admit. Anyway, you should stop now with the drug."

"I need it to see this through. When it's over I'll stop. I haven't done enough to become dependent again. I can stop."

"Physically dependent," she says.

"What?"

"Not enough to become physically dependent. But you have to be able to let it go, Adrian. In your mind you have to be able to stop. Can you?"

He can't believe he'll have trouble. He's been clean for so long. This is just a brief aberration, an extraordinary experience. When it's finished, he won't even want to use anymore.

"Afterward, I promise. I can stop then."


Later they move to the bed. She lies with her face on his chest, one of her legs thrown up over his own. Blackness seals the bedroom, and nothing outside her voice can be heard but the freezing rain tinkling on the window glass.

"Can you talk about her? I mean what it was really like. Was she easy to live with?"

"I can talk about her," says Lancaster. "No, she was not an easy person."

"She never was."

"But I wasn't looking for someone easy. I wasn't looking for anyone, really. But I was young and she was the sort who just took you over."

"Yes. That's exactly right."

"If she wanted you, you had no choice. You had never been loved like that, never been taken care of, or made love to, or coddled, or made to feel luckier, than when you were with her. And when it was bad you felt like you'd never made a bigger mistake than to hook up with her."

"I never had that choice. She was just mine."

"Yes."

"Would you have stayed with her?"

After a moment he says, "I think so, yes. I think we would have gotten clean, and that would have been very hard, that could have ended things. But if we survived that, then yes, in the end I think we would have just kept going on."

There was a time early on, in the Ann Arbor days, when Denise was still living with Bobby, not too long, maybe a month or two, after the first time she and Lancaster had slept together. They'd gone, just the two of them, to the botanic gardens in west Ann Arbor. She brought along a lunch. When she spread it out on the blanket, though, he couldn't believe this was her idea of a picnic. The lunch included a bottle of Moët, a lobster salad made with her own home-made mayonnaise, thick-crusted bread bought fresh that morning, a wedge of a soft French cheese he'd never had before, and hard, sliced d'Anjou pears.

She laughed when she saw his expression, then proceeded to finger-feed him his lunch.

"But that was early on," Storm says.

"That's the thing," he says. "She kept it like that. The last year, in '84, when we were both impossibly busy and nervous, we'd had a pretty vicious fight about something and then right afterward I had a run at the hospital that lasted almost forty-eight hours. It was a weekend in the winter, and a couple of residents were sick or something, and one of the staff docs couldn't get in from his suburb. So I just kept working, catnapping now and then, but never more than an hour. And we had everything that weekend, auto traumas, an electrocution, heart attacks everywhere, ODs, freezings and frostbites, a couple stabbings, a gunshot to the groin. You name it, they just kept piling in through the door. And we just kept working. I felt like I didn't look up once the whole weekend. And when I could finally go home, early Monday morning, about six, I was beyond exhausted, you know. You kind of go into a numbed state, where you don't feel anything.

"So I get home to the apartment and let myself in. I'm being quiet because I figure she'll be sleeping, or getting ready to drive over to Ann Arbor. But there in the middle of the living room she has a sheet spread out, and on the sheet she has a breakfast, coffee, juice, waffles, fresh strawberries. Where did she get fresh strawberries in the middle of winter in Detroit? How did she know I was coming home just then?

"But it was great. I ate some, and then she stayed with me until I fell asleep. And I know she was tired and stressed. Now I realize it was even worse than I thought then, with Bobby and Straw into her. But she'd do that sort of thing. She had that instinct and that capacity."

"She loved you."

From the kitchen he brings them each a tall glass of ice water, because their mouths are dry from the day's drinking, and cigarettes and an ashtray for her.

"Tell me about Holt," he says.

She sits up in the bed and lights a cigarette. "I think Holt set everyone up for them," she says. "I think he was a mole."

"Why not get Straw out alive, then?"

"I don't know. We don't know what happened that night."

"That doesn't explain his calling me, or the letter."

"Sure it does. He was trying to flush you, like you said, because I dropped your name. He'd called me before, thinking I might know who the chemist was. That's what he was after. Nobody knew what was going on, Adrian. Try to understand. When this drug hit the street, they must've gone out of their minds. Then, when you got arrested and became part of it, how long before they figured out you were really Denise's old partner, that you had worked for Bobby? Not very."

"You're right," he says. "Holt knew who Straw was when he called me. He knew about the scar, about our past. That means he had to be tapped into them, whoever they are."

"But there still remains the question—who are *they*?"

"I was serious when I said you were going to help me find out. You've got your own self to save now. This is one of those no-looking-back situations. Either show who's behind it or take the fall yourself."

"I don't know what you expect me to do."

"Go to Brandon. Tell him everything. Then tell him I'll be the bait. Hang me out there and I'll draw them in. Just like Denise, only this time you'll be there, and the police will be there."

"But think about it. Denise was set up in the first place. The people she went in to, the cops or feds or whoever, were in on it. Brandon believes this. There's no way they could have known without a leak."

Storm doesn't say anything for a long time. In the orange light when she drags on a cigarette Lancaster can see tears on her face.

"That can't surprise you too much."

"No."

"Last week in my house, you told me narcs were onto Kevin. Was that true?"

"Yes and no. I think Petie Boncaro, who worked for Kevin, who was Kevin's lover, was also ratting him out."

"Why?"

"He was a coward."

"Know what I think?" he says. "I think you should just get out of here now. You've done what you set out to do. You made the drug, got it out there. The hell you were after came to pass. You've had your revenge."

"I can't, Adrian. I have to know who was behind it."

"Brandon knows, I think."

"Who is it?"

"He knows. I don't. You want to go in to him?"

"Only him?"

"Yes."

"You trust him?"

"Yes."

She rests her chin on his shoulder so that he can feel her breath on his face. "Use a pay phone. Just to be safe."

## THIRTY-TWO

The house is too quiet with Lorraine gone. No humidifier steaming away, no coughing from the bedroom. Even though she was crippled and couldn't speak, her presence alone kept it from being so damn quiet.

Susan made him a nice big dinner of sausages and sauerkraut and boiled potatoes. It's a heavy meal and feels good. The task afterward is to make it to the reclining chair in the living room. After that nothing matters.

But the phone rings between the second and third helpings.

"Who is it?"

"Lancaster. I'm at a pay phone. You get the package?"

"I got it."

"I have some answers. I can tell you where the drug's coming from. I found the chemist. But I need to know now what you know, who was behind it then."

"Then you'll tell me?"

"Not now."

"That's not a fair trade."

"Has to be this way."

"Can you deliver Holt?"

"No."

"Then we have a problem. I don't really care about the drugs at this point."

"One step, then another."

"Lancaster, I don't know what you're doing or what you think you know. Whatever it is, I hope you're right. Because there are things happening here that tie back to powerful systems. The toes being stepped on can step back very hard."

"Whose toes, Brandon?"

"Let's meet. Just me and you. You'll let me have your information. I'll give you mine. All of it."

"But, Brandon, the moment you and I meet, at that instant, I'm exposed. We don't know what's going on, and we don't know who knows what. There were leaks before, and there very well could be again. That's why I want to know now who's behind this. You said you know."

"I said I can't prove anything. You'll have to believe I have this under control. No one knows I'm talking with you. But what about you? I don't know who you're with. I don't know who you've been with, who you've talked to, who's seen you."

"If we meet it'll have to be a safe place, and no one but us."

"We'll make it a neutral ground, isolated, away from town." Brandon squints and peers out through the kitchen window at his yard, bordered at the back by Elmer Creek. "Where Straw was found. The place they call Suicide Park. You know it?"

"Yes."

"Nothing's there."

"Tomorrow morning, first light. Say seven o'clock. And we'll both be alone."

★ ★ ★

Brandon polishes the .44 and loads it with his hot rounds. He wonders, of course, what Lancaster's information will be. He hopes it's good. Because he knows that if it's not, if it doesn't go far toward explaining things, then regardless of the file and tape he turned over today, Lancaster himself will be the primary suspect in the manufacturing of the new Fang. And from there it may be a small step to the murders themselves.

# MONDAY

## THIRTY-THREE

**L**ater, she awoke. He was looking at her.

She sat up and pushed her hair back behind her ears. The fire in the living room had died, but the coals glowed hot in the darkness.

"It's set."

"We need to anchor ourselves. We may get separated. It may get nasty," she said.

"Anchor how?"

"We'll set up a couple times and places. If possible we'll go to each and check in. If we both show up, everything's fine. If we need to find the other person, we know they'll either be there or can be contacted by leaving a message."

"What if one of us can't make it at all?"

She reached for the pack of cigarettes on the nightstand and lit one. Its tip illuminated her face when she dragged on it. "Then by not showing, we've left a message. We've communicated. First, there's this apartment. I've kept it as a spare. I have two keys. No matter what happens, we can't let anyone else know about it. It's our fail-safe. The other spots, if we need to bring someone else, we can."

"So what's the first meet?"

"The diner where you found me last night. I noticed that inside the front door there's a public bulletin board where messages can be left. Tomorrow afternoon, five P.M."

"Make the second out of town—the same spot where I'm meeting Brandon. Suicide Park. The Overlook at the river."

"On the day after tomorrow—at noon, let's say."

"Okay."

"But I want to go tomorrow too."

"You can watch, but you can't be seen. If I remember, there are woods. We'll get there early so you can hide. But you can't chain the smokes out there. You'll get spotted."

"Indulge me now," she said. "And then trust me."

It was 4:00 A.M. They could sleep for another couple hours.



He fixed himself good when he got up. Today there could be no nerves, no flinching. For the first time since he'd bought the smack, he decided to inject. Using a TB syringe and a 25-gauge needle, he popped a bolus under the skin of his forearm. It was a far cry from mainlining, but even so the effect was intense and he knew it would last. He needed it to last.

They were too early by more than half an hour, and it was so cold out, he didn't think he could stand it.

Besides Storm hiding, Lancaster wanted to be early to this meeting to see what was there, to see where he could run if he needed to. But there is no place to run.

They drove his rental LTD. When they arrived it was still dark. They stood for a moment looking out into the void where the frozen river lay hidden.

"The woods are to our left, to the east," she said. "I'll be somewhere in there if you need me." She wore the black hooded shawl again to cover her red vest, so she'd be less visible.

He nodded. He had Brandon's .38 Special tucked in his belt, under the overcoat. She had kept the longer-barreled .357 for herself because, she said, if she had to fire it would be at a greater distance.

"You have anything on you?" he asks. "For nerves?"

She hands him a couple Valium. He swallows them both.

"Kiss," she said. He kissed her once, twice, then she was gone.

At 6:30 the blue-black sky started to give way to a rising glow on the eastern horizon. Lancaster has always marveled at sunrises, especially those few moments before it really starts to get light, when it's more an erasure of the darkness than anything, a sensation that night will be gone soon.

At 6:45, the dusky daylight growing stronger, he's frozen already, his feet numb all the way to the middle of his calves, his fingers solid ice. He breathes smoke. Brandon's not due for another fifteen minutes.

Then Lancaster hears a car pull up in the parking area. The engine dies and a door opens and closes.

A man appears at the top of the rise, but this man is not Brandon.

The man walks gingerly toward him, his street shoes slipping on the snow. He wears a wool trench coat and silk scarf, and there's no doubt that underneath he wears a suit and tie.

He is not tall. He smiles when he gets closer. Lancaster does not know this man, but he knows that something has gone wrong.

"Dr. Lancaster?"

"Who are you?"

The man's blond hair is curly and he continues to smile. He wears red-framed eyeglasses.

"I'm here for Brandon. He couldn't make it."

"How—"

"I'm special agent Kline. DEA." He holds up a badge, which seems genuine enough. "He might have told you we're investigating the series of murders here. He got into some trouble this morning and asked me to meet you, to take you somewhere to talk."

"That wasn't the deal. Goddamn him. Is he all right?"

Kline looks around at the iced-over snow. "He's not exactly all right."

"What happened?"

"Can't say now. We want you in protective custody."

"Was Brandon shot?"

"Can't say. But it looks like the pressure we're laying on is having its effect. You'll need protection."

"I don't need protection," Lancaster says. "I told him I'd see him alone. I'll do that when I can." Lancaster begins to walk back up the sloping grounds toward the parking lot.

"I can't let you walk away. I have my orders. Let's just go somewhere and talk. I'll buy you breakfast."

"No," Lancaster says back over his shoulder.

"You want me to arrest you?"

He stops.

"I'll do that. I can. Or do you want to be civil?"

"Can I drive?"

"No. But if you don't want our protection, I'll drop you off after we've talked. I'll agree to that."

Lancaster turns to face the man again.

"Do you have a gun?" Kline asks.

Lancaster's not sure what to say.

The man walks to Lancaster, steps around behind him, and pats him down. He finds the .38 and removes it.

So what choice is there? As the man puts him in his backseat, Lancaster manages to slip the keys to the LTD from his coat pocket and drop them. Then they begin to drive.

In this backseat Lancaster notices that there are no handles on the doors, and that the lock buttons have been removed.

It is happening now. He can feel the end beginning.

From the pitted dirt road they turn onto 57 and head south, toward town. When they make this turn, Lancaster risks a casual glance over his shoulder. There, a quarter mile back, the LTD follows. Its presence is obviously not lost on the agent.

He drives slowly, careful not to lose the tail. Instead of following the detour around the downtown they head into the tight, narrow streets that compose the central city. The occasional horn honks. The streets are full of slush.

They cut into a narrow passageway between the refurbished Morgantown Theater and a bank building that leads several hundred feet through to a public parking lot. At one point they are pretty well hidden from general view by the buildings and the snow and the trees. Kline stops the car, blocking the alley.

Lancaster turns to watch. Storm has pulled in behind them.

Too late she sees she has driven into a trap.

Kline gets out, lays a silenced pistol on the roof, and aims.

Storm dives to the seat. But he is not aiming at her. The gun makes little noise. The LTD's right front tire bursts.

He jumps back in and they take off. No sweat.

"Questioning?" Lancaster says. "What the fuck is this?"

"You were supposed to be alone. That was your agreement."

"Tell me all about it."

They continue south until they've passed entirely through the city, then turn east, and at the next crossroad, south again, until there is nothing but fallow crusted fields and the low gray sky and distant copses of barren trees marking property borders and ravines and creek beds.

After a few more miles they turn again, onto a small snow-packed spur between fields, and stop alongside the road in front of an isolated old clapboard farmhouse sitting close up on the berm. Behind it a barn rests in its slow but inexorable collapse. Lancaster sees no evidence of habitation.

"Breakfast," Lancaster says.

"The best," says Kline. He pulls the car into the barn, closes the door, and leads Lancaster to the house.

Inside is another man, more elegant by far even than Kline. His hair is silver and well cut. His clothing looks expensive. He wears a business suit and silk bedroom slippers under a long white apron. He makes no change of expression at Lancaster's entry. He is cooking breakfast for three, and doing it very well, Lancaster judges from the smell.

# THIRTY-FOUR

**I**t's well after eight when Brandon pulls into the gravel parking area at the Overlook and sees an LTD with a rental sticker and a temporary doughnut tire on its right front.

He's out and running before his car is even stopped.

As he comes over the embankment and down the slope toward the railing, though, the only figure he sees is that of a woman huddled on the ground, hugging herself and rocking back and forth. He slows to a walk, then stops altogether and watches.

Storm is crying. He kneels down next to her. The bruise on her forehead from the wreck has faded. The stitches are gone.

"What's wrong?"

"I hurt my knee. I'll be fine. They have Adrian."

"What happened?"

"Someone came for him. A man. I knew something was wrong. He was waiting for you, wasn't he?"

"Yes. What did this man look like?"

"Short and blond."

"Kline."

"He flashed a badge. I was in those woods over there, hiding. I came running out, telling them to stop. I slipped on some ice or something and fell. He just took Adrian up to his car and drove away."

"Come on. I'll help you."


At his empty house he finds some bandages and ice for her knee, then boils water for tea. He helps her into an easy chair where she can keep the foot elevated.

"What time did he get there?"

"It was just light. I sat in the car for a while and got warm. Then I decided to walk a little. Then I fell again. I knew you'd come. Where were you for so long?"

"Two of my tires were slashed."

She thinks about this. "You think—"

"Yes."

"He only called you last night. Who could—"

Brandon holds his fingers to his lips and cuts her off, and then she understands. "Were you with him?" Brandon says.

"Yes."

"You've been with him."

"Only for the last day or so. He was away before that."

"Why are you helping him? What's between you?"

She shrugs. "I'm not too much help. I tell him things I remember about Kevin. I'm in love with him."

"Oh, Jesus." The teapot shrieks. "What was it he thought he was onto?" he says from the kitchen.

"I don't know. You think I told someone else you were going to meet him, don't you? I couldn't have told anyone. I've been with him the whole time."

"So you say."

"Would I set him up then come out here and sit in the snow and wait for you?"

"I don't know." He hands her a cup of tea.

A van pulls up out on the berm of the road, and a man in an overcoat gets out and walks toward the house. He carries a fat briefcase. Before he gets to the front door, Brandon has it open, and without either of them speaking the man enters. He glances at Storm, then turns his attention to the house.

He removes some electronic equipment from the case, including a sort of doubled-over wand, which he plugs into a meter. Then he begins walking around the room, moving the wand near lamps and pictures. When he's finished in the living room, he moves back into other parts of the house.

"Someone I hired," Brandon says quietly to her.

She nods.

"We might as well get out of here."

She nods again.

He takes her with him and heads into town. He doesn't trust her an inch, but figures he'll wait to see what the surveillance man finds. If there's no tap, for sure this girl set him up. In any case, he figures, if she's playing games she knows something he should know. And if she's not playing games, she was the last one to see Lancaster and maybe she heard something significant. Either way, she's all he's got right now.

At a pay phone he dials Ellen's number and leaves a brief message on her machine about Lancaster getting snatched.

Next stop is the justice building with Storm in tow. He wants to be seen with her. If anybody knows who she is, if they saw her when they grabbed Lancaster, he wants them to think he's onto something, maybe flush them into saying something.

But no one pays much attention. Kline is out; Lou's tied up on the phone; the other feds are all busily hunched over their various tasks.

To Storm: "So what do you want to do? You got any plans?"

"No."

"Any ideas on how to find Lancaster?"

She pulls out a cigarette and digs through her purse.

"Here," he says, holding out a light. She inhales and exhales, nicely.

"Depends on how Adrian can lie," she says. "I might have some ideas."

"Brandon." Spinner walks up. "I been trying to reach you." Spinner looks at the girl once, then back at Brandon. "Jimmy got some results on . . . could you excuse us?"

"Sure," she says. She walks over to stand by the elevator, where there's an ashtray attached to the wall.

"Who's that?"

"Never mind," Brandon says. "What's up?"

"Here," says Spinner, handing him a report. "Print from the clip of the 30.06 in the Washington. Jimmy got a clean match."

"Yeah?"

"It's weird. I don't know what to make of it."

"You know we're the only ones who know about this," says Brandon. "You, me, and Jimmy."

"I know."

"That bother you?"

"No. Should it?"

"Jimmy?"

"He's okay with it. He'll do anything you say, you know that."

"I'll just hold it a little while. Then I'll turn it over."

"Whatever."

"Kline has Lancaster."

"No shit?" Spinner says. "What's he—"

"I don't know. I think they wired my house. I had a clandestine set up this morning. When I came out, my front tires were cut. Lancaster had been snatched. Kline didn't show here?"

"Not at all. I been here all morning."

"Then he's got the doc stashed someplace. I'm starting to get nervous all over again. This doesn't smell right at all."

Brandon gathers up the girl and leaves.

## THIRTY-FIVE

While the tall man cooks, Kline takes Lancaster into a barely furnished living room. He sits on a wooden chair across an old yellow coffee table from Lancaster, who is given the slightly more comfortable folding lawn chair.

"I'm Julian," he begins. "You are Dr. Adrian Lancaster."

Lancaster doesn't say anything.

"Right?"

"Yes."

"You're one of the heads of the emergency room of the Morgan-town County Hospital."

"Are these questions?"

"Yes."

"Oh," Adrian says. "Yes."

"You were arrested eight days ago. . . ."

And so it goes, the man naming the facts of Lancaster's life, Lancaster correcting any minor inaccuracies. They work backward to the time of Denise—the setup in Adrian's apartment, the addiction, Karnowski, Straw, the move to Detroit, the bust. All the high points. As he did earlier with Brandon, Lancaster denies having known anything about Denise's involvement in manufacturing synthetics.

"Okay," says Kline. "Now. Do you know Elizabeth Richards?"

This one freezes him for a moment. "She was Denise's sister."

"Was?"

"Is, I guess."

"You don't know her."

"No."

"Ever meet her?"

"No."

"Ever see her?"

"For the first time two days ago."

"What?"

"I found a picture of her when she was about twelve or thirteen. I'd never seen her before that. Denise never talked much about her family."

"Where is that picture?"

"Back at . . . in my house."

"Who was following us?"

"A girl named Storm. Just a friend."

"Kevin Babcock's friend, who came to you in the clinic."

"Yes."

"She said she had spoken with the man named Arnie Holt. Later, Holt contacted you in the emergency room. Had you ever seen him before that?"

"I've never seen him at all."

"Spoken with him before that time, or since?"

"No."

"But you received a letter from him."

"Yes. That's all."

Julian Kline sits back, locks his fingers behind his head, and glares
at Adrian. "Shit," he says.

"If you tell me what you're looking for, maybe—"

"James."

The cook comes into the room. Lancaster wonders how much
he could overhear from the kitchen. Everything, probably.

"You know my theory," James says.

"Double alias," says Kline.

James nods. "Now, if I can interrupt?"

"Ready?" Kline says. To Adrian: "Let's eat."

The breakfast is exceptional. Porridge and veal sausages, fried potatoes
and soft-boiled eggs, fresh cinnamon rolls and squeezed juice. James
dishes up huge platefuls and serves them. Lancaster can't remember a
breakfast like this, and can't quite get over the incongruity of being
held captive in a semiabandoned farmhouse in the middle of the
Michigan tundra and having this kind of lavish meal.

"Even in the wilderness, in a hideaway, good food is the necessity," says James the cook. "One simply must insist on refusing to do
without it."

During the meal Kline says very little and James says nothing at
all. The three of them simply eat. It is very strange.

Afterward, Lancaster is taken back into the living room, and this
time given the wooden chair. Kline sits opposite him and James on a
stool across the room.

Kline says, "Let's begin where we left it. Do you know anyone
who might be Elizabeth Richards?"

"I'm sorry?"

"Anyone who might go by another name but might in actuality
be Liz Richards. Maybe she, or he, bears a resemblance to the earlier
photo. Maybe a resemblance to Denise."

"No," Lancaster says. "Sorry. You want to tell me what this is about?"

Kline reaches inside his jacket and removes a small pad of paper. "Series of killings, obviously related. One or maybe two killers. We have access to a big smart computer that does all kinds of bitchingly complex things like running fingerprints for matches nationwide, checking for similar MOs in other areas, comparing specific types of chemicals, fibers, glasses, metals found at the crime scenes around the country. But this computer also does some simple stuff that can bust cases open sometimes. In this case the simple route was the answer.

"Your packet of information from Denise came to us through Brandon. Also the letter from Holt, and the notes you took on the phone conversation. We've kept a list of every name that's come up from the beginning."

"So?"

"So the computer did a standard little maneuver it always does with names connected to a series of crimes. It analyzed the names."

"And how does one analyze names?"

"For spelling, Doctor. For letters." He pauses, obviously pleased with himself and his brainy computer.

"And?"

"This may seem like a bit of a stretch to you, but bear with me. And keep in mind the mentality of the sorts of people who commit bizarre series of crimes. They're sometimes very intelligent, and very Byzantine in the ways they think."

"I'm listening."

"When Holt called you in the ER, he said some unusual things. He said, 'Arnie Holt is the perfect name, you'll discover . . . the name of a king, of a beast.' Then his message to you was from a Regal Crusader."

"Something like that."

"Arnie Holt has nine letters. Letters that can be rearranged to spell other words. It happens that one respelling of those same nine

347

letters is the term *Lion Heart*. One name is an anagram of the other."
Kline tosses a pen and the paper pad at Lancaster. "Try it yourself."

Lancaster feels woozy.

"Coincidence?" Kline says. "Impossible. Common for a serial
killer to use anagrammatic aliases. It comforts them somehow."

"Lion Heart," Lancaster says.

"A king, a beast," Kline says, leaning forward, smiling. "The
king who is a lion heart, Doctor, a crusader. Who was that?"

"Richard," Lancaster says.

"That's right. King Richard. Richard. Richard's crusade. As in
Denise Richards? Elizabeth Richards? We flew the voice tapes of Holt
to Washington, where our audio guys ran them through some high-
tech diagnostic loops. They tell me the voice had been altered elec-
tronically. They think it was a woman's voice beneath the masking."

"Arnie Holt is Denise Richards?"

"We don't think so. We think Holt is the sister, Liz. We didn't
know about her until we got your information."

Arnie Holt is Elizabeth Richards. Lancaster's mind runs with
this, playing it over, thinking about the raspy voice on the phone, this
strange man whom no one ever saw except in the semidarkness of a
bar or outside at night, but who Storm said spoke to her several times.
Liz Richards was an actress.

But Liz Richards is Storm.

So Storm is Arnie Holt.

He knows it is true.

"Oh, God," Adrian Lancaster whispers.

"I didn't have to kill anyone," she said to him. "That was the
beauty of it." But did Arnie Holt kill anyone? Did she use the alias to
separate herself from the killings? Does she have a multiple personal-
ity? Is she psychotic?

On Saturday night, just before returning, Lancaster reached the
McGivvons Institute, where, according to the receipts Denise left,
Elizabeth Richards had been in ongoing treatment. McGivvons, a

night-shift nurse finally told him, was a psychiatric hospital. Most of their patients were severe and long term.

Straw had to have been killed by her. And Karnowski. No one else would care about them.

That's what this is all about. Storm wants to know who else killed her sister so she can kill them.

But what about the others, Kevin Babcock and Petie Boncaro? She had nothing against them. They were spreading her drug. They were working for her. Or Tommy Winter, whom Brandon had told him about. Or Seth Babcock? Holt, or Storm, was on the snowmobile, not shooting.

Adrian Lancaster feels ill. His face is damp with cold sweat. Trembling, nauseous, and a little dizzy, he excuses himself and finds the bathroom, where he washes his face in cold water and sits, head in hands, trying to think of what to do. But his head is muddled.

A bit later comes a pounding on the door. "Doctor." It's Kline. "You've been in there twenty minutes."

Twenty minutes?

"I just got here."

"Look at your watch, Doctor. You went in at nine thirty-five. It's almost ten o'clock."

He looks at his watch. It's blurry. He can't focus. Then he understands and stumbles back into the living room.

"What was it?" he says.

James smiles up at him. Kline looks stony and says, "Sit, Doctor. Let's talk some more."

"What was it?"

"Triazolam. It'll just make you drowsy, less hostile. Then we'll run a little truth serum into your veins and we'll have a discussion. See if anything kicks loose. It's so easy to forget things, to repress them. I think you know who Liz Richards is, whether you've acknowledged it or not."

Lancaster drops into the chair. The room swims. Kline's voice is soothing, though, a point of stability in a sea of confusion.

"Well, you're very clever," Lancaster says. His words are slurring badly. "But I injected myself with a good dose of street heroin this morning and took Valium on top of that, so at the moment I'm medicated out of my fucking mind."

And with that he pitches forward unconscious onto the floor.

In the late afternoon he comes to. He's in a bedroom, which from the angle on the trees outside he guesses must be on the ground floor, strapped to the bed. His head hurts so badly that when he looks at the weak light in the windows he sees colors each time his heart beats.

He isn't awake more than a minute or two when they come in. They must be monitoring. The overhead light comes on, sending the headache up to the next screaming level.

"Why are you doing this?"

"Do you know who Liz Richards is? Where we can find her?"

"No, I told you."

James holds Lancaster's left arm, which is already strapped down and immobilized. Lancaster feels the cold swab of alcohol or Betadine, whichever they're using.

"I told you I don't know who she is. I've never seen Arnie Holt. What do you want from me?"

"I want to plumb your mind," Kline says. "Somewhere you've met Liz Richards. Maybe you're lying to me, or maybe you truly don't realize it. But you've met her, and I want to know where."

Then there's a tearing pain as James drives a needle awkwardly into the antecubital vein.

"You're inhuman," Lancaster says. The room begins to swirl and blur. "Pentothal?" he says.

"Close," whispers Kline. He's squatting, his lips next to Lancaster's ear. "Surital. It's a favorite of ours. . . ."

Then Lancaster is under again.


When they were in love and living together, Lancaster and Denise fought one evening. The subject of the fight has been long ago forgotten. The reason for it was the tension they were feeling from the effects of their withdrawal. They had run out. Wherever Denise had been getting their drug, from whatever source, it had dried up. Lancaster felt nervous that evening. His skin felt wrong, it hurt, and he had a headache and he was cold. They had done their last fix that morning. He was not close to full physical withdrawal. But the symptoms were beginning.

"I'll take care of it if you can't," he remembers saying.

She looked at him with red-rimmed eyes. She wanted them to quit. There was a methadone clinic, she said. They could go there, take a couple of weeks off. But he knew how well methadone worked. Not very. He knew those junkies and they were the most pathetic. They didn't even have the courage of their addictions.

He laughed at his little internal joke.

"We'll run our own goddamn clinic. We've done it before."

"What will you do?"

He didn't want to kiss her. He didn't want to be close to her. He didn't want to be close to anything. He itched. His skin was dry and flaky and cracking, he felt great chasms just beneath the surface waiting to open. He would split along the arms and legs and abdomen and his fluids would run out.

But she was trying to get close, she was trying to put her arms around him.

"What will you do?"

He stood still, in order to feel less, as she undressed him. He had two hours before he had to leave for the hospital.

Naked, a hint of chill in the air, he lay on the bed, on his back, staring up, not moving, trying not to participate. She moved over him, up him and down him. She moved in him and out of him. She moved and she moved and finally he could not lie still. He grabbed a handful of her hair and dragged her head back and bit her neck so hard, he drew blood. She moaned and hugged him closer.

They rolled with the torment. She wrapped herself around him and would not let go, would not let him come up for air, and she worked on him, she worked him until he was so agitated, he was nearly uncontrollable.

Then she pushed him onto his back and got on top of him and pulled him into her.

The intensity, the high-tension arousal—she, a tiger-lady growling and scratching him, her hair hanging over her face, was out of her mind. And he felt this and the maddening effects of his condition, the skin crawling, the head pounding, the stomach knotting; at the same time he had never felt more powerful, more sexual.

They rode up higher and higher. As he waited to crest he rode higher with her still, the waning effects of their drug delaying, impeding, and so heightening their deliverance he thought there would be no end to it. He had never risen this high. He had never felt anything like this.

Finally, though, they arrived together. At the moment of climax he lost all control. He screamed. He bit into his lips. And her—he remembers choking her, wrapping his hands around her throat and squeezing until her face turned crimson and her eyes bulged and drool ran down from her mouth. And still they rode their wave together. Then he let go of her neck, drew back his hand, and slapped her so hard, he knocked her from him, knocked her clear off the bed.

"Don't stop!" was all she said.

He crawled off after her and finished fucking her on the floor.

Only years later would he remember this and understand what he had seen in himself, what demon he had glimpsed. He had never hit a woman before. He understood how people could kill people. It was a small step. He understood something, only a little, but something of Bobby Karnowski that he hadn't understood before. And he wondered if he and Denise could ever have made love again.

He knows what she would have said, if he'd had the chance to ask her: "Always. You can always make love again. Making love is different than that. You can always follow violence with love. I'll show you." That's what she would have said. But that night he stole the morphine, and he got arrested and he was sent away from her. His life changed. He was saved. And he was condemned.

## THIRTY-SIX

S torm and Brandon have dinner together at Bunnies' Restaurant, this at Storm's suggestion. She explained about the prearranged contact. No note from Lancaster, however, is waiting for her on the bulletin board.

"I'm worried about him," she says.

*Me, too,* Brandon thinks. There's no predicting what the feds unfettered will do to him. But still, they're law officers. There are limits of conduct even they cannot cross. "Where's the next meet?"

"Noon tomorrow, where you found me this morning. You're out in the cold on this one, aren't you?" she says. "On your own."

"Looks that way."

"You want to tell me about what you know? Just because I'm curious about who's behind this."

"It's an open question," Brandon says. "Has Lancaster told you about his past, about Denise Richards?"

"Pretty much."

Brandon eyeballs her pretty face, then lights a smoke and says, "Let's blow."

In the parking lot, in his car, he does an odd thing. While she's buckling the seat belt he reaches over and rubs her hair between his fingers. She freezes; she does not move.

"Fairly short," he says. "Fine. Dark."

He drops his hand into his lap. They both stare forward into the dusk. When the hand comes up again it holds the .44. He presses the muzzle against the side of her neck.

"What is it with men?" she says. "When they want to talk, they pull a gun on me."

"The car Friday night, after you were chased by Seth Babcock. Anything come to mind?"

"No."

"There was a gun under the passenger seat of that car, a .25-cal auto. It was yours, right?"

"Maybe."

"Your prints were all over it. Yours and no one else's."

"So what?"

"Room six thirty-eight in the Washington Street Hotel, which is where Arnie Holt was living, was full of munitions. From the clip of a 30.06 we lifted a beautiful index print. Perfect match, my friend, to the .25 cal. It was your index finger. It was Arnie Holt's."

She says nothing.

"You."

"Yes. I knew your men were watching the place. You people, you're all so obvious. All of you."

"Makeup. Beard."

"Accent. Dentures. A little padding here and there."

"How about the voice? How'd you do that?"

From her purse she pulls a small electronic device adapted to fit over the mouthpiece of a phone. "Digital voice changer. You can buy clunkier versions of these in stores. They're for women who live alone, so callers think a man lives there. This one is a little more advanced. I bought it from an electronics engineer I know."

"Over the phone that's fine. But in person?"

"Who'd I talk to? Who was I with? Kevin, but Kevin knew. He helped me set it up. We'd use Holt as the mythical chemist, seen but not heard from except when we chose. I dressed up and went with him a couple times to the bar. He took me in, we had a drink, and I left. People saw us. I ran the operation, Petie and Seth, over the phone. Later I made a few other calls, reported a few incidents, spoke with a certain doctor. Poof, I'd created an entire persona. You'd be amazed at how easy it was."

"You went with Seth to the airport."

"Yes. And as Holt I met Petie and Straw each one time. Those were the only times I spoke with people directly. All three were at night, outside, without lights. Each time I conveniently came down with a terrible sore throat, and could only speak in whispers. Most people are too unimaginative to question what they're told."

"I could take you out somewhere and kill you."

"That would be stupid. You'll never get out of it alone."

"Who'd you kill?"

"Straw and Karnowski."

"That's it?"

"So far."

"Straw killed Kevin?"

"Yes. I don't know exactly what happened, but Straw said it was Kevin who got scared and attacked him first, that he hadn't planned on killing him. That may be, because Kevin was worthless to them dead. Anyway they fought and in the struggle Straw lost control and killed him. I, as Holt, didn't get to Kevin's house until some time after it happened, but Straw had gone back there to try to cover it up, make it look like a suicide. I convinced Straw I wasn't angry, that Kevin had been cutting in on me, and now I wanted to move the dope myself. Of course, he thought he had me, that he'd get the drug and then kill me, too, or turn me over. Of course, he was wrong."

"At the Overlook you lit him when the deputy got there."

"Just when he was pulling up. And I only put the napalm on his sleeve, so he'd be sure to survive. Even so, look how he burned."

"He was unconscious?"

"Semi. I hit him with the tire iron. You know you're not through yet. You thought you'd figured something out, but you have murders left to solve, Detective. Who killed Petie? Who shot Winter? Seth? Who was that shooting at me and you at the airport?"

"Do you know?"

"No. It was a man."

"So we thought about Arnie Holt."

"This was a man. It was the same man who threw Petie off the bridge. He lifted Petie right up."

"Those were your tracks on the other side of the bridge. Going up partway, coming back down."

"Yes."

"Who in the hell are you really?"

"There's a question."

"Did Kevin know?"

"No. He thought I was just Storm, a chemist."

"Will you tell me?"

"If you guarantee me one thing. Either you arrest me—in which case you're on your own, in which case you fail and die—or you fill me in on everything you know. Everything. I have to know everything, then I can help you. Then I can finish this."

"One or the other," he says. "You have my word. Now talk."

He parks the gun and lights two fresh cigarettes, one for each of them.

★   ★   ★

Before going back to the house Brandon stops at a pay phone in a gas station and makes a call.

"You got a definito on the tapski," says the man who answers, the same man who ran the sweep earlier that day.

"Someone's been listening in. It's only on the line, though. I don't think they ever went into the house. There's no bugs inside, so you can converse freely. Just don't use the phone."

Brandon hangs up.

So not only does Kline have Lancaster, he's running taps on Brandon. And on who else? Probably everybody involved in the case. It's clear Kline has divorced himself from any locals—this is his operation now. He's trying to control everything. What's not clear is who's controlling him.


Storm's settled in Susan's old bedroom, napping and quite unarrested. He noticed the limp she'd affected had disappeared. The fall in the snow, the twisted knee, was all an act.

The house is dark except for a night-light in the kitchen when Brandon hears a noise outside, then someone knocking.

He peeks out the window and sees Byers at the front door.

"Hurry," she says. "I'm freezing."

"What're you doing here?"

"I told you I'd be here if you needed me."

"I need you?"

"I called over here today. They said you were on indefinite sick leave. I asked about the case, being involved as I am. They said it was all a DEA matter now. *Bullshit,* I said to myself. You have any news?"

Brandon laughs.

★   ★   ★

He and Ellen sit at the kitchen table. They talk first of Lorraine.

"Everything's different," he says. "I've started thinking maybe she should stay in."

"Maybe as much for your sake as for hers. You're allowed to lay down some burdens sometimes, you know. You've paid your penance."

"It's as much Lancaster as anything," he says. "When I see him now, or think of him, it's as just another casualty of the shit that's come down on all of us. Nothing more. He's probably done more good than most people. Than me."

"A different kind of good," Ellen says. She slides her hand across the table and over his.


They're getting ready to go over the blowups of the photo of Denise Brandon found in the archives when Storm appears in the doorway.

Brandon watches Ellen watching Storm. There's something in her eyes as she looks at this mad girl. Brandon guesses it's in large part admiration.

"You okay to look at some shots?" he says. "Might be difficult."

"I can look." Storm nods at Ellen. "Is she in?"

"She's all the way in," Brandon says.

Ellen pulls a manila folder from her bag. First she slides a blowup of Denise's face across the table. Storm doesn't react; she hardens her face as she picks up the picture.

"It's probably the last picture taken of her," she says. "I want a copy."

"You can have that one," says Ellen. "I brought several."

Storm takes it into the living room.

"What else?" Brandon says.

"Wait for her."

A minute later Storm is back, composed, stone-faced.

"This is a pretty remarkable shot," Ellen begins. "It never should have been taken, not because it got Denise on film, but because it also got these interrogators."

"The outside deep covers."

She lays out the original archives photo Brandon saw.

"What are you thinking," Storm says, "—these undercover agents sold out Denise?"

"One of them, we think," Ellen says. "Le Seure was still at the DEA at this time. This was a few months before the election. But of course he wasn't involved in the actual mechanics of the investigation. He would need someone inside, someone actually with the informant to suppress what might come out about Le Seure's own involvement. We don't know if Denise knew of Le Seure or not, but he wasn't taking any chances."

"So he planted someone to kill her."

"Yes. And we know from the tape she left Lancaster that she was still being handled by Karnowski and Michael Straw. They were the ones who took her in at the end. She thought she was going to a high-level meeting with the man behind it all, with Le Seure. She was wearing a wire. It's just that the people who wired her, these DEA agents, or at least one of them, knew she would never come back. Who killed her? Karnowski and Straw? The undercover agent? Le Seure? We'll probably never know. As far as I'm concerned they all killed her."

"So who was the agent?" Storm says.

"That's why we're here," says Brandon. "To look at each of them."

"Right. We know the man standing in the doorway was a DEA special agent brought in from Chicago." She slides an eight-by-ten blowup of him onto the table. Brandon's surprised at how clearly the enlargement reproduced. He can see the man's eyes squinting from cigarette smoke that's risen from his hand. His head is turned slightly as if he's straining to hear what the girl's saying.

"His name was Roger Markover. He was dead within six months of this."

"Dead how?"

"Heart attack, labeled questionable. He had no history of heart disease, no overt signs of cardiopulmonary disease or distress. A recent physical showed him to be in great shape, low blood pressure, et cetera.

"The second man, on the couch, facing us, is a federal marshal." She slides out the next blowup. "He did not go in under cover. He was really a monitor, a neutral hand. He retired about three years ago, lives in Key Largo, Florida, now. I spoke with him last night. He claims to know nothing. He got into this, got out. He had no knowledge of anything illegal."

"He telling the truth?"

"Probably," Ellen says. "There's no reason to suspect he's not. Now, the three sitting side by side at the table are more problematic. They can't be identified. They were all clandestine, presumably DEA, but we don't know where they were from. They were probably all people who worked under cover anyway. They would have been impossible to trace."

She slides their pictures one at time toward Brandon. First, the picture of the woman. It's not as clear a shot as the others. She's writing something so her face is down, not turned toward the camera. Her hair is blond and tied up on top of her head.

The second is the man nearest the window. His chin rests on his hand as he watches Denise. He is balding; his face is turned partially away from the window.

The final shot, of the third man, is also less clear, but his face is turned toward the window and held low, near the table, as if he's listening to something coming from its surface. He wears glasses, a beard, and turtleneck sweater. He's younger looking than the others, certainly younger than he looks now. But Brandon recognizes the handsome face and curly hair.

Storm recognizes it, too, from the Overlook at the River Sorrow.

It is a picture of Julian Kline.

# TUESDAY

## THIRTY - SEVEN

Morning. It's cold in the bedroom. Or he's cold and the bedroom's warm. Lancaster's teeth rattle; his knees bounce. The straps are still on. His wrists burn from the leather. The headache's gone, though, thank God for that. He tests himself, straining against the bands, feeling his muscles and his bones. No great pain anywhere, nothing seems broken or torn.

He can smell another of the breakfasts cooking. He wonders what it is with these people and breakfast. It seems bizarre to him that they would go to the trouble of hauling all the food out here, taking the time to cook. If it were him, he'd just eat bread and coffee.

He calls out. "Hey!"

Kline sticks his head in. "You hungry? Would you like some of James's breakfast?"

"Sure," Lancaster says. "Make sure you get the dosage right this time."

"Who knew you were medicated?"

"Exactly."

"Seriously, would you like to eat?"

"Fuck you," says Adrian Lancaster.

In the living room Lancaster sits in the wooden chair, hands strapped behind him, feet strapped together. Kline leers at him, then turns and swings a backhand into his mouth. The force of the blow sends him and his chair over sideways. He spits out blood and tongues the hole in his lip.

Kline sets the chair up again. James the cook is on his stool across the room again, watching.

"We searched your house. There's no picture," Kline says. "And you knew more than you told. You watched the drop behind the airport. You saw the shooting. And Elizabeth Richards is here. You know her."

"You son of a bitch," Lancaster says. Inwardly, though, he's thrilled that Kline didn't say the name Storm. Even under the needle maybe it didn't come out.

"You said something about an apartment where she'd been staying. You were staying there too."

"She's not there."

"Just tell me where it is."

"I'm telling you she's not there anymore. She was staying there with me."

"How do you know she's not there?"

"Because I have the only key. Dig?"

This time Kline punches straight forward from the hip, hitting Lancaster in the face and sending the chair over backward. His head cracks against the floor, and he goes dizzy again for a moment. Blood pours from his nose back into his throat and he gags and turns his head trying to clear the airway.

"Careful," James says, from his stool.

Kline rights the chair again. The blood flows down Lancaster's shirt. Lots of blood. A good broken nose. The pain's fine, though. It resolves. It sharpens. He holds his mouth open so he can breathe. He coughs out blood, which sprays onto Kline's white shirt.

Now Kline flips open a knife. "I'm telling you, Dr. Fix. I want to know. If you don't tell me where I can find this woman, and right now, I'm going to start taking body parts off you."

"She ran. How can I know where she is? How can I?"

Kline nods. He steps beside Lancaster. With little more than a flick of the wrist he strikes. There's a flash of intense pain, then a horrible burning on Lancaster's ear and the warmth of blood running down his neck. He says nothing.

Kline holds up a grayish bit of flesh. "Earlobe. Get it? Next: a finger? Eyelid? Penis?"

He didn't show last night at the restaurant. That should have been taken as a warning. Would she go to Brandon? Would Brandon know anything? Would he know Kline was a madman? That these goons were crazed and out of control?

And then, in that moment, Lancaster understands.

"You killed Denise," he says.

Kline breaks for an instant, freezing and then glancing at James. It's the answer.

"You fucking murderer. It's you who've been doing it. You're the killer here, too, who wore the black mask."

"Shut up," Kline says.

"You're the one."

"Shut up! Where is she?"

"Eat shit."

Kline spins the chair around so Lancaster is facing the window. Grasping Lancaster's left index finger, he places his thumb on the top of the middle knuckle and bends it upward until it cracks.

Lancaster screams.

Kline undoes the strap, freeing Lancaster's hands.

His finger is ruined. He squeezes the back of his left hand with his right and presses it into his thigh. With his palm flat on his leg the broken finger points bizarrely upward.

He weeps after that, huge racking sobs that move up from his belly through his chest and out.

Holding his breath, he forces himself to snap the broken finger back into place. It moves with a grinding click.

Then he bends forward and vomits between his legs.


Storm has the gun. Storm has the control. Storm started this. Storm can finish it.

Lancaster can think of no greater revenge than to turn her loose on these men. They have no idea what they're asking for.

He's calmer, although his hand hurts like no pain he has ever known.

Kline's blade moves toward his face again, toward his left eye.

"I'll tell you. You have to believe me."

"What."

"The place where you picked me up yesterday."

"Yes."

"I'm supposed to meet someone there today at noon, the girl named Storm, the one whose tire you shot out. She's Liz's friend. She was supposed to take me to her. She knows where she is."

"You're lying."

"I can't afford to lie. I don't want to lose anything else. And I don't care anymore. What time is it?"

Kline looks at James.

"Little after ten."

"So let's go there at noon. If no one shows, I have a phone number. You can trace it, get an address, find Storm."

"You were never to this girl Storm's house?"

"No. I only met her a couple times."

"She knows Liz?"

"They're good friends, from my understanding."

Kline looks at James again and James motions him over. They whisper.

"All right," Kline says then. "We'll try it. If you've lied, you'll never end up regretting anything more."

"You're wrong," Lancaster says.

# THIRTY-EIGHT

## I

At the Overlook the sun shines as if winter is finished. It reflects from the crusted snow, giving the world a hazy cast. The river still flows in its icy embankment.

At the west end of the park, just off a pathway that leads through a copse of trees, Brandon kneels behind a stump. The .44 Mag is in his coat pocket. A police-issue 12-gauge leans against the stump. He knows if Lancaster shows it will be a setup. Lancaster will not be alone.

Ellen is at the opposite end of the park, in the heavy woods that begin there. She wears one of Brandon's Kevlar vests beneath her coat.

Storm leans against the railing at the edge of the cliff, exposed as she has chosen to be. He knows she has a gun tucked into her jeans. All the guns they confiscated at the Washington Hotel and still she manages to get her hands on a piece. She was shivering when they got here—in anticipation, he assumed. She wears his other Kevlar vest.

It is just noon.

## II

Lancaster is fully awake. The drugs have worn off. His hand is terribly swollen, so much so that he can't fit a glove over it. James helped him tape it to stabilize the break. He keeps it inside his jacket. His nose, too, has swollen out across his face; his eyes are only slits, and they are quickly turning black. His ear burns. His mind is as empty as he can make it. He has never been one to think much of death, except as an invisible force to be defeated on the emergency-room tables. His own death has never preoccupied him. He does not dwell on its possibility now.

Kline rides in the back with him. James drives.

A beautiful day. Lancaster remembers Storm's description of the day Denise died, how nice it was that autumn. It's funny that this man next to him was there then. Maybe he even killed her. Maybe both of these men were there. One of them may have been the last person to touch her alive.

"Do you remember her?" he asks.

Kline, who today is wearing boots and jeans instead of his suit, doesn't react.

"I just wonder what happened, who did it to her. I just wonder if she saw it coming."

"You want more pain?" Kline says. "You want me to cut you again?"

"No."

"Then shut your mouth."


"It's my car," Lancaster says of the LTD. "She must be here."

"Good," Kline says. "Excellent. Let's see what this girl has to say."

"Just get her," James says. "I'll wait here. It's warm."

The two of them, Kline and Lancaster, walk over the edge of the parking area and down the sloping snow-covered park toward the railing. A girl wearing a red down vest waits there. She's toward the far woods, near the end of the railing, maybe fifty yards from them. She waves at Adrian, then stops, noticing the other man. She looks around, looks as if she is suddenly frightened that he is not alone.

*Good for you,* he thinks. *Suck him in deeply.*

They plow through the snow toward her until they've covered about half the distance and she calls out, "Stop there."

"Listen, girlie," Kline says, slowing not a bit, walking up until he's a few yards away, Lancaster at his side.

"Adrian," she says, "what've they done to you?"

"Storm, this man is a federal officer. He's looking for Liz Richards. Liz is Arnie Holt."

"I want you to come with us," Kline says. "We're going to put an end to this."

"He knew Denise," Lancaster says. "He really knew her, Storm."

"Shut up!" says Kline. The silenced .22 materializes in his hand, trained on Lancaster. "And you," he says to Storm. "Get your hands out of your coat where I can see them. Hurry, or I'll kill him."

"Then you'll die," she says.

"What—"

"Kline!" Brandon calls out. "Put the gun down. Walk away from them both, hands on your head."

Kline, wide eyed, looks beyond Lancaster. Brandon has the shotgun leveled across the top of the stump.

"Back away and put your gun down."

"You'll kill him if you shoot that thing," Kline says.

"Slugs," Brandon yells. "Like you used at the airport, remember? Much more accurate."

"I'll kill him if you don't put it down." Kline holds his gun to the side of Lancaster's head.

"And then I'll kill you, and I'll like it. If you back off you can live."

## III

In the open spaces, with the hard crust on the snow and the coldness of the air, sound travels easily. A light breeze blows, playing in Brandon's ears. Otherwise it is silent.

"Bullshit," says Kline.

"I've got men in the woods behind you. I've got men sealing off the cars right now. You're cornered."

"Cornered? I'm a federal officer, Brandon. I know where your men are, and they're not here."

"You're a murderer," Brandon says. "You threw Petie Boncaro off the bridge. You shot Tommy Winter. You are the man in the black mask."

"You're insane."

"I have an old photo of you. Six years ago. You set the whole thing up, working for—"

"That's right," Brandon hears then, from his left, from up the hill toward the parking area. A silver-haired man is smiling at him. He holds a scoped hunting rifle, a nice-looking piece of equipment, the stock a dark wood, the barrel and action a flat shineless black metal. "This is the end of it, Detective. I wouldn't miss it."

"Le Seure," Brandon says.

Le Seure fires, the bullet cutting through some brush that stands between them, continuing on into Brandon's body, sending him rolling backward across the path, to the edge of the precipice beyond which lies the river. The sound echoes from the snow and the trees and from the far side of the river, reflecting from the hard rocks and ice, rolling away into the distance.

# IV

"Brandon," Lancaster says, but quietly, almost to himself.

"Le Seure," says Storm.

Several things happen simultaneously then.

Ellen Byers calls from her hidden observation post, "Kline, put the gun down!"

Le Seure, across the park from her, jumps behind a tree and swings the rifle toward her voice, training it on the woods.

Kline had been looking, of course, at Brandon and Le Seure, then at the woods where Ellen is hidden. When he turns back, Storm has the .357 in her hands, pointed at his face. It gleams in the early-afternoon sunlight.

"One move," she says.

Kline freezes.

"Drop the piece and turn toward Le Seure, slowly, or I'll kill you where you stand."

He does what she says.

Lancaster bends and picks up Kline's gun.

"Kneel behind me, Adrian," says Storm. He crawls through the snow, Kline's gun hugged against his chest with his broken hand. He is in shock from his torture; he shivers so hard, he can't see clearly.

As Kline turns, Storm grabs his hair and pulls him back toward her.

With Ellen's backup from the woods, and Kline as a shield, Storm and Lancaster are strangely protected.

"Tell him to hold his fire," she says. "You'll die if anyone moves."

"Who are you really?" says Kline.

"I'm who you've been looking for. My name is Storm. My name is Elizabeth Richards. My name is Lion Heart."

"Your sister was Denise."

"My name is Death," she says loudly, so it carries.

"Kill him," says Lancaster. "Kill Kline."

But she doesn't kill Kline. Kline is the only thing keeping them alive. They all wait, Kline blocking Le Seure's shot at her, Lancaster kneeling in the snow behind her, she with her gun pressed against Kline's neck.

They have reached a point of momentary stasis. It is the moment they have all, each of them, been coming toward for years.

"Now you know who I am," she yells. "And I know who you are, James Le Seure. I know that when Denise and her attorney went to the DEA, they could not know that the man who was its district head was also the man who was behind everything she was doing, the man she was working for."

"Yaaas," Le Seure says.

"But you still needed a ghost. Someone invisible and vicious and inside to be your eyes and ears and to do your dirty work. And that was Julian Kline."

"Bright girl," he says.

"What the fuck are we doing here?" Kline screams.

"We're satiating ourselves," says Le Seure.

"What'd you do with her?" Storm says. "That's all I want to know."

"Julian injected her with her own drug," Le Seure answers. "She was ODed, in case anything went wrong and she was discovered. But it didn't go wrong. Bobby and Michael gave her a right proper burial, a real down-home affair up in some marsh country by Battle Creek."

Lancaster has crawled off toward the railing, which he uses to pull himself up. He's come back into his head somewhat.

"James Le Seure," Ellen Byers yells, her disembodied voice floating out of the woods, "you have no way out of this. I want you to put down your weapon now and surrender yourself."

Le Seure steps out from behind his tree a little and trains the scope on the woods, trying to catch sight of Ellen.

"This is where I burned Michael Straw," Storm says.

"He was an idiot," Kline says. "Babcock could have told us everything we needed to know. But Straw thought he was solving our problems by killing him."

"I loved watching him burn," Storm says. "I wish I could have stayed and watched longer. He thrashed and screamed."

"But he lived."

"Only by design."

"You must be pleased with yourself."

"Not as pleased as I'll be when I burn you too."

Lancaster is on his feet now. He notices something the others don't off to his left, down the railing from where he stands. He raises Kline's gun toward Le Seure and yells to distract attention. Le Seure bites, turning his aim toward Lancaster, who tenses for the shot that must follow.

A shot does sound, a roar which comes not from Le Seure or Ellen or Storm but from Brandon, who has crawled around and pulled the .44 Mag with its awesome load from inside his coat. The mercury-core bullet hits James Le Seure high on his well-cared-for face. His scalp peels back and his skull comes apart, brain matter spraying back out over the snow behind him. The report rolls across the snow and out over the iced-up river.

But this distraction gives Kline his opening. He knocks Storm's gun away and spins into her, toppling her over backward. They wrestle in the snow, rolling over each other toward Lancaster so quickly, he has to scramble to keep from being knocked down. As he tries to dodge them he slips on some hard pack and stumbles, dropping Kline's pistol. They roll on top of it.

Then Kline has her up against the railing. She pushes her bare hand into his face, and reaches back to hit him again, then suddenly stops, going cold. Kline's fist has come up into her, and now Lancaster can see the knife he's holding. He shoves Storm away from him, knocking her to the ground.

Ellen runs down the slope at them.

Kline picks up his own gun, and runs toward the woods that border the western edge of the park.

Ellen fires once at Kline. The bullet whangs off the railing and whistles out over the river. He fires back, then disappears into the woods.

Ellen goes after him.

Storm looks up at Adrian, pain and anger crossing her face.

"Well, go," she says. "Finish it."

He finds his father's .357 lying where she dropped it when Kline tackled her, and stumbles toward the spot where Ellen and Kline went in.


# V


Brandon lies bleeding in the snow. His neck is twisted in such a way that although he's lying on his back his view is out over the river at that beautiful quiet place.

He listened to them talk, Storm and Le Seure and Kline. Having heard it all pleases him. He was not wrong. His gut was true. His sense of his people and his city was what it has always been—dead on. He feels a kind of deliverance. He is calm. He is in no pain. The snow holds him.

He closes his eyes.

And then he is not lying in the snow at the edge of the precipice over the River Sorrow anymore. He is moving up through the air, looking down at his old body as it bleeds. Up the slope is the body of James Le Seure. Storm is bent over, holding herself, walking along the railing toward the spot where he lies.

He rises.

An opening appears before him, an entrance into the air. He is drawn toward it.

Someone waves at him, beckoning him, encouraging him to come. It is a woman. It is his youngest daughter, May.

She is beautiful, as she was when she was alive. She is young. And he is young.

## VI

When Denise came to visit Lancaster the last time in the rehab clinic in Royal Oak, they sat together at a table in a small, cheaply furnished conference room. The only window was constructed of thick glass blocks, so the sunlight bled in but it was weak and dissipated. He hadn't been outside for a month, had only even glimpsed the outside a couple of times, since most of the windows here were of the same glass block.

Harpo Epstein had come with her, but after a few minutes left the two of them alone in the room. She lit a cigarette and offered him one, which he accepted although he hadn't smoked much since coming in. Most of the patients here used cigarettes and coffee obsessively, these being the only drugs they were allowed, the only weapons they had to calm their nerves. But after the first couple of weeks, the withdrawal during which his mind shut down, cigarettes had started giving him headaches. With her, though, he smoked. He needed to have something to do with his hands, to keep from touching her. He knew if he touched her it would be much more difficult to finish here.

He wore jeans and slippers and an old T-shirt. She was in a dress and jacket, as if she were going to some important meeting.

"I just wanted to look nice for you," she said.

"Don't," he said back. "It's hard enough as it is. It's easier if I don't have reason to think about you."

He waited for her to chastise him, to say it wasn't her he was withdrawing from, only the drug, that she would be there for him when he got out. But she didn't say anything.

And then a thought occurred to him that he hadn't had before.

"What about you?" he said. "Why aren't you in treatment?"

"I will be. Just not yet. I have some things to finish."

"What things?" he said, and then asked, "You're still on, aren't you?" He reached for her arm so he could roll up the sleeve and look, but she pulled away.

"Aren't you?"

She looked at him.

"Adrian, I have to go away for a while. You might not see me when you get released."

"Where?"

"I don't know. Really I don't. But I'll be in touch. And you'll come visit soon. I promise."

"Denise, how are you still getting drugs?"

"Please let's not talk about that. You shouldn't talk about it. You have to forget it. It's your job now, to forget."

"But why? Why aren't you in treatment?"

"I'll tell you when you see me again. It's a long story."

"I got caught, Denise. They were waiting for me, outside in the parking lot. I took it for you, so you wouldn't have to suffer so much." He'd done it before a couple times, stolen morphine because their supply was so low. "I did it because you wanted me to."

"No," she said. And he could see that her eyes were filling with tears now. She pulled a tissue from her purse.

"Who told them, Denise? How could they have known I took it? I was careful. I followed procedure. I know how to steal drugs."

She smiled at him through her tears, which did not stop flowing.

"How, Denise?"

"I called them, love. I called."

He did not say anything then. He looked down at the Formica tabletop, at the cigarette pinched between his fingers, at the smoke curling up in the small stuffy room. He dragged on the cigarette and blew out the smoke, and then he nodded.

"I did it because we had to be forced. Do you understand that? Someone had to make us stop."

"Don't explain," he said. "You can't put something like that into words."

"But I want you to understand."

"I understand." He smiled back at her and wiped a tear from her cheek. Her skin felt warm against his cold hand. "I do. I love you too."

Lancaster learned a little about hunting when his mother moved them from Cleveland to this backwater. Friends would take him out, loan him a gun, and he'd tramp around the woods, mostly watching them get their deer, then helping with the cleaning and the packing out. The stillness in these woods reminds him of those hunts, trying hard to stalk noiselessly, listening for some snap of twig or crack of crusted snow.

The only noise is the breeze above him in the tops of the trees.

And then he hears it, the sound seeming to come from several directions, but close, the whisk of a branch whipping, the noise of a large body crashing through the underbrush.

He hears a shot, and then the answering hiss of the silenced .22. The snow and the trees absorb the sound.

After following the footprints through a dense bank of brambles and saplings and dried grass, he comes out on an open trail three or four feet wide and cleared to a height of maybe five feet. Snowmobile tracks run here, and down the middle fresh boot prints.

Ellen is lying across the track, slumped against a tree trunk, her head driven into the snow, her legs sprawled apart.

Lancaster turns her over.

"Get away," she says. "He's right there." Her left shoulder is ripped open and her head is gashed where she fell.

Then a hunk of lead whumps into the tree, and afterward comes the flat ugly hiss of the silenced .22. He drops and rolls forward, landing on his broken hand. The pain drives the wind from him, but he looks up in time to see Kline running, aims the .357, and fires four rounds.

Kline disappears around a tight-banked curve.

Lancaster crawls forward along the trail, then moves up into a running crouch. When he gets to the bend in the trail he moves to the inside, pauses, moves a step, watches. He notices blood in the snow at his feet. Dark blood, venous, not life threatening.

"Kline!" he screams.

A high whine passes near his burning and bloody left ear, and again the sound of Kline's gun echoes and is absorbed.

Instead of moving forward around the curve in the trail, Lancaster crawls into the woods. Saplings and branches whip his face. He feels caught, trapped stupidly, unable to run. Then through the trees he sees a movement of color, raises his gun, aims, and fires twice.

No sound comes, either of a body falling or a body running away.

He crawls back onto the trail and creeps forward on his knees so he can see around the turn. He sucks in his breath. Kline has come back to him. They find themselves face to face, not six feet away from each other.

Both have their guns pointed.

"You're empty," Kline says. "It holds six shots. Count them."

Lancaster squeezes the trigger. The hammer snaps on an empty chamber.

Kline lowers his gun to his side and watches.

Again Lancaster thinks to fire, again the hollow benign snapping of metal striking metal.

Then he, too, lowers his gun.

It doesn't matter. It is finally finished, he can see. Bright blood pours from beneath Kline's coat, down his legs, and soaks into the snow at his feet.

Julian Kline steps once forward and then falls dead.


The pilot places the bird perfectly at the opposite end of the stone-covered parking lot from the two cars. No trauma doc or flight nurse has come along, at Lancaster's insistence. He would be the flight doc, he told them. He has a lot of people to transport and there will be no more room.

When Lancaster came out of the woods, Storm was holding Brandon's head in her lap.

"Did anyone call?" he said.

"No."

He made the call from the phone in Kline's car. When he came back, he looked at Brandon, who had stopped breathing. The rifle slug had hit him in the lower right chest, puncturing the lung and its rich blood supply and probably the liver. It left a terrible exit wound out the back. With equipment he could try to close the hole and insert a chest tube to reinflate, but Brandon had lost a vast amount of blood. Lancaster looked up at Storm and shook his head.

Kline's knife hurt Storm but was deflected down by the Kevlar and prevented from penetrating too deeply by all her clothing. The blade entered her lower abdomen. It would have to be cleaned and sutured, but she was in no immediate danger.


Sheriff Donner, his deputies, and the Morgantown police have started to arrive. Spinner Wharton is there, staring out in astonishment at the blood-spattered snow of the park.

He looks at Brandon on his stretcher. He looks at Lancaster with his black and swollen face and his bloody ear and his bandaged hand, at Ellen and Storm, who are being loaded onto stretchers.

"The woods," Lancaster says, pointing. "Kline's dead in there."

Soon Lou Adamski arrives and breaks down when he sees Brandon.

Then a second chopper lands, the life flight from St. Rita's in Ann Arbor, which was in the area to transport out a preemie.

"We heard you had a mess here," the flight doc yells to Lancaster. "But, Christ—"

Ellen, who is conscious but losing blood, asks to see Brandon. She has been told he will not make it. From her stretcher she reaches over and takes his hand. She says something Lancaster cannot hear, then raises Brandon's hand to her cheek for a moment. The Ann Arbor bird takes her alone, because she needs the most immediate attention. It lifts off only seven minutes after it landed and heads toward Morgantown.

"We'll go with you," Lancaster says to his own pilot. "Brandon and Storm and I."

The pilot revs the engine and unfeathers the rotor blades, and the air whips faster around them.

When Brandon and Storm are strapped in, Lancaster gives the thumbs-up and the pilot lifts them off. Once they're in the air, though, Storm undoes the belts and sits up.

"Brandon?" she says.

"Gone," Lancaster says. "He stood no chance."

"I'm sorry, Adrian."

Lancaster snaps open the red metal case that serves as the onboard crash cart, which contains the drugs and equipment needed in critical situations.

He removes the vial of morphine and a prepackaged syringe and needle.

Storm says, "You can't anymore. It's over. You promised when it was over."

"I can stop," he says. "Just right now—" and then he hears himself, as if for the first time, as if all the hundreds of times he's heard others say those empty bullshit words, as if the dozens of times he said them himself, never happened. But he can hear it now, in his own voice, the lie. *I can stop.* It has always been a lie, always an empty utterance, because when you're in need you can convince yourself of anything. But nothing is true, nothing has any meaning at all, except where the next dose is coming from.

He stares down at the roads and traffic below.

"I need it," he says.

"Now," she says. "Right now you have to start facing it."

"I can't just quit."

"That's all right. But then do it with sanctions. Just don't keep shooting yourself in the arm. You'll never come back this time."

"It's going to be harder than before."

"Promise me—you'll wait until you get in, then call someone. You'll still get a fix, but someone will be there with you, someone who can help. And every time you take one, you won't be alone."

"I will."

"Just keep it in your mind."

He nods.

"Will you give me that?"

"I haven't had anything since yesterday morning. I hurt."

"I know."

He opens his hand and holds it palm up toward her. She lifts the bottle of morphine and slips it into her vest pocket.

"What do you want?" he says, finally. "Will you stay?"

"Would you want me to?"

"Yes."

"I'd be in jail for the next thirty years if I stayed."

He nods.

"Why don't you come?"

This is a good question, he realizes. For a moment he can imagine it, being free, living on her royalties and her interest, the two of them. It is a heady and seductive thought, this freedom he envisions. It is the source of her power. He understands that. But as his imagination opened to this vision, so it closes again in the next moment. Right now, right here, no one else can do what he can do. He is needed. This is his own power. He is bound by it. And that is the way he knows it should be.

"I can't," he says.

"It's finished now."

"So much destruction," he says.

"Just tell them I pulled a gun on you, I hijacked your helicopter. You won't get in any trouble then."

"Do you need help?"

"This?" She taps her belly. "I'll get it taken care of."

"That's not what I meant. I know about the McGivvons Institute. I know you were treated there. What was it?"

"Severe chronic reactive depression, they said. It started after Daddy went, but I was just an outpatient."

"Until Denise died. Did you have any other family at all?"

"No. She was it. They admitted me then."

"How long were you in?"

"Almost three years on and off. I'd get out for short periods, get through another semester at school. I made four attempts on my own life, one of which nearly succeeded. I was on a respirator in intensive care for two weeks. Pills and whiskey. But I don't need help now. Especially now."

He looks into her pretty eyes and wonders if he will ever see them again.

As if in answer she says, "Maybe someday."

He shrugs, then leans forward and taps the pilot's shoulder.

"Can you set down for a second? We'll go right back up."

"What gives?"

"Just do it. I'll tell you later."

The pilot nods, turns them into a tight circling pattern, and corkscrews the bird down into a snow-covered field. Off to the east a few hundred yards lies State Route 57. Lancaster points to it.

"Get to a doctor. You'll get infected."

"I'll be fine," Storm says.

"I know you will."

"Denise thanks you," she says. "Wherever her soul is, she knows." Storm leans over and kisses his cheek, and then the door is open, wind and snow swirling in, and Storm is on the ground running. As is her constant fashion, he imagines, she does not look back.

She moves quickly away from them as they rise, and soon all he can see is the red nylon of her vest, a tiny dot now nearing the road that will take her back into the anonymity from which she came.

Lancaster reaches up and takes Brandon's stone cold hand in his own. When he can no longer see Storm he looks forward through the front window.

Soon Morgantown rises on the horizon, and soon after that they are home.

## ACKNOWLEDGMENTS

I must thank especially James Ellroy, Gail Hochman, and Leslie Schnur, first for their endlessly energetic and generous efforts and advice in the shaping and reshaping of this book, and then for general guidance that has proved invaluable. Great thanks also to Judy Clain, for early and ongoing support and perfect matchmaking, to Dr. Ruth Ann C. Opdycke, for sharing her formidable professional expertise and judgment (with the notation that I didn't always heed this information, so any inaccuracies of biochemistry, pharmacology, or medical technology are entirely my own), and to Frederick Holden, for always having at hand whatever esoterica seemed to be needed at a moment's notice.